FAILURE TO CURE

A HEALTH CARE CONSPIRACY

Vanderblumen Publications
P.O. Box 626
La Mesa, California 91944
619-465-3400

FAILURE TO CURE

This books is a work of fiction. The characters and incidents were created by the author and are used ficticiously. Any resemblance to any person, living or dead, events or circumstances is entirely coincidental.

Cover Design by Paula Micallef
    The Write Stuff Studios, Carlsbad, California
Graphic Design by Alexandra Y. Orazi
    Escondido, California

Printed in the United States of America
ISBN: 978-0-615-43724-8

This book is dedicated to the memory of my Mother. She instilled in me the confidence to face adversity, the understanding of the right to speak your mind and the expectation of expressing yourself professionally. Her tireless pursuit of life and liberty were a constant inspiration.

CHAPTERS

Chapter One - Death of the Scholar

Chapter Two - I have a Dream

Chapter Three - Meeting the Research Team

Chapter Four - Christ the Redeemer

Chapter Five – Government's Role is to Protect the People?

Chapter Six - A Young Boy's Hope

Chapter Seven - Your Government at Work

Chapter Eight - The Treatment of Rigoberto Ayala

Chapter Nine - The Scholar Verses the System

Chapter Ten - Inside the Investigation

Chapter Eleven - The Government's Resolve

Chapter Twelve - Investigation Without Progress

Chapter Thirteen - The Consequence Phase

Chapter Fourteen - Paying it Forward

Chapter Fifteen - In Conclusion

CHAPTER ONE
THE DEATH OF THE SCHOLAR

1

Jude Scott and Chris White are seasoned professionals in the art of crime scene investigation. The two partners are currently assigned to the Hennepin County Sheriff's Department Homicide and Criminal Investigations Unit. They are well respected detectives who have spent many years of service in their respective roles.

Jude is a life-long veteran of the Hennepin County Sheriff's Department. She had been with the Sheriff's Department for almost twenty years and consistently worked her way up through the ranks and earned her way to the position of detective after her many years of faithful service to the county.

Chris was a recent immigrant from Great Britain where he had been a detective for his entire career. Prior to his move to the states, Chris had previously served as a detective with the Manchester police department in Manchester, England for the last twenty-two years.

Together, they have grown to complement each other professionally and have grown to know and understand each other well. Chris was assigned to Jude a year ago. To be sure, they were polar opposites when it came to their perspective on the job. To date, they are the most successful investigative team the county has to offer.

The two veterans had very little in common when it came to their ability to connect with people. Conspicuously, there was one common thread. While they certainly loved their career choice, domestic or abroad, they both understood one compelling fact, this job did not always bring out the best in them, their assessment and opinion of people, or their perspective on human behavior as a whole.

At a minimum, the collective time on the job enabled them to see how far people would reach to prove their point, act out in passionate rage or to just even an old score in the most basic and primitive of ways. It was a role that was both intriguing and bothersome to each of them.

Throughout the last year together, they had become better than just good friends. Their relationship currently was not, and had never been, physical. They worked together exceptionally well as partners and respected each others' opinions and competence immensely.

Their professional relationship was clearly a case in how opposites can be attracted to each other and be great partners on the job. There was; however, always an undeniable underlying tension. Nothing corporeal, but an emotional tension nonetheless. A tension that seemed to be rooted in the very principles upon which they stood. A tension based upon perspective.

There was always a conflict in terms of their individual judgment. It was a tension where assumed guilt began and where presumed innocence was allowed to be applied. They would each think through and react to a given circumstance differently. The way the two were able to process information and evidence individually complemented each other very well. Chris would shoot from the hip and be quick to work out his theory almost immediately. Jude was all about seeing some substantiation.

2

Tonight, Jude and Chris dined at *Maynard's*. It was their first anniversary as partners and they were out for the evening to enjoy some light celebration.

Maynard's is an institution in Excelsior, a small artist's community on the shores of Lake Minnetonka, in the Minneapolis' suburbs. *Maynard's* is a great place, particularly in summer and fall, to celebrate memorable occasions in a comfortable and unassuming seaside atmosphere.

The dining room restaurant seating at *Maynard's* had begun to slow after what looked to be another very busy fall supper crowd. The food tonight, as usual, was outstanding. The dinner conversation was light-hearted and the views of the lake as night fell had been nothing short of spectacular. The night was blessed with clear blue skies, a light breeze and a moderate temperature.

The fun seekers on the large bay had headed for shore and although the hours leading to sunset were not particularly windy, you could see plenty of full sails on the lake which were sure to have made the boaters very happy this late in the season. The sun had just set and they were ending with dessert when the call came in. It was an unlikely interruption to an otherwise perfect but unremarkable evening of fellowship.

Chris set down his fork and answered his Blackberry phone, "Detective White," he said in his usual slightly intolerant voice.

Jude could only hear one side of the conversation, but insofar as she knew Chris did not have much in the way of family or a social network in this country, she was pretty confident it was the department calling.

"Sure," Chris said casually, as he pulled a small spiral pad from his pocket and reached out for the pen from the tip tray the server had left on the table. He was writing with one hand and gracelessly holding the phone ackwardly to his ear with his shoulder.

"Yes, Sir, I know where that is. Minnetonka Blvd, Greenwood, sure. Street address again?" he asked as he wrote in his tablet.

Chris was looking at Jude with a bewildered look on his face. He continued writing with one hand while the other hand was palm up waving slightly, inquisitively, as he nodded back and forth while looking at Jude. The phone was still pinched between his shoulder and his ear.

"Greenwood," he asked again for clarification. "On St. Alban's Bay. Right?" he asked a third time.

There was a pause as he listened. Jude waited for some sign as to what exactly the call concerned.

"Okay, well, it won't take long, Sir," Chris relayed to the caller. "Jude and I are probably right across the street, give or take a few hundred meters."

After a brief silence, as Chris continued to listen and scribble in his tablet he spelled out, "Last name of the deceased again was K-e-l-l-e-r, correct? Dr. Garrison Keller?"

"Yes, Sir. I got it, Sir. Have they secured the scene this time I hope?"

Jude shook her head. She was constantly making half apologies for her partner. Chris was just as good at identifying barriers as he was at building barriers. He bordered on being rude in his manner of getting his point across in virtually every conversation. Chris had no concept of what the locals referred to as "Minnesota Nice".

"How long ago did this take place Sir?" Chris asked.

"I see. That seems to be quite some time ago now," Chris continued in an English accent as he re-adjusted his phone and looked at his watch.

"Okay. Are the city cops keeping people out of the house? I don't want to have all of the evidence trampled on like the last time I dealt with those guys. It would be nice if everything in the home was accounted for this time, including the dead guy."

"Yes, I see," Chris relayed to the caller.

"We would like to speak to anyone who has first hand knowledge or anyone who was involved in discovering the body this time too," Chris added.

Chris listened. Who would that be exactly, Sir?"

Chris continued to motion to Jude in a questioning manner. He was not exactly sure what the caller was telling him.

"Uh, huh. I see. The Federal Government has already been at the scene for several hours and why is that Sir?" Chris asked descriptively intending for Jude to start following along with the conversation.

"Okay. Can we assume that at least our officers in the home are not contaminating the scene? I am tired of asking the lab to disqualify our own people and now we will need to account for the feds prints and fibers too?"

Still on the call, Chris stood from the table. He hastily put away his pen and notepad. He took his jacket from the chair as he continued to hold the phone with his shoulder. He looked at Jude and pointed to the door indicating they were leaving. He then pointed to the credit card receipt, made the ok sign with his free hand and nodded silently. The bill had been paid.

"I know. I understand. Thank you, Sir! We will be over there in just a few minutes. Thank you, Sir," Chris said as he hung up and cradled his Blackberry.

Chris was a cantankerous Englishman who, having immigrated from England only a year earlier, still carried a heavy British accent. He wanted to get his twenty-five years of service in and move on to another more positive career.

He had moved to the States thanks to an exchange program that was intended to help cross-train law enforcement members. In a post September 11th multi-cultural, multi-national world, many programs were put into effect that would increase cross-national cultural awareness programs. Chris was a beneficiary of one of these programs.

He had another two years in America before he would be headed back to the U.K. where he would have only one year to go before the benefits of full retirement would kick in. By then, he would have some real decisions to make about his career. For now, those decisions seemed a lifetime away.

Chris is easily irritated, tetchy, and often times unreasonable. He is skeptical of people. In this line of work, being a cynic is a necessary character trait most of the time. At times his skepticism could be confused with a lack of any and all sympathy to any given situation.

Chris has a unique investigative style. As far as Chris was concerned, the closure of a case was just a matter of things taking their course.

Unlike Jude, he is not driven to close every case or know every detail. If you could give Chris only the easy cases, it would be fine with him. After forming an immediate opinion, he would make a reasonable effort to get the details, find conclusive evidence and get a conviction. If the resolution was not readily available, he would move on. The case he was about to embark upon would compel him to be more uncharacteristically committed. Time would tell if that extra commitment would prove fruitful, or if he was best suited to stick to his hunches and put maximum effort into readily solvable cases.

To sum it up, let's just say he was not a good candidate for cold cases. This lack of detail orientation was only complicated further by his feeling that the cumbersome nature of American laws made the job of law enforcement and attaining justice self-limiting by nature.

As a rule when investigating, everyone was guilty in Chris's eyes. You would then be eliminated one-by-one as a suspect. He found it difficult to see the good in people. Understandable, I suppose, given the lack of local family in tandem with him spending virtually every waking moment at work; therefore, not really being exposed to a lot of the cities law abiding inhabitants. He was a single workaholic. People, to Chris, were largely fakes and hypocrites.

However, Chris is a professional at his job and carried himself marginally well as a detective. He just couldn't help making a habit out of conducting investigations in a manner that was abrasive and alienating of his partners on the force. He was very difficult to befriend. He presumed guilt and was very hard to impress.

Amidst all of this negativity, he did have an uncanny ability to stay logical and objective by not allowing any emotional communication to filter in.

Whether it was positive or negative, emotional, verbal or non-verbal, subjective communication would not be allowed to sway his ideas or his investigative trajectory. This method of operation for Chris had served him well in his twenty plus years on the job.

All in all, he was dedicated to the job and to getting the truth as long as things were investigated on *his* terms and on his timetable. With Jude being the exception, he did not get along with people very well and it was obvious.

Chris constantly complained about how much immigration was ruining our country just as it had ruined Great Britain, yet he was now the immigrant trying to improve himself and this country. It was an anomalous argument.

3

"Back to work Jude," Chris said as he finished putting on his jacket and positioned his Blackberry on his side. "Looks like we have a dead man across the street named Dr. Garrison Keller. They want us to come over and take a peek at him."

"Garrison Keller?" Jude replied.

"You know this character?" Chris asked, surprised she was familiar with the name.

"I think so," Jude answered. "If it is the same man I am thinking of, he is a big time researcher at the University of Minnesota."

"Researcher of what?" Chris asked.

"He is into a lot of stuff. Cancer mainly, I think," Jude informed.

"Was into!" Chris exclaimed. "He is not into anything anymore."

"He lived across the street?" Jude asked.

"Guess so. At least, he died there. We need to go. Let's walk," Chris insisted impatiently as they left their table.

"Who was on the phone?" Jude asked, as it seemed like an oddly lengthy line of questioning this time of the night.

"The Sheriff himself," Chris replied with a chuckle. "You must be right about him being a big-time guy. The Sheriff said this was a high profile case and he wanted his finest on the job from day one."

Jude smiled.

"I am sure he was talking about you Jude," Chris continued in a self deprecating fashion. "He thinks this may be a particularly challenging case, but didn't exactly say why. He just wanted us there as soon as possible."

Jude was contemplative.

"He said the federal government already had some investigators at the crime scene."

Chris stopped for a moment, looked at Jude and added, "Which is odd. Why would the Federal Government have agents at the crime scene? On this crime scene? On any crime scene before us?"

"Federal agents," Jude replied inquisitively, shaking her head. "No idea!"

The two thanked their server as they made their way to the front door, down the steps and out onto the street. At the corner, only a couple hundred feet from the restaurant entrance, they looked down Minnetonka Blvd from Old Log Way. They could see the squad car at the entrance to what was likely the Keller residence.

Chris was thinking over the call. He was machinating through the one-liners the Sheriff had given him and assessing the scene before he even was on site.

"Feds were there investigating already, but it was his case? What the hell does that mean?" Chris added.

"It sounds pretty conspiratorial to me! How long have they been there and how long do they think he has been deceased," Jude asked as she smiled while intentionally pressing Chris's hot button. She knew Chris liked a good conspiracy theory and she was purposefully antagonizing him with the question.

"Awhile, I think," Chris said without hesitation or acknowledgment of Jude's satirical query.

"I think the Sheriff has also known for awhile. I think he took his sweet time deciding if or when he should call us," Chris theorized.

"Hmm," Jude shrugged and looked at Chris with a crooked grin. "Sounds serious," as she continued her playful exchange.

"Yeah, I know," Chris chided as he looked further up the street after stopping at a second mailbox to check the number to be sure he was headed in the right direction.

"Wow," Jude continued, "You sound like this case might really have you engaged from the start."

"I doubt it," Chris added. "The easy ones are more my style and this one looks like it will be a stinker from what I know so far."

"That sounds more like the Chris I know," Jude responded jovially.

"Looks like that is it, right down there," Chris said as he pointed to the squad car again. Jude was keeping pace right along side.

They would be walking the equivalent of three city blocks. As they walked, St. Alban's Bay was on the right and the big lake, Minnetonka, was on the left. It was just past dark and while the sun had set, there was some light from an exceedingly bright fall moon. The air was typical Minnesota in early October, cool and crisp.

There was a sailboat marina on the left and a dock for outboards in rows on the right. Both marinas were well lit and all but empty this late in the season. There were very few people on the docks as the boaters on the lake tonight were some of the last of the season. The lake and bay would be filled with ice houses in a matter of a couple months.

4

They crossed the bridge that straddled the causeway between the lake and the bay. A couple of houses later the two approached the Keller home. There seemed to be a lot of commotion visible from the street as they looked up the long driveway that angled towards the bay. There was definitely more activity than usual for a fresh crime scene. There was a moving van and numerous men with "Federal Agent" screened on the back of their thin navy blue windbreakers.

Chris approached the local police officer standing sentinel at the end of the driveway leaning, cross armed, against his cruiser. The officer appeared affixed at the hip to his squad car, leaning on the rear quarter panel, closed postured. The car was blocking Dr. Keller's driveway.

Chris pulled out his badge and flashed it at the officer as if he were trying out for a part in an old *Kojack* segment and stated, "Chris White, Sheriff's Department Homicide. What the hell is going on here?" Chris said in an abrasive tone of voice that was sincerely confused.

"Everyone knows you are an asshole," the uniformed officer instructed as Chris advanced.

Chris, not giving the officer even the slightest bit of satisfaction by acknowledging the comment, kept walking. Jude smiled at the officer as she approached, lagging a few steps behind Chris. Chris did not even break stride. He just kept walking up the driveway towards the house.

"Feds have been here for hours. We were wondering when you were going to show up," the officer said speaking louder with every step Chris took.

Chris and Jude continued briskly past the officer, up the drive and towards the home.

"Hey," the officer beckoned towards Chris without a break for a response, "You can introduce me to your little friend though," while the officer continued to watch Jude's backside as she followed Chris up the driveway.

"Piss off," Chris said over his shoulder, not missing a step as he put more ground behind him and the officer.

Jude was silent and didn't look back. She just kept pace with Chris.

"English prick," the officer said aloud as he once again focused his flashlight on Jude as she continued to walk along the narrow drive.

Jude had come to accept that the attitude and frequent retorts were just part of working with Chris. It came with the partnership and, by and large, it worked. Chris would joke about making the *thin blue line* of officer partnership and commitment to each other *a thick blue line* right through the names of many of his peers whom he felt were incompetent paycheck takers. There just weren't a lot of his fellow officers that he cared for and visa versa.

It was obvious. Chris did not get along well with other officers and detectives in the office or in the field. He did not feel the American system was a *high integrity* system. Local law enforcement seemed particularly incompetent. They seemed to be without lenience or kindness to the local *subjects in the kingdom* while at the same time not willing to really take down the hardened criminals.

They would hassle people at traffic stops and then forget to document your work correctly when you get a real offender. This was a real difficultly in principle for Chris. To date, he was unsure if this standard was prevalent at all levels of law enforcement in the United States, or just locally.

He was steeped in the lack of tolerance and greater discipline for serious crime in Europe. He was intolerant of laws that allowed for handguns to be in every home in America and he wanted to make society here more accountable, but it just was not to be.

When it came to the matter of what other officers thought of Chris, they thought he was lazy and grossly under committed. By and large, they were right.

5

There are some extraordinary homes on Lake Minnetonka and the bays that surround the main lake. Company executives, record producers, movie stars, have all laid claim to extravagant seasonal homes on the lake.

It was dark, but you could see the exterior of the home was of contemporary design and professionally cared for with an abundance of the appropriate shoreline and lavish landscaping.

Insofar as it was on the bay, there was a shallow water dock down the narrow walkway on the left side of the home.

Dr. Garrison Keller was a researcher, teacher, philanthropist and an accomplished sailor. Everyone knew he loved his summers on the lake. He insisted on staying at home during the summer months and spending as much time as he could on the lake. Garrison's boat was always one of the first in the water in the spring and one of the last to be pulled from the lake in the fall. This season would prove to be no different.

His sailboat was still docked across the Boulevard on the main lake and his speed boat was still conveniently tied down adjacent to the home.

Chris and Jude walked briskly towards the home. Their pace and interest had intensified due to the flurry of activity outside the home. What was going on here? This was a crime scene!

As they approached the home at the end of the drive, Chris was uncharacteristically calm, but intently scanning the landscape and asphalt driveway as he walked. Jude was focused on the home ahead.

The garage doors faced the driveway. The contemporary two-story home, as well as the property the home sat on, were long and narrow. The entrance to the front door was accessed by a custom raised cement tile deck walkway to the right of the home. The front door was open. There was a closed screen door.

Every light in the house was on.

"Great!" Chris audibly said to himself. "Just great!"

Jude stood silently by his side.

"I sure hope that they did not forget to contaminate absolutely every God damn room in the house. It would be a shame if they missed one," Chris commented to one of the agents as he passed him on the way to the front door. The agent was carrying a box of files.

Chris and Jude traversed the raised walkway and stopped at the screen door.

"Hello," Chris bellowed into the home.

Within a moment, an older ungloved uniformed city officer came down the stairs that were just inside the door.

"Hey, Matlock, I suppose there isn't a need for gloves here eh?" Chris said sarcastically.

Chris, and anyone else, would usually need to be gloved before touching the door or entering the home. He could see the box of footies along with an empty latex glove box sitting on the floor just inside of the doorway. Although from what he was seeing so far, he was not sure why he would need either at this point. After all, no one else was wearing them.

The officer did not say a word as he opened the door.

"Do you have some gloves for us?" Chris asked in a more serious tone.

"This is your first crime scene White?" the officer asked mockingly.

Chris and Jude did not stop back at their car before they came to the scene. They were not prepared with a set of gloves as they would be usually.

"Just give us the damn gloves and save your sarcasm for your little sister. I think we just saw her taking a waxing out on the lake by some middle aged unemployed used car salesman," Chris replied.

The officer ripped some gloves from his vest and slammed them into Chris' hand. Not surprisingly, Chris' reputation had preceded him to the scene. The bad news truly was this. Both of the officers he had confronted so far were Greenwood police officers. They were not even a member of his own Sheriff's Department. The distaste for Chris knew no departmental boundaries.

"My sympathies ma'am," the officer said to Jude as she put on her gloves and footies just outside the door before entering. Clearly, the Officer was inferring that it must be a tough assignment working with Chris.

Jude, in contrast to Chris, was energetic. She was reserved in comment and she was an idealist. She was able to relate to almost anyone. She took pride in her ability to get the most from people. She was compassionate and, unlike Chris, she was consumed with bringing closure to the details and justification to the facts.

To her community's credit, like Chris, she was single and devoted to the job. Jude enlisted a tireless dedication to the citizens of Hennepin County. She had a commitment to see things through. These characteristics all played a role in her multiple promotions through the ranks and the effectiveness in her current position.

Jude was always calm and collected and did not get into the antagonistic banter that Chris seemed to attract and enjoy. She was non-confrontational. That is part of what made this relationship work.

There was a comprehensive approach to each situation; a sort of tag team that played off each others' strengths and weaknesses very well.

6

Chris and Jude entered the residence and stood on the interior tile entry. The home was appointed tastefully, albeit with a minimalist's style and design. Two more men passed them, carrying two more boxes out of the home. The boxes were filled with paperwork, a computer and various miscellaneous things.

It was not clear if this was truly a minimalist environment, or had things just been cleared out already. It was getting frustrating to watch and Chris had yet to ask the all too obvious question and therefore had yet to get a good answer. Who was directing this scene and where were they taking this potential evidence?

From the entry, even with all the activity, it appeared that there was a place for everything and everything was in its place.

The two began to walk the main floor of the home. The floor plan was very open. There was a living room, dining room and a kitchen. From all of the windows and the position of the home on the lot, even when guided only by the moonlight, one could image what appeared to be dramatic and sweeping views of the bay.

The home was obviously not opulent by high-end metro lake standards, but would likely cost somewhere north of a million dollars. Adorning the walls were conservative pieces of art. The tables and mantel were tastefully appointed with pictures of Garrison, family, friends and Garrison's wife, Sally. Nothing really appeared missing or out of place on the main floor.

The two bedrooms and a study were on the second floor. The bedrooms and the common areas were all neat as a pin. Although the various drawers and closets were open, they appeared not to be disturbed. Again, no items appeared to be out of place.

So far so good! Or so it appeared on the surface. Perhaps this was not as troublesome of a crime scene as it first appeared. However, where were the boxes of paperwork and computer hardware coming from and who was asking that they be removed?

There was one room to go, the study. It was there, when they entered the study, where they would find the body of Dr. Keller.

"Whoa, Nelly!" Chris said as he turned the corner into what appeared to be a home office.

In front of him was Dr. Keller, face down on the desk, arms outstretched on the desk above his head with a handgun clenched in one hand. Chris was looking at Dr. Keller's back. Dr. Keller had been sitting at his desk, the front of which faced the window overlooking the bay.

The unobstructed view during the day would have been outstanding. There was a coagulated pool of blood on the desk that ran visibly off of the desk, onto Dr. Keller's lap and then onto the floor.

Chris scanned the office. Thanks to the federal agents, the room was practically empty with the exception of a desk and the man sitting behind it, the deceased Dr. Garrison Keller.

This room was filled with certificates and achievements, a stark contrast to the rest of the other, austere and contemporary, rooms in the home.

Throughout the home things appeared to be in order. Then out of nowhere, you have a well-educated solitary man, in a million-dollar home, in a peaceful neighborhood, shot in the head presumably by his own hand. Complicating the matter was the arrival of the federal agents who had virtually cleaned out one room while obviously waiting a tenuous amount of time to call in the investigators.

As it was in grade school, when you had to pick which one of the four pictures did not go together with the others, this pick was too obvious.

Do you remember in grade school when you are asked to name which object did not fit in the picture? There were three farm animals and then an airplane. In the grade school version, the airplane just did not fit. In this case, it wasn't necessarily the deceased, it was the federal government who did not belong there.

By nature, Chris did not need a reason to be skeptical during any investigation. This investigation would at least be easy to explain why he would be incredulous right from the start.

7

The same officer from downstairs had followed them through the house, up the stairs and into the study.

"Your first suicide, White?" the officer asked.

"Are you still here?" Chris replied, having no interest in making conversation with this officer.

Jude was standing to the side of the desk while Chris studiously looked at the body from the one side and then from the other. Garrison sat fully clothed at the large burl wood desk, hands outstretched, in a medium height diamond tufted red leather nail head chair. His shoes were still on.

There appeared to be a single gunshot wound to the right temple which was delivered by a .357 Magnum revolver that lay in a sticky pool of blood on the desk. Chris was hunched over the right side of the body. Looking up by moving only his head, pointed to the wall on Dr. Keller's left noting silently a corresponding bullet hole in the adjoining wall.

There was no apparent struggle and there were no defensive wounds on Dr. Keller's hands. From what Chris could see by moving Dr. Keller's fingers lightly with his pencil, circumstances were what they appeared to be.

Chris stood upright from the hunching position he was in when examining the body, "Is this the man you were thinking about?" he asked Jude.

"Appears to be," Jude replied, as she gazed across the remaining identifying accomplishments that adorned the shelves in the study.

Chris pulled further back from the desk and walked around the room. The drawers we mostly empty. The room looked as if it was in the middle of being relocated. This was the one and only room in the house that was filled with a lot of *informational décor*; albeit even though much of it was conspicuously missing.

Judging by the intermittent open spaces on the shelves and the open file cabinets, the décor had been departing and departing rapidly. The items remaining stood in silent testament to the life of a very accomplished man.

Dr. Keller was a man with no shortage of personal achievements. It seemed he had done it all; computer technology, cancer research, medicine, mathematics, M.I.T., M.D., and a Ph.D. You name it. He appeared to be an accomplished scholar.

Looking up, Chris noticed the agents who continued to dart in and out of the room and past the open doorway. This created a very anxious feeling for Chris.

Chris opened the desk drawers only to find there was nothing in them except for various office supplies. The top of the desk was void of any paperwork or computer hardware.

Was his work or work-product information already packed and removed? Chris asked, almost rhetorically, yet hoping someone would answer as he thought through the crime scene before him.

Jude replied, "Like I said, he worked at the University. He was active and well regarded, I think."

Chris scanned the room from a stationary position. He pointed to a picture on the shelf, "This is the woman in the picture downstairs too? Is she his wife? Where is she?"

The uniformed officer replied, "According to the maid that found him, it is his wife and she died sometime in the last couple years. I don't exactly recall what she said."

"The maid that found him? What maid?" Chris asked abruptly as he spun around, eyeball-to-eyeball, and drew a laser focused bead on the officer.

"Where is this maid now?"

"They sent her home," the officer replied in an incompetent, indifferent and sheepish manner.

"Good one there, Columbo. Who are *they*?" Chris snapped, taking another stab at the officer's age, proficiency on the job and attention to the question behind the question.

Chris did not wait for an answer.

"I was across the street when I got the call. I literally walked over here in less than ten minutes and the person that found the body has already been dismissed," virtually dismissing the officer verbally.

"Look, White, there have been people on this crime scene all afternoon. When you got the call, and from who, is not my problem. The body would also be gone by now if the Sheriff had not pulled rank on the Feds," the officer stammered.

Chris looked at Jude. He did not understand what that meant exactly as to how the Sheriff could pull rank on the Federal Government. Jude nodded her head up and down ever so slightly. Chris was not about to show a moment of weakness and ask the officer to explain his comment here on the spot. He would ask Jude later what this meant.

Chris looked back at the officer and delivered a collection of one line satires.

"Man killed and found by the maid? Killed himself and found by the maid? Killed by maid?" Chris continued.

"Man killed by officer who was screwing the maid and as an act of envy over the fact that the maid had a real job that she was good at performing? Officer let the maid go home before detectives spoke to her because officer was afraid of what the maid might say," growled Chris. "This presents quite a problem, don't you see?"

Chris shook his head back and forth gently as he mentally processed his continued distain for the officer and began to walk around the room. Even the officer had thought the comments from Chris were funny at first.

Chris was angry.

"Answer me buddy…and stop jacking me around. This is a problem. Who the hell is *they*? Who was the *they* that sent the maid home?" Chris asked again as Jude continued to look at each of the few remaining items left on the shelves attempting to understand more about the man that lay dead before her.

"*They* would be the lead federal officer in charge of the investigation that was here," the officer responded to the question as to who sent the maid home.

"The Fed who *was* here? What Fed leader? Did he leave too? What, is he some kind of imaginary friend of yours? Did the Fed have a name? Did you let the Fed go home early too?"

Chris followed Jude around the room as he spoke. Picking up and looking at the remaining individual items in the office, Dr. Keller's lifeless body peacefully slumped over the desk facing the bay.

"Jude, tell me what you know about this man," Chris asked as an agent cut in front of him and began to take more items off the shelves and pack them into boxes.

Chris was growing more irritated, "Will you stop taking things off the shelves and get the hell out of here."

The agent promptly left the room empty handed.

"Well, as I recall, he pioneered cancer treatment research. I read a couple of articles about him in the *Tribune*. He had a great medical and mathematical mind."

Jude was not fazed by the sight of Dr. Keller's lifeless body or the attitude that Chris was getting. She too was processing the crime scene mentally.

"What do you think?" Chris asked.

"Well," she replied, "If he killed himself, why is he sitting at his desk with his shoes on? People seldom kill themselves with their shoes on. More importantly, if I was thinking like you, why would this man even own a gun?"

Chris nodded affirmatively, "Exactly, and if he was going to own a gun, why would he own this *big daddy,*" referring to the .357 Magnum made famous by *Dirty Harry* in the 1970's.

Jude continued, "My guess is that he has plenty of money. It could have been that he was despondent over the loss of his wife? I don't know when she passed."

The uniformed officer added, "When I interviewed the maid, she said he had been very withdrawn the last six to eight months and was spending a lot of time at the office. A lot of time for him, given it was summer and all."

"Columbo, really? Now you tell us that you interviewed her," Chris said as he stopped and turned to the officer waving his hands dramatically.

"You are just full of surprises! How about you tell us everything she said or let us do the interviewing!"

"Well, I really didn't actually interview her," the officer added nervously.

"I just overheard the conversation. I did not personally interview her," he repeated.

The officer added. "The interview was done by Federal Agent Edward Cuda."

"You interviewed her. You didn't interview her. Have you even been a witness before? You're pathetic. How about you do as your daddy said Columbo and speak when spoken to? For Christ's sake. Get out of my sight before I fire myself for just being here in the same room with you," Chris barked disrespectfully.

A new agent came into the room carrying an empty box, accidentally running into Jude as he entered. Without comment or apology, he passed them by, stopping to set the empty box on the floor at Chris's feet, presumably to fill with more items from the open file cabinet.

"Tell me who you are?" Chris asked angrily.

"I am a federal agent," the man replied as he got on his knees to start packing.

"Great. That was helpful. Are you Agent Cuda?" Chris asked in a baby talk fashion.

"There was no sign of a break in," Jude added, attempting to take Chris's attention off of the officer and the soon to be packing agent.

The agent laughed, "I am not Agent Cuda, that's for sure!"

Chris inadvertently turned towards the door as if looking for another answer and there was a man standing in the door way, "Well, hello. Now who are you? Just another anonymous packing agent perhaps?" Chris asked.

"My name is Ed Cuda," the man replied.

"Nice," Chris responded with a chuckle. "The interviewer of the maid I understand? Maybe you are going to tell me this is your crime scene and not mine now?"

"I didn't know Sheriff's detectives had personal crime scene rights, particularly if they were from Manchester," Cuda replied.

"Do I know you?" Chris asked with a sneer.

Cuda had nailed down Chris' English accent right down to the township after only a couple sentences. Cuda was a gamer. Of course, unbeknownst to Chris, the hours leading up to Chris and Jude's arrival certainly helped Cuda be prepared to meet the investigators on the scene.

"No, you don't know me," Cuda replied.

"The Sheriff can command a crime scene over and above all other agencies, even the federal government. This will remain a county crime scene," Jude replied.

Chris looked back at Jude in appreciation, but remained silent.

"So I have learned," Cuda replied. "So I have learned. It is my hope that you excuse my ignorance and appreciate the fact that I have packed a lot of what I thought would be relevant to the investigation and will deliver it for your review. As you can probably see, we started to pack a lot of things before we were made fully aware this would not be a federal crime scene."

Chris was not appreciative of the help. Moreover, he remained unaware of exactly how the Sheriff's jurisdiction played into this scenario. What he did know was that he had also taken an instant dislike to Ed Cuda.

"Back to my original question then. Why are you here and what made you think this was a federal crime scene to begin with?" Chris asked.

"I believe that this is the first time you have asked me why I am here. Your original question was 'who are you'?" Cuda replied mordantly.

"Nonetheless, I am here because Dr. Keller was a very high profile person due to his research grants from the United Stated Government and the President has asked if I would offer my assistance in the investigation. There may be sensitive national security issues involved."

"President," Jude said with a confused look, "President of...?"

"The President of the United States of America," Cuda responded.

"Wait a minute," Chris commented. "Are you telling me that the President of the United States wants to get involved in this investigation? The President is investigating a dead researcher from the University? Seems he would have bigger things to manage these days, wouldn't you say Jude? Maybe he could start with the economy."

Chris was clearly asking Jude a question, but did not take his eyes off of Ed Cuda, not even to blink.

"Can we see some identification?" Jude asked.

"Sure," as Cuda handed over his Secret Service badge and photo I.D. identifying him as Edward Cuda, a Special Liaison to the President of the United States of America.

Cuda reassured Chris, looking back at Jude. "We will be glad to offer you all of the resources available to the United States government in an effort to help bring timely closure to this investigation."

Cuda continued solemnly, "Dr. Garrison Keller always strived to make an impactful contribution to people and to society. He had made such a big difference in the lives of so many Americans. He will be missed. That is why he moved from mathematics to medicine, you know. He was all about quality of life."

"It is tragic that he would take his own life. Tragic! Please know that we are prepared to help if you need assistance," Cuda continued with a somber non-emotional look on his face.

Chris was not impressed with Cuda's cool behavior or his attempt to inform him about the great significance of Garrison. Chris was indifferent to Cuda, Presidential Liaison or not, Cuda was right up there with the missing maid. He was just another potential suspect.

Chris continued to look around the room with his back to the door where Cuda was standing. Speaking as he gazed. He would pick up and make comments on each of the remaining awards and commendations that were displayed. Most of the items he had already inspected. While doing so he would make brief remarks loud enough so that Agent Cuda could hear.

"So, the President of the United States is interested in this fellow's death? Why do you think that is Jude?" Chris said rhetorically as he set down a picture of Dr. Keller having dinner with Governor Pawlenty. No reply.

Jude was diligently looking over the body with her back to the door and her back to Chris.

"And you, Mr. Special Agent man, just surreptitiously happen to be in town, and at the crime scene I might add, on the day that Dr. Keller committed suicide. One hell of a big coincidence, Mr. Cuda, I would say," Chris added.

Chris was finishing his thought and now standing over the body with his back still to the door. He was looking at Jude who was now fixedly examining the wound.

"It is interesting that you know so much about this guy. Have you met him before?" Chris was gaining confidence and self assurance.

"Maybe I should be asking to take a gunshot residue test from your hands, Mr. Cuda," Chris advised as he turned to make eye contact with Cuda.

Cuda was gone. He was no longer standing in the doorway. The only three persons in the room were Jude, Chris and Dr. Keller's lifeless body.

8

Chris charged out the office door and to the stairwell where he called down to the officer below, "Where is that Fed that was here. Ed Cuda?"

"He just left," the officer called back.

"Stop him," Cuda implored as he scampered down the stairs exiting the front door and giving chase down the raised concrete tile decking towards the driveway where he met several agents loading the last of a few boxes into a small moving van.

"Where is Agent Cuda?" Chris asked slightly winded from excitement.

"He is gone," one agent replied.

"Where is he staying?"

"He never says," the agent replied as the other agents continued to work.

"Who is his supervisor? How can I call him?" Chris asked frantically. "I need to see him tonight. No. I need to see him right now!"

"Supervisor? You want his Supervisor?" They all laughed. "Do you have the phone number to the Oval Office?"

"As far as we know, he is a liaison to the President and a member of the Secret Service. Call the President if you like," the agent lauded.

Chris took a deep breath and put his arms to his side. He was perturbed by the run around he had just received and began to walk determinately back to the house.

9

Chris walked back into the house and back up to the room where Jude was still taking a few last pictures of the crime scene.

"I don't like that guy. No not even a little bit," Chris again growled.

'You don't like anybody," Jude responded with acceptance.

Looking over the events of the last hour Chris felt justified in his dislike. This crime scene was in an evidentiary shambles. Cuda scurrying out unannounced was certainly suspicious enough even though the last words he heard Cuda say before departing were words of well wishes and assistance.

Chris definitely thought robbery was out of the question as a motive. The thought of a well-educated, society-centric fellow killing himself when he had everything going for him, just did not sit well.

Chris continued to reason that Dr. Keller had everything to gain and nothing to lose, assuming Dr. Keller did not kill himself and everything to lose and nothing to gain by assuming he took his own life. This was not a simple suicide in Chris' opinion. There was a lot more going on here, but Chris certainly seemed a little more committed than usual. He thought he could see closure to this case. He would expend a little more than his usual perfunctory effort to prove it.

The plain fact and circumstance that Cuda was coincidently here in town and simply left as quickly as he appeared was a materially incriminating fact Chris just could not seem to get past.

Jude was more objective. She was a *follow the money* investigator. Jude would always look to follow the money. Money and love, or the love of money, or both, was the root of ninety-five percent of violent crimes.

Jude's direction would be to follow up on Garrison's financial situation and research grants. The *follow the money* theory was a sort of *all roads lead to Rome* philosophy. In this case, Rome was Dr. Keller and the almighty dollar was the road.

The Coroner had just arrived and entered the room. Surprised at what appeared to be an aging and ransacked death scene, he immediately started the examination of the body. He was careful to bag Garrison's hands. He then took an inordinate number of photos of the body and of the room including the gunshot hole in the wall adjacent to the body.

This investigation would be complicated. All of the contents of the study had been packed. One of the Agents from downstairs came up to say that everything was packed and awaiting direction as to where Chris wanted it delivered.

In the room was the coroner, Jude, one agent and; of course, Dr. Keller's lifeless corpse.

Chris took another deep breath. "What I want to know is," Chris paused, "Where is the maid?"

The agent replied, "The maid was sent home."

"Perfect," Chris replied. "Do we know where home is?"

"I do not!" the agent responded.

"Why did I bother to ask? I already knew that would be your answer," Chris concluded, resolute to the incompetence of the agent.

Thankfully, the Sheriff had somehow pulled rank on the United States Government. The Sheriff was a wise leader. He knew something was not right. He had the wherewithal to take action and manage the situation in an upwardly mobile manner.

Unfortunately, the investigators and the coroner arrived on scene many hours after the body was discovered and after much of the evidence had been compromised in this case. There was the potential that critical evidence would end up missing. The custody of evidence trail, if any were needed, would be virtually inadmissible.

However, somehow the main suspect, at least in Chris's mind, was a liaison to the President of the United States who could not be immediately located.

As a final thought, Chris turned to Jude and asked in a moment of reflection, consolation and solace, "Does the United States government cover up a lot of things here in this country Jude?"

"The federal government is here to help," Jude replied.

"You are naive Jude," Chris reprimanded with a smile. "Naive, but a great American. I'll give you credit for that."

"And you sound committed to the case," Jude replied.

"We'll see," Chris replied

Once again, they agreed to disagree.

CHAPTER TWO
I HAVE A DREAM

10

Nine months earlier, the able bodied, young and assertive new President knew he was just what the country needed as he walked through the narrow halls of the West Wing of the White House. He was recently elected to the highest office in the land by an unprecedented margin.

These indeed were challenging times in America. The country had nearly been thrown into an economic depression through a series of fiscal miscalculations by the Congress and by Wall Street.

To be more precise, there was a monumental financial implosion in the United States of America. The implosion was largely created by a Congress unwilling and unable to control their spending.

More recently, they have been equally unwilling to compromise on their various policy platforms in the new post world wide war on terrorism that was ballooning out the deficit geometrically. The current situation needed to be addressed, whatever the stakes, on every level possible. This new President was the *chosen one* in what were clearly not the best of times in America's triumphant and storied past.

The self confidence brought on by the election, his youth and his rocket ship ascension to the nations top leadership position would show, not so inconspicuously, oozing from every pore in his body.

At a brisk pace, he walked with a long gait given his six feet, two-inch, frame. He was well spoken, well-read, well-educated and immaculately groomed no matter how formal or casual the occasion. Definitively, he was a statesman by every definition of the word. Looking back on the campaign trail, many would say, he was a stickler for micro-managing details on many levels below his own.

Outside the four walls of the White House and throughout the country there was a feeling, a not so easy feeling, that his self-assurance and poise were being misapplied, misrepresented and perhaps were not in the best interest of the fiscally troubled nation as a whole. What some saw as confidence, objective, worthy opinion and true leadership, others saw as arrogant, self-centered and inflexibly damaging to the country. Recklessly looking to the future, he was hell bent on being a *change* agent.

You could see it in his stride as he passed the cabinet room and approached the entrance to the Oval Office. There was a swagger in his step. There was a self-appreciating superiority he carried about him. So much so, that he could not even bring himself to acknowledge the Secret Service members who were noticeably positioned outside the Oval Office door and at the end of every corridor.

He had worked what seemed his entire life, controversial as it may be, to lead this country into prosperity and out from underneath the heavy hands of the conservative right, conspicuous consumption, presumed religious segregation and the big business establishment of corporate America.

It was obvious, he knew he was brought here by the people to be the most powerful man in the world and he was going to play it for all he could. He was going to leave a legacy that was his and his alone. Now that he was here, he intended to lead this charge for change on his terms; all others, be damned.

The White House, the Oval Office, and the Presidency in total, are all dynamic, respectful and procedurally driven institutions. Very few could come to the Oval Office in the American White House and simply speak their mind, unless they had been asked to do so by the President himself.

People arrived on time, when scheduled, prepared and ready to discuss their business with the man, a nation of independents had elected to lead the richest society the world had ever known. The scope, the breadth and the consequence of the conversations and decisions that have been generated and confirmed by this Office has been globally sweeping and awe inspiring.

Recently elected to the Presidency and unbeknownst to him at today's early hour, this would be one of the more impactful hours this President would have during his term. What he did not realize was how impactful it would be for him principally, before it would eventually impact the people who had chosen him and those he now had pledged to faithfully serve.

This President in particular brought to his administration a series of pre-determined ideals. The ultimate ideal and dominating principle of this administration was that all men, all women and all children, have a right to have what everyone else has.

This administration's ideal was to exemplify that the United States Government should provide for all who, willing or unwilling, able or unable, cannot provide for themselves on their own. The lazy, the poor, the committed, the rich, the infirmed, the physically challenged along with the healthy and gifted, are all seen as equal beneficiaries of American privilege in this President's mono-chromatic tapestry of this great nation.

No matter the cost to the economy or the populace en masse, everyone should have a nice home, a new car, universal health care and the standing that comes from being an American by birth, deserving of the title from a patriotic or moral standpoint not withstanding, including himself.

It was a time in American legislative power that socializing government was all the rage with the new and up-coming non-traditional capitalistic generations.

11

The President was scheduled to meet with two men this morning. The meeting was set for 8:00 a.m. sharp and would last one hour. One man was Edward Cuda, who was a Special Agent and liaison to the President. This was the first time the President was to meet with, or had even spoken to, Edward Cuda. The other man was Dean Taking. Taking was the new head of Homeland Security.

A couple days earlier, both men had inched their way into an unscheduled emergency issues slot on the President's early morning calendar. They needed to speak to the President today regarding the security of various members of the government's executive and legislative branch. The concern was brought on by the growing unrest around the country associated with the inability of Congress to represent the constituents, make financially sound policy decisions and deal expeditiously with the President's number one initiative, health care reform.

Across the states, there were town hall meetings that were turning into shouting matches. The verbal altercations were targeted at both local and Federal representation, from both bodies of Congress and from both sides of the isle. This was a bipartisan divide. A divide which was getting deeper as every day passed. Call it free speech, free will, organized chaos, whatever the matter, people were speaking freely and the Congress did not like it.

One could presume they never did, but the Democratic Party in particular really disliked the intolerant animosity it was getting these days in light of the fact that they had control of the House, the Senate and the White House. The Democrats thought this was time for real, undeniable and deservingly needed long term change.

The overall feeling today was that it was the President's own party's turn to govern now.

Practice in the field often differs from practice in the office. As we all know, in Washington, Congressmen and Congresswomen on Capital Hill meet in small groups with people who have been approved for a spot on their calendar by a juvenile aid, barely wet behind the ears and unsure of what the real priorities or concerns are back in their respective districts.

Legislative members are accustomed to being respected. Yes sir. No sir, you're right madam Congresswoman.

On the contrary, in the field, they are not accustomed to being confronted in person, in their districts by every day citizens who may be down right angry with the decisions they are making.

Many assume that the political maneuvering and method of distraction that many members of Congress use satisfies the majority of constituents. Be assured, there is a big difference in decorum between meeting with a constituent in the field and meeting with someone who is lobbying in your office.

Applying this principle to the negative side, the town hall meetings were becoming a real problem for the President and his policy reform efforts. In some of the senior staff member's minds, a potential threat to the stability and peacefulness of the nation as a whole may be in play. Of course, the President's safety was always a concern.

What the President wanted more than anything was to get past what he saw as the limited civil unrest which was mainly attributed to health care reform, and to discuss the remedies and ameliorations with the two men present, and then move on.

In the President's inexperienced mind, the unrest as well as the security meeting today was merely a speed bump on his high speed race for health care policy reforms. The President's intentions to date, with regard to the health care debate and restructuring, did provide for universal coverage in the most sincere and unassuming manner possible. The President had very big vision in terms of what he intended to do in principle, without regard to the cost, even though he was not getting credit for those intentions.

As the morning would proceed, the root of the intentions would change and the roots would grow very deep and very fast.

For Edward Cuda and Dean Taking, the purpose and surface objective of today's meeting with the President would be about national security and not policy. This too would change today.

After the election, decorated with fresh paint, fresh flowers, tidily dusted and arranged, the Oval Office was awaiting the arrival of the President and his guests.

The President entered the Oval Office to meet with the two men, exhibiting his standard uninterruptable high velocity, upbeat and well rehearsed tempo. The President acted as if the cameras were always rolling.

"Good morning, Mr. President," Dean Taking said as both men stood up from the two chairs that were in front of the President's desk. Dean was still inspired and intimidated by the presence of a sitting United States President.

There was an original portrait of George Washington on the wall. In the center of the room stood the desk of John F. Kennedy which the President had requisitioned as his own.

Taking was slightly short of breath and nervous, despite the fact that he had been here a couple times before. He was the head of Homeland Security and was in what was most likely the most secure place in this or any other country, but was nervous nonetheless.

"Allow me to introduce you to Ed Cuda, Mr. President. Mr. Cuda is a Special Agent and liaison to you, Mr. President," Taking described.

"Special Agent and liaison to the President!" the President exclaimed. "That title itself does certainly provoke further inquiry. The position sounds like it has some pretty lofty responsibilities. I would like to hear what those responsibilities include; that is, insofar as I am the person for whom you are the liaison," the President said in a metered, pompous and virtually dismissive tone of voice.

"Thank you, Mr. President. Thank you for setting the time aside in your full schedule to see us today. It is an honor to meet you. We all have great responsibility to the people of our nation Mr. President, in many different yet interconnected ways, we all are here to serve," Cuda replied in a confident and respectful manner.

"Yes, we are all chosen to serve at some level and I am happy to serve at the highest level," the stately President said with a smirk as would a boy who had beaten everyone else to the tree house and was looking down at them after pulling up the ladder.

The President completely overlooked the fact that he had been outplayed in the very first volley from Ed Cuda. Nowhere in Ed Cuda's response was there an answer to the question that the President had just asked him.

In the President's own office, he asked a question and you answered the question directly. Those are the rules of play here. He *was* the President after all. The insincerity and disinterest in the answer to his own question was strike one for the President in Edward Cuda's master plan.

What the President did not know, and should have known if he had been properly briefed by his staff, was that this was the fourth administration with which Mr. Cuda has been involved. Cuda was no stranger to the game afoot.

Cuda was a certified covert insider looking in and a power player in Washington. He represented the United States Strategic Planning Commission, a heavy hitting Washington, D.C. think-tank that had great, but in the eyes of the public largely unknown, impact on policy. He was a very young man many years ago when he started his career in politics.

Today, without question, he is a fearsome competitor who has a "leave no man behind that will compromise the battle plan" and "take no live prisoners, they will just slow you down" operating style. He is seasoned. He is tough. He is committed. He is extremely well connected and he will not be intimidated by a new, first term, and likely one term, President.

The United States Strategic Planning Commission was, as think tanks go, a very deep tank that had a heavy undertow in terms of policy and planning management. It was; however, much more. It was the mother and father of all special interest groups. It managed the master plan for the governmental control, the manipulation of all policies, cause and effect, as related to the long term fiscal management and the solvency of the nation. Everything came through the Strategic Planning Commission office. The oversight and influence was nothing short of massive.

The President walked around his desk and stated while being seated, "I am glad that you are here on time. The President waits for no man," as if that statement was not inferred already and speaking about himself in the third person.

The two men then sat down while the President shuffled through a few papers of little consequence on his desk. While paying half attention to the two men in the room, he asked, "Let's get down to business. How are you going to deal with these people who think that they can run rough house at all of the town meetings that my people are going out of their way to come to. The Congressmen and Congresswomen are very accommodating it seems to me."

The President thought that he was bigger than the job. Strike two, Cuda thought to himself. We have only been here for a couple minutes, staring at the President who was himself now locked on Taking for an answer.

Your people Cuda was considering silently. These are not *your* people and *you* certainly are not accommodating them by allowing the constituents to have their say. Cuda would soon be maneuvering into a position of letting the President know who was really in charge here, and it was neither the President nor the office of the Presidency itself.

"Mr. President," Taking stated nervously and stuttering, yet still calm, "The particular situation to which you are referring, I mean regarding the town hall meetings and mild unrest, well, is one that we need to allow to play out. We should be careful not to make a big 'operational imperative' of these town meetings at this time."

The more emphasis we put on quieting the ground swell of resistance, history has shown us, the more aggressive and defiant the crowds become. It would seem to me that we need to allow this to run its course, keep adequate levels of security on the Congress members as they travel to insure safe passage, perhaps add additional screening at these meetings where Senators are attending, and let the unrest burn itself out. If you wish, we can surely discuss it further as part of the reason we set up this meeting today. This will…"

"Mr. Taking," The President interrupted in mid-sentence and calmly laid the distractions of the tangential paperwork aside, "Are you telling the President of the United States to relax and be patient while these angry organized right wing nut job mobs hijack what is likely the most influential and powerful collection of governing legislators this nation has known in industrialized times?"

Taking spoke during the President's brief respite, "Would you advise…" Again, cut off by the President who continued, "Do not interrupt me in my own house. Are you telling me that I have control of the House of Representatives, the Senate and the White House and we are going to let some grass roots bunch of thugs dictate legislation to the people in elected positions that by the very definition of their roles are empowered to propose, create and generate new policy and law for my personal, I repeat my personal, signature and approval?" the President continued.

"Is that what I am paying you for? What am I to expect from you, a strategy of 'let it play out' and 'run its course'. Are you kidding me? Let it play out!"

The President was temperamental to say the least, often acting like a spoiled brat and a bully. He has acted this way for his entire political career.

He was flailing his arms and hands about, "Let it play out and I would not be President. Let it play out and I would be uneducated. Let it play out and I would be just another poor Black Muslim man."

"Perhaps you would prefer a woman had represented my party and had become President. Maybe she would be happy letting things play out for you," the President scolded. "Perhaps you would have liked that better."

Taking was perceptibly shaken now and understandably so. He was sweating profusely. He was being reprimanded by the President, in the President's office in front of a guest no less. He was surprised by the immediate turn in the discussion. He was clearly unprepared. He did not have a good solution, and not many did, to the complex problem to which the President was referring.

Making it even more complicated, Taking was new in his position. It was as if he went to the President for direction instead of coming prepared with issues and solutions to discuss and have them approved by the President. He looked back and forth between Cuda and the President looking for a break in the thrashing he was receiving.

The arrogance that the country felt was undeniably evident in the President's mannerisms and actions today.

The President was fully engaged and locked on, eyeball-to-eyeball with Dean Taking, "Need I remind you that you are in the Oval Office of the White House, speaking to the President of the United States of America. When most people come here they come to play it up. They come with a plan, a program, a solution, something; at least, a proposal!"

"Does this appear to be an office of action or an office of wait and see? I govern from this chair, with my opinion, and with few exceptions, to the exclusion of all other opinions. I do not give advice, I make things happen from this chair," the President mandated as if to clarify the roles and an almost maniacal fashion.

Cuda on the other hand sat calmly, patiently and without emotion as he watched the nearly totalitarian tirade that was taking place before him. Strike three, Cuda thought to himself. This mans ego was in control here and nothing else. He would be an easy mark if faced with embarrassment or consequence, Cuda speculated. He was a bit of a bully in the preadolescent sense of the word.

Cuda had been here before, although, in less ego enthusiast administrations and under convincingly different circumstances. He knew what he was doing. This was another afternoon on the job for Cuda. Cool as a cucumber; dispassionate as you would think a twenty-first century public policy mercenary would be.

Taking responded to the outwardly verbal reprimand, "I suppose that we could put a stop to the town hall meetings citing security concerns. We could then arrange for smaller, not public, by invitation only, town hall meetings and only invite news crews we know will be editing our material favorably. We certainly would not invite *FOX News*," he said with a strained smile that he thought might help the overall undertone of the meeting as he scrambled for a course of action in an effort to attempt to please.

Taking was trying to be helpful by stepping out of his scope of responsibility and area of expertise in an attempt to meld his security priority with the policy redirection the President was guiding the conversation with.

The President was leaning aggressively forward at his desk, "You suppose?"

It was hard to tell if the President was just frustrated or if he was down right angry. Either way, this was not going well for Taking.

Dean Taking had come to this administration well endorsed by many of the President's top advisors. He had come from a law enforcement background where he was usually in charge. His role in law enforcement had not prepared him well to deal with the politics and pressure at a Presidential level. He was prone to sweating and was out of shape. The ability to handle the difficult demands and challenging responses on the fly did not come easy for Dean. He did not think fast on his feet.

In the final analysis, Cuda felt no sympathy for Taking. He didn't need Taking to complete his assignment involving the President today. Taking was merely the price of admission.

Unlike Taking, Cuda was in shape. He controlled his emotions and ran daily to alleviate the stress of his high impact job. He was a strategist and clear thinker. Observing the two of them was like watching the Kennedy-Nixon debate on television in September of 1960. It was clearly a mis-match and Cuda was Kennedy.

Cuda and Taking did not know each other well. They were barely acquaintances. Taking was a real rookie when compared to Cuda. Conversely, Cuda thought Taking was totally out of place in the big leagues.

Looking at the question the President had initially asked, understanding the nature of executive discussions and the strategy of diversion, this should not have gone so far astray. This one issue, the issue of the unrest at the community level, was a big one to the President. He rightfully needed to understand what could be done and what was being done.

The point that was missed due to the nervousness and the intensity of the moment was this. All Taking needed to do was to state that the security issues were his concern and his area of expertise. The nature of the meeting today was to address security related matters and it was someone else's area of expertise to address the town hall meeting schedules and their content more specifically.

If the President would like, he would arrange to have those people brought in as soon as possible for his counsel. Had Taking done so, they would have discussed security and he would have been off the hook. Regrettably for Taking, that was not the case.

To Cuda's good fortune, Taking was caught up in the moment. As it stood at present, the meeting conversation was irreversibly off the original target, at least as long as Taking was present. The President had him on the run. Taking kept digging deeper and deeper and the President was going in for the kill.

"At what point in this meeting should I question your qualifications to provide security direction? For that matter, should I question any direction you give to this office in a forward thinking, preparatory and futuristic fashion. Perhaps I should just start by questioning the people who referred you to this position in the first place," the President asked Taking.

"If I may, Mr. President," Cuda answered for Taking in an attempt defuse the situation and to provide a solution before Dean was flat out fired on the spot. Besides, Cuda needed the President alone.

Surprised by the interjection, "You may," the President said failing to take his eyes off of Taking as Cuda spoke.

"May I suggest that perhaps you allow Mr. Taking to be excused from the meeting today? He will need some time to consider your comments and seek the comments of others before attesting to a satisfactory plan of action that will serve the security of this office, the Congress persons' security and the security of the people most appropriately."

"You and I can finish up on the most pressing issues regarding what immediate safety concerns may need to be met with regard to you personally. I will follow up and share them with Mr. Taking separately."

"That will be fine. Mr. Taking, please see yourself out," the President said without respect and still intently focused on Taking.

Taking got up to leave, thanked the President for his time and made his way to the open Oval Office door. The office was silent. Every step Taking took was running in slow motion in his mind's eye. Each step he made seemed to have echoed in the small office.

The awkward silence was interrupted just prior to actually leaving the Oval Office proper. The President called out, "and Dean!"

Taking stopped and turned to the President, "Yes, Mr. President?"

"You may want to take your friend, Mr. Cuda, here out to dinner and thank him for intervening on your behalf today. He probably allowed you to stay in the job that you have yet to grow into," the President said in his usual supercilious manner.

New batter or strike four Cuda thought, he wasn't sure. This will be easier than Cuda had anticipated. Deep down, past the election and the office, this President had an indifference to people as individuals. The President saw the American citizen not as an individual with rights, but as a collective group who had an obligation to follow his lead.

Accompanying his indifference to individualization, there is a self-significance that will be likely to get in the way of controversial decision making. He will be committed to the ideal of his public perception and will not likely show any humility. He will have to be right all the time. This would be a perfect combination for the conversations that would be happening next.

Furthermore, this President would not take well to criticism or being told what to do…unless he could quickly weigh the options and avoid public controversy and the humiliation that may come from being wrong or the need to backtrack on previous commitments. He would have to see a path where he himself would not be seen as failing.

"Yes, Sir. Thank you, Sir," Taking said in an embarrassingly meek tone as he walked out of the room a defeated man.

"Well, that is twenty minutes of my life I am never going to get back," the President said contemptuously to Cuda as he sat upright while comfortably leaning back at his desk looking out over the White House gardens.

12

Cuda was now alone with the President. With some minor unpredicted adjustments, things were right on schedule. It was time for Cuda to engage in some candid conversation with the President.

"Do you mind if I close the door Mr. President?" Cuda asked.

Sitting comfortably and preoccupied with his view out of the window with the chair still turned away from Cuda, the President made a waving hand gesture and replied, "Can you believe the view from my office? I don't care. Close the door if you like."

Cuda walked to the open door. Standing in the doorway he looked out into the hall. Standing right next to the door was a Secret Service Agent. The agent turned and looked at Cuda as he peered out from the office. Both nodded at each other as though they were cordially, silently greeting one another as professional courtesy and more than the agents generally received from the President they were there to protect.

Cuda withdrew himself back into the office and closed the door. The two men were all alone and Cuda walked towards the President who still had his back to Cuda.

Cuda had been here before with other sitting Presidents. His comments would likely be relatively short with some of the same predictable dialogue. The conversation would be generally one sided. This President's presidency would not be the same after today and, for better or worse, there were very few ways around that simple fact.

Cuda sat back in his original chair vacated only moments earlier.

"Your administration is really caught in a tough spot these days," Cuda said as he looked at the back of his own hand smug and conceitedly.

"And how is that, Mr. Cuda?" The President asked as he broke his gaze and turned his chair back to face Cuda, giving him his undivided attention.

Cuda replied, still composed and still looking at his hands as if avoiding eye contact, "I am speaking of your health care plan passage. I mean, you know, it will pass eventually in some form, right? I mean, *your* people will have to see to it. Right? It is your plan, right?"

It was quiet.

"I understand it is challenging," Cuda continued still looking at his hands, picking his finger nails and nodding affirmatively. "These are issues that are complicated and the issues are further complicated by complicated times. It is too bad that your predecessor left you in such poor financial health, specifically with the war on terror and the huge deficits and all. None of us were expecting this cost to get so far out of hand."

Weighing things out, hands palm up in front of him like an animated human scale of justice, Cuda made eye contact with the President and continued, "On one hand, the rapid expansion and socialization of medicine is a real job killer for small business if it passes especially in an already struggling economy over the short term. On the other hand, if it passes, in the long term, it will need to be a real killer of people in our society because we simply will not be able to afford the care. It is a short term long term dilemma, don't you think?"

"Both hands show passage it sounds like to me," the President replied. "It will be great for all Americans everywhere."

"Are you sure, Mr. President? Did you hear what I just said?" Cuda asked.

13

From where Cuda sat, the people had reached their limit on what they were willing to pay in taxes. From the perspective of the Strategic Planning Commission, there were acceptable losses in how heath care was delivered to Americans. Losses that would need to be logically assessed financially as individual care is approved and dispensed.

In theory, medical services will need to be *assigned* in such a fashion that would keep the system solvent. To do so, the system would need to purposefully deliberate over what procedures would be done to whom and what return there would be to society for having invested in the applied care.

There are no even trades. The government will always want the best deal for itself. As an example, someone in their thirties who is well educated and that could have a high likelihood of contributing to the system for many years to come would be a good investment.

Dissimilarly, someone who is in their seventies and will no longer contribute to the system, and worse yet, just take benefits from the system, would be an acceptable loss.

To practically apply this theory, the system would have to set standards. There would need to be standards that would stipulate, on a multi-axis curve, procedures, ages of the people receiving a procedure and the ability of the recipient to contribute to the community. If these curves intersected outside of the acceptable range, the treatment would be denied.

It sounds harsh, but in many ways it is in practice already. Care is already metered out. In the United States, to some degree, it is metered out by the ability of the recipient to pay for the care. Abroad, many government care systems provide services and continue to do so in the fashion that Cuda proposes. They do so with restricted access to certain treatments, to certain groups, to maintain solvency.

More than nationalization, it would be *rationalization* as care is rationed to the best candidates. The more years you have behind you, the more restricted your access and ability to get the appropriate care.

In the final analysis, you cannot treat old people differently just because they are more frail and young people differently just because they are less experienced. That would be discrimination based on age.

However, there is a need to treat them differently based on the elderlys' use of medical services, particularly among legacy benefit users. Their contribution to the stability of the community and the financial position of the health care system, have to come into play at some point.

14

Cuda awaited the reply from the President.

"I do not know what you are talking about. The killer of people?" the President asked.

Yeah, I know," Cuda admired. "You're new here."

Cuda continued, "Please, allow me to explain. You will have to get your legislation to pass. It is a priority for you. The Strategic Planning Commission would like to see your health care plan pass too. It is a priority for us also. It just will not be in the spirit that you have dreamed of during all of your liberal life."

The President felt the pain of a direct body blow to the ego and was not amused to hear it in his own office. Remember, the rules are different in the office than they are in the field. He was not at the pub with a bunch of college buddies, he was in control mode. This was his time on his turf. The President was not sure what a liaison of his was doing in his office to start with, much less attempting to be mandating policy.

"Mr. Cuda, first of all, what is the Strategic Planning Commission? Second, are you going to be the next one to make the mistake of coming into my office and dictating policy to me? I thought you might have had enough education on politesse after being a student of Mr. Taking before he was dismissed. Do I need to start over now with you on etiquette in the White House?" the President questioned. "Or will I have the pleasure of seeing two people fail and be thrown out of this office today?"

There was a momentary verbal hiatus as the two men kept eye contact. The President asked, "Perhaps you can explain what it is that you are doing here and why?"

This was a critical point in the conversation and Cuda gladly replied confidently, "What I am telling you is this. Bluntly put, in our current financial times, a decision has been made. Within that decision there is the subject of health care costs. These costs must come down so that the country can again find the equilibrium it had in the 1990's."

"In short, I am speaking to your dream of a cradle to grave, one payer system, and the *same care for everyone* type of health care system. It will not happen as you see it happening," he explained.

Through his gesticulation and his commentary, Cuda could tell he had the President's attention. There is no substitute in all of civilized business for what an experienced veteran with knowledge and understanding of their role and state of affairs can bring to the table. This was big business and Cuda was an expert.

The President was unresponsive and intended to put an end to this needless engagement and provocation. Why was he listening to this jabber jawing anyway?

"I do not understand what you are talking about Mr. Cuda....and I will ask again, why am I having this conversation with you anyway? What is your area of expertise as liaison?" the President queried as he scrambled in his mind to recall why Cuda was even in his office and just exactly what it is that he does. Only now was he recalling that his original question to Cuda about his *pretty lofty responsibilities* was not answered.

"My area of expertise is to give you a message, as it has been given to Presidents before you, and as it will likely be given to Presidents after you in one manner or another I suspect," Cuda added.

"You are giving *me* a message?" the President replied in disbelief. "Really!"

"I am," Cuda responded. "These are not the best of times and the fiscal intake, liabilities and assets of the system are out of balance. A decision has been made that the health care costs must once again be a major area of cost containment in the United States overall budget."

"Is that so?" the President replied. "I will have cost containment in my plan."

"I am sure you will, but not to the extent and definition that will be needed," Cuda added.

"Is that so?" the President replied again in the same tone still wondering why this man was in his office.

Cuda continued, "One of two things will have to happen here. We will need to continue with the health care plans and dysfunctional legislative process related to health care the way it is, or preferably, we need to get to a strictly controlled government plan that actuarially caps out human life at just under seventy-eight years of age. No longer."

"What on earth are you saying?" the President said as he stood up from his desk. Are you another one of these uneducated crackpot skinheads that say I am out to kill your grandma? That is not the purpose of my plan and never was. I am sick and tired of people coming around here telling me what I intended. This is a plan that will give comfort and dignity to an aging population and basic coverage to the underprivileged children. It will add quality years to human life."

"I know what I have stated was not the purpose of your plan, but that will be the purpose of our plan, Mr. President. The system plan," Cuda cautioned in a firm tone of voice.

The President was quick to take offense, "Are you coming in here telling me what to do? I am the President of the...."

Cuda cut the President off, "Respectfully, Sir, I know who you are. You are the President of the United States of America. I am well aware of where I am and who I am talking to. I have been listening to you tell me who you are for the last half hour. As a matter of fact, I hear you say *me* and *I* more than I have ever heard any other President use those words."

"I will have you removed from this office!" the President ordered angrily and increasingly more motivated to have Cuda forcibly evicted.

"By whom?" Cuda questioned with a smile and still staring straight ahead towards the President who was facing him from behind his desk.

"My Secret Service Agents," the President instructed as he stomped to the closed Oval Office door and opened it with a rush to speak to an agent who was dutifully positioned outside the door in the hallway.

Cuda called out, looking at his hands again in contempt, "My guess is that they are unavailable at the moment."

He was right. There was no one outside the door. As the President looked up and down the hallways, there was no one positioned at the end of the corridors either.

"You should come on back in here, Mr. President. Every system has a weakness and every rule has at least one exception," Cuda counseled.

The President stood in the doorway not sure quite what to think. This was the first time in a year that he was actually vulnerable and was quickly weighing every ego obsessed, control driven option.

In haste he replied, "This room has an automated voice activated recorder. Unfortunately, you must have forgotten that in your liaison training. I will be more than willing to play the tape recording at your court-martial. I will even see that you get a copy to play for your regretful entertainment in your prison cell."

"Let's get past the small talk, Mr. President. You seem to think everything around here is yours. It's not. You sound like you think I am part of *your* military. I am not. I have a civilian job, so a court-marshal is pretty unlikely. It's funny to me that you seem just arrogant enough to make me believe you really think you are in charge around here and, well, you're not. The *system*, the *establishment* is in charge here Mr. President. Don't you get it? I am here to help you adjust to that premise. You are just the temporary face of that establishment that occupies this office. As President, you really don't preside over anything."

The President stood silently as Cuda continued the exchange from his still sitting position, "With respect to the position, Mr. President," Cuda said sarcastically and without the respect outwardly spoken he reiterated, "the system is in charge here, Mr. President. Not the President, not the people's representatives, not the people and certainly not you."

"Who knows what would happen if the people would actually be in charge?" Cuda mused shaking his head inferring all out anarchy would be at hand.

Like the lion that had misplaced his courage, the President was still silent, listening, and unsure of what to do as he weighed his options. The Secret Service was no where in sight. There was a phone he could use. He continued to process the situation.

"Mr. President," Cuda continued condescendingly, yet understanding the President was mentally searching for what to do next. "The system is focused on the long term financial survival of the nation as a whole. This is not a personal discussion. Things have taken a huge turn for the worse in the last couple years and the last year more specifically. With the banking crisis, the war on terror, loan guarantees, you name it. Like I said, these are not the best of times. Health care is a place that we need to make some sacrifices."

Cuda was actually caught between enjoying the full frontal assault on this President and educating him on the gravity of the situation.

"And about the tape, it is really a digital video disc with infrared underwriting capability and not a tape. I am pretty sure it is not working right now. It is just you and me. Man-to-man. I am just explaining to you what has to be done," Cuda, the teacher, continued to instruct.

15

The President had now humbly made his way back to his desk. A look of incredulity, mistrust and skepticism was on his face. The President was tactical. For the moment, he would continue to listen to Cuda as he continued to process his options and course of action.

"Suppose I was to take the time to listen to you Mr. Cuda?" the President asked inquiring superficially.

"Now who is the one *supposing*? I thought that you have been listening?"

"I have been listening," the President replied and repeated. "I have been listening!"

"Please, call me Cuda, Mr. President. My good friends and colleagues call me Cuda," Cuda replied.

"Fitting," the President said standing at his desk.

"What is it that you have come here to say to me?" the President asked.

"Where do I start?" Cuda continued. "I think I will have to start briefly at the beginning."

"I have an appointment in less than ten minutes," the President interrupted.

"Then you will have a decision to make in ten minutes," Cuda replied. "It will be your call to make a decision by then! After all, you are the President. Your security detail will be back in place and your assistant will call and ask if you were ready for your next appointment. You can continue to talk to me, or you can call in security to have me removed or you can meet your next appointment. It will be up to you."

"I see," the President said.

Cuda continued, "I have sat in this chair before. I have sat in this chair to hear different matters, which in most cases were less serious and certainly less impactful from a cost standpoint. Others before you have had the same decision to make. It is my hope that you will choose as wisely as most of them have done."

The President sat quietly. His palms flat on the desk, elbows straight out in front of him like a school boy on restriction. The President was now the one who was *letting things play out*.

Resolved, at least for the moment, to taking the time to hear from Cuda, the President merely said, "Begin."

Perfectly orchestrated so far, Cuda had worked himself into the same position with this President as he had three times earlier. Cuda was indirectly in charge of the President's own Secret Service detail.

He was armed with critical data and almost unlimited influence from the United States Strategic Planning Commission, for whom he has faithfully served for years, and to whom he is currently accountable. From this position, he knows he has more power and persuasion than the President himself.

He also knows he is playing from a position of great strength having had such power since the mid 1980's. He would never tire of the task of being with a sitting President telling them what their priorities would need to be. It was not just about the power and control for Cuda in total, he was also acting as a patriot for his country. This is what needed to be done for the benefit of the government, and the economy of scale, if the Country was to survive and prosper.

It was a bit of a self-fulfilling prophecy for him personally, the task transcends one man, transcends one term and transcends the President's office. Make no mistake about it. This has been a critical role for Cuda over the years. The experience he brought to the job along with the data he had collected regarding the economic sustainability of the United States was compelling.

Cuda stated as a matter of fact, "I am not going to bore you with too many details, Mr. President, but let me briefly bring you up to date. Over the last sixty years, we have been seriously trying to execute an appropriate strategy for health care solvency in the United States. This priority seems to come and go based on other economic factors and trends. Our Commission first proposed universal health care in 1948 during the Truman administration."

"Since that time we have had a number of strategic objectives that, in one way or another, were able to manage human life expectancy in a controlled, socially acceptable and fiscally sustainable fashion. In the last couple decades, this has become particularly challenging due to the increased costs of Medicare and Social Security, an aging population and many life extending medical advancements and treatments."

"I see," the President said.

"Longer life expectancy and the cost of legacy health care are huge expenses that will need to be managed as a series of trade off maneuvers. There is an enormous economic pay off if things are in balance and a mammoth economic burden if there is an imbalance," Cuda continued.

"The system, as it currently operates now, is a system that creates wealth and incentives for services that are provided. There are services that your government currently pays for. Logically, the more services that are provided, the more your care will cost and the more jobs that are created. The more the government will subsidize those costs, the more costly the overall care for an aging society will become. In good times, when we have the money, that is an acceptable result because it creates jobs. That is, as long as we are paying for procedures and not paying for end results. In this case, a result would be a longer life."

"Are you following me?" Cuda asked.

"Not exactly! How do you mean?" the President asked.

Cuda continued, "Medicare pays big when you do a test *to* someone for something or you provide a service *to* them. Any slice, dice or scan is usually bigger money than if you do something *for* a patient; and, as we know, it does not net you any money to do something *for* someone. That is the imbalance and why the system is so costly. Again, that is okay in good times and you have planned for it. It gives people a sense of well being, you know, like they are getting good care."

"I am trying to fix the system that you are defining as *broken*," the President reminded Cuda. "I am going to have everyone covered with preventative care and have more than a sense of well being. The people will actually be in better hands with my plan. We will be the most progressive and the healthiest nation on earth."

"Sure you are. I understand what you are trying to do," Cuda responded.

"You are missing the point. The system will not be able to afford cost of the long-term benefits being received by the people who are siphoning off the cash from the care programs. The cost will be great and the people are already over taxed. By and large, those people who are taking the most from the system are no longer paying into the system they get the benefit from. Get it! The most benefit is being received by those who no longer contribute and we are getting more and more that do not contribute everyday. Then you come along and tell me that you want all these non-contributors to live even longer."

"I see," said the President.

"C'mon man…talk about passing it on to your children. Where were all of those AARP constituents when you asked them who will pay for a lifetime of services, hip replacements and prosthetics, regardless of whether you are healthy enough to even be surviving the procedures?"

"Right or wrong, Mr. President, someone has to decide and that someone *is* the system and that system *is* the United States government. The way it is today, in these times, these are circumstances that we can no longer afford."

Cuda continued. "Do you understand me so far?"

"Are you saying that the current system is doing too much for the patient already?" the President asked.

"Winner, winner chicken dinner! Please allow me to go on," Cuda said with a hint of excitement. He felt the king was actually listening to the peasant.

"This is immoral and is not the right thing to do," the President said.

Cuda needed to get a little more aggressive. He raised his voice and converted to a more serious tone, "This is big government. You have been all for it in the past. Now all of a sudden it is not such a good idea? Let me refresh your memory on a few facts on the status of the health care now in this country. Facts that you and your *free for all party members* may not remember," Cuda said.

"My party members?" the President inquired.

Cuda quickly corrected himself, "I should have said *the* party members. I have had this conversation on both sides of the isle and the response is largely the same with everyone. You will not like what I have to say, but you will understand. Let me continue."

"No, please, continue," the President listlessly waved him on as he gently rubbed his forehead.

Cuda began to add some detail, "Eighty-five percent of Americans have health care now. Sixty-one percent of those get it through their employer and that has been an okay system in the past. Your plan seeks to insure the other fifteen percent of the American population. As you are aware of in your quest for equality, some of these are the uninsurable. These are the most expensive of the most expensive. Many of this fifteen percent are either illegal immigrants or legal citizens to sick to save from certain death."

"Too sick to save?" the President snapped.

Without recognition of the President's comment, Cuda continued, "Government already controls one sixth of the American economy thanks to many of the new takeovers. That does not even include the loan guarantees you have rushed through via public panic. To control health care will bring it to be less than one fourth of the economy. Do you really think that is smart? That is an additional two point five trillion dollars a year. I mean to have that much government control is that okay?"

"That depends," the President responded.

"Exactly," Cuda replied. "Exactly! Control is good. You are a quick study. Control is good. We are making progress."

Cuda elaborated on his point, "The health care plan will need to be written in such a fashion that it will accept all people with all conditions. Pre-existing conditions…"

The President interrupted, "Okay, and …"

Cuda finished his sentence, "Hang on. Let me finish…but not cover numerous high dollar target issues specifically and certainly not cover low return high termination value events."

"Termination value? Conditions like what?" the President asked confused and shaking his head.

Cuda responded vaguely, "Oh, I don't know, I am not a doctor. Conditions like hips and cancer treatment after sixty-five years of age. Conditions like birth defects prior to birth, irreversible coma, and cancer treatment for people who are deemed to be terminally ill at any age or too old to make treatment worthwhile, you know. Conditions like that."

"This is unacceptable, Mr. Cuda. It is not possible to make these types of demands on people. Who will decide?" the President exclaimed.

"Call me Cuda, please," Cuda responded and continued.

"Mr. President, this is where you are wrong. You of all people, an African American President in the United Sates, should surely know that anything is possible. After all, you yourself are here in this office. Anything truly is possible."

"And if I don't follow along with your plan?" the President asked.

"You don't have to go along with anything. As you frequently point out, you *are* the President. You can do as you please. You must also be aware that there may be consequences," Cuda reminded the President.

"Consequences?" the President asked.

"Let me tell you. I had a great conversation with forty-two. What a showman. What a politician. He was amazing. Amazing!" Cuda joked as he reflected back on another Presidential intervention.

"Forty-two?" the President said as he shook his head again showing a lack of understanding.

"Yeah, forty-two. The forty-second President. He understood things. He made a big push to reform things. He got the message…and he was happy to just stay two terms and manage the status quo. He had a good run at it too. Things stayed in balance," Cuda continued.

"I see," the President said staring at Cuda and recalling his history.

"Forty-three was a surprise to me. He did not seem to care about much at all. He was just surprised he was actually here in this office to begin with. He went along with everything. All we had to do is ask. It would have been okay, like forty-two, if he had not had to get all caught up in that whole terrorism thing. Forty-three wanted to get even. I think. It's a shame, all those people in the twin towers…," Cuda added.

"And the towers, did that have anything to do with…," the President said, still staring at Cuda whose eyes were glazing over.

"We did not have anything to do with the September 11th attacks. Makes me mad people actually think we would stoop that low," Cuda answered before being asked or allowing the President to finish his question.

Cuda was steam rolling. He was comfortable. He had the President right where he needed him to be mentally, virtually comatose.

"There have been some big achievements though," Cuda said as he prepared to explain to the President the system through which he was elected.

"Really?" the President stated in an almost disinterested manner.

"The big one though…I mean the big one, Mr. President, is how we got you here!" Cuda storied on.

The President listened, eyes straight forward as he came to attention. He was beginning to be convinced that anything, I mean anything, just might be possible. This story was all fitting together too nicely to be fiction. The President added, looking at Cuda indignantly, "Go on."

Lightly chuckling out loud Cuda continued the story, "Well, when we found out that forty-two's wife actually had a chance at winning your election, we had a big problem on our hands. You see, she knows the system all too well and she was not her husband. She was going to cause some real trouble for us. Big problems! We were going to be forced to enter the consequence phase, maybe even before the actual election, and we just did not think that was smart. So Alan had this great idea…"

"Who is Alan?" the President asked.

"Oh, sorry. Alan Hoard is my Director, my other boss who is over at the Planning Commission," Cuda replied.

"I see," the still stunned President acknowledged.

An excited Cuda resumed his documentary, "Anyway, he had this idea that, who best to compete with the first woman than the first African American. Outstanding Strategic Planning Commission stuff, don't you think?"

Cuda was fascinated with how the Commission, and Alan Hoard particularly, saved the nation from the unfortunate demise of a former first lady. A real *win, win* resolution.

Lethargically, the President asked about the previous comment, "You mentioned consequences and the consequence phase?"

"Oh, sure, consequences like a country that collapses financially from within consequence phase. Well, we were going to have to take her out," Cuda replied casually.

The President thought he saw a weakness in Cuda's argument. "This Government has sustained two hundred years of growth and prosperity, turmoil and chaos," the President instructed.

"That is correct," Cuda replied, "but that does not mean that it will not collapse tomorrow. None of us has the promise of tomorrow," he suggested seriously.

The President was contemplative.

"After all," Cuda said jesting, "Rome was not built in a day, but it burned down in just a couple days."

"It may be a risk I am willing to take."

"Is that so?" Cuda replied.

"People need honest care, good care for all and long-term care for the elders who made this nation great. It is what I campaigned on. They trusted me. I took an oath!" the President repeated.

"Truth be told," surprised by the answer, Cuda responded. "I suppose you think that you will be the first candidate that did not live up to their campaign promises. Is that it, do you think you will be the first?"

Cuda continued, "There is a very good reason that past Presidents, just like you, are better at *becoming* President than they are at *being* President. It is because the system is in charge, not you! The system is the biggest reason why Presidents do not deliver on what they promise. Believe me, you will not be the first to walk away from your campaign promises and you will not be the last either."

"I do not think that I can compromise on this. The people and the party will never forgive me," the President added.

"Well, that is disappointing," Cuda shot back in a snidely tolerating sort of way, "I would not plan on any Presidential trips to Dallas if you know what I mean. There could be a consequence phase!"

Thunderstruck by the comment, "Wait a minute, are you

threatening my safety?"

"You decide what I am saying," Cuda replied with greater indifference.

Are you saying that Kennedy was not cooperative and that the government...?" the President attempted to inquire.

"I am saying that thirty-five would not take the time to understand or compromise on anything. I mean anything. Ironically, it was about health care, I understand. Neither would his little brother and neither would his son; who were both planning to run for office. We tried to avoid that same unfortunate circumstance with forty-two's wife," Cuda replied. "Compassionate, I think."

"On the bright side, we did get through to one of his brothers," Cuda added. The President had a stare that looked out for a thousand yards. He was literally looking right through Cuda.

"You bastard," the President lamented.

"Like I said, there was one of his brothers who had a good run and really understood why it was so important to compromise. It was so important to him, understanding the consequences, he became known for being a great compromiser. He lived a full life, don't you think?" Cuda said as fiddled with a paperweight from the President's desk.

The President attempted to clarify what Cuda was saying, "Are you saying that...?"

Cuda again cut off the President, "I am not the bastard here. It is *your* government after all. All I am saying is that people can be marginalized or eliminated from the equation all together depending on their ability to follow the direction of the system. Some people may not have been cooperative enough. I could not say for sure, it was not on my watch."

"We have to get serious and make some tough decisions here. You see, social security and medicare cannot handle all these old and sick people hanging around the system while not contributing anything to it," Cuda continued. "You must understand the convergence here, Mr. President. You want people to live longer and healthier lives right?"

"Correct," the President said.

"And the system is saying that we cannot afford to have them live any longer, healthy or not, than they are now. Your party's legacy benefits, healthy or not, are not sustainable. Even if they are healthy, they will have social security until they hit the grave. Be grateful, some think we should roll the average life expectancy age back," Cuda added.

Saying somewhat as a tease, "Even if we had a choice, and we don't, and even if citizens had to live longer, which they cannot, we would need them to be healthier and not accept any social benefits. It is simple mathematics. Now, thanks to the global recession and the war on terror, there is less, much less, to spread around. Either way, healthy or not, we still could not afford to have them around due to the legacy costs."

"It is a game of actuarial averages. It is a give and take process, a series of trade-off's, as I said, to keep the average age down. We just cannot afford it," Cuda said cocking his head to one side, being thoughtful of the associated costs and intriguing him with the bifurcation of the choices.

The President's phone began to ring. He looked at the phone and then at Cuda, and then back at the phone. The President was departing from information absorption mode and went once again into the mode of calculating his options. The phone continued to ring.

The risk was high and the potential for reward was low. It was a very poor position for the President to be in. He would have his health care, likely contribute to the solvency of the nation, but would sacrifice many Americans lives in the process.

Presidents have caused the loss of life before. He would not be the first. This time, there would not be any blood involved.

"Hello," he said to his secretary.

Cuda listened with poise.

"Yes, yes, I understand," the President paused.

Cuda waited confidently for the President's next words.

"Please tell them that I will not be available and please clear my calendar for the balance of the day. Yes, I said the rest of the day. Thank you."

The President hung up the phone.

"Good call, Mr. President. Good call. Now, let's get on with business."

Cuda was relentless and determined. At this moment, he must have felt like McArthur as he walked back onto the beach when he returned to the Philippines. Old soldiers never die, they just fade away. The President had begun to fade.

Cuda picked up the pace of the conversation. He knew now that the new President was committed. Cuda needed to delegate.

"It will not make you feel any better, but I have some direction for your friends on Capital Hill," Cuda instructed. "Here is what you will need from them. You may want to take notes."

Glaring at Cuda with contempt, the President retrieved a pencil and pad from the desk drawer and prepared to write.

Cuda dictated the objectives of the Strategic Planning Commission as follows,"You will demand a single payer system."

"Everyone must be on the government plan. We do not need any individual plans out there. No patient-centric plans. You have been telling everyone that they can keep their private plan...that's fine, we have come up with a solution so that you do not have to go back on that. Something like taxing the hell out of a private plan, the company and the individual, should suffice. You will have to make the public plan so good that employers will bail out of the private plan.

"As we said earlier, eighty-five percent of people are insured through their employer. No company plans. People will need to convert. We will then be back in control of procedures and more importantly the outcomes. We will be able to keep the system in balance that way.

"The federal pre-emptive language that will eliminate the alternate lifestyle partner plan will be needed. Unmarried people will need to be tracked individually, as we have done in the past. Some states have gotten carried away.

"The costs of all plans will need to be borne by the government so that we can control what is happening *to* the patient. We will take the patient out of the equation and; therefore, we will decide what care is best for them when balanced with what is most economical for the system. We need to pay for probable outcomes on middle-aged recipients and not an infinite number of procedures. Procedures with high cost and limited probable outcomes will not be given to the very young, which there is little invested in to date, and will not be given to the old who are no longer contributing to the system," Cuda explained.

"The patient as a person needs to go away," he continued. "Patients are numbers. They will need to be treated in accordance with their age and their sustainability of the treatment. Their care and history will need to be definitively tracked."

The President cut in, "Hold on here, Cuda. This will be worse than doing nothing at all. No one is going to make better decisions about your personal care than the individual!"

Cuda responded, "Listen carefully, Mr. President, I mean carefully. This is important. We will never, and I mean never, truly be able to support public health care with public health. It is a bad fiscal decision. I thought I made the fiscal cost of treatment decision clear already. You cannot afford to see how long you can stretch out life as long as you have the legacy benefit issue in place. It is simply not sustainable."

"This will be worse for everyone!" the President repeated.

"Depends on from what angle you are defining worse. Let me continue," Cuda retorted and continued.

"Government assisted euthanasia is nice to have. The older patients that are receiving care now, those near expiration, are getting a disproportionate amount of man hours and dollars from the health care pie."

Cuda interrupted himself, "Okay, maybe just patient requested euthanasia. By all means, when they are ready to go, let them go. There will be good estate tax implications here too in the shorter term. There should be some revenue associated with revising the tax code for estates or at least allowing the temporary tax cuts to expire."

The President continued to write.

"Did you know that we could save almost one hundred billion dollars over the next ten years if we could just manage the care of terminally ill people better in their last sixty days of life? Sixty days! Unbelievable?"

"Those too sick to save?" the President asked.

"Exactly! People are getting to much low return care in their final days,"

Cuda replied and continued with his list.

"The issue of euthanasia and end of life care directive counseling needs to be part of the bill Mr. President. People need to know the options early on, before they need to make a decision about their own expiration."

"In the bill language, when we consider any treatments, people need to die from the disease, not the treatment. Let them go. We need less sick people burdening an already busted system."

Like a programmed machine, Cuda went through his list of demands. He expected the President to faithfully follow through on his requests, item-by-item.

"I want to all but eliminate high probability medical research testing for major ailments like cancer and heart disease. What we don't need is someone to make a big discovery in one of these heavily weighted mortality ailments and we will throw the entire matrix off again. Someone gets close on a treatment, God forbid, a cure, we will then need protocols. Clinical trials must be eliminated if they get close. In the short run, all clinical trials must be drawn out, expensive and exhaustive in terms of extension hurdles."

"Unbelievable, you are throwing God in on this," the President said under his breath.

"You know, Mr. President, your own people have said that we should accept a *hopeless diagnosis* and forgo experimental treatment. They have even said that the *use and overuse of technologies and treatments* have contributed to runaway costs. Your own people, in your party, have said this. I know, I have spoken to them in person. Many of them have said it in public," Cuda said.

Cuda added, "Even the Hippocratic Oath says, 'Do no harm'. It does not say take every extreme measure at any cost."

"My colleagues are mistaken," the President corrected.

Cuda angrily continued, "What you don't understand about your preventative plan Mr. President is that people without means only consider preventative assessment when there is insurance and; from where I am sitting, in our current condition, people without means can and should be allowed to expire in the Darwinian fashion of survival of the fittest and natural selection. Got it!"

"And what about all those patients currently in hospice who are dependant upon the government for their care," the President added.

"Some of those people should not have been kept alive so long anyways," Cuda argued. "They suffered too much and we paid millions to allow them to continue to suffer. Think of it as natural selection as I said," Cuda replied.

"You can work it out with the G.A.O., let the people have front line preventative care if that will make you feel better or let them have hospice. I really don't care much either way. It does not matter to me. However, you should know that on the backside there needs to be limits to long term health care given, shall we say, hardship cases and there will need to be specific calculable limits on long term care and longevity, period," Cuda added.

The President sat meekly.

"Let's take a moment and talk about the bill itself. In the strongest terms possible, I would suggest that you make the language of this bill as long and as complicated as possible so that we can get the disciplines we have outlined run through without undue scrutiny," Cuda continued.

"I mean make this bill a fat cat. One thousand pages at a minimum, maybe even two thousand pages. We need the loopholes in this thing. I am less worried about people getting around the system than I am concerned about us having the latitude to manipulate care to our economic satisfaction. The longer the verbiage, the more room there is to navigate the interpretation on the government's part and to the government's advantage," Cuda instructed.

"And get me some language that eliminates the medi-gap reinsurance. We have to be able to start plugging the loopholes in the coverage," Cuda reprimanded.

"Back to your earlier point, are you saying that there is a sort of treatment advisory panel that will decide who gets treatment and who will not?" the President asked.

"You can call it whatever you want. You are the President," Cuda replied to the request and continued, "No one is arguing the medical system is fine the way it is. The health care system is broken and you are going to give the appearance of fixing it while at the same time helping to manage this comprehensive spending, entitlement and deficit issues."

"You said that you spoke to a lot of people in my party," the President said drumming his pencil nervously on the desk and looking at his notes. "Are these *people* that you have spoken to ready to get on board with your plan?"

"This is to be sold as *your* plan Mr. President. This is your plan now. In answer to your question, well, maybe they will sign on," Cuda said with a grin from ear to ear. "Take control man, this should be an easy sell for your party…and I mean *your* party this time."

Cuda added in a calm and grandfatherly voice, "Think about your colleagues in the Congress, Mr. President. How do you think so many of these incompetent old bastards and withered liberal hags stay in office? Huh!"

Without pause for a response Cuda continued, "I will tell you how. They have prostituted their principles to the system for the face of a prestigious position. That's how. Just like you will do."

"You want it all," the President said. "These directives will stifle all innovation in the medical fields and take cancer treatment back to the 1970's," the President reminded.

"Okay," Cuda replied. "That's okay, and that's not all. This could be a very good year for me. I am an incrementalist, Mr. President."

"A few more things," Cuda again began to dictate after a brief uncomfortable silence.

"You might as well try for these too since you are so flamboyant about controlling the House, Senate and the White House."

"The Government will need to set the pricing for all care plans and care services. Participation will be compulsory. You will be mandated by law to carry a care plan, preferably the government plan and charge what the government will pay. This alone will help us determine what services get done on what patients."

"By all means, tell them they can keep their own doctors. That will help sell the program. What we will fail to tell them is that we will make the payments to the doctors so poor, the doctors will cancel the patients," Cuda explained.

"There will need to be electronic recording of all medical records. E-records deliver trends. Trends give us probability. Probability will then allow us to know what will be likely impediments in terms of life expectancy in the future."

"Impediments?" the President inquired.

"Impediments, yes!" Cuda replied. "Do you not know what impediments are?"

"I know what an impediment is," the President replied in a disgusted tone, "I just do not understand the context in which you used it."

Cuda tried one more time to explain the situation to a President in denial, "Mr. President, as I have said. People need to have limits on life span due to the legacy benefits the government has been committed to. The likely impediments in terms of life expectancy I just referred to will come as a result of analyzing data. This data, in the future, will allow us to calculate what obstacles and barriers in research, development, health care and health coverage need to be enacted or retracted so that we can keep the system in balance."

Cuda got off track and tried to give some justification and explanation for his action, "Remember in 2001, just before 9-11, during a prime-time televised address when the President imposed a stem cell testing ban on embryonic cells? Remember?"

The President did not respond.

"At that time, just a month before 9-11, it was the biggest issue of the presidency, health care, I mean. We were on the right track. The deficits were low and things were getting into balance. Then we were derailed by this whole terrorism issue and we have yet to get back on track."

"On that note, by all means necessary, terminate the stem cell research you recently approved."

"Why?" the President asked.

"Like I just said, we were able to get your predecessor to see that the ban stayed in effect. And then you come along and over turn it in a matter of weeks. You surprised us on how fast you acted on that one."

The President asked, "Why does stem cell research matter so much?"

Cuda responded to the naïve question, "We stayed on top of it and twice your predecessor vetoed lifting restrictions even after it was passed by Congress, just as we asked him too. Why do you think that was?" Cuda added.

"I don't know," the President answered.

"It is because we certainly do not want to know how disease regenerates in the body and we certainly do not want overall reparatory regenerative medicine to advance. That's why!"

Cuda continued, "And there was a 1996 bill that banned embryonic research and prevents funding for new research even on embryos slated for destruction at fertility clinics. Make sure that ban also stays in effect."

Cuda took pause and the President stopped his feverish writing and looked up. "Is that all?" the President queried.

"I would think that would be enough. Your colleagues will add hundreds of pages to this I suspect," Cuda replied.

"I am sure," the President conceded.

"Look at the bright side, Mr. President. You said that the runaway costs are unsustainable. You will be managing costs now. You only have to live here in this house a few years and then you will pass the baton. You and all the people who make this legislation will set yourselves up with a pretty tidy plan for yourself I would guess," Cuda advised.

"There will be thousands of people, mostly legislators I imagine, who will not have to have the standard government plan crammed down their throat. You and your self-serving public policy cohorts will be gravy sucking pigs feeding at the preeminent medical health care trough all the way to the grave," Cuda admonished.

The President sat silently knowing that, if true as described, he would be one of the thousands that Cuda was referring to. He would see to it. In the end, politicians, like most all of society are a *me first* collection of people and are always looking to take care of themselves. Government politicians just have greater access and; therefore, greater ability to write themselves into the most favorable outcome.

Cuda got up from his chair and stood next to the President who was still seated at his desk, "I hope I leave you today with the thought of a better America on the way," he said.

Still standing and now at the front of the desk facing the President, "Like Cronkite says...," Cuda turned his back to the President and began to walk to the door, "and that's the way it is."

"But don't be like Cronkite, Mr. President. Don't sign off too early in your career," as he continued to walk to the door. "You need to get the job done here. I am counting on you. We are all counting on you to get the job done."

"Oh, one last thing," Cuda said as he opened the door to leave and turned to the President who was again looking out the window towards the garden with his back to Cuda, just as he was positioned when Cuda closed the door earlier, "just for the record, I would have fired Dean Taking on the spot. He is a gutless little hack of a man who has no business being in charge of securing anything. As a matter of fact, I would say that he is a living, breathing example of the Peter Principle applied in practice. Check the references next time."

The President turned in his chair and got up from the desk, following Cuda and meeting him at the doorway. As Cuda passed through the doorway he gave another pause and then a comment, "and I will see that the Oval Office recorder is back in operation immediately," he said looking back at the President face-to-face.

Cuda walked out of the office as the President stood at the threshold. The President could see that all of the Secret Service agents were back in position, which, knowing what he knows now after his encounter with Cuda, was not a comforting feeling. More unsettling perhaps, he watched as Cuda strolled casually down the hall, greeting each Secret Service agent by name and each agent doing the same. They simply called him "Cuda".

Each Secret Service agent shook hands with Cuda as he swaggered passed, making small talk. Most disturbing of all to the President, as Cuda moved on, each agent would look back at the President exhibiting an all encompassing and unnerving Mona Lisa type of smile. Unlike in the case of the Mona Lisa, a smile that, to the President in this case, said all that needed to be said.

CHAPTER THREE
MEETING THE RESEARCH TEAM

16

Garrison awoke early to the chill of the frosty bedroom air on his face. According to the news report the night before, the overnight forecast was expected to be unseasonably warm for Minnesota in mid January. Lows were anticipated in the mid to high thirties. He had decided to sleep with the window cracked open. There was little opportunity to reintroduce new air into the house during the winter months. A night of fresh air was certainly welcome.

It was cool once out from under the covers. Stumbling from his bed and into the hallway to check the temperature, there was little doubt the thermostat had been calling for heat all night to compensate for the open window. Garrison returned to close the bedroom window standing for a moment overlooking the beauty of the lake before heading into the bathroom.

Garrison and Sally had loved life at the lake together. The summers on Lake Minnetonka were fabulous and life on their small bay just off the main lake was even better. A permanent timber dock for the speed boat, along with a sailboat docked on the other side of the Boulevard on the main lake, afforded them access to both the bay and the main lake without the hassle of having to constantly launch and recover their various water craft. The combination of the lake front living, along with the numerous water front restaurants located just blocks away, made the year round *in city* lake living particularly pleasant for them.

Their modest contemporary home had served them well over the years. The conservative exterior did not look like the home of a wealthy and very well educated couple.

Inside, the home was conservatively appointed and comfortable as well. Neatly organized and clean. Underneath the soaring ceilings, there was large abstract works of art adorning the interior walls. On the perimeter walls, there were floor-to-ceiling views of the dock and bay. One of Garrison's favorite and most treasured spots on this earth was an office on the second floor.

After starting a cup of coffee in the coffee maker, Garrison put on a jacket and boots and walked to the mailbox that was about fifty yards down the length of the narrow yet generous lake front lot.

It was winter. Under the light snow, the landscape looked a bit untamed.

Although barely enough snow to cover the ground, the new snow was so wet and heavy it was obviously weighing down the lower tree branches of the numerous towering cottonwood trees that dotted the property. The snow appeared to have left a white outline, as if highlighted, on all the bushes, trees and shrubs.

The footing was wet and the temperature was quite comfortable now that he actually had some clothes on. The snow only amounted to a few inches of coverage on the ground. The snow, which had fallen overnight, had melted just enough over the warm night, to be slushy. It was one of those classically wet and sloppy Minnesota mornings.

Once at the mailbox, you could see that Minnetonka Boulevard was salted and sanded courtesy of a recent trip through by the County. Garrison pulled his copy of the *Minneapolis Tribune* from the mailbox and walked back to the house thinking first about the peacefulness of the quiet early morning and then about the length of his pending commute due to the slapdash road conditions. Entering the front door, he could smell his fresh brewed coffee was ready and awaiting his return.

He was thinking he would be best served by getting cleaned up, taking his newspaper with him, and leaving for the office early. He wanted to start his day on time, as usual. The traffic would be unpredictable and probably delayed due to the road conditions.

The substrate warmth and chemically induced thaw had created wet streets as Garrison traveled into the city. The traffic coming into the city from the western metro on Highway 7 and Interstate 394 was particularly challenging today. It seemed that over the summer and fall, Minnesotans had once again forgotten how to drive on slushy streets and freeways.

Listening to his favorite local D.J., the time in the car passed quickly as the traffic went through the many fits and starts of the less than ideal conditions.

Fortunately, after compensating for what he had anticipated would be a slow commute, it was 8:00 a.m. Dr. Garrison Keller was arriving on campus at his usual time.

Being a member of the senior staff at the University afforded Garrison many privileges, not the least of which was a designated parking spot that was very close to his office building. This time of year, it was a perk that was very much appreciated and widely envied among the not so privileged faculty and students.

Arriving at the Medical Research Center office, on the campus of the University, today would start as a typical day. There would be a second cup of coffee and some small talk, followed by various meetings with other research professionals and perhaps fund administrators. Not necessarily in that order.

Today would start with a meeting with internal staff. This was to be, for all practical purposes, an average day.

17

The Cancer Center was founded in 1991. Garrison had been associated here for all but the first few years. They are part of the Universities Academic Health Center which also includes the Medical School, Dental School and College of Pharmacy to name a few. The Cancer Centers Research partners also include, among others, the University's Stem Cell Institute, Center for Magnetic Resonance Imaging, the Institute of Human Genetics and the University Children's Hospital.

Clearly, this facility and all of its tributaries was a research powerhouse. Garrison was an influential figure, having been instrumental in their receiving designation from the National Cancer Institute (N.C.I.) in 1998, and renewed designation in 2003, as a comprehensive cancer center. They held the designation that makes them one of only thirty-nine institutions in the United States who consistently make on-going and significant advances in all aspects of cancer research. This is a very highly regarded teaching and research facility.

This facility, housing over five hundred faculty and staff members, is home to some of the world's top cancer researchers in all types of bone, blood, genetic, pediatric oncology, immunotherapy, soft tissue and new therapies development. Garrison's team was on the cutting edge of forward looking cancer and health research. Garrison's seat was without a doubt, front row in his field.

Despite what you hear, there is no shortage of funds in today's college research facilities. It can be argued that the money may or may not be spent correctly, but there is plenty of research and endowment money to go around.

However, from an administrative perspective, the immediate offices Garrison and his staff occupied were modest and somewhat non-descript.

From the exterior, the facility looked like a dated brownstone. Insofar as it was built in the 1960's, it was a standard fare state building before the excesses of the 1980's architectural construction on campuses across the country. The office area was typically modest and representative of an analytical and administrative arm of a research department. These spaces had the look and feel of administrative offices and Garrison was the head of the department. The research laboratory was located on another part of the campus and was largely part of the hospital.

The office furniture in the receiving area was in *like new* condition. There were not a lot of visitors to the office. The walls were freshly painted and the woodwork was all in good condition. The décor and colors were traditional and fairly sterile. The art in the common areas of the office was contemporary, yet traditionalist conservative.

There were a total of four persons including Garrison working in the department's administrative office.

Dr. Randy Pell was Dr. Garrison Keller's research partner. Randy had grown up in southern Minnesota and attended Mankato State University, a small regional university. After graduating, he received a medical degree from the University School of Medicine.

Randy was fluent in Spanish, single and a novice traveler. His dry sense of humor was appreciated by Garrison who has been a good friend and mentor for many years. Beneath his light humor was an intellectual. He is a very smart, talkative and a somewhat unsophisticated academic. He tried to choose words carefully when challenging Garrison's wisdom and authority, but he lacked the care and restraint in his everyday conversation with strangers.

Craig Lynd was a Research Assistant. Craig was a middle-aged man who, if you did not know him, may seem so challenged that you would wonder if he could tie his own shoes. Fortunately or not, he is a very matter of fact person with no real personality or interpersonal skills to speak of.

Craig is a bit of an unknown, a bit of a recluse. He never speaks of his family or professional affiliations. He was blessed with an almost supernatural knack of being able to clear through the mindless clutter most of us are bogged down in.

Craig has the unique ability to see what everyone else sees, but he sees these things in way that others casually overlook. He is gifted in his ability to analyze issues and data. He is exceedingly futuristic, realistic and methodical, a very rare combination of strengths to find in today's workforce. Craig has been with Garrison for many years dating back to Garrison's time in the information technology start up business.

Nan Kady was the Administrative Assistant for the office. What a nice lady. As far as Assistants go, you could not ask for a better person. She is a real "jack of all trades". Whether it was to plan a meeting, make dinner reservations, create spread sheets or plan logistics, Nan could do it better and more accurately than anyone Garrison had worked with before. He truly loved their working relationship.

18

Everyone had made the commute to the office safely and on time. Nan, Garrison and Randy, were collectively standing at Nan's desk that was in the center of the small office. Garrison and Randy were signing off on some routine financial allocations.

From behind his neatly organized desk where Craig sat upright on his ergonomically correct chair came a comment, "Garrison, I understand you are going to Brazil in February. Is that true?" It was an odd personal question from Craig.

"That is true. We are going on a cruise," Garrison replied. "I am really looking forward to the trip. Randy is going too," not looking up as he continued to sign the documents.

Nan had helped amend the previously made reservation several months ago.

"Why did you pick Brazil anyway?" Nan asked.

Putting down his pen and taking off his glasses, Garrison responded, "Sally and I had always wanted to go to Brazil. We had heard it was a beautiful country. There is so much emphasis there on environmental conservation and responsible uses of energy. It sounds so interesting. We wanted to see it for ourselves."

"It sounds like we could take some lessons from them," Nan replied, collecting the documents from the counter and clipping them together.

Garrison added, "Could be. I understand there is very little pollution and the people have a real stake in their country in terms of managing the need to be responsible for their people while at the same time understanding and respecting their environmental surroundings. They have been green since before Americans even knew what 'going green' meant; not to mention the fact the countryside is beautiful."

Garrison continued passionately, making a "Clintonesque" fist for emphasis, "The government sounds so connected and forward thinking. They recognize the need to be proactive in managing the preservation of the planet for both the people and future of the environment."

Garrison really loved the forward thinkers. Regarding people and their governments alike, he was impressed with the concept of being able to anticipate and plan. This was particularly true as it related to efforts committed to improving the quality of life in the world for his and future generations yet to come. In a personal way, though he never really said, quality of life was his self proclaimed personal quest and signature.

Garrison's convictions ran deep when it came to ecological conservation. The beliefs he held on the environment were second only to his commitment to the health and longevity of humanity. The guiding principle and overriding train of thought he used on these subjects was simple. Success follows when people and the environment come first.

"What you can conceive and believe, you can achieve," he often stated to colleagues.

His concept was basic in terms of having people come before profits and environmental perpetuation ahead of capitalistic indifference and complacency. You have to be able to chart your course with these fundamentals keyed into the navigation system, sticking to the principles of an idea and to see those ideas to a logical, ethical and productive conclusion. You must have the planning in place to actually see the concept through, stick with it through the roadblocks and bring closure to the ideal.

This was the very straightforward and compelling application of the *concept of perseverance* Garrison possessed. Garrison was truly a living lesson in what the commitment to a good idea can bring.

Still behind his desk and without looking up, Craig asked inquisitively, "That does not seem like much of a vacation. Are you going there to explore their governmental policies on the environment?"

Garrison turning to Craig replied, "Well, Craig, the culture also seems so interesting. There was great emphasis on family and spirituality. Overall, I think I am intrigued mainly with the environmental responsibility and vision, but we were also intrigued with the natural beauty and the excitement of Carnival', so we will be going to the Carnival' Parade and celebration also while we are there."

"Hey, Craig," Garrison continued. "Maybe you will be willing to check in on the house a couple times while we are gone. I would hate to have a frozen pipe or a leak or something go undetected for a whole week. I can get you the key and you should still have the code to the alarm from the last time."

"Sure," Craig replied.

"What is Carnival'? Is that the cruise line?" Nan asked as Craig sat back in his chair, placed his pencil in his mouth and listened intently as he fiddled with his keyboard.

Randy replied, "Since Garrison asked me to go with him, I have done a little bit of research and here is how I would answer that question. First of all, Carnival is a cruise line, but that is not the one we are traveling on. We are going sailing on Royal Caribbean. The pronunciation of Carnival' is different from the cruise lines name, Carnival," he explained.

"Carnival' is a celebration combining parades, folk drama, and feasting that is usually held in Catholic countries during the weeks before Lent. It is a festive season that usually starts in February or early March. How was that explanation Garrison?" Randy asked as if looking for an "A" on his report card.

Garrison added, "Normaly, the Carnival' season begins early in a new year and ends in February on fat Tuesday, like Mardi Gas."

"Says here," Craig added as he read from his Google search, "They rejoice the passing of the winter season and the regeneration of nature, a new beginning, and at the end of the day recommitting all creatures to the spiritual and societal codes of the culture. Carnival' promotes mockery of, and affords transitory liberation from, community and spiritual constraints. Feasts of fools, blasphemous masses, and naked women on parade, sexual and social restraint is not recommended and …"

Garrison interrupted, "That's enough Craig, I know you well enough to know that you are no longer reading, but just babbling on and creating your own Wikipedia-like response."

Craig sat back grinning.

"There are a lot of celebrations, events, culture and scenery. Let's not pigeon- hole my vacation as one of an international deviant behavior marathon just yet," Garrison added with a pensive smile.

Going to Carnival' this year would be particularly difficult. Carnival', after all, was a celebration of life and of new beginnings. *Viva la Vida*. A celebration of life.

19

The celebration, for Garrison, would, in fact, be bitter sweet without Sally.

There was an unspoken uneasiness to the conversation. An unspoken word everyone knew and no one wanted to acknowledge. These continued to be challenging times for Garrison.

He had been happily married to the love of his life for many years. A marriage to Sally which bore no children. He and Sally were tireless travelers in the winter months. They traveled the world compulsively as time and their busy careers permitted. They loved to travel the world together seeking out new events, new experiences and new cultures. They were adventurous together and had been discussing going to Carnival' together for many years. Her untimely death almost a year earlier would take Garrison to Brazil without her. He was going this year in her memory.

A trip originally reserved for he and Sally would now be taken with a trusted colleague, Randy. They were after all, good friends, good research partners and, on the whole, good for each other.

20

"I understand it is a difficult place to visit?" Nan asked.

"Difficult is relative," another comment coming from Craig as his fingers pitter pattered on the key board of his desk top.

Randy jumped in again to answer. "It was difficult in the sense that you needed a visa to enter the country and there were many time sensitive restrictions and conditions on the application and uses of the visa."

Garrison added professionally, "And roughly three hundred dollars in fees!"

"What do you mean by restrictions and conditions?" Craig asked taking his attention off the computer screen almost as if he were inputting the responses. Craig was a great multi-tasker.

Randy turned to Craig, "For starters we had to complete a lengthy application. We needed a notarized letter from the University stating this was a pleasure trip and needed confirmation we had a job here at the University to come back too."

Craig stood up and came into the circle of his associates, "The Brazilian Government doesn't want you doing research in their country without their knowledge. They know people generally cannot be disciplined enough to tend to being on vacation during vacation time."

"In this case, your objective is to be on vacation and they know it, but they just want to remind you of it. This was particularly true when it comes to Americans."

Craig continued at a more breathless pace, "and the United States Government does not want you to do research there either. They know, Randy. They know where you are when you go there. There is a very tense relationship between our countries. Why do you think they make it so difficult to go there? They know. You know! I know!"

Randy, ever amused by Craig's almost autistic tendencies carried on, "Easy Craig, we are not going there to do any research."

Randy continued his explanation, "We then had to send our passports and fees to the Brazilian Embassy in Chicago for the actual visa stamp."

Craig asked, "You surrendered your passport to a foreign jurisdiction? That's unnerving!" as he walked to his desk and sat back in his chair. He occasionally grunted in disapproval while he typed away on his computer keyboard.

Nan, changing the subject slightly, "I hear Brazil is a dangerous place."

Garrison commented, "Downtown Minneapolis can be a dangerous place. Memphis can be a dangerous place. Be aware of your surroundings and you will be fine."

Garrison was excited about going on the trip. He was somewhat reserved in his expectations internally. While he had so many things he wanted to see there, he too had heard it was a dangerous place. Garrison understood he would need to be careful.

Craig was staring purposefully at his computer screen, "Says here you better not get hurt while you are there or you may be in trouble. They have nationalized health care and it is the largest enterprise java application ever built with well over two million lines of code and over three hundred and fifty domain model classes."

"Wow," Nan replied. "Sounds cumbersome."

"Sounds like 'Big Brother'," Craig replied.

"Also says here you are likely to die while waiting to get in to see a doctor," Craig added as he was snuggled up close to his over sized twenty-seven-inch flat screen monitor.

On that positive note, Garrison thought the small talk had gone far enough. While he enjoyed the fellowship of his office staff, this informal snowy day conversation seemed to have taken an irreversible turn towards the sarcastic. Now was a good time to get to work.

21

"Okay, everyone, gather up any pressing issues and let's meet in my office. Time to go to work," Garrison requested as he slid the last of his paperwork across the counter to Nan.

As they gathered around the large maple meeting table in Garrison's office that was adjacent to his oversized maple desk, the atmosphere became more disciplined. From the table you could see the numerous tributes to Garrison's achievements around the room. Garrison was not a vain person, but he was very proud of his accomplishments and he was certainly very nostalgic.

Like badges of honor, and some were, covering every wall and shelf, were plaques and awards recognizing his various triumphs, degrees, certifications and accomplishments. Garrison was a well-educated man.

Dr. Garrison Keller was an M.D., PhD., M.B.A., past President of the Medical Research Council, and past director of the Medical Research Council, Medical Fellow, and many more organizations. His titles and accreditations went on like alphabet soup.

Like Randy, he also grew up in Minnesota. Widowed, single and without children, now more than ever, he pursued his true legacy.

Though his previous education and interests as a Professor of Mathematics at M.I.T., he had been an early pioneer in computer technology and micro chip evolution. After achieving much success as a founding member of silicon chip computer technology, his yearning for a greater gift to mankind continued. As such, looking for that lasting contribution, he went back to the University to become a doctor.

Although a board certified Physician and Oncologist, he did not actively practice medicine outside of a research facility. His emphasis and intent was on research and medical application rather than medical practice. He was a powerful force in the research community. He was at a point in his life that he had money. His interests now were directed towards the common good.

On a more personal level, having never had children, he was generally not very patient or understanding of children. He was equally not well versed in dealing with strangers. He understood how others perceived these character traits and consciously tried to overcome them, at least in public.

By way of his education, he was very deliberative and chose his words carefully. This was in part due to his teaching experience, where impressionable young students would take his ideals and words as fact. His medium build, and taller than average stature, could be imposing to people who did not know him well.

Garrison is a stickler for timeliness, punctuality and accuracy while preferring not to have tight deadlines himself. Garrison had always been a man that plays by the rules of the system. He has always been of the conviction that it is infinitely more satisfying to win playing fair than to cut corners even if he himself did not always agree with the rules.

Garrison brought the informal office meeting to order, "Randy, tell me about your visit to the genealogy symposium on aging."

Randy responded anxiously, "It was fascinating, actually. There are theories out there that are hypothecated on the basis that with some genetic engineering around hereditary disease, there is a likelihood that exists, within the next two generations, people, and women particularly, could have a life span of one hundred twenty to one hundred thirty years."

Craig commented, "Was personal responsibility part of the discussion?"

Garrison asked Craig, "How do you mean?"

Craig responded, "I mean that the engineering on a cellular level is critical. Meanwhile, no one is addressing the obesity, the heart disease, the sedentary life styles and the pervasive smoking issues. Personal responsibility! How will people manage themselves and their personal environment? What will the patient do to help themselves?"

"Interesting sideline," as Garrison challenged a theory he knew and understood well. "I assume any query into hereditary diseases would cover both the cellular and the psyche."

Randy replied, "Psyche in terms of Alzheimer's, yes, even though it is all cellular in nature. In terms of the specific behaviors, it was not. Are you asking me about genetic memory like you might find in predatory wild animals? I am not sure what you are asking me Craig?"

Craig continued, "No. I am saying that there is a huge gap in personal accountability. There is never, and will never be, any real incentive for any medical provider, in any system, to help control your behavior. That is why there is so little emphasis on it. It is a self-perpetuating system. People don't take care of themselves and the system medical establishment gets richer."

Garrison was a stickler for accountability. He wanted people to have the freedom to pursue their development, but it had to tie to the objectives in the current research focus and that focus was on expanding the human life cycle, which by nature is very complex and even more variable. Garrison's team was out to find the high impact common cellular denominators. More specifically, they were on a quest to reduce the number of cancer deaths. This required tough questions at times.

Garrison responded, "I hope we are sticking to the physical and not getting into the metaphysical Randy?"

Garrison remanded, "Randy, can you explain to me how this directly ties to the Protein Suspension Radio Therapy (P.S.R.T.) or the Glucose Microwave Therapy we have been working on?"

Craig's question and comment seemed to have been bypassed.

Responding, Randy reassured Garrison, "Aging deteriorates all living things on a cellular level. This seminar was about genetic engineering to avoid hereditary disease. Sure, it was about genetics, but in any cell deterioration, regardless of what is causing the cell deterioration, we could potentially see more diseases like cancer that the P.S.R.T. and Microwave Therapy can potentially remedy?

Garrison was a bit agitated. "So, you went on a fishing expedition with research funds, probably because it was in a warmer area of the country in December, to see if there was anything of any value to learn. This does not seem like a good use of funds or your time."

Randy replied "Not true. Isn't all research a fishing expedition? This was foundational education."

Garrison, calm but still agitated and gently tapping his pencil on the table, "No. No, it is not. We are focused on the treatment of existing disease here. We make educated estimates as to what will be fruitful. Then we formulate a hypothesis. Only then do we test our theories, make new assumptions and monitor and adjust based on trends and results. It is at that point you can test until definitive results are achieved, documented and repeated. That is research.

"Let me tell you both what research is not. Research is not collecting a bunch of sage old philosophers, sitting in a conference session fantasizing about how long people could live in a world without bad personal habits or disease," Garrison said.

"People will continue to have bad habits."

Craig was put in his place along with Randy. While the symposium was educational for Randy, and Craig had a point about personal responsibility, neither point was relevant to the research they were discussing. Their research was treatment. The issues were clearly separate in Garrisons mind. His concern was not prevention and it was certainly not personal responsibility.

Garrison continued, "Furthermore, while all diseases may some day be prevented all together, rendered genetically extinct or remedied post onset in their entirety, the unfavorable personal health habits and behaviors of humans may never be eliminated. You may want to make a note of that Craig."

"So noted," Craig said with restraint.

"So, in summary, as we have talked about at this table in the past, we need to stay focused on the high value, big picture treatments which can cure broad swatches of public disease, communicable or otherwise. Individual personal behavior is too variable and is not, in and of itself, a treatable disease."

Garrison's response indeed seemed very out of the ordinary. He was suggesting that we could cure the major diseases, but we could not prevent the people's behavioral habits that in some cases caused the disease in the first place. It was a *treat the symptom not the cause mentality*. Strangely, but perhaps captivatingly true.

Garrison's conviction was on the cure and not the prevention. It was a compelling premise that flew in the face of personal responsibility and prevention. Garrison knew, left to their own devices, people can be very self destructive to themselves and to the planet.

Garrison knew, like it or not, there was the inferred role of government. The government would always be around to help regulate behavior, good and bad, and promote balance through legislation. Garrison was not a fan of government regulation.

Nan sat listening to the exchange.

Craig, objective, smirking and indifferent to the emotional passion of the verbal volleys, just listened intently. Within himself, he knew he had other priorities.

Picking up on Garrison's comment, Randy attempted to defend himself, "Are you profiling good researchers from bad based on age and education?"

Garrison completed his thought, "You are changing the subject from the research to the researchers, but I guess I opened the door for both," as he turned the chair and gazed into the blankness of the January Minnesota outdoors.

"Profiling? Sure, I suppose it is profiling, at least based on the poorly thought out response you provided. However, profiling rooted in the premise of probability and outcome and guided by justifiable performance metrics. Even in the most liberal establishments, discrimination based on performance will still be recognized as acceptable and where appropriate, rewarded or reprimanded."

"Craig asked about personal responsibility as a factor. I agreed. It is a factor. What I did not say was that I think it needs to be factored out because it is to variable for this research."

The grin slid from Craig's face.

"Can we get back on information sharing rather than attacking," Randy asked.

The awkward silence at the table was felt by all.

Randy regained his excitement and continued, "There was perspective into aging as a logical pathway. Sure, there is deterioration as a course of a natural action that is material and interrelated, but not mutually exclusive to a creature, a body part, a soft tissue, a cellular component, or a particle. There are the impacts on the aging process within a family over time and over generations."

"Go on," Garrison requested softly.

"Besides genetically, there are traces culturally, as a function of practical use. There is the environment and things that happened historically based on world events that have an effect. There are even political events that need to be overlaid. Then, there was an emotional factor. As an example, is depression brought on by one's environment a causation of further disease over time if untreated?"

Craig commented derisively, "Wow, are you suggesting we pave the way for political cellular degeneration research?"

Randy responded with what was becoming a less tolerant tone, "That is not what I said. Let me give you an example, Nagasaki. Did those people want to be exposed to somewhere in the neighborhood of three to four grays of radiation? No. That was political. Blame our government or theirs, you choose. I don't really care. It was political. Governments play a role. Governments play a big role both positive and negative depending on their motivation."

"Back to personal responsibility," Craig added.

"And back to the reason we have to treat the disease because we cannot possibly overlay every possible variation," Garrison replied.

Garrison realized this was a very interesting debate, but that it was not productive towards accomplishing the day's agenda. The tone that started as small talk in the lobby had now extended to the office staff meeting. Debating aging theory was not the reason for the meeting, but somehow became the focus. The mood was not productive. It was time to hit the reset button.

In a somewhat reprimanding tone, Garrison stated, "Randy, you need to be in greater control of the use of your time. By that I mean this, and listen carefully, spend your time collecting knowledge and data that will help us understand the physical treatment of malignant diseases. There will always be a cause and an effect. Our role is the treatment. No piddling around."

"Use better discretion. Get to the meat of the conference theory and then consider all of your options, applications or consequences of what you might be hearing. Then, and only then, decide if it is worth attending."

"If you have a great thought, don't sell your ideas short if they are good ones. Prove them right or wrong, but be sure you are sticking to a subject matter and related course."

Nan was feverishly trying to decide what comments were noteworthy for the minutes of the meeting.

Randy, feeling a bit chastised, "What do *you* recommend?"

Garrison asked of himself, "What would *I* recommend? Let's see, what I would recommend?"

Garrison was a bit restless, but still wanted to be a good researcher, friend, good mentor and supervisor.

"What I recommend is what I have learned. I have learned that many of life's triumphs and successes are much more satisfying when you have achieved them through your own hard work and as a part of your own thought," Garrison explained.

"What I have learned is that my ideas are not always the best ideas, but they are generally good ideas. Seek out input on your hypothecations from others either directly or indirectly. Be prepared for some set backs, don't waste your time, but lead courageously.

"Most importantly, foundational learning can be gained at these symposiums, but great research cannot. People are communicating their ideas. This is not the place for research direction so to speak. This is a place to add perspective to relevant ideas and a forum to stimulate thought and formulate directional parameters. That is, as long as the topic is on subject and this particular symposium was not."

"Like the fact that we are going to be focused on treatment because the variables of the cause are too great to establish trends in a credible control group?" Craig added.

Craig appeared to be back on the team.

"Exactly," Garrison replied. "I am not saying the causes cannot be addressed or that prevention is not a worthy cause. I am saying that it is not your cause to follow. That is someone else's responsibility."

The medicine was not easy going down, nonetheless it was good information for Randy and Craig to hear. Randy has learned so much about life, research and doing the right thing from Garrison. Incongruent as it may sound, Garrison would never intentionally give Randy bad advice unless he thought it would help him.

This time was no exception. Garrison wanted Randy to "be the best Randy" and to put him on notice that he would only amount to being the "second best someone else" if he gained a dependence on the coat tails of others.

There was some other general business discussed at the meeting which entailed numerous operational and logistical issues that needed to be addressed today.

Having completed what seemed to be a standing daily agenda and update, Garrison dismissed Craig and Nan with a simple, "Craig and Nan, you can go, Randy, I will need to speak to you privately."

As the meeting came to an abrupt end and everyone got up Craig asked, "Do you know what the health care is like there?"

Randy replied even though he was not sure who the question was directed at, "Where?"

Craig replied in a genuinely apprehensive tone, "In Brazil? You should know!"

Garrison popped off a response as he walked by, "If it is anything like their environmentalism, it is a hell of a lot more efficient than it is here. It is probably less expensive too."

Garrison stopped as if in mid-thought, "That reminds me though, speaking of money, today would be a good day to walk over to the bank and purchase some *Reais*."

22

The standard currency in Brazil is the *Real*. The plurality of the Real is *Reais*.

Reais is pronounced *hey-eyes*. Garrison had found it much easier to travel abroad with at least pocket change in the local currency. The Brazilian currency is not particularly strong against the dollar so a few hundred bucks worth should be enough.

Garrison asked, "Randy, grab your coat. We are going for a walk."

Randy and Garrison both collected their jackets and exited the office. As they left, Craig and Nan continued a conversation relative to the apparent state of Garrison's agitation.

Nan asked Craig, "Does Garrison seem a bit short?"

Craig replied, "No, he seems about the right size to me?"

"C'mon Craig, you know what I mean."

Craig snapped, "Nan, I don't know what you mean." Craig became agitated as if preoccupied.

"Everyone is busy. Everyone has a lot on their mind. There are personal and professional strains on everyone and the state of the economy doesn't help. Each person expresses stress and motivation in a different way. I have found that you should input the facts only as you know them and process the resolution with the facts you have and not with the *seems like* speculation added in."

Nan interrupted, "Can't we?" but was interrupted after only two words by Craig.

"Ask intelligent questions specifically of the people who should know the answer Nan. If people do not know the answer, but need to know the answer before proceeding, help them get the right answer. Any questions like 'did he seem short' is idle conversation and does not foster a creative work environment."

Nan was speechless.

"Nan, your question was just filler and conversation filler is not something I want to make time for."

By now, Nan was not interested in making time to pursue this further either. She knew Craig, with his *Spock* like tendencies could not relate to the personal evaluation she was tempting to make.

"Okay," she replied. "Let's get back to the fund request from the R.W.T. Foundation we were working on."

"Perfect. That's more like it. I have a very important call to make first," Craig replied.

23

As Garrison and Randy walked down the slippery stone steps that exited the building, it was challenging to keep their footing. The sun was out, but the north side of the building did not get much direct sun and was always prone to having slick steps.

Nan was correct. Garrison was testy and preoccupied to some extent during their meeting. He was not an irritable person by nature, but his focus on work related matters made him come off as somewhat indifferent at times. Similar to Craig, but with a lot more interpersonal skills, Garrison was driven by the merits of an issue overlaid by the rules of play. His objectivity and *play by the rules* attitude was often misinterpreted as lack of interest in personal perspectives.

"Let's get right to it, Randy. The clinical trial involving Protein Suspension Radio Therapy (P.S.R.T.) and Microwave Glucose Therapy for both systemic and soft tissue malignant diseases have been concluded," Garrison said in his usual matter of fact style.

Randy's look was somewhere between amazed and devastated.

Garrison continued, "While the research appeared to show some promise, the FDA is not convinced that there would be value to moving further forward with the clinical trials at this time and would not support our doing so in any environment. Therefore, the medical grants have been terminated. We will need to schedule a review with the clinical researchers, wrap up the documentation on what we have found to date and put it to bed."

Randy was surprised by Garrison's indifference.

"Garrison, these protocols showed some of the greatest results we have ever seen in the treatment of all tissue cancers. Maybe even with hematological presentations. How could they have possibly come to this conclusion?" Randy asked.

"Randy, the thought was that our findings were circumstantial and not conclusive enough to justify taking up the government's time, money and energy overseeing our trials," Garrison replied.

"Are you saying that that these findings and our trends were just lucky?" Randy asked.

Garrison responded, "I am not saying anything other than that there is not a willingness to continue to nail down the behavior, the results or the effects of this treatment regimen in the eyes of the people who are funding it or the people who have to follow the trials. I suppose you could interpret what they have said as surmising our deductions were ones more of luck than cause and effect, sure."

"That's B.S.," Randy said. "We prepared ourselves to be lucky. We did the right things, the right way, with the right hypothesis. We are on to the right track this time. We have treatment for millions of people at our finger tips. It is that close, I can feel it."

Garrison again replied, "Randy, you are taking this personally. You are not always right. There are a lot of people who have looked at this data and come away with differing thoughts on how rewarding the outcomes will be."

"Garrison, you know how much promise this has. You know! You have seen our laboratory results. You know it is. You know that if it is not us now, who will it be and when?"

"Randy, what I know is that the funding drives the research and the F.D.A. drives the approval for clinical trials. As of right now, we do not have support from either one."

They continued to walk down the sidewalk past a few of the campus buildings and towards the bank a few blocks away. Again, the late morning was really turning out to be quite pleasant for January. The sky was clear and the temperature had warmed up to almost forty degrees.

As they stood at the crosswalk, a panhandler was on the opposite corner. The temperate weather had obviously brought him out for a chance to make a few dollars.

Randy was frustrated. While looking across the intersection he pontificated, "We are struggling with something here that can save a lot of lives. Then there is this guy, who has a life he is willing to drink away and discard."

Garrison responded, "Personal Randy, not so personal. Listen to yourself. You are mono focused. Think things through before you blurt out such silly and disrespectful comments. Sound bites like that will stunt your growth."

"What do you mean?" Randy asked.

As they crossed the street, "Consider this Randy," Garrison continued. "That young man over there was someone's little boy when he was born. His mother probably placed all of her hopes and dreams, and maybe the hopes and dreams of the world, on his shoulders. Somewhere along the way, something went off beam. Be assured, when he was born, he was someone's perfect baby boy."

"What is your point, Garrison?" Randy asked.

"My point is one of moderation. Everything must be viewed in moderation Randy. Things operate on more than one plane in life. This man has lost his moderation and has worked his way into a land filled with excess and imbalance on a very fundamental scale," Garrison said.

"However, this is the path he has chosen for himself. You must exercise some restraint in your ambitious pursuit to be right. Like I said at the staff meeting today, we may cure disease, but we will likely never cure the behaviors that in many cases cause it. That man over there just represents another lesson in self management for you Randy. He is a lesson in decision making. That is how you have to see it."

Randy was not interested in a life lesson or any other lecturing from Garrison today. He was really not listening to the good advice he was getting.

"C'mon Garrison, there would not be a lot of cost outlay to continuing on with the trials without the grants or the F.D.A. Should we continue on without their support?"

Garrison replied, "You're not listening to me. We cannot do that!"

Randy responded, "Why not? We have the equipment, the facility. Hell, the equipment we need is readily available in any major medical facility."

"Randy, you and I both know we cannot do that. That would fall far short of making luck and be a lot closer to just being foolish."

Repeating himself Randy mumbled, "If not us, who? If not now, when?"

"It takes patience my friend, Randy. It would be a mistake to forge ahead on our own. What you are proposing is the equivalent of the toddler biting the dog to get even after having been bitten himself. There is little good that can come from taking an unsanctioned and non-traditional approach. Our time will come."

Garrison was not one prone to tactical errors. He had seen numerous colleagues many years his junior make what seemed to be minor strategic mistakes that cost them their careers and ability to complete further research.

Randy admired his mentor, but he was hell bent on disagreeing, "I thought you learned by making mistakes?"

Garrison was ready with a reply, "You learn more by foreseeing the probable chain of events on the path you are taking and avoiding mistakes rather than carelessly rampaging forward, consequences be damned, and hoping for the best result. Worse yet, the path you are proposing will rely mainly on forgiveness after the fact."

24

Garrison went into the bank to make his foreign currency exchange. Randy stayed outside soaking up what little warmth there was coming from the winter sun as he paced contemplatively back and forth in front of the bank. It seemed ironic. A forty-degree day seemed like it was sixty degrees when it was mid-winter.

The transaction seemed to take a long time, but finally Garrison emerged from the bank with his exchange receipt and money. Another "to do" item ticked off of the travel checklist for their upcoming trip. The bank, for whatever reason, documented the entire transaction including name, driver's license, address and social security number. Overkill it seemed when exchanging three hundred dollars of American dollars for what will be local Brazilian currency. He did not check the exchange rate today, but was certain that the bank took their cut in the deal. Everyone seems to want a cut of the deal.

Some deals you see up front. Some deal cutting exchanges make it a lot harder to follow the money. This principle was also painfully evident in clinical medicine and research.

"I had such high hopes for where this was going," Randy said as Garrison came out of the bank.

They began their walk back to the office. The sloshing on the sidewalks and the sloshing in the street as the traffic went by made for interesting background effect on such serious conversation. This was a sharp contrast to the life enjoyed at the lake on the narrow seaside lot.

"I did too, Randy. Particularly with the lymphomas and the slower growing soft tissue carcinomas," Garrison reassured.

Randy said, "I thought this would be our legacy Garrison. I thought this was it. I thought this might be the cure. This could be a cure with very few side effects and limited healthy cell destruction to boot!"

Garrison relayed, "Randy, we will look elsewhere for our contribution, achievement and legacy."

"But Garrison, who decided to pull the plug?" Randy asked.

"What, you want a name? Let it go Randy."

"Think about it Garrison, that is what you tell me. What do we have to lose? We spend billions of dollars on baldness in this country. Is that because it is an affliction of the rich and the rich can afford to pay for the treatment themselves?"

"What do you mean Randy?" Garrison asked.

"Baldness is a sickness of vanity. Rich people who think their level of testosterone can be measured in follicles? Yet now, we have to give up on this research that shows promise to so many everyday people?"

Garrison stopped the conversation, "That was only two thirds of the news Randy."

Garrison continued, "The work we have been doing on active cellular immunotherapies has also been canceled. There will be no more work on this advanced prostatic cancer cell and prostatic antigens research either."

Randy, now even more frustrated, "Now, who is selling this idea short?"

"This is an F.D.A. denial of trial continuation as well," Garrison answered.

Randy knew that Garrison was a conservative and thoughtful man. A man who said what was on his mind, but meant what he said when he said it. If the grants were over, so were the research and the trials.

Garrison was a company man, regardless of what he thought as an American, he was a patriot. He was an advocate of the establishment and a committed champion of making the world a better place even though the intersection of the two conflicted at times. Randy would have to accept his direction and would be resolved to do so, but only after a few more questions.

"Garrison, I know you are boxed in here, but hear me out. You always say that we have two ears and one mouth so that we can listen twice as much as we speak. Tell me, do you agree with the plaque in your office that quotes Thucydides when he said, 'Surely the bravest are those who face the unknown, glory and danger alike, yet not withstanding, go out and meet it'?"

Looking both ways for traffic and looking over at Randy wondering where he was going with his train of thought this time, "Yes, I do," Garrison replied.

Randy continued with Garrison's approval, "Chemistry has to be on the same page and level as humanity here. You know it and I know it. This trial is being intentionally discharged without good reason. What about thinking of what *could be*? Isn't that what you tell me? Isn't it?"

"Yes," Garrison replied, continuing to watch himself put one foot in front of the other as they walked down the busy street.

"Then why…," Garrison interrupted Randy's latest thought and rumination.

Garrison was good at being non-emotional in very trying situations. He was also pensive when it came to how one circumstance related to another.

"Randy, listen to me carefully."

Randy hated it when the conversation came to this point. This discussion was coming to an end and these would be the closing comments, the likely final response from Garrison.

"I understand people have to be in a frame of mind to accept information and knowledge when it is being presented to them. People then have to be of the frame of mind to act on that information. It is human nature. You were not in that frame of mind when I conveyed the initial news, so let me try again."

"For whatever combination of reasons, the F.D.A. and other financial and governmental facilities are not willing to continue to support, or fund, the P.S.R.T., Microwave Glucose Therapy treatments for cancer or Active Cellular Immunotherapy for prostatic presentations."

Randy tried to get in on the commentary, "But…"

He was promptly restricted as Garrison continued, "No buts and for whatever combination of reasons, the financial and governmental facilities are not in the frame of mind to receive our appeal. Their decisions in these matters are final. This has nothing to do with you. This has nothing to do with me. This is how the system works."

It was now Randy's turn, "And you Garrison, need to know that I appreciate your long standing perspective. What can be dreamed of, can be achieved. This is a battle we can win. Hear me when I tell you, we can win this one on our own."

"On our own? There is no *on our own* in this scenario," Garrison replied with a slight chuckle.

Randy was going in for an attempt at the last word as they approached the steps to the office, "Garrison …you tell me not to take this stuff personally and you frequently tell me I do not think things through. What I am telling you is that you are not taking this personally enough and that you are not thinking this through with the universal greater good and the probable end in mind. That's just not like you."

Garrison looked at his apprentice with appreciation for his youthful exuberance and approach. "I know Randy. I know." Heading up the stairs, Garrison had one more comment as he opened the door for Randy, "and here is the final answer."

This *final answer* approach was a trademark in Garrison's management style. Garrison often waited, heard all of the relevant input, and determined the next steps.

"We will not carry on from here with the Protein Suspension Radio Therapy, Microwave Glucose or Cellular Immunotherapy. Only a fool destroys the life, integrity and reputation he has worked a lifetime to obtain. Understood?"

Randy nodded his head. While indignant and in disagreement, he was respectful of the traditionalist order of things. Garrison was his boss.

"I would like a verbal response."

"Yes, I understand," Randy replied.

"Very good," Garrison concluded.

CHAPTER FOUR
CHRIST THE REDEEMER

25

A very busy couple of weeks had passed since the conversation regarding the discontinuation of the clinical trials for the Microwave Glucose Therapy and Cellular Immunotherapy (P.S.R.T.). The conversation had struck Randy like a lightning bolt from a clear blue sky. From the weather to the attitudes of the team, things were different today than they were a few weeks earlier.

The stress on Garrison and Randy after the cancellation notification had been enormous. There had been many difficult conversations with the research staff and even more challenging documentation which needed to be completed in order to close out not only these projects, but this time in their lives.

This closure was made even more difficult, whether expressed openly by Randy or not, expressed by Garrison at all, or expressed by a strong under current, there was a feeling of misdirection. They both knew they were not doing the right thing by ending these trials so abruptly and without being convinced of the merits of the cancellation.

Personal feelings not withstanding, Randy had successfully brought closure to the documentation and they were all ready to get on with other business. Although all of their research was in some way interrelated, re-focusing was difficult. The thought of having to abandon several projects you believe in so strongly, and which showed so much promise, was very frustrating indeed.

Both Randy and Garrison were ready for a vacation and ready to take their minds off of the work that had consumed them for the past few years. Perhaps the long awaited trip to Brazil would be just what they needed to repose and revitalize their spirit, and moreover, renew their commitment.

When preparing for any travel, by way of his nature, Garrison would much rather leave home early and relax in the Crown Club before a trip, rather than feel rushed to get to the gate right on time. Neurotic perhaps, and not good time management for sure, for someone whose time was so valuable?

As a matter of every day practice, planning ahead was one of Garrison's most cherished characteristics. Throughout his work, he was consistently able to avoid the inevitable obstacles through careful study and thoughtful planning. Garrison was notorious for traveling in such a fashion to get to his destination a day ahead of his actual commitment.

In this way, he was assured of being well rested, fresh and engaged in the event, sport or challenges of the day. In retrospect, there was always plenty of work to be done on the computer that would make good use of his time. The next couple of days would prove challenging to his requisite travel planning history.

26

Garrison and Randy arrived at the Minneapolis/St. Paul International airport early. As a research scientist, Garrison is a consummate thinker and planner and never likes to be rushed in his timelines or his strategy. Regardless of the circumstances; the flights, meals, business appointments, research or otherwise, they would be early, prepared and always planned ahead for the unexpected. This discipline was just another example of Garrison's many hallmarks.

It was a quiet afternoon at the Lindbergh terminal. Everything appeared to be on schedule. The Club was not too busy and the small talk with Randy was light, but enjoyable.

They departed the twelve below zero February overcast and grossly typical Minneapolis winter weather in the mid afternoon and arrived on time in Dallas. In Dallas, they boarded the ten-hour overnight flight to Sao Paolo, Brazil. The trip to Brazil, while long, went without incident. That is, aside from Garrison's recurring frustration with parents who could not, or would not, counsel the child next to him on how to behave in public.

Garrison had never been very committed to spending time with children. He did recognize; however, that children, after all, were future guides to societal, as well as cultural, evolution and needed direction and guidance especially in their formative years.

In this wearisome and sleep deprived case, the parental lack of interest was assigned directly to the father of a five-year-old who was thoughtlessly tossing and mashing breakfast cereal into the floor and onto the seats around him on the less than crowded flight. The child certainly had plenty of energy on the overnight flight; that was for sure. Harmless, but irritating nonetheless.

Randy on the other hand, was able to get some rest during the all night flight. Garrison was not as fortunate. Randy was rested, Garrison was a bit tired.

Albeit restless, both had gotten some sleep. Perhaps, looking towards the day ahead, just enough sleep to make a productive first day out of their trip to Brazil. However, the lack of sleep would leave the pair at odds for the day ahead.

They arrived late morning after the red-eye flight. The time change, which was four hours ahead of the central time zone, along with the fitful sleep added to the jet lag.

Their travel plans called for them to go directly from the airport to their cruise ship. The ship departed from the shipping port in Santos a couple hours away. This created a little extra tension for Garrison as he was not accustomed to having to make tight deadlines when traveling.

Walking off the plane in Sao Paolo and walking through the airport, they could feel the humidity in their lungs as they drew each breath. The air was hot, heavy and thick. This improved slightly as they transitioned through the customs area which was a little cooler and provided some relief from the heat.

They had not yet taken possession of their luggage. The line for the customs and immigration inspection was long and very slow moving. As they approached the checkpoint, you could see that the agents were inspecting each person's documents carefully and with the same dedication with which they procedurally dictated the documentation for the visa application process. Garrison and Randy were up next.

The young lady at the custom's desk did not look a day over sixteen. Both Randy and Garrison handed over their slightly worn United States Passports. She scrutinized the passport and the visa stamp imprinted by the consulate in Chicago where they had sent them sixty days earlier. She then ran the passports through the electronic reader. She stared blankly at the visa and then leaned forward to closely examine the stamp. She looked intently at Garrison.

Assuming that she did not speak English, he did not comment. Garrison stared back at her, raised his bushy eye brows and lifted one shoulder trivially as if inquiring back at her in the international non-verbal expression of a question. She looked back at the visa and took out a magnifying glass to view both Garrison and Randy's visa stamp more carefully.

Apparently satisfied, she picked up the numerically reciprocating stamp, crashed it on to both passports on page fifteen, initialed them and, in perfect English with a Portuguese accent, stated, "You will be enriched by your trip to Brazil. Enjoy your time here. Next."

She handed the passports back to them and motioned to the next in line to come forward.

Enriched, Garrison thought. This was an interesting choice of words from a person who was undoubtedly speaking English as a second, or maybe even a third, language. The two of them proceeded to the baggage claim, acquired their luggage and were off to catch the shuttle to their cruise ship which was waiting for them in Santos.

They would board their ship in Santos and begin the true purpose of their travel adventure, experiencing Rio de Janeiro's Carnival' in a South American fashion, as well as stroll through the beach communities of Buzios and Illius.

After gathering their well-traveled and beaten bags, they easily located the cruise ship representative, made their way to the shuttle, and started the two hour trip to the port. Garrison was tired. Randy was leading the way. Both were in pretty good spirits.

27

The road from Sao Paolo to Santos was very slow, narrow and wound determinedly through the mountains. Many times they experienced the fear of over extending the road and careening over the side of the guard rail free mountain highway.

At a minimum, there existed the constant possibility of striking some local pedestrian as their shuttle sped along the mountain side. There seemed to be no shortage of foot traffic on the well traveled and poorly crafted highway.

Garrison thought of his wife, Sally, and what her eyes must have seen in her last moments less than two years earlier as her bus ran along the slender hillside road on the Greek coast just before slipping over the steep grade killing all but one on board, including her.

The irony of the moment haunted him. Could he have the courage to some day travel to Greece to see the exact spot on the road from Paphos to Limassol, in sight of Aphrodite's rock, the mythical place of Aphrodite's birth, to look upon the place where the love of his life had perished?

Garrison and Sally were tireless travelers together. By some paradoxical twist, was he looking at the same fate in Brazil? Was he in the wrong place at the wrong time like his good natured and warm hearted Sally? Would this be how they would be connected for eternity in one of life's gross little ironies?

Not being one prone to compulsive behavior or compulsive thought, these images soon left the tired and introspective Garrison's mind. He did love and find solace, however fleeting, thinking of past life experiences and comparing the relationship of what one of life's events has to another.

Randy sat quietly looking out of the bus window. He was amazed at the contrast and contradiction between the rain forest and the world wide conservation that Brazil emphasizes versus the poverty and rampant pollution he was seeing from his perch on the shuttle bus.

As the bus passed by the local residents, Garrison was closely watching the faces of the people on the road, there was a sense that the people had given up, or given in, to the inability to manage their environment or maybe even to manage themselves. Again, this was not what Randy or Garrison had expected to see in the country that he had heard so much about in terms of personal pride, ecological preservation and environmental vision.

They arrived at the Port of Santos around three in the afternoon following their long, nauseatingly winding, and culturally enlightening rural trip through the steep grades of the coastal Brazilian rain forest. With little time to spare, they were on board and ready to start their holiday. Together, after checking in, finding their state room and attending the compulsory muster drill, their ship was scheduled to sail for Rio de Janeiro at 5:00 p.m.

28

Garrison was a little anxious after having to travel on an over night flight and having arrived at the port just in time to board. Relieved to be there, but not yet relaxed. This was not how he preferred things to be done. He liked a lot of leeway in his timing and wanted to be in control of the clock, not visa versa. He was getting more tired by the minute.

On board the ship, and always the one who needed to be looking to what was happening next, Garrison had just enough time to wash his face and head down to their early dinner seating assignment scheduled at 6:00 p.m.

Garrison and Randy needed a good dinner and a good night's sleep. Garrison, in particular, needed rest to be ready to look forward to the next day's activities, which was sure to be a twenty-four-hour day of sightseeing and night life at the Carnival' parade.

They were seated at a large table. A table set for eight, provided dining with some nice, but not very interesting, people. Dinner was leisurely, but strained. Randy and Garrison were intellectuals, they did not have a lot in common with the two plumbers, their wives, and their two clearly dysfunctional and heavily tattooed children from New Jersey.

Garrison was not the type of person who could go to a party and know everyone in the room in thirty minutes. With strangers or children, he had never mastered the art of social networking. He was more of a people watcher than a people person. He was an observer and a thinker. He very much enjoyed his colleagues and family, their personal and professional development and accomplishments, as well as how he could help them grow, but he was a real introvert with strangers.

It was hard to get into Garrison's inner circle. The longer he knew you, the more trusted you would be and the more accessible he would be to you. He was just not very good at making new friends.

As they dined, they could see Santos through the large windows in dining room. The ship had departed for Rio de Janeiro on time. It was expected into port tomorrow by 8:00 a.m.

After dinner, Garrison and Randy enjoyed the welcome aboard show and a cocktail in the Schooner Bar. They watched and listened to the other guests in the theatre and around the bar. It was clear that the ship had assembled a very wide range of travelers from around the globe. The popularity of Carnival' must have driven the diversity of the voyagers. Surprisingly, there were only a few hundred Americans on board the twenty-eight hundred passenger *Vision of the Seas* from the Royal Caribbean fleet.

The post-dinner cocktail, combined with their lack of sleep induced giddiness and semi-delirium, created some comic relief in each others company.

The evening was finished off by laid back conversation and ended with the rebuking of their dinner companions. The *plumbers* were not the type of people that Randy and Garrison would be exposed too very often back home, but they did seem to be fun people. Randy had quipped that it would appear that the two teenagers had put the *fun* in *dys"fun"ctional*. They laughed and called it a night.

They had discussed that perhaps the lesson for the two of them as non-parents was that it was a good time in our social history not to have to deal with the technological and community pressures that were piling on today's children. They were both glad to be outsiders looking into the art of child rearing in today's world.

Retiring just before midnight, it was the first time since his first years of college that Garrison had shared a room with someone other than his wife. This may prove to be taxing, he thought, given the tight confines of a cruise ship cabin, but Randy was like a son and Garrison had an undeniable soft spot for him. Of course, being with Randy, there was no one he would rather be here with, other than his wife, Sally.

29

The wake up call came early Saturday morning. This was the big day that Garrison had been planning with Sally. Carnival' in Rio! The ship had arrived in Rio early and the two men had missed the sail into port. By doing so, they had also slept through the spectacular view of the harbor on their way to making port and tying off at the dock. Garrison was groggy. Perhaps still at a sleep deficit from the all night flight the day before.

Randy sprang out of bed with all the youth of a Brazilian boy headed for his first soccer match with his friends and without his parents. The day had been intentionally planned to be very full. The two would be going to *Christ the Redeemer*, which is one of the Modern Seven Wonders of the World, followed by grandstand seating at the Samba Carnival' Parade scheduled to start at 9:00 p.m. The parade was expected to run until early in the morning the following day. This meant another all night adventure for the duo.

This was the day that Garrison and Sally had planned for so long. For years they had spoke of seeing another of the world's great wonders here in Brazil. There was a mood of sadness and reflection overshadowing the fact that he was here and his wife, Sally, would only join him in spirit.

Breakfast consisted of one of Randy's all time favorite delicacies, smoked salmon and eggs. Garrison too seemed to like the light; however, smoky breakfast. He was confident he would taste it all day.

Sated for the time being with their light breakfast, and once again right on time, they walked down to the theatre where the first of their two tours today would depart.

As they entered the large auditorium, there seemed to be confusion. There were two groups. Randy and Garrison were assigned to the first group. Their group was over booked. The second group had room for extra passengers and they needed volunteers from group one to go with group two. A few travelers seemed agitated that they would even be asked to go from one group to the next.

Garrison and Randy had just come in and were hearing the slight discord for the first time. There was a young women from the cruise staff who approached them and asked if they would be interested in going from group one to group two. Calmly, Garrison simply listened, non-emotional as he was, and asked her two questions.

"Does this second group leave and return at the same time?"

She said, "Yes."

"Does this second group go to the same places?"

She said, "Yes, but it goes to Sugar Loaf Mountain, an attraction that was first included in the tour and *Christ the Redeemer* second."

It sounded like the two attractions were just in reverse order. Garrison gave this little consideration. This was a simple transaction he thought. Facts are the same. Let fate take his hand.

Being the pillar of objectivity that he is, "Sure," he answered.

With that one word, a thank you from the cruise staff, and a sticker stating "Tour 2" slapped on the breast of their shirt, they were off. Collecting a bottle of water as they passed the gangway, they used their SeaPass card to log off of the ship. After a short walk down the pier, they joined their group, boarded their bus, and were headed to the aerial tram at Sugar Loaf.

30

The string of motor coaches departed the port area and went directly onto the streets of Rio. Immediately the two men were struck by the vastness of Carnival's impact on the city. There were banners, signs, tables and chairs, and huge beer tents advertizing "Nova Shin", the domestically produced beer whose name seemed to be everywhere. There were masses of people scurrying about on the downtown streets. It was only 9:00 a.m. on Saturday.

The streets, though crowded, had a look of casual abandoned. Not unlike the road they took from Santos the day before. The amount of trash on the streets was compelling and reminiscent of the 1975 trash strike Randy had seen while vacationing in New York City as a boy.

The buildings had character. The structures themselves were similar to those on the streets of Santa Barbara, a city on the Central California coast where Garrison and Sally once lived for a short period of time while Garrison was on one of his many sabbaticals at the University of California at Santa Barbara.

The sidewalks along the streets were adorned by an intricately laid montage consisting of black and white stone tile pieces about three inches across and in various inconsistent cuts, but predominantly square. The stone tiles were set in place in a simple waving mosaic design.

Unlike Santa Barbara, there were bars on the windows and graffiti on almost every wall they drove past. Sally used to have a saying, "take bars on the windows and graffiti for what it is!" Translation; be careful and be aware of your surroundings.

Garrison had heard from many sources that Brazil was a dangerous, unstable and beautiful place…another strange collection of contradictions he thought. On a recent flight to Kansas City for a seminar, he was seated with an Austrian business man in first class. In conversation, he and the gentleman spoke of Garrison's upcoming trip to Brazil. The business man had said he used to do business in Brazil, but had chosen not do so any longer.

When asked why and if the economics of his business had changed, the response Garrison received was not reassuring. He was told, "Leave your jewelry, your children and your wife at home," the man lamented in a tone as serious as bankruptcy itself. "They will steal all three in Brazil."

Usually open-minded, he was having trouble seeing anything but cultural instability at the moment, much less the *enrichment* spoken to him yesterday by the reserved, juvenile looking, customs agent.

The traffic was horrifically slow. There was plenty of time to take special note of the city life surrounding the motor coach. Was this a function of Carnival' or was this just the way things were in Rio year round? At this point no one on the bus was quite sure. The coach was quiet as the obviously diverse multi-national group of travel enthusiasts took in the sights, such as they were.

The pair continued to soak up the local environment. Regardless of the celebration, Rio was clearly a people watching smorgasbord during Carnival' and an architectural wonder year round.

Hardly a word was spoken between the two on the bus. The coach rolled on as they made their trek through town on their way to Sugar Loaf. With each red light, more details came into focus. There were people covered in light blankets sleeping on the street. One woman, she must have been in her seventies, sleeping in a black and white checkered blanket, only grey hair and a weathered face with eye glasses still in position, sticking out from under the light cover.

"That could be my mother," Randy stated, as he broke the noticeable silence and as if speaking to someone.

"Yes," Garrison replied matter-of-factly without taking his eyes off the street, "but it's not."

While his comment smacked of a lack of sympathy, it was just another example of his objective nature. Perhaps too much time with Craig in the office was rubbing off on him.

The bus continued through the seemingly endless maze of wandering people, roaming dogs and ambitious street vendors all having left their respective waste as they departed. Nothing really seemed to be happening with any purpose.

Finally, they were emerging from the inner city streets and onto an expressway. The coach felt as if it were racing. They had reached a speed of about forty miles an hour now and, for the first time since they left the Port, it did not seem like they were going to crop the edges of cars in the adjoining lanes any longer. The bus, at last, felt as if it fit on the road it was traveling.

Along with the entering of the expressway came the introduction of the tour guide. It was as if the guide knew that she would not have anyone's attention while traveling on the skeletally thin local avenues due to all of the activity and the stress of such confined streets. The guide stood up and spoke in broken English to the group.

31

The native language in Brazil is Portuguese. Her attempt at English was respectable, but metered. Randy was fluent in Spanish, which you might think is linguistically close to Portuguese due to the close geographical proximity of their native countries in ancient times. The fact is they were very different. Randy understood about two words of every three that were spoken.

Motoring along, the coast again reminded Garrison of the Santa Barbara Riviera. However, it was missing the multi-million dollar homes. The coastal configuration of the mountains and foot hills here were very similar. The guide pointed out what looked to be a shanty town in the foot hills as they traveled along the coast. The name of the shanty town in this part of the city was Rocinha.

As a side bar to the tour guides commentary, Garrison and Randy briefly discussed their travel history. Neither could recall a place in the world they had visited where the most impoverished had commanded the highest ground. They agreed this was very interesting socio-economically.

The shanty town was expansive. From a distance, it appeared to be a mass of falling down interconnected shelters that went on for as far up the valley as you could see between the foothills. From this vantage, one could only imagine the living conditions up there. Except for the scope and density, this was not unlike the poverty they had seen on the trip from Sao Paolo to Santos. The sheer number of dwellings, while finite, appeared to be uncountable. The living conditions looked to be unimaginable from where they sat on the bus.

Garrison's thoughts were in conflict with the triangular inconsistency. There was the living conditions, the social excesses of what he had heard about Carnival' and the role of the Government here in terms of the poverty as well as economic and social responsibility.

Is this a society that speaks of ecology, humanity and conservation to the world and then allows so many of their people to live in the throngs of squalor? Does it just look worse from a distance or does it look bad close up too?

Garrison thought silently. What would be the real Carnival' lesson to be learned here while he visits this culture, the celebration and the public policy? Would it be the *Viva la Vida*, celebration of life he had expected? Will the lesson be symbolism over substance and not to believe everything you read?

Surely the homes on the hill are not a function of the celebration. Are the citizens here indifferent to the less privileged? Are these the acceptable loses in every society? Is there a case made for acceptable loses?

32

The coach turned off the road and headed into the central terminal parking lot at Sugar Loaf. The parking lot and the attractions were obviously very busy. It was from here they would board the gondola to the top of Sugar Loaf Mountain. As they exited the motor coach and looked up, you could clearly see the length of the lift. There were two legs to the gondola ride.

The first lift was to the smaller mountain in front of Sugar Loaf where you changed gondolas, and then the second lift up to the top of Sugar Loaf Mountain.

The line was surprisingly long, but the wait was not. Garrison checked his watch. Their plan was to see Sugar Loaf and *Christ the Redeemer* today before the parade. There seemed to be plenty of time.

While waiting in *queue* for the gondola lift, there was much laughter and many local families enjoying each others company. There was a great deal of celebratory spirit while waiting. A very positive and almost infectious spirit was in the air. Family interdependence is big here in Brazil. Unlike society in America these days, the family unit and the gathering of family and friends on a regular basis, is a very large part of their daily and weekly life in Brazil. It is a key to the national culture. The connectedness was palpable.

At the risk of Garrison predetermining his expectations, the environment he was witnessing here was more consistent with what he had envisioned the spirit of Carnival' to be like. Family ties, personal responsibility, moderate celebrations and a lot of laughter and fellowship.

Conversely, what he saw on the way here via coach, was the Carnival' spirit that appeared to be stained by excessive substance abuse, vagrancy and environmental disregard.

Predetermining expectations always seemed to be a set up for disappointment. In research, it is a precursor to bad data and a bad determination. He will let the face value of his entire trip here take him to the final determination. For that end result, he would have to wait.

As they waited in line, they continued to be surprised by the language barrier. Almost everyone was speaking a language other than their own. They assumed it was Portuguese. Garrison thought of Sally intermittently.

They entered the gondola. A gondola ride almost always creates some apprehension. The level of apprehension can be calculated by the distance from the ground, the wind and the relative turbulence created by the inevitable anticipation of the bumpiness as you cross the support towers.

The gusty coastal winds today would be the most unnerving. The ride was generally smooth and the scenery out every window was nothing short of once-in-a-lifetime beautiful.

The views from atop Sugar Loaf were equally spectacular. There was a wonderful view of the Atlantic Ocean, Copacabana Beach and the city below. The time at the top was adequate, but short. They descended down the mountain, through the mid-point gondola connection and back to the central terminal parking area.

It was lunch time now, so they grabbed a quick sandwich from the on-site concessionaire. The coach was loaded promptly and without delay for the short bus ride to *Christ the Redeemer*, the highlight of the day's city tour.

33

Garrison must not have gotten totally caught up on sleep. He was already getting tired. Randy, fresh from the adrenaline high of the four segment gondola ride from which he psychologically and without merit surely cheated death, was ready for more.

The coach traveled through Ipanema on Delfirm Moreira Avenue a district made famous by *The Girl from Ipanema*, a Grammy winning song from 1965. The guide continued her attempt at merging English and Portuguese as both Randy and Garrison took in the domestic sights passing the bus.

What a difference it was compared to the initial start as they departed the port. The bus was full of laughter and chatter. The streets in Ipanema were clean, generous in size and well maintained. There were mosaics and cobblestone amid well maintained buildings. Some of the art deco buildings were splendid. This was the nicer end of town for certain.

Their sight seeing entailed traveling through a little city named Barra da Tijuaca. This is where the bus turned around and headed back north towards Rio. Barra da Tijuaca, like Ipanema, must be a place where the people of higher means lived.

The bus passed the Barra Grill. Randy understood enough of the guides personalized English to know that the guide was strongly recommending this restaurant and referred to it as the best of all Brazilian cuisine as they passed by. The two were in port for a couple more days as part of an extended visit to Rio by the cruise line to honor Carnival'. Maybe they would come back and sample some of the local fare before they left the city.

It was early afternoon by now and they were miles away from the ship as they headed to *Christ the Redeemer*. They both saw this as one of two main highlights of their trip to South America. Sally was checking off her "Wonders of the World list" and this was one of a few that were remaining.

Randy and Garrison had to be back at the ship by six. They had planned to attend the all night Samba parade. Surely the stop at *Christ the Redeemer* will be one stop where people will want to linger. Garrison did not want to get back to the ship only to have to leave right away. Some time to freshen up and get something of substance to eat would be nice. The schedule now appeared rushed for the rest of the day.

The coach turned in at Corcovado Hill, where the statue of *Christ the Redeemer* was located. After a short line up, they boarded one of three red cog trains that would take them to the top. Everyone filed in gently and took their seats. Without warning and with one sudden jerk of the train as the cog took hold, Garrison and Randy were headed up two thousand three hundred feet to the viewing area at Christ's feet.

The ride was smooth, slow and steady. It had started to rain. The rain too was steady. Not a downpour, more like a misty tropical rain through the seventy-five degree Fahrenheit balmy Brazilian air. The sound of the rain drops falling on the metal roof of the tram had a calming effect. The tram went up the mountain through what was a pretty dense and apparently undisturbed rain forest in the middle of town.

As they climbed, the sound of the cogs combined with the rain drowned out most of the background conversation. It was a comforting combination of sounds which, amalgamated, were almost trance inducing. Garrison drifted off, blankly staring into the rainforest. How quiet the jungle must be he thought. Brazil is a vast country.

This is not the rain forest so many come to see. They were on the coast, near the city and only a couple hours from Sao Paolo, one of the largest and most dense cities in the world.

Then again, just a little further inland and into the unincorporated forest itself, lay the rain forest so many people travel to in an effort to escape the city, the hustle, the responsibility and do so in the name of conservation. Or is this really just a place for fantasy and soul searching?

Garrison contemplated. Do people really come here to go *Green*... or does that just sound good? Perhaps they have figured out what I have not, Garrison thought.

Have they found the cure for the human condition? What is the human condition? Is the human condition merely the betterment of mankind or is it more personal?

Should you worry about your own happiness first, no matter what? As Ricky Nelsen sang, "You cannot please everyone, so you have to please yourself?" Had Garrison missed that lesson? Does the human condition need a cure, and if it does, is it possible? Maybe the human condition needs only treatment?

Does the government here or elsewhere care about the human condition much less how to treat it if it needs treating? If it is possible to treat, by whom and by what means would social or medical ills be remedied? Was there a limit to a government's tolerance when searching for a remedy?

This rambling thought seemed to leave Garrison with more questions than answers. That is the usual course for his mental wanderings and machinations. Slow and steady, always the theorist, seeking what has not yet been discovered and perhaps, in this case, the undiscoverable.

Could Garrison seek to find in Brazil what he had not yet lost at home?

He was snapped out of his abstract internal argument when the little red tram shuttered over a trestle that spanned a large ravine. To Randy and Garrison's surprise, after assuming this sanctuary and park was a pristine area in the middle of town, there was a river of trash that flowed from what appeared to be a gathering of nomadic tents. A few of the inhabitants were present.

More homeless it appeared. No one else seemed to notice, just Garrison and Randy. The contrast between the *have's* and those that *have not*, the *conservation* and the *pollution* was inescapable. Acceptable loses along the coast perhaps where the population is so dense. He reminded himself that Sao Paolo is one of the largest cities in the world.

Maybe the real conservation was in the interior of the country he deliberated. There are often degrees of commitment to public policy, health and conservation geographically within any large country.

34

After a brief stop, pulling off to the side of the shared track to allow a second tram to come down the mountain, they had arrived at the top. The fog was lifting slightly, high clouds had appeared and it was starting to rain a little heavier.

At the main entrance there was a sign.

Ben Vendo ao Cristo Redentor
Welcome to Christo Redentor
Beinvenido al Christo Redentor

Everyone was wise enough to know that this was an international welcome for people from around the world.

As a Christian, as most Brazilians are, and in a society much more religious than in the United States, Garrison knew this was truly a place to be cherished.

The two hundred and fifty stairs which lie ahead would lead to the base of the Christ statue. These steps looked to be easily managed. There were several switch backs that came in segments of about twenty stairs at a stretch followed by a landing. The landings collected the out of shape, the elderly and the slightly infirmed as they paced their way diligently to the top. The rain continued to come down in a slow and steady fashion.

About half way up the stairs there was an assortment of small cafés. The workers were present, but the rain was keeping the prospective patrons from the al fresco dining that was sure to be a great experience on a sunny day. Randy headed to the restroom at one of the Cafés.

When he caught up with Garrison towards the top, he recounted he had never had to pay one dollar to use the restroom before. Although Randy had traveled abroad, he was so naive for such an educated man.

The view from the top was spectacular, even through the light rain and slightly foggy vantage point. Randy set off for the railing so he could get a better look down the sides of Corcovado Hill and out towards the city below. You could see Copacabana Beach, the coastline, the cruise ship and the islands of the archipelago in the distance. The weather was not ideal, but it had not totally ruined their trip to the top. It was still an impressive sight.

Garrison on the other hand, a pensive and not generally guilt ridden or penitent catholic, was mesmerized by the site of the one hundred and twenty-foot statue of the Christ itself. He was not particularly committed to religious participation although he was a believer in one Christian God. For Garrison, this was a site that almost compelled one to confession. It was a spellbinding place.

With arms outstretched, the Christ was an imposing figure. The statue was a much larger figure theologically than here, merely a statue in effigy, but none the less an amazing site. The Christ's head appeared to be covered in a shroud with full length clothing.

In spite of the light rain, the atmosphere was again teeming with laughter and happiness. People of all shapes and sizes and from all over the world were rushing about to make good use of their time at the top of Corcovado Hill. Positioning, posturing and repositioning for pictures followed by pointing to various sights in the city and beyond. Of course, there were plenty of respectful admirers of the Christ statue. Maybe it was the site, maybe it was the exercise up the steps that had everyone's heart pumping, but the endorphins were definitely flowing.

The rain had all but stopped for the time being. Garrison stared upwards at the figure. Slightly dazed and in one of those great moments of admiration and reflection, he had wondered. How did they build this in this place? How did they build it here in 1931? Why did they build it and why here? Was this more evidence of the strong ties to family and commitment to Christianity here in Brazil?

Was this actually a manifestation of the *Redeemers* work? Perhaps it was in appreciation of the loyalty of *His* following. Was this symbolism over substance too? How and why is this impactful to me?

As he stared at the statue, there appeared to be a darkened spot, perhaps a weakness in the stone, where the rain looked to have soaked in or stained the Christ's clothing. The wetness, as if it were heavy tears on the garment went from the left shoulder and gradually tapering slightly larger as it washed out about mid thigh. It had been raining and the entire statue was wet, but the staining from the face down the side of the garment was coincidentally darker and consistent with how tears would flow. It was a clearly identifiable resemblance of tears.

Garrison again had more questions than answers. He would always try to assess and apply logic to his experience in the here and now. This visit to *Christ the Redeemer* was on the verge of becoming a spiritually moving and life changing moment for him, a very uncharacteristic moment.

His daze was broken by the startlingly sudden appearance of a helicopter which came from the south side of Corcovado Hill. With Copacabana Beach in the distance and a helicopter flying directly over head, snap out of it Garrison, he thought. This was a statue. Clearly a worthy sight, but this is only symbolic, albeit significant, reminder of a cultures dedication to an ideology.

Looking off towards Copacabana, he had thought briefly about how silly it was to think he had actually seen what could be interpreted as tears on a symbolic statue of Christ. It was raining after all. In the past, he has scoffed at people who had sold their French toast on E-bay just because it looked like there was a holly image on it. How gullible he felt at the moment. To a man of logic and structure, it was almost laughable.

As he rounded the back side of the Redeemer, Garrison would embark on

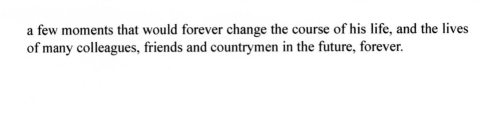

a few moments that would forever change the course of his life, and the lives of many colleagues, friends and countrymen in the future, forever.

35

Sitting at the base of the statue, on the back side, was an older woman who was holding a young boy. The boy appeared to be about seven years old. The itinerantly dressed mother was rocking the emaciated young boy as she sat on the wet marble substrate that covered the rear of the observation area. She was whaling in low, faintly audible tone.

As she wept, she was pitching slightly back and forth. The boy, pale and gaunt, with face and hair wet from the rain, only stared blankly, and without emotion, into the foggy overcast sky.

Garrison attempted to ask if she was alright. Speaking only tourist survival Spanish, and not the native Portuguese, his inquiry was largely inconclusive.

He motioned to Randy, who was admiring a group of Brazilian girls piled in for a photograph along the railing, to come over. In the last twenty-four hours, one thing Randy had not noticed until now was the legendary beauty of Brazilian women. Never wanting to keep Garrison waiting, Randy came over directly.

Garrison had asked for Randy to see if there was anything he could do for this woman and her child. The boy was obviously in distress. Helpless as the situation may be, he felt it was his duty as a doctor, even though he was in a foreign country and was not a practicing physician as such, to assist. Had the boy fallen?

In Spanish, Randy explained that they wanted to know if she needed assistance. Tourists and locals alike seemed to just pass by the woman and child without comment or even a second look.

The woman explained that her name was Marguerite Ayala and her son's name was Rigoberto. She would refer to him as her little Rigo. They were from the shanty town of Rocinha in the mountains. This was the same earth tone dull, but colorful, transient looking collection of interconnected run down villas they had seen on the way here in the motor coach.

Through a combination of Garrison's English and Randy's Spanish, along with the woman's shallow knowledge of English and native Portuguese, Marguerite had explained in what sounded like a grouping of run on sentences, that this was her only son and that he has been very sick for a couple years.

The doctors have told her there was nothing they could do for her son. Her husband, who was originally an American from Texas moved here in the mid-1980's, had passed away a couple years earlier just before Rigo had taken ill. Marguerite was frustrated. No one seemed to listen to her because she no longer had secondary insurance after the death of her husband.

It was common knowledge that the care in Brazil is very good. That is, good unless there are a couple of conditions you are unable to satisfy. If you were under the age of ten or over the age of seventy and had a hereditary or otherwise incurable disease, your care from the government was going to be very limited.

Lastly, the medical care in Brazil is poor for those who do not have supplemental insurance or for those who are in a pool of the secondarily underinsured. Without secondary insurance or independent financial care, you had to totally rely on the governments socialized care and discretion.

The discretionary component was critical. The government could decide what level of care you would be getting and moreover, whether you were a better candidate for home hospice and comfort measures care than you were for treatment. Everyone knows comfort measures, as you fade into certain death, are much more economical than extended periods of treatment.

Marguerite explained that, Rigo continued to get weaker, lose weight and would sweat profusely at night. His disease and the malnutrition had almost completely taken his sight. She had run out of hope and had been praying in her home. As a last resort, she was able to put a few Reais together to make the trip here to the Redeemer today. She felt her son was reaching the end of his time here with her. This might be her last chance to once again ask for God's Devine intervention.

What possessed Garrison to say what he said next was, at a minimum, uncertain to Randy at the time.

Garrison said to Randy, "Tell her we are American doctors and tell her we may be able to help her son. Does she know what is wrong with him specifically?"

Randy turned to him abruptly, "Tell her what?"

"Go on, tell her!" Garrison repeated in a matter of fact voice staring at the boy and the woman, waving his hand at her, and intermittently looking around.

Randy reminded Garrison they were in a foreign country. They were not licensed to practice here and in no position to help anyone medically, particularly someone with a progressive and long term disease. Given the language barrier and the short time here in port, much less customs and what ever unknown regulations they would encounter, how could they really be of any assistance?

"What can we do for Rigo?" Randy asked

"Tell her Randy," Garrison said restlessly as he nervously looked around showing signs of losing patience with his good friend.

Garrison further chastised by telling Randy, "You really have to get past this self-limiting thing you have going on. I said maybe we can help. We have to understand our options before we know if we can potentially help. We need more facts at this point."

"You simply do not know enough yet to determine if we can help him or not," Garrison restated calmly, "Now tell her! Let's see what is wrong with him."

With a confused look on her face and a deep frown line furrowed on her forehead, Marguerite concentrated on listening to Randy's attempt at gathering more information. As Randy began to explain that they were doctors, within seconds, the furrows were dissipating and there appeared to be a smile emerging on her face.

By the time Randy was finished speaking these brief couple of paragraphs asking about the specific clinical condition of her boy, Marguerite was beaming. She stood up and transferred her son from her arms to the reluctantly accepting unmarried and childless arms of Randy.

Marguerite, now simultaneously joyful and tearful, engaged Garrison in a full body hug. Marguerite began to speak at a rapid clip. Her tiny frame had a death grip embrace on Garrison. She sounding like a speed reader running through the Lords Prayer, Hail Mary Full of Grace and an entire Sunday sermon all wrapped into one.

Randy, holding her seemingly lifeless son tried to translate as fast and as best as he could. She was thanking the Christ for hearing her plight about Rigo and for sending the American doctors to help cure her son. How thankful she was the Redeemer had chosen to intervene on her son's behalf on this day, yet no words about his condition.

Garrison was speechless. In a matter of five minutes, he had gone from being an intrigued American tourist to the pseudo surrogate savior of this Brazilian woman's only son and the only worldly genetic record that her husband had ever lived at all.

Garrison stuttered through asking if she had information on Rigo's condition, an address, a phone number, someway to contact her, anything that could be helpful. Assuming that she was very poor based on where she lived, Randy inquired about some additional specifics.

The best Marguerite was able to supply from the shopping bag she used as a purse was a dog eared business card of a woman she and her husband had been friends with. Her friend, DiDi, painted women's nails at a shop in Ipanema.

DiDi had tried to help Marguerite and Rigo when she could. She too was of limited means, but had a phone number. Marguerite and DiDi met about once a month when DiDi would try to meet and buy her friend lunch. Usually, this was the best meal of the month for Marguerite.

In return, Garrison scratched out his name and e-mail address on a small piece of paper he found in her bag, although he was not sure what she would do with it.

The doctor's calling card was also in her bag, so Marguerite was also able to supply the name and number of the doctor whom her son had seen some months ago. This may be helpful Garrison thought, as he accepted the additional contact information.

As fast as this chance meeting had started, it seemed to come to an end. The final translation from Randy was one of Marguerite saying that she was sure she would hear from them. It was Gods will, sent through God's son. She continued by saying they could not avoid the fate of helping her now. They were sent to save her little Rigo. It was meant to be this way. These things happen purposefully and with a predestined path for good reason.

"We all have a pre-destined path to walk," Marguerite recounted as Randy translated.

36

Randy and Garrison started to navigate their way through the crowd and make their way down the steps, leaving mother and son to the terminal and paradoxical *loneliness in a crowd* that she was experiencing when they first saw her. The gross contradictions of Garrison's Brazilian life experience continue.

Randy reminded Garrison, as it started to rain heavier now, of what they had seen and heard about Brazilians. There was spirit in the Brazilian people, there is resolve in their religion and there is strength of their families. She would be fine.

Garrison snapped back, "Unfortunately, Marguerite had no family to help. Were you listening at all?"

Clearly disappointed with Randy's obvious disregard for the obvious, he ranted on as if to reprimand, "You cannot tell the difference between this young boy and the one on the plane last night or yesterday, or whenever it was, smashing cereal? They are the same age! You cannot see the difference?"

Ouch, Randy thought. Now who is taking things personally? He took a shot directly at what Randy was able to see and comprehend. This was really out of character for Garrison. Why was the generally non emotional Garrison acting with such unbridled passion and making this circumstance personal.

"C'mon Randy," Garrison continued, "The next thing you are going to tell me is that he didn't have insurance and who was going to pay for his care even if we provided it. Your priorities are not in order here, Randy, and I find your indifference and swift dismissal of this boy's clinical dilemma to be irresponsible."

Randy was up for the challenge and replied, "Oh, so have you looked around in your own country lately? It is the same way at home, Garrison. You just don't see it anymore. You are too busy being focused on the research to know what the actual care is like. When was the last time you had a claim denied with your insurance."

"Better yet, when was the last time you had to face a terminally ill patient and tell them there was nothing more you could do for them. You, the one who gets everything paid at one hundred percent through the University faculty state subsidized wonder plan."

Compelled by an intellectual *tit-for-tat* all out volley, "This place was meant to be enjoyed for the view, the spirit of Christ, the people who built it and the fresh air. It should be a place of hope and not a place of heartache," Garrison answered off subject.

Randy replied, "Who are you to say why this place was created?"

Garrison let him have the last word this time. Both men were content to retreat to their respective philosophical corners and end round one of the sparring over Rigo and Marguerite.

Having traversed the stairs back down to the transportation station, they entered the little red tram for the trip back down the mountain. Garrison and Randy got the last two seats. They were seated in separate cars. Garrison was in the back where he could see the jungle foliage and an intermittent view of the beaches to the south.

37

So many people seemed so inspired by their visit to the top of Corcovado Hill. Garrison did not feel inspired. His mind was racing and his heart was pounding. He needed to take a deep breath and calm down.

The rain became heavy. Thankfully, the roar of the rain hitting the tin roof of the tram was once again having a calming, satisfyingly depressing effect on Garrison just as it did on the ride up the hill. The rain has always had an unusually sedating effect towards helping slow Garrison's gears down. The rain helps him relax, think and separate the issues that would frequently race through his mind. The balance of the tram car travelers were once again teeming with merriment and joyfulness just as they were in front of the Christ statue.

Garrison tuned out everything but the sound of the rain beating the roof of the tram car. He was drifting into another thoughtful and abstract, almost dreamy, state. Despite trying to use the sound of the rain to help slow him down, his thoughts were still coming fast. Garrison was torn between his racing mind and his need to slow down.

What was wrong with Rigo? Exactly how long had he been sick? What had he gotten started for himself and potentially Randy? Was he the person that could help this boy? Could this boy be helped at all, by anyone?

Was this really Garrison's predestined path to walk? That was sure a good question? The attitude of "You cannot please everyone, so you have to please yourself" was never his style.

Like Craig had asked back in the office, what was health care really like in Brazil? Garrison didn't know. Was that affecting the treatment Rigo was getting?

Still faster the thoughts came as he tried to file and sort out his perspective. He was totally struck by the circumstances. Was it the appearance of the tears on the Christ, the sorrow of a helpless mother's love, the rain and the sanctity of the *Cristo ao Redentor* site in and of itself? Why me? Why here? Why now? Was this truly Divine intervention?

Was it the soothing rain as he walked up the steps to the statue of *Christ the Redeemer* that put him in a receptive frame of mind, the *enrichment* comment from the young customs agent, and the lack of sleep the night prior, all in combination that made him so susceptible to this one person's troubles?

Do we have a predestined path? Is this why he was on the "Tour 2"?

The cog train was getting close to the bottom of the mountain. The train ride seemed like it had been only a minute long. Garrison continued to be introspective and reflective. As long as he could remember, he had always been a good listener. He was accustomed to hearing the issues, the merits and the facts, the objectives of resolution, whatever they may be, and in the end, being decisive. When patient and thoughtful listening was employed, he was always able to find the best path and give practical solutions to the task at hand.

This circumstance was morally, ethically and culturally challenging not to mention, the personal, political or legal consequences of whatever some of his actions might be.

He steadied himself on being focused. He was well-educated. Not fearing the consequences, glory and danger alike as Thucydides said, he would take on new challenges when needed. These were all character traits he has been committed to as an adult so that he could be a better person in this generation than his father was in the last. He had an ability to know the right moves. Right now, his morale and ethical compass was spinning wildly, unsure of direction, but he knew this would be a character building, perhaps character defining situation.

Interestingly, Garrison had the ability to think things out in a way that made you believe he could see around corners. Always being careful, he would find the equilibrium between being too cautious and not being too aggressive when accepting risk. He was either very lucky, had very good timing or was just exceedingly intelligent and therefore good at tactically plotting his way through his many career mine fields.

Garrison did not know any other way. In truth, it was probably some combination of patience, street smarts, being well read and having very high level of intelligence and education. He made his own luck and made very few mistakes. No one likes a supervisor that panics. Garrison was the boss you wanted when the chips were down.

To his credit in this situation, he was very well versed in understanding the relationship between the reactions people have to the events they encounter. He would need all of his experience if he was to have any impact at all on little Rigo's situation.

Although Garrison was able to always keep his ego in check, this time, he was faced with something greater than he was. Something more knowing than he was and more powerful than he was. If you were a believer, and Garrison was, it was like being watched by the all knowing, all seeing eyes of *Christ the Redeemer*. Garrison did not want to disappoint the mother, the son and especially himself.

Randy, well, he was just glad to be with Garrison, but Randy had a lot less experience to draw from.

38

Garrison had not even realized that he had exited the cog and was already in his seat on the motor coach. As if by auto pilot, he had gotten to where he needed to be, next to Randy, on the coach. He could not retrace his trip from the tram to the coach if he had to. His mind was elsewhere.

The motor coach left the lot and was making its way through the heavy city traffic on the way back to the ship. Garrison's mind was still silently processing at full speed. The distraction of the day's compact timeline was having a disquieting effect. It was after 3:00 p.m. It was getting late. He was looking forward to the time he had planned to clean up and clear his mind in anticipation of his all night adventure at the Carnival' Parade. Now pre-occupied with Marguerite and Rigo, he needed time to check his thoughts.

Just then, the guide came on the intercom. She said it was their lucky day. There had been one more stop that had been added to their tour today. She asked the fully loaded bus if they wanted to see the Metropolitan Cathedral. The response was a reverberating *yes*.

The thought of another stop, another distraction, was not what Garrison wanted to hear. He was probably the only one on the bus that did not want to see the Cathederal. He was not in control of the clock. He was out of his element. He was very distracted now. Garrison was trying to arrange what he had experienced in his mind while he prepared to be out all night.

Thankfully, the trip to the Cathedral was short. He was not sure if the Cathederal was really as close as the guide had stated, or if it was his racing thoughts that just passed the time faster.

The Cathedral was striking. It was built in the 1970's with a prominent stained glass and dark walnut colored interior. The exterior was raised in a concrete construction and fashioned a bit after the ancient Mayan ruins at Chichen-Itza.

Luckily for Garrison's piece of mind, the stop was brief and they were once again headed for the ship. The stop for Garrison reconfirmed something. One more time, if nothing else, this stop solidified and reinforced the impact and emphasis of religion in this society. This is unquestionably a committed culture of believers.

The stop back at the ship was equally brief. The day had been hot. Randy and Garrison were really sweating as they took in the sights of the day. They did have a chance to get something to eat and take a shower. There was limited time for food and beverages, so a quick buffet style early dinner in the Windjammer Café was welcome indeed.

Garrison and Randy, both somewhat quiet and thinking to themselves about the day's events, gathered their rain gear, some local currency from their state room, and were back to the gangway where they would be catching their shuttle to the Sambodromo to watch the parade. This is the site of the annual Rio de Janeiro Samba Parade. The pace of the last couple days was getting physically, and now emotionally, exhausting.

39

Time was flying by. They were on a new bus headed back towards the downtown area. Randy had not said much since they left the site of the statue of *Christ the Redeemer* several hours ago. Along the way to the parade, Randy seemed consumed with thoughts about what Garrison might be asking him to do next as respects Rigo. However, he did not have the courage to bring it up. He knew his father like friend very well and this was a time of contemplation that is best when not interrupted.

After a similar motor coach ride as the trip earlier in the day through downtown, they arrived and were uncomfortably positioned in the over crowded Sambodromo by 8:00 p.m. The Sambodromo is a several block grandstand structure consisting mainly of bleachers. On the side of the Avenue where they were seated, people were packed in to watch the parade. Across from them on the other side of the street sat the corporate and media representative's seats which were more of a box seating type of layout.

The Samba Parade is a traditional competitive event. The spectators were loud and fanciful in the lightly misting evening rain. Many of the parade watchers in the stands were in Mardi Gras attire and most had already been drinking for hours. This parade is a rain or shine event.

Tonight, there would be six competitive groups performing for the crowd and the judges. The groups were replete with floats and dancers. Each group contained about four thousand to five thousand actual performers and ten to twelve two-story floats.

They would have one hour and fifteen minutes to traverse the one half mile street from end-to-end. Going over or under that time limit would cost their group valuable points in the competition. The first competitive group would start at 9:00 p.m. with a brief intermission in between groups. The last group would finish around 6:00 a.m.

As they waited for the event to begin, Garrison initiated the conversation with Randy. "So, what do you think about our trip to the Redeemer today?"

As was customary, these were probing essay questions intended to gain perspective. A simple yes, no or one word question would be unlikely and a one word response would not be welcomed.

They discussed the circumstances of the day. Garrison mostly listened to a battery of all too obvious gauntlets and logical obstacles that were being laid out by Randy. He listened faithfully to his valued colleague.

Totally out of the blue, as if not even listening, Garrison interrupted Randy, "What about the weeping Christ?"

Randy replied with a look of puzzlement on his face, "What weeping Christ?"

Had he missed it? What was Garrison talking about? This was the first he had heard of a weeping Christ. Was this a figment of his imagination compounded by a lack of sleep and the inviolability of the place he was in?

Garrison did not reply.

Randy continued, "I am a good Catholic too Garrison, but you have to be kidding me, a weeping Christ? Listen to yourself…and Rigo, you never talk to strangers. You cannot even make conversation outside of the office, much less with parents and their kids. Are you out of your mind? What is driving you to help these people?"

Randy, now shaking his head, continued as he took a sip of his beer, "A weeping Christ! Wow, you have to be kidding me."

Garrison was reserved. Now they had both made their comments personal. Garrison had to get in the last word this time. "Randy, it is easier to categorize people than it is to try and understand them. Calling them *these people*, when you know their names, is disrespectful. Did you not do well in grammar *or* manners?"

Throughout the evening and into the morning hours, in a deafeningly loud Sambodromo, Garrison continued to be thoughtful of Rigo, Marguerite and the apparently dire situation they were in. As he watched the parade, which in spirit is a transformation of life, spirit and season, he sorted out the challenges ahead of him.

He could not help but think about the time, effort, money and man hours that went into the thousands of costumes and wave after wave of floats. Not to mention the time, the effort, and planning that had to be in place to pull off an event of this scale. It was all exceptionally wasteful, he thought.

Compounding this wastefulness, was the fact that the excess he was seeing, on a scale only a Roman Emperor could look up to and appreciate, was taking place while a nations youth was suffering due to a poor or ineffective health care system. How could that be?

He mused sheepishly to himself as to whether the community and their government had their priorities straight. Their own children were dying in their mothers arms without major medical care or care management. He saw the elderly sleeping in the street. He had seen both circumstances first hand today.

Was this a civilized society?

Shouldn't there at least be managed care for the terminally ill?

Is not the first and most important role of the government in any civilized society to be to protect and care for their people?

Was the government doing this intentionally to people of little or no means and to people who were thought to have a marginal expected impact on society? Was this natural selection with the government playing the part of nature?

Doesn't the principle of *expected impact* apply particularly to the very young and the old?

He could not bring together the connection of the parade to the culture, the culture to the people, and the people to the policies that were at the expense of the citizens.

Garrison recalled the trouble his staff had trying to get people to volunteer at the hospital, much less spend the days, evenings, weeks, months and the hundreds of thousands of hours it would take to promote and execute such a vast and extravagant event.

Carnival' is an event that is known around the world, in one of the worlds more financially stable countries, for its beauty and fanfare. The world does not appear to fully comprehend what this experience has created and at what consequential expense.

As the final grouping in the parade passed at 7:00 a.m., the stadium still stuffed with festive chants and flag waving celebrators, Garrison was resolved to believe he was in no position to judge his culture or theirs in and of themselves.

After all, there were generations of men and women before him that created both. He must make one decision at a time. The cumulative effect on cultural customs is only culturally significant when viewed over time. He knows that he is one man. He also knows that one man can make a difference, particularly if that one man is himself.

Randy appeared ready for another nine hours of cheering on his feet while enjoying the sights of women in costume, the drink and the song of this years Carnival' celebration and parade.

At the end, the two men walked with the crowd to exit the stadium and onto the prearranged coaches that were traveling back to the ship every hour.

Arriving at the ship they were hungry. A few overnight beers would not be a substitute for dinner. They decided a good breakfast would be a great way to cap the eventfully long day and night.

The hot breakfast was soothing after having been out in the cool rain all evening. Spending a half hour in the hot tub after breakfast would prove to be even more comforting still.

The excitement of the night and the fanfare of the parade were officially over. They went to their shared cabin to get some sleep. Exhausted, stomach full, and relaxed as they could be given the experiences and length of their day. They should sleep well. It had been a physically and emotionally draining time since they had both slept last.

Both continued the silence. A "Do Not Disturb" sign was put in place on the outside of their stateroom door, thought filled and tired, tomorrow should be a day of rest.

CHAPTER FIVE
THE GOVERNMENT'S ROLE
IS TO PROTECT THE PEOPLE?

40

Garrison awoke from a restless night's sleep with a sweaty pillow and a kink in his neck. It was one of those "I was too tired to sleep" nights where a good rest is fitful at best. His strained slumber was interrupted by some conversation in the hallway outside of their stateroom. Rolling over in his small single bed, he was face-to-face with Randy who was already awake.

Randy muttered as he sat up, "I heard them too. They have been at it for a half an hour."

Randy stumbled out of bed and walked to the bathroom. The mid-ship inside cabin was crowded. Inside cabins were preferred for Garrison. They were a better value. The lack of a window did not bother him in the least. After all, how much time does one really spend in their cabin on a cruise anyway.

Sally had almost always insisted on an inside cabin. She was a night owl and she liked to be on the go all day. She liked to stay up late and enjoyed the dark peaceful quiet of the inside cabins until well into mid morning.

Inside cabins were better for sleeping in, she always said. Sally was not an advocate of an alarm clock and only used one on vacation when there was a commitment. She used to say she liked to get up when she was done sleeping.

The other major exception was; of course, when there was the interruption like the one they had been awoken by this morning. In this case, they had both forgotten they had just recently gone to bed at almost nine in the morning.

Randy emerged from the restroom breaking up Garrison's day dream about Sally, as he tried to shake off the sandman.

"So, are you ready for some breakfast or do you need some additional time in the sack?" Randy commented as he stretched his arms as if to try and recover from his all-nighter at the parade. The morning hours had been ticking past without them.

Garrison said as he yawned, "What time is it?"

Randy replied, "12:30 p.m."

Garrison questioned, "It is 12:30? I am pretty sure our shot at breakfast has long since passed. I should probably get up and get something to eat."

Garrison was now sitting on the edge of the bed. Randy was still standing in the doorway to the bathroom. Garrison sat looking at him.

"Well," Garrison said. "Can I get in the restroom now, or are you just going to stand there guarding it? My prostate certainly has less discipline than yours!"

Randy moved from the doorway making way for his friend.

After Garrison finished his business, the conversation resumed.

Randy asked, "And, about that breakfast?"

Garrison replied "What is the plan for the day? Let's start there."

Garrison was always starting with the end in mind, Randy marveled at this trait. He himself did not have the patience to be so deliberative. The two decided they would spend a leisurely afternoon on the ship hanging out. A light breakfast was in order.

The highlight of the day, they agreed, would be trying to make their way back to the Barra Grill for dinner. It really sounded like a great way to spend their final evening in Rio. It was hard to pass up the glowing recommendation from yesterday. It would be pretty easy to skip dinner with their shipboard table mates.

After they had both showered, they agreed to meet back in the Windjammer Café on Deck 10 at 1:30 p.m. for a bite to eat.

41

Randy had showered first and was waiting at the entrance to the Café when Garrison arrived. They were flamboyantly greeted by a young Asian host.

"Welcome to breakfast!" he exclaimed in high pitched, drawn out and amusingly distressed English. He could clearly see Garrison and Randy had just awoken and were indeed breaking their fast.

As a matter of sanitary practice, and for the safety of the crew and guests, they had to apply sanitizer gel to their hands as they walked into the Café.

"Did we have to do this before," Randy asked as they entered.

Not waiting for a response, Randy answered his own question, "I don't recall."

"Me either," Garrison replied. "It is interesting though. The lengths they are going through to keep the microbiology on board in check. You have to know that these ships, with their confined quarters and humid South American or Caribbean itineraries, must be floating Petri dishes brewing up almost every conceivable human migratory pathogen, virus and bacteria."

"It would be very challenging, don't you think?" Garrison continued, looking around intently at all the nooks and crannies of the ships physical structure as well as the guests in various degrees of dress.

Garrison ran his fingers on the window sill along the entry discovering it to be almost dust free.

He continued, "This reminds me of what Craig was saying a few weeks ago in the office. You cannot manage each individual's personal hygiene habits. In this case, to keep the ship clean and safe, it is probably more beneficial to focus on prevention rather than treatment. The hot tubs, confined cabins, hand washing, excess alcohol, fecal choloforms…"

"Stop it," Randy jutted in. "We are going to sit and eat breakfast, or lunch, or whatever, we are on vacation. I have every confidence that the ships medical staff, environmentalists, housekeepers, or who ever is in charge of living conditions on board, are competent enough to take care of us and do a good job. I want to be able to get something to eat without your microbial commentary."

Garrison, looking a little confused by being cut off, could not see why someone else did not share his intrigue. He could not understand why a fellow scientist like Randy could not appreciate why he perceived this to be such a fascinating environment. Garrison as an advocate of treatment for serious disease as the prevention was simply to much of a variable. This was a case where prevention was clearly beneficial.

Garrison merely closed out the discussion by saying, "Like we discussed in the past, the continuing challenge will always be managing and anticipating the ultimate variable; human behavior. It is very difficult to anticipate and compensate for, at least in terms of cause and effect on the human body."

Together, they walked through the buffet and found a seat. Light fare was in order given their dinner plans and the late hour. Both took only cold salads on their plates along with bread. The Greek salad was Randy's favorite.

The Café was not very busy. Port days usually aren't busy as people are off exploring the town, countryside and local culinary fare. They sat at a table by the window. Even given their nine story perch, the views were mostly unremarkable. The dock was old and run down. You could see they were delivering a lot of trash portside. The trash was colorful and beginning to accumulate as if being staged for secondary transportation.

Randy, predictably impatient, thought he would take a chance and see if Garrison was interested in talking about yesterday. For all he knew, although unlikely, yesterday was all but forgotten.

"What are you going to do today? Anything you want to talk about?" Randy asked.

Garrison looked up from his salad, raised an eyebrow, sat back and shook his head. Smiling, he let out a quip of a laugh, "Ha, you are too funny, Randy," as he continued to chew his most recent mouthful.

"What do you mean," Randy asked.

"I mean you're funny! I mean that was a pretty feeble attempt to see if I was thinking about our day yesterday. You wanted to see if I was thinking about Rigo and Marguerite. You are so eager sometimes. It is so obvious."

"But," Randy tried to interrupt.

"Stop it. Relax, Randy! We have time tonight to talk," Garrison sagely stated as he continued to eat almost as if uninterrupted.

"But Randy, please think about what you want to say!"

After their lunch, the two went their separate ways. Garrison was off to wander the ship on his own. Randy was going to the pool deck. They agreed to meet back at the room around 5:00 p.m. From there, they could catch a cab into the city where they would enjoy good dinner conversation and a great meal at the Barra Grill.

42

Randy, overly sensitive at times, was smarting a bit from a comment by Garrison. He was a doctor. People always looked up to and respected his opinion. They rarely would question if he had thought through his comments.

Not surprisingly, Randy would spend the afternoon alone by the pool, fading in and out of sleep, but obsessively preoccupied with thoughts of his dinner conversation tonight with the man that had taught him so much about life, research and doing what was right.

Garrison walked the stairs down to the promenade deck. From there, Deck Four, he could walk the length of the ship. He was about two stories above the dock. He wanted to take a closer look at the weathered port seawall, the architecture and the piles of trash he had seen from the café.

Walking through the automatic doors and leaning over the banister, Garrison was dumbfounded by the sight that was before him. The sight to see was jaw dropping. Stunning. The trash piling up dockside was the collective remains of the floats and costumes from last night.

All shapes and sizes. All colors in the spectrum. There were large parts and small parts. These were definitely the floats from last night's parade he commented under his breath. Unless you were at the parade, you may not have known what you were looking at. They were bringing the trash to the port by the truck load. Presumably, they were getting it off the streets.

Where were they taking all this trash for disposal? Garrison walked up and down the railing on the port side of the ship looking down at the piles of trash. Last night this trash was meticulously assembled into eye popping arrangements. Now, it was nothing more than refuse. The amount of material that was now nothing more than debris was, well, overwhelming to say the least.

Were they taking it out to sea? He supposed not. Burning it in Rio was another unlikely possibility, at least not here in the city. The most likely explanation was that they were probably barging it down the coast to another part of the country for incineration or land filling somewhere in the country's interior was his guess.

More importantly, and what was more on his mind, was the waste. It was inescapable. Granted, he continued to see the same waste from the same event, but the money alone could have been used for so many great things. Thinking back to what he had seen at the parade, the absolute number of man hours invested alone was monumental. He kept coming back to the same conclusions about Carnival' and the misappropriation of priorities. The scale was epic!

He walked through the ships interior beam and to the same balustrade on the starboard side of the ship. Looking out, you could see a few of the islands that dotted the bay and the Atlantic beyond. It was beautiful. The razor-sharp contrast was brilliantly apparent. The contrast was unmistakable from one side of the ship's hull to the other.

He pulled up a lounge chair from along the superstructure of the ship and placed it by the railing. Sitting back in the chair and looking out into the enormity of the ocean, he put his feet up. He wanted some time to himself. He needed some time to himself. Some time to think.

He was sure that Randy would want to talk tonight. Maybe all night. If for no other reason, Randy would want to know what his mentor was thinking. The next few hours would likely be the only time today that he would truly have to himself. He too, like Randy, would spend a solitary afternoon in a chair.

While he tried to rest, though the air that was thick and heavy, his mind was completely occupied. He thought of his concern for Rigo and Rigo's mother, Marguerite.

He thought of his own spirituality and how it played into his place in modern medicine in these trying and controversial socioeconomic times. He searched his heart for where these contemplations intersected. Then, there was the Redeemer and the power he felt when he visited the statue first hand.

Despite the heat, time had passed quickly through the afternoon. The men had both been able to get some additional rest. Randy had indulged in some limited local conversation, and before they knew it, it was nearly 5:00 p.m. It was time to get ready for dinner.

43

They met in the room as planned. On time, refreshed from their time to self reflect they made their way back down to the gangway, off the ship and onto the street. A cab was hailed portside where they directed the local cab driver to the Barra Grill.

Travel through the streets was now a familiar sight. The cab ride, unlike the lumbering coach, was swift and fluid. The streets were still busy, but were so much more easily navigated in a smaller vehicle. The cab driver was quiet, with only some careless conversation about the city as they drove. Garrison and Randy were both reserved in their speech. Neither Randy nor Garrison wanted to start something they could not finish in transit or make a comment that would potentially be misinterpreted.

After negotiating some side street and freeway travel, they exited in Ipanema. Their cab traveled down Delfirm Moriera Ave through Ipanema, where the two had been yesterday, and onto Ministro Ivan Lins Ave stopping at the famed Barra Grill in Barra da Tijuca. The ride was uneventful. They had made this trip several times now, looking at the locals, Rocinha and marveling at the Ipanema architecture one more time.

At the end of the virtually silent thirty-minute ride, they arrived at the Barra Grill. Appearances from the outside suggested a nice, but modest, restaurant. They were both surprised by the fact there was a valet service at the curb. The cab driver let them off at the door and agreed to return for them in two hours for the return trip to the ship.

They walked in the front doors of the restaurant and found the décor to be slightly masculine, yet inviting. The lighting was low. The furnishings were rustic and functional. The décor and uniforms were tantamount to some of the finer conventional steak houses in the States.

They discussed the décor which was very similar to the original Manny's Steak House in Minneapolis, which they both enjoyed, before the local landmark steakhouse moved to the Ivy. The floor plan was more open and spacious. Their eyes were feasting on the ambiance and operational feel when the gregarious hospitality of the host interrupted.

"Welcome to the Barra Grill! Thank you for coming to dine with us tonight," the portly young man said in English with a sincere open smile that stretched from ear to ear. They replied that there would be only two for dinner.

Garrison had seen enough bad dining situations to know when he was going to be in for a good one. He abhorred insincere politeness and could spot it a mile away. The restaurant felt inviting and fresh. The people were friendly. The greeting, decor and cleanliness, assured Garrison, right from the start, this was going to be a good dining experience. Present company with Randy would make it great.

Randy had requested a table. His long legs were the central reason he had always described himself as a *table person* as opposed to a *booth person*.

However, everyone knew Randy had a theory. There were *booth people* and there were *table people*. No one ever knew what that meant exactly, only that he was a *table person* because he had long legs. Many close friends suspected there was far more conceptually to the seating theory Randy always referred to when asked about his preference. He always seemed to snicker as he responded, "I am a table person."

It was his personal musing, created and enjoyed mainly with himself. Colleagues were not sure what other interpersonal references and social connotations Randy was deliberating when sorting people this way. Craig seemed a party to his thinking one day at lunch when he attempted to qualify the theory. He speculated there were actually three types of people. Craig had added *counter people* to the list. Craig then concluded that all of mankind could be accommodated in these three categories.

To say the least, Craig moved up on Randy's *good to great* list that day. He agreed with Craig completely and wondered how he could have overlooked so many people, Randy confirmed, Craig was right, from here on out, there would be three. Nonetheless, Randy would continue to be a table person.

They had arrived at prime time. The restaurant was busy. As luck would have it, they were seated at a table towards the back of the dining room. Perfect Randy thought. They had a good deal to discuss and as much privacy as could be afforded in a large and congested dining room would be welcome.

The waiter approached the table promptly. In perfect English, took their order; two bottles of Nova Shin. They were looking forward to an ice cold beer. It was cool and comfortable in the restaurant but still very humid outside.

The method of service at the restaurant was out of the ordinary. The service was one of a traditional Brazilian style. After you served yourself at a salad bar, which offered substantially more than just salad, there were waiters who made the rounds through the dining room with long stainless steel skewers of meat.

The skewers must have been between two and three feet in length. There were various cuts of lamb, beef and pork served by different waiters touring in the dining room. The waiters would set the bottom of the skewer in a small stainless drip pan and hold it with one hand at the top. With the free hand, they would carve off slices of the meat which you picked off with small tongs as it was carved. The food looked wonderful.

Perhaps they were lucky. They were spoken to in crystal clear English at the door and in clear English at the table. This was a switch from what they had become accustomed to over the last couple days.

44

When the waiter returned with their two ice cold beers, Garrison asked, "Does everyone employed here have to speak English?"

"Oh, no, Sir. Everyone here does not speak good English at all. There are some that speak no English," the waiter said as he poured the ice cold beer into Garrison's frosted glass at the table.

"It is part of our training," he explained. "The host carefully profiles each guest as they enter. He is listening to what language they were speaking when they come through the entry and seats them for service accordingly."

Garrison was fascinated. "Now that is really thinking things through. I love it. They are starting with the end result in mind. I love that! I love that! That is what I have been talking about," Garrison exclaimed as his open palm spanked down on the table.

This was an unusual show of emotion for Garrison. Pretty simple Randy thought, but it was a real intellectual move. It was a preemptive service imperative in a multicultural society during an international event like Carnival'.

"Randy," Garrison said, "This is evidence in real time. There are parts of individual human behavior that can be managed. Not always predicted, but managed. If everyone could think things through at this level, how different things would be for all of us. Think, Randy, think. Probability, planning and outcome Randy. That is the train of thought you need to be applying here. Think! Probability, planning and outcome! Sometimes people have to be managed."

Using information they already have, the management here has done just that. This is fascinating stuff Randy. Human behavior can, in many cases, be predicted when based on repeated exposure and the intensity of their programming. Throw in a pinch of ego and, bingo, predictable behavior that may even appear to be compulsive behavior.

"Are you following me Randy?" Garrison asked.

"Not exactly."

"What I am saying is that there are many things that can be predicted and anticipated, and many things cannot be predicted. We should take advantage of what we can reasonably expect. However, it is our role, our research and out commitment to prepare the treatment for what cannot be predicted. There will always be people who take care of themselves. There will always be those who don't take care of themselves," Garrison explained. "And third, there are the ones who have some misfortune, genetic or otherwise, who will need treatment."

The waiter was now standing at the table and asked, "Can I bring you anything else or are you ready for a great dinner?" he said in a soft voice and a Brazilian accent.

Randy said, "I will have what everyone else is having."

Jokingly, the waiter responded, "Good thing! The salad bar and the meat at the table are specialties of the chef. It is also all we have, but there is plenty of it."

The waiter smiled, "It is all excellent. Help yourself to the salad bar."

Clearly, this comment was a shameless plug for the restaurant by a seasoned sales and service professional.

45

Randy was ready to take another shot at getting Garrison to open up with his thoughts. He would be a little more direct this time.

As they returned from the salad bar and began to eat their meal, thankful once again they were not with the plumbers for dinner this evening.

Randy faithfully began to test the waters regarding how Garrison's mind had sorted through the events of the last couple days. Randy was pretty confident Rigo, and the trip to the Redeemer yesterday, were consuming Garrisons thoughts too. However, he wasn't at all sure of what action, if any, Garrison would propose.

"Let's get started," Randy said, again showing his impatience.

"How can you help?" Continuing on before Garrison had a chance to answer, "Let's be honest here, at least between the two of us at the table."

Randy assumed Rigo and Marguerite were something Garrison wanted to discuss. He was right, but not so fast. Garrison continued to cogitate on the question. He answered as he ate his well chilled fresh shrimp and cilantro salad.

"I was asking you about the behavior and predictability of the training here at the restaurant. Were you listening?" Garrison asked.

Randy was silent.

"Can one man make a difference?" Garrison said.

Randy was sure that one man could, but was content to let Garrison carry on. After all, this was a rhetorical question and Garrison wasn't really looking for an answer. Garrison too knew one man could make a difference. Either favorably or unfavorably, one man can change the course of any event. History has proven this too many times to count throughout both civilized and uncivilized world history.

Garrison continued, "You know, the shortcomings of a parent in any society often revolve around their secrecy and mishandling of family matters. People worry too much about appearances. Parents need to become honest with themselves first and about their problems second if a family and their friends are expected to grow, accept what is real, and help the personal development of the overall family in any culture. Most parents want to hide the imperfections in their immediate family."

Garrison continued to speak as he ate his salad. Randy was listening carefully, but was perplexed by the commentary.

Garrison added, "Although the imperfections may be less critical than Rigo's, parents want to keep problems to themselves. Marguerite was willing to make her plight public, but still only as a last resort and in a less than optimally effective way. She was tired of following the herd. She was tired of being trustful of what the government and professional caregivers were telling her. It is frustrating for me to see people suffer when there are options available to ease their physical or emotional pain."

Randy had to ask, "I am not following your train of thought. What options do you see for Rigo and for his family?"

Garrison responded, "There was no family support for Marguerite. More importantly, the public system failed to support her. Don't you think we have an obligation to little Rigo; an obligation to help him? To help those who cannot help themselves. Should it matter what country we are in or what the government policies, practices and procedures are? Should a parent have to result to virtually ineffective last resorts to be heard?"

Randy saw unreasonableness to the way that the conversation was going. He saw that look in Garrison's eye. A look he has seen before when his boss started to dig in.

"I think there are certain responsibilities parents have to children, children have to their parents and responsibilities that people have to themselves and to each other," Randy responded.

Garrison listened.

Randy added, "I think there are vulnerable adults and there are vulnerable children in any society. Vulnerability could be due to money problems, poverty, substance abuse, genetics, handicapping, there are a lot of reasons."

Garrison responded, "That is not an acceptable answer Randy. I am not talking about vulnerability and you know it. You are slanting your comments towards a world of dumbing up government intervention and perpetually escalating acceptable loses.

"I was not talking about the government at all Garrison. I was just stating personal variations."

"No. You are starting with the premise there are acceptable losses in every society. That is what you implied."

Randy replied, "You cannot save everyone Garrison!"

Garrison was upset by the flippant response Randy provided. It was negative. A fatalistic view was not in tandem with the principle of "how do I make the world a better place than when I found it". Garrison was troubled and disappointed by Randy's comments.

Garrison stabbed at another oversized shrimp and asked, "Would you rather start by attempting to save or improve the quality of life for everyone and calculate losses backwards or would you rather start your day thinking you could not save or help anyone and calculate your successes forward?"

Garrison added, "Which is better practice? I sure think it is the first one. Start with the lofty goals."

Randy Responded, "Maybe we should be realistic. Maybe we should take every success as an individual accomplishment?"

"Maybe that's not good enough," Garrison quickly corrected.

Randy followed up, "Garrison, I think you are sounding like a do-gooder now that you are getting older and now that you figured out that you will not outlive your bank account."

Garrison's dislike for Randy's tone was going from bad to worse. He did not like being called out by a colleague twenty-plus years his junior and formed a timely reply.

"Randy, I have always wanted to *do-good* as you put it. Whether you knew it or not, as far back as I can ever remember, I have always had money in my pocket. I worked hard for everything I have. While my adversity has not been financial, I have hardly led a sheltered life. If you want to be critical, know what the hell you are talking about."

Tell me Randy, "What is the Government's role? Isn't the Government's role to protect the people from plagues and invaders both foreign and domestic? Seems I read something like that in a civics class somewhere along the line. Tell me, isn't that the Government's main role to protect the people?"

"Better yet Randy, tell me this, who protects the people from Government? You Randy, will you protect me?"

Garrison was rarely this animated and aggressive in his commentary. He had caught Randy completely off guard. With a shrug of the shoulder and a brief cock of the head, he had to agree.

Everyone knows governments around the world have turned into huge bureaucracies riddled with corruption. Many governments are rampant with theft and filled with the misappropriation of taxpayer dollars while squandering the spoils of great revenues from natural resources and business. Brazil, like America, was probably no different.

"Randy, like I have told you before, you need to open your mind. Set loftier goals. Think about how great things could be in the future and not just how comfortable things may be at the moment. Think in terms of absolutes. Think about how great our culture or a countries quality of life can be. Think about how long people could possibly live if they were given the education, the research and the ability to pursue life in their own best interest."

"I am not talking about aging symposiums and think tanks here Randy. I am talking about taking the regulator off of your perspective. Take a longer view of life. Challenge yourself to have an unsullied perspective. How big is big? What shape will your dreams take? How can you shape and live up to your dreams? How can you shape the dreams of others?"

Randy sat silently with an empty fork in his hand. Like a young boy in school, he was impressionable, listening and processing every word conveyed by Garrison. This is the very reason Garrison had always chosen his words carefully when lecturing. Impressionable students and faculty would take his words as fact. Yet, Randy was unsure of where this lecture was going.

Garrison continued, "You see Randy, our oath is to humanity, to mankind. We have seen and participated in great break throughs you and me. We have had the benefit of enjoying many quality of life enhancing innovations over the last hundred years. I am confident there have been great discoveries made which you and I, as well as the public at large, are not aware. Discoveries we may never see. Some have been kept from the public for good reason I am sure."

"Conversely, Randy, I know that I have done some great research and made some great discoveries in my career which would help the masses and yet I have struggled to get them in the hands of the public. The system has failed to be able to provide a practical and *accepted* application for them in today's society. The great social hierarchy and the current political leadership stand guard on new discovery these days. Great discoveries have to be tested, implemented and shared with the public in a timely manner."

"What on earth are you talking about Garrison? I thought we were talking about Rigo here. Where are you leading me?" Randy asked impatiently.

The waiter interrupted. "Are you through with your salads?"

They were finished. The waiter removed the soiled plates from the table. In an instant from behind the waiter, appeared a truly spectacular serving of perfectly prepared beef brisket on a stainless skewer. The brisket was barbequed, hot and juicy, fresh from the broiler.

The service personnel were now lined up three deep at their table. Each server carried a skewer with a different cut of meat; one beef brisket, one lamb roast and one pork shoulder. Each would be carved off the skewer and removed from the blade of the knife with the tongs from the table. The quality and presentation of the product was wonderful.

Trying to be tactically elusive but still answer, Garrison was contemplating his response carefully. This was now becoming a very serious conversation on uncharted ground. To continue on, Garrison knew he would not be able to un-ring the bell. He could not take back his comments once he shared them.

"We discussed the work we have been doing on active cellular immunotherapy's a few weeks ago right?" Garrison asked.

"Yes," Randy replied. "That was the killer T-cell that would seek out prostatic cancer cells through prostatic antigens in prostate cancer patients. The treatment would condition cells to recognize prostatic malignancies. It was a sort of vaccine for prostate cancer. We had to stop the research because we had lost the grants and the pharmaceutical funding."

"Exactly," Garrison snapped. "That is at the root of the point I am trying to make."

"I am still lost here. What does that have to do with this conversation? Rigo doesn't have prostate cancer."

"This is the twenty-first century Randy. There are ways to cure many of life's ailments. Many cures could be available."

"Could be," Randy asked.

"By could be, I specifically mean there are obstacles. Obstacles like the fact that the F.D.A. regulations are so stringent. You have to prove unequivocally that there are favorable outcomes for *everyone* during early testing. Many products don't pass that standard early on. They never have a chance to get to market. In some cases, tested compounds and great regimens make the standard so quickly. They are labeled as quackery and immediately discarded. It simply makes no sense."

Randy was naive. He could not follow Garrison's rambling train of thought at this point in the conversation.

Randy, trying to understand commented, "There would be millions to be made if there was a discovery of a vaccine for any form of cancer. Why would anyone stand in the way of such a great discovery?"

Garrison replied, "There may be more money to be made or saved if a failure to cure the major diseases occurs and a cure isn't made available to the people. It just depends on whose money you are counting."

Garrison patiently began to explain. "Research grants are a commitment to tell the government what you know, how your research is going and, in some cases, when you are getting to close to an outcome or innovation the government does not want discovered. This is one of the ways they maintain control of medicine, mortality and so much more."

"And so much more?" Randy asked in his usual unassuming and naïve way.

"It is the research Randy! The research! The discovery! C'mon man. I am painting by numbers here. Do you remember when the funding ended on that comprehensive cycle cryo-chemotherapy project a couple years ago?" Garrison exclaimed.

"Yes," Randy responded.

"I told you I was contemplating the continuation of the work on the cryo-chem project and how it could be a great discovery for the University?" Garrison continued.

Randy replied, "Sure."

Garrison continued on, "I was told that I would be terminated from the University and black-balled from researching at all major research venues, both public and private, around the country. I would be labeled a quack and a spend thrift by the entire Board of Governors and potentially be prosecuted by the federal government, not to mention barred from medicine. Basically, I could get jail time and never have another F.D.A. trial again for as long as I lived if I continued on with the research."

Randy was following along.

"What I am saying Randy is that I have devoted my life to innovation. I have given in to the wicked ways of high-end research in the past. You need to know the government and the research system are synonymous. It is time that someone steps up and does what is right. That someone might as well be me."

Garrison continued, "So back to your question. I think it was along the lines of "how can you help?"

Randy replied, "I think I get it. You think that Protein Suspension Radio Therapy (P.S.R.T.) is heading in the same direction and to the same fate. You think they are shelving it on purpose?"

"Randy, your innocence can be irritating. Liberating, but irritating. Listen carefully. I will try to make this as simple as I can."

"Let me ask you the same question you asked me a few weeks ago Randy. If not us who? If not now, when?"

Garrison continued to make analogies in an effort to explain, "Randy, listen here. You see, there are funding limits to how long people can live. Funding limits established from the perspective of your government. There is insurance, social insurance in the form of Medicare and Medicare reinsurance. There is Social Security and a national economy to consider. Both the States and the Federal Government have health care budgets. The Federal Government has a defined benefit plan for retirees and citizens all of which start at a certain age and only terminate at the grave."

"Do you think that there is any coincidence in the fact that the average life expectancy in America has not changed in the last several decades?"

Garrison was steam rolling his thoughts, "First of all, we have ensured that babies are surviving longer. This was a political *must have* in the eyes of the people. Particularly when around the world mortality rates for new born babies are higher than they are in the United States. Think back to your education, even in the mid twentieth century, children were dying of diarrhea and mothers died giving birth. Society would no longer accept this. Once this element of survival was improved, they had to look at other reasons to unfavorably affect mortality because this alone would improve the average life expectancy rate in America."

Randy questioned, "Who are *they*?"

As if not even acknowledging the question, Garrison continued to eat and talk.

"Looking back in time, the average age of a person born in 1900 could expect to live to about fifty years of age. Remember, I said average. That same person born in 2008 may live to be an average of eighty years old."

"Okay," Randy confirmed.

"During the middle of the last century, there were great discoveries. I mean great discoveries. People were living longer and healthier lives. Think about polio, smallpox, surgical sanitation, penicillin and antibiotic derivatives, all showing huge gains. The list can be overwhelming in both scope and breadth."

"Life expectancy numbers have risen due to the saving of young lives. The lengthening of old lives has not budged in sixty years. Why do you think that is? Why Randy?"

Randy replied, "Tell me why?"

Garrison gladly continued, "You see, the maximum life expectancy has not moved. The average life expectancy has improved because of the young living longer. You are being duped with averages. Think Randy. Think big picture here!"

Garrison continued, "In the 1960's, there were people who predicted the long term trend of higher life expectancy would start to improve. People were starting to live longer. They saw this trend improvement as very threatening. A possible threat that could, by itself, potentially topple the entire United States economy or even topple our government some day in the future."

Randy listened intently, "Who are *they*?"

Without acknowledgement, Garrison answered Randy in sentence. It was a mouthful, but Randy began to understand, "Your government has a vested interest in regulating how long you will live. The cost of your survival, greater than a pre-determined actuarial estimation of age, from a benefits perspective, cannot be afforded by the people or the tax structure.

"This was particularly true now with a post WWII aging baby boomer coming on line and needing more legacy benefits, coupled with the very low birth rate. These post war generation citizens are all due to receive maximum benefits at a time when less and less people are paying in. You can see this is principally true in an aging country like the United States with a culturally unsustainable birth rate."

"What do you mean a culturally unsustainable birth rate," Randy asked.

"Americans are not having enough children to sustain the culture. They are not having enough children to even out pace immigration. The average American family is having just over one child. The average immigrant family is sprouting over four children."

"I see," Randy replied.

"You see what I am saying Randy? But what do you do? Answer, you create socially acceptable trade off's."

"Trade off's?" Randy inquired.

"Looking back, you cure polio, so you subsidize tobacco. This is an example of a social trade off. Looking forward, there will be new trade offs," Garrison continued.

"Do you think that example was a reasonable trade off in the eyes of the public?" Randy asked.

"You bet it was?" Garrison replied. "Smoking was even glamorized in the movies and in ads. It was cool to smoke."

"Let me give you another example of government meddling and trade offs. Legislate seat belts then approve faster speed limits and faster cars. These are more trade offs which are intended to counteract one another. While doing so, they seem to be giving a net favorable outcome to public opinion."

"Randy, do you see this as manipulation? Is it greed? Or is it just one big coincidence? Now who is the *do-gooder*? Is it me? Is it the Government? You tell me!"

Randy was surprised by Garrison's docudrama, "This is quite an assessment. This is quite a conspiracy theory you have here Garrison. Do you have any facts to support this theory, or is this just a hypothetical wandering you have. It sounds like *magic bullet* material to me."

Again, as if he was totally ignoring Randy's misgivings and query, Garrison continued to speak. He was on a roll. There was so much he had kept to himself over the years. He wanted it flowing like a direct kinetic conduit from his mind to Randy's mind.

"Randy, you still are not seeing the big picture here. This is not about survival and quality of life. This is about control. Think about it. Think of the monumental gains that have been made in statins, heart health and smoke free environments. Great stuff huh?"

"They are," Randy conceded.

"The problem is that you will now have the young living longer and now the old are living longer too. This will result in to many people living off the system in old age," Garrison reaffirmed.

"The government now has decisions to make and they need to start making them in a hurry."

"Decisions like what?" Randy asked.

"Your government has approved these potential improvements to these previously deadly threats. But, can't you see, they have had to replace them with new epidemic threats while simultaneously standing in the way of other life prolonging discoveries to help compensate. They are targeting *life expectancy reducers* and you are buying into it in the spirit of freedom. They have to target life expectancy with a great deal of urgency. They have a real problem on their hands right now."

Randy asked, "What new epidemic threats?"

"It is a twin epidemic of obesity and diabetes to name one. The older people are taking better care of themselves now, so we are reverting back to young people diseases. Over time, this will start a new wave of diabetic problems and cardiovascular disease deaths. The young will not be offered the statins by physicians or they simply will not take the statins because young people think they will live forever.

"Meanwhile, the damage is being done. Day-by-day, silent and deadly over many years, the damage is being done. Years that will make the analysis very difficult until the cumulative effect has taken hold. In turn, over time, these people will not live to a ripe old age due to the cumulative damage they are causing. Your government works in cycles.

"Obesity has exploded in our country and we are watching it happen. This alone is an epidemic. We are the fattest nation on earth. You might take note that the United States has the fattest poor people on the planet. That's ridiculous."

"How about this Randy, the government does not even track or publish information about eating and the American diet. There is no data."

"Really, I didn't know that," Randy said.

Garrison continued, "It's true. Who gave you the food pyramid which leads directly to diabetes and obesity anyway? Eat all the carbohydrates you want, grains and breads at the top. Your government did. And there is not even any tracking of the results. How convenient!"

A perplexed yet attentive look was on Randy's face.

Garrison was still on a passionate, emotional energy high. He had wanted to get this off his chest. He needed to confide in Randy so he persisted by adding, "Randy, how about this one. Remember when there was a 'Presidential Physical Fitness Award' in the sixties and seventies? Of course, you don't. That was before your time."

"I remember," Randy replied.

"We used to reward kids for defined physical achievement that promoted overall exercise and physical activity. Not any more. Why not, I have to ask?"

"Why," Randy asked.

"Why? Because instead, we cancel the physical education classes due to the 'funding' being needed elsewhere and we wonder why the kids get fat. Then we decide we need to regulate schoolyard food rather than encourage the physical activity. All the while the funding is going to big government, big waste and the big retirement benefits of tenured teachers and staff. It is self-perpetuating, big government looking out for itself. That's all it is. It is big government yearning for big control."

"You are one of those faculty benefit recipients," Randy reminded Garrison.

"Funding my ass! Now we give every kid a trophy just for showing up. You don't even have to win."

"Look at this yet another way Randy, you place a frog in cold water and gradually turn up the heat. The frog isn't sure when to get out until he is cooked. Toss the frog into warm water and it knows right away it has to get out. That is what government does. Gradually, without you seeing it, strategically, they turn up the heat. In this circumstance, continuing to find equilibrium with regard to age. I will bet they did not tell you that at your symposium?"

Garrison did not wait for a reply, "Why? I will tell you why, because the research is done in the field by free thinkers, not at symposiums."

"Surely you are not suggesting that people will be able to live forever? Are you looking for a modern day Methuselah?" Randy asked.

Garrison was feeling vindicated in his view and was now in the mood for a two-way conversation.

"There will always be a fundamental challenge in providing services to the oldest members in any community. They are the elderly and being old takes greater care," Garrison explained. "The question is, at what age will you be able to stop paying to comfort and care for the most senior members of our countries citizens. They have left their prime. In some cases they can no longer care for themselves, contribute to private service or fight in our wars. They are a physical and economic liability, plain and simple."

"Human longevity should be more elastic than we give it credit for, but no one has incentive to change the system or the standard. Why, because our health care is no longer about the level of service we receive or the service standards. Mark my words, I saw this one coming. Health care from the government's perspective is all about control. In our lifetime, it will cease to be about the care."

Garrison added, "If the drug companies are dependant on the government to pay for the drugs in the twilight of one's life, and the government decides it cannot afford to pay, who has incentive? As the population ages, the costs of health care will escalate. Imagine Randy, a society of the infirmed elderly, unable to work or contribute to the system they were taking from, siphoning off the resources of an already strapped government."

Randy interrupted, "You are saying the government is attacking the young and the old longevity at the same time. Which is it?"

"Answer me Randy. What would cost more? Caring for a million patients in their nineties, maybe as many as ten million by 2040, with Alzheimer's or some other totally debilitating disease, or letting them die of a myriad of other average and accepted causes in the early eighties. It is a numbers game. Here are the variables in these final ten years. We can add or subtract ten years of Social Security payments, by *allowing* people to live longer. We add or subtract ten years of medical costs. This is a ten-year case that is extrapolated over tens of millions of people. You tell me the obvious answer!"

"Have you ever seen any clinical trials for developing any reputable anti-aging drug Randy? Seriously, do you think that is a coincidence? The government does not want any part of that research. They will generally sell it to the public as quackery. It is the same threat that was made to me if I proceeded a few years ago with cryo-chem intervention. In the event they already have a protocol to slow aging, you can be sure you will never see it."

"Did you know Randy there is not even a protocol set up for the development and clinical testing of anti-aging drugs?"

"Better yet, when the time comes that regenerative cellular medicine outpaces aging, you will see a potential slingshot effect in mortality. It will take a lot of money. It will take government funds, cooperation and approval. Do you think they will give it? Why would they?"

"Remember all of the speculation on the human genome mapping. How we could virtually eliminate hereditary defects. Remember all of the literature on stem cells?"

"Stem cells. Let's talk about stem cells, Randy. Who is preventing that research from moving forward? Who? Now they are "metering" the programs. Some compromise."

Randy answered, "The Government?"

Garrison replied with a snarl, "That's right Randy. The Government.

Our Government!"

Garrison stated again snidely. "They are metering it in the name of religion. Please. You have got to be kidding me. You can go to China and Eastern Europe and be treated with stem cells."

"Instead, and less practically, we address one aging issue at a time. We address dementia, cancer, chronic obstructive pulmonary disease, and other diseases. We address them one at a time. If we were to roll enough of these together, you would have an anti-aging protocol, but no one wants to talk about that."

Randy interjected, "You are saying that the government is controlling age to the low side by controlling the various larger components of mortality."

Garrison replied, "That is what I am saying."

"Can you picture a world Randy where people could be vaccinated against Alzheimer's, cancer and diabetes? I can!"

"You can? I don't see that," Randy said in disbelief.

"Take a look at the leading killers of people. Cure cancer and you gain about five years on to the human life span averages. That would have a huge impact. Cure degenerative heart and vascular disease and you have gained another five years on life span. This is what medical research needs to be focused on Randy. These are the big picture items. These are the same big picture items the government does not want to improve."

"Like I said, this is a number's game. Don't you ever forget it. Humans will never be able to live forever, but imagine if everyone lived to be one hundred years old, on social security, soaking up benefits. What if they lived to be one hundred and twenty? It is the failure to cure their ailments that is so lucrative. Much more money can be made from supressing the cure than can be made from creating a cure."

Randy sat silently as Garrison continued.

"Think of this Randy, can you picture what an average life expectancy of one hundred and twenty would do to the tax structure in the United States. A rising tide lifts all boats, right? In this case, the rising tide may sink all boats."

Randy asked, "Doesn't race and poverty come into play in this?"

"You sound like Craig, but it doesn't change the big picture. Sure it has an impact. If I remember right, the gap between men living in the economically best verses the economically worst counties in America were factored at an eleven- year variance in life expectancy. That was a point being made back at the office. I think you were the one making the point about the connection between Governmental implications and aging."

"What point was that?"

"I think you referred to Nagasaki and Governmental natural selection."

"You're right. I did."

"Look at how the government handled Katrina. That was one of the poorest areas of the country. The aid was slow in coming and inadequate when it came.

That was done on purpose, I suspect. These people were taking more benefits than they were contributing in revenue. I am not saying that was the right thing to do, I am just making my point."

Garrison truly enjoyed good food. He sat for a minute and examined the generous portion of meat along side the leftover salad ingredients on his plate. He continued to be passionate, but his emotional state was beginning to level off. He stared at his food, moving it side to side with his fork.

"Here's another one, think about this Randy, a low calorie diet promotes good health. We know that. That is what we teach these days, right?"

"It is," Randy answered.

"Yet, people are more overweight now than ever. Right?" Garrison explained.

"They are," Randy responded.

"Here in lies one more example of the disconnection between behavior and learning I have been talking about. People fall into the food that is most convenient. We do not enforce or reward what we are teaching. We do not manage behavior to the expected outcome, like the host did here when we arrived. No one wants to see apples in vending machines. We intentionally look the other way."

"How do we get around all of those variables?" Randy asked.

"You can't. You can't because no one wants you to get around them. That is what I have been saying. That is why we need to focus on the processes that treat and processes that cure. It is shameful to focus on cures rather than prevention, but we are being out positioned by the government on the prevention."

Randy was speechless.

"Don't get me wrong, people should not go hungry for the balance of their lives just because a low calorie diet is better for you," Garrison instructed.

"Agreed," Randy said with a full fork and a big smile.

"What if there was a pill to help the arteries with all the excess, cheap, fast food fat. Oh, silly me, we have that pill now. Enter the statins," Garrison confided.

"In summary Randy, young people are taking worse care of themselves now more than ever. Smoking is on the decline, obesity related disease is increasing and older Americans are taking better care of themselves. Trade-off's, all of these are orchestrated trade-off's that will need to be analyzed and counter-acted on a go forward basis by our government. It's a numbers game and the legislative conduct of the Congress proves it.

Randy was listening intently and focused on Garrison. There still remained a look of disbelief on Randy's face.

"Are you still listening?" Garrison asked as he noticed a glazed look on Randy's face.

"Yes, of course, I am," he answered, "I am a bit overwhelmed with your perspective on our Government."

Garrison replied, "Why do you think the F.D.A. is so rigorous in the clinical trials? Do you think it is to protect the people or to protect the government? I think they are just slowing things down so great advancement cannot be put into practice? Or, at least slowing the process down until something is positioned to off set any progress. Government is the largest of all self-serving and self-preserving environments. I can say that without question."

"Randy, do you know that obesity alone will cause a decrease of between three to six years in human life. That puts them back to even verses several years ago. Do you see what I am saying here?" Garrison continued.

"There is no good or evil in what I am telling you Randy. There is just power and control!" Garrison sighed. "It is just power, just control. It is just a numbers game! I know. I have seen it in action first hand."

Garrison reclined in his chair. Sated, yet contemplating another round of the chef's roasted pork.

"Well, Garrison, you have certainly given me plenty to think about. Plenty to consider," Randy said.

Garrison replied angrily, "I have given you nothing to consider."

"You may have some things to think about, but there is no consideration by you to be given here. You did not think we could help."

Randy added, "I assume you are talking about Rigo. If so, that's not true Garrison. I did not know how we can help. I am still not sure how we can help. What you have relayed here is a far flung socio-economic health care conspiracy that, on the surface, sounds paranoid, a little psychopathic and excessive."

"Excessive," Garrison responded. "Excessive," he said again as he looked around the room.

"Excessive is what I have seen here in the last couple of days. Excessive is spending without true purpose as citizens suffer. Suffering when there are alternatives."

Randy replied, "Celebration has its place Garrison. Just because you are not running through the office waving your pom-poms, does not mean that other people cannot have a good time."

Garrison was quiet, and then, you could see in his expression that the flood gates were about to open. His head moved side to side. He was done trying to convince Randy. A moment of clarity had arrived. Direction was coming. Garrison had spoken his piece.

46

Throughout the day, Garrison had considered the many options and even more potential consequences. He was not prone to wild speculation or making careless mistakes. He had a plan sketched out roughly in his mind and he was preparing to share it. He had made himself just mad enough tonight to take action. By regurgitating his observations over the last few years, he would take action this time.

"I have taught you to think about all of the circumstances surrounding your decisions Randy. I have asked that you listen to the data and not to your heart, to be objective. I have asked you to prepare for every eventuality."

Randy waited for the direction he knew was coming.

"You must look as far to the future as your information will take you as long as you did not make your interpretation of the information personal."

"That is all true," Randy agreed.

"We are involved in research. Research is objective. There is no need to make it personal. Think of the glory and the danger alike as you make decisions. Be cautiously courageous and professional in all of your findings and commitments. Does that sound right, Randy," Garrison asked as he prepared to end his counseling and bring closure to dinner.

"Yes," Randy said. "That sounds right. That sounds like you."

Randy thought. Where was the direction? What are we going to do?

Garrison carried on, "This is one time I need to make it personal. I have seen enough. I have caved in enough. This is a time when I will need to make a contemplated tactical mistake on purpose. I am going to act consistently with my principles."

"What do you mean? You hate to make mistakes?" Randy asked.

Garrison repeated, "I mean just what I said. Sometimes you are better served by doing things in a non-traditional way. Sometimes you must be prepared to take the road less traveled and speak the words not spoken. Do the deeds no one else will do. No matter how far off the beaten path your decision takes you, you have to see what is out there, glory and danger alike. This is how true discovery is made. This is how change is made."

"Our nation was created by a legion of dissenters," Randy added.

Randy was listening. Sponging in this new, revitalized, and yet still calm and reserved, introspective perspective from Garrison.

"I know what I need to do. Men like us, well educated and from a nation as powerful as ours have a moral obligation to fulfill," Garrison said as he sighed again.

"Yesterday, standing at the base of the statue of *Christ the Redeemer,* set me on a new course. A course I should have taken years ago," Garrison stated contently as he set down his fork.

The waiter arrived with more roast. They would each have just a little bit more. After all it was so perfectly prepared. While the waiter was there they had ordered some Bananas Foster for dessert. That would be a perfect end to a great meal. Garrison realized the great conversation he had anticipated had turned into personal manifesto and monologue.

47

"What do you plan on doing Garrison?" Randy asked.

"I plan to find out what is clinically ailing Rigo. I will need to work fast. He does not have much time to live I'm afraid. Depending on what the diagnosis is, we will come back here, or bring him to the United States for treatment somehow."

Randy had the thousand-yard stare. He was not sure what to say or how to say it.

Garrison noticed Randy's law abiding and clinical discomfort.

In a reassuring voice, Garrison told Randy that he did not have to be involved in any way. Randy assured Garrison that he would be up for the challenges that lay ahead.

"You can count on me," Randy replied.

Garrison confidently spoke, "We have to be in control of our time now. We have started a clock ticking without being knowledgeable of the situation. That is never a good way to practice medicine."

"Randy, our research and our lives will never be the same after tonight. You know that, right?"

"Rigo will be challenging. What you have told me this evening will also be challenging for me to accept," Randy complied.

"We will need to be careful now. There will be people who will find out what we are doing and they will not know how to react at first, but believe me, they will act," Garrison warned.

"People like who?" Randy questioned.

Once again, Garrison did not bother to acknowledge the question posed by Randy.

"Their ego and their training will compel them to take action. Remember, it is about control and we will appear out of control. There are manipulative people out there. Not necessarily violent people, but bureaucrats whose fascination resides with the control they have over people and events."

"I understand," Randy confirmed.

"There are many unwritten rules that governments employ to insure compliance. I do not know where the limitations on peoples' hunger for power will end. I do not know everything I need to know at this time to help Rigo. I am fortunate to have your help. More importantly, I will need your confidence and confidentiality."

Randy seemed to pause. Randy did not confirm his confidentiality. He had always had confidence in Garrison's wisdom and ability, but he would need to decide where he would need to draw the line if the going got rough. How much could he keep to himself and who was he willing to deceive just to keep up appearances?

The conversation was coming to a close. Garrison was sure he had overwhelmed his colleague and friend. For some reason, Garrison was sensing Randy's discomfort. He needed to close out his thoughts.

"Randy, I am not saying what is right or what is wrong here. I am only saying that this is how it is and this is what I have to do. I have to help Rigo. Tomorrow we will make a plan."

They finished the last of the Bananas Foster as their credit card receipt had been returned to them. They got up from the table and made their way to the door. The same pleasant host thanked them for their visit and wished them an enjoyable remainder of their stay in Brazil.

Garrison responded to the host and laughed, "My dinner was enriching."

The host had a strange look on his face. He thought that was an unusual comment after dinner. Garrison knew what he meant. The comment was for Garrison's own personal satisfaction, his connection to Randy and his commitment to a little boy in Brazil.

Finally, Randy realized, this may be, just maybe, the start of the legacy that Garrison could leave to medicine. He was not sure why helping this one boy would be so important to Garrison. It was an answer Randy would need to find out.

The cab was waiting. They were a bit early, but luckily, so was the cab. As they made their way back to the ship, the two were quietly thinking of what steps to take next. The ship would depart at noon the following day.

Once on board, they were both ready for bed. It was late for them given the limited sleep they had the evening before.

CHAPTER SIX
A YOUNG BOY'S HOPE

48

The travel alarm that Garrison had packed was hammering at exactly 7:00 a.m. the next morning. The loud, intermittent throttling noise sounded more like a distress signal than a wake up call. It was not the very best way to wake up and start your day.

Randy, startled and annoyed by the initial blast, sat on the edge of his tiny twin bed wondering what it was that was so important that they needed to get up early in the morning. This was a travel day, an at sea day, with no plans to be off the ship this morning.

He watched as Garrison made his way silently to the bathroom, closing the door behind him. He listened as the shower started. Hands rubbing his face, what had he forgotten about their plans for today? Surely, there was a plan.

Randy turned on the stateroom television to get a glimpse at the news back in the United States. After some brief channel surfing, eyes rolling back in his head, he was able to find an international news channel.

Garrison soon exited the bathroom in his underwear, still rubbing his wet, thick head of hair. Randy inquired about their plans today by asking, "Are we going somewhere?"

No answer.

"Hungry?"

Still no answer.

"Dirty?"

No answer.

"Did I forget we had plans this morning?" Randy asked one more time.

The response from Garrison was clear, crisp and matter of fact, "Pack up only what you are going to need to take care of yourself for a few days. Medication, your passport, a tooth brush, a change of clothes, make it a small list, you know what I mean. Your cruise is over. We will be spending a few more days in Rio. We have very little time to help Rigo. We will not be coming back to this room."

"What?" Randy exclaimed as he found himself wide awake now, although not sure if he was asking a question with his response or just replying in disbelief.

"We are going to miss the ship's departure time today. It will be our way to spend a few days in Rio without suspicion to gather some facts on Rigo. If we take our luggage, they will think something is up. If we miss the ship, but have our passports and visa stamp, we are here legally," Garrison said hurriedly as he stuffed a few items into his back pack.

Randy replied, "Define 'here legally' for me please. We stated we were here on a pleasure trip. Now we are saying we are here on a business trip. How do you explain that?"

Garrison stopped, "We won't have to explain anything…you're asking too many questions."

Garrison continued his pause and looked back at Randy. "I suppose that is good; your asking questions, I mean," nodding his head slowly as if agreeing with his own direction.

He continued, "I am pretty sure I have thought this out already. We will not have to be explaining anything. As we found at dinner last night, human behavior can be predicted and managed. We will not leave much of a trail, if any, and we will be on our flight back home before anyone really knows or cares that we are missing."

Randy questioned, "And how exactly are we going to do that?"

"Pretty simple really," Garrison said as he continued collecting items, selecting needed items and setting aside unwanted items that were expendable as he stood cramming items into his rapidly filling backpack.

"We will employ predictable human behavior, training, and repeated exposure to a situation, just like we saw at dinner. People miss these ships with some regularity. The ship will notify the local authorities that we did not return in time for the ships departure."

Randy asked, "…And?"

Garrison was determined and focused, "So we will tell them the same thing. When asked, if asked, we will tell them we missed the ship and that we will try to meet up with the ship at the next port or find a hotel here or somewhere. The officials will think that we have ruined our vacation which will most likely be amusing to them. It may even give them some authoritative satisfaction."

Garrison, pausing for a moment to see if he had brought some closure to the question for Randy, "As long as we make our plane at the end of the week, or any plane for that matter, case closed."

Garrison explained, "After all it was Carnival' week! They certainly have more pressing issues here this week, don't you think?"

Garrison was right Randy thought. This was a difficult week in Rio for law enforcement. Opportunists and criminals from all around South America come to Rio this time of year. They know there are big crowds, a lot of tourists with money, a lot of alcohol and a lot of people who are out to have a good time with a low level of awareness and an equally low level of familiarity with their surroundings. Like the man told Garrison on the plane a few months earlier, "hang on to your wife, your children and your jewelry," because they will steal all three in Brazil. They will need to be careful.

Randy also thought, while apprehensive of the plan on exactly how they would actually get out of the country and where exactly they would actually be able to sleep given the fact that every hotel along the entire coast of Brazil was full, it would be challenging but potentially humanitarianly rewarding to be consumed with what they could and should do for Rigo.

The next few days of vacation would most likely not be fun and would definitely not be restful. They may be personally fulfilling, they may be adventurous and they may be dangerous, but they would definitely not be business as usual. Most importantly, as seen by Garrison's abrupt actions, time was of the essence and he would be, once committed, anxious about the little time he had left on Rigo's ticking life clock.

The two scurried about their stateroom gathering up and determining the few essentials they needed for what may amount to a three-day camping trip. Once packed, they were careful to leave daily staple items lying about as if they had intended to return.

49

It was a quarter to eight as they walked across the gangway and past the ships security, each carrying a slightly overfilled backpack. They were reminded that the "all aboard" time was 11:30 a.m.. They responded to the agent that they were just going out for breakfast and to buy a few souvenirs. They would be back shortly. With an unassuming Philippino smile, the security agent logged them off the ship and watched them walk past the stacked debris from the parade and disappear into the port terminal. Little did he know they had no intention of coming back.

Randy asked as they walked, "You remember that conversation last night about 'starting the clock ticking before you were in charge of the situation'?"

Garrison corrected, "Control."

Randy asked, "Control what?"

Garrison explained, "Control of the situation. Not *in charge* of the situation. Interesting Freudian slip though."

"Whatever," Randy said. "You know what I mean."

"What is the plan now? We are definitely not in control of the situation," Randy said, slightly winded from nerves and a marathon walkers pace as they made their way through the terminal.

Garrison stated, "It is quite the opposite Randy. We are in total control right now. I actually feel liberated right now. I sort of feel like I did when I got my driver's license and was able to drive alone, with my own car, at my own pace, for the first time."

Interesting comparison Randy thought. Garrison was always good at these life comparisons to give an every day perspective to complex concepts.

Garrison stopped at the curb at the end of the terminal and took a deep breath. He looked around. He took another deep breath.

"Liberating," Garrison said. "Healing."

"What is the plan?" Randy asked again.

Randy was startled by the tone and volume of Garrison's response as Garrison shouted, "CAB!!" and waved his hand to the oncoming traffic on the street.

"Where are we going?" Randy asked.

A cab, looking brand new, pulled up to the curb in front of them.

As Garrison entered the cab, he pulled the dog eared business card from his front shirt pocket. This was the card he had gotten from Marguerite two days earlier. Garrison sat staring out the window in the back seat of the cab, with the business card in hand. There was a thoughtful recess. He was holding the card in one hand and flicking it gently with his index finger from the other hand.

"Where are we going?" Randy asked again as the cab driver looked back over his shoulder for direction.

"We are going to Ipanema to see DiDi," Garrison replied.

The cab driver, clearly not savvy enough to read his guests like the restaurant host, had asked them in Portuguese where they were going. Not interested in attempting to communicate through Randy in broken Spanish, Garrison handed the business card to the cabbie and pointed to the address on the card in silence. The cab driver turned his body in the seat to get a better look at Randy and Garrison, as if in disbelief as to where they wanted to go. They could not tell what he was thinking. He nodded in the affirmative and said, "Ipanema."

"Si," Garrison replied.

Randy, listening and watching said, "Si. That was impressive. I have never heard you speaking such fluid Spanish before. Now tell me, who the hell is DiDi?"

Garrison said, "I thought you were with me at the statue of *Christ the Redeemer* when we met Marguerite and Rigo?"

Randy answered, "I was, but there was no DiDi there."

Garrison replied, "You need to get better at this than you are right now. DiDi was the friend of Marguerite's that paints women's nails in Ipanema. She is the only connection to them we have right now. To find DiDi is to reconnect with Rigo."

Randy, as if rethinking Garrisons plan for him sat nodding and said, "Okay, okay. That makes sense. Shouldn't we tell them we have missed the ship first?"

Garrison smirked, "Shouldn't we let the ship leave without us first?"

Randy, still nodding, "Sure, that makes even more sense." He was irritated with himself that he could have said something so stupid when he just walked off the ship less than ten minutes ago.

The car ride was brisk through the streets of Rio, back onto the freeway and briefly along the coast. As a whole, the cab ride was, at the very least, unnerving. It was so much faster than the bus.

The driver had the ultimate confidence in his skills. He was no longer a youngster, maybe in his fifties, his jet black hair was slicked back. He had a bit of a Michael Jackson curl to one side. The hair, the "Members Only" jacket straight out of 1983, the black driving gloves and the billowing smoke from the font seat left you feeling like you had turned back the clock twenty-five to thirty years.

The driver traveled side streets very fast and managed to smoke and talk on the phone at the same time seemingly paying little attention to the actual responsibility he had to his fare.

Needless to say, for the entire twenty minute ride, which consisted of several cigarettes, two phone calls and numerous radio station channel changes, the cabbie was not aware of their discomfort. The two men did not say a word to each other the entire trip.

The cab pulled over as they arrived at what appeared to be their destination. The fare converted to exactly forty U.S. dollars. Two twenty dollar bills, what a coincidence. Garrison jumped out of the car and took out the business card, validating with the driver, on the street sign and on the building address that this was the street and street address in Ipanema he was looking for. It was as it appeared to be. This was DiDi's place.

50

They were on a side street a couple blocks off of the beach. The entrance was merely a clear glass door with floor to ceiling glass windows along the roughly twenty-five feet of frontage to the road at the base of an apartment building, or maybe it was a hotel. There was a street address clearly printed on the door along with a cursive script message. *DiDi Para Nails* which loosely translates to *Nails by Didi*.

As fate would have it, they were here and the shop had a sign in the window which read *Obrierto*, open. As luck would also have it, there was another script message on the door, *Si habla English*, they spoke English inside. Excellent!

It was early, but the sun was starting to beat down, the humidity was high and the air was thick. The cab ride, with windows rolled down due to the smoke, afforded very little comfort in the way of air conditioning, not to mention the nervous energy they were burning due to the driving habits of their cabbie. They entered the air conditioned shop and found the cool environment to be very refreshing. A door bell chimed one time as they entered. The bell was a lot more inviting than the wake up alarm bell earlier. Garrison was wiping the sweat from his forehead and stood just inside the door with Randy.

The shop was simple. A couple of beauty shop style chairs, mirrored along one wall, clean and tastefully decorated in mainly red and white. There was a counter on the left that was constructed at a right angle to the front door. This appeared to be where the business transaction end of the service took place. There was not anyone visible in the shop.

Garrison turned to Randy raised both eyebrows and shrugged.

Randy said, "Well, there is a door bell, surely they heard us come in."

"I am not interested in any *they*, all I need to do is spend a few minutes with DiDi, you can stay and get your nails done if you want Randy," Garrison said.

It was at that moment that Randy figured out why the cabbie turned and looked at them when they got in the cab. They were two Americans, leaving for a nail salon at 8:15 a.m. It was probably a strange fare, even for Carnival'.

"Very funny," Randy said. "I think I will wait and have them done by you in our Brazilian prison cell."

Garrison replied, "No one is going to prison this trip."

"This trip, what do you mean, this trip," Randy asked.

Just then a woman entered the room from an open doorway at the back of the shop. The woman was dressed in tight pants and an equally tight fitting shirt. This is typical for Brazil where the majority of all women tend to select clothes that are smaller than their physical frame. In a lot of cases, it looks great. In DiDi's case, it was not as flattering.

DiDi was too big for the clothes she was wearing.. Her hair was flamboyantly teased and put up on top of her head as if put up just to keep it contained for a short period of time. She wore fire engine red glasses that were horizontally thin, but of a heavy, thick frame, construction. There was an excessive amount of wrist bracelets on each arm.

"Buenos dias," the woman greeted.

"Hello," Garrison replied. "Are you DiDi?"

"I am DiDi," the woman replied.

Yes! Randy was thinking inside as he clenched his fist with approval. As he stood next to Garrison looking around the shop waiting for Garrison to tell her who we were and how we would connect with Rigo, he knew they were both relieved to be speaking in English.

Garrison began to explain, "My name is Garrison Keller and this is Randy. I met Marguerite and Rigo a couple days ago and she said that she did not have a phone. She also said that if I wanted to see her, I could do so through you. She said that you would be able to take me to her home."

DiDi's English was very good, her sultry Brazilian accent not withstanding. As she started to arrange and shuffle things on the counter and obviously avoiding eye contact she said, "You do not sound like you are from here?"

Garrison replied, "We are not."

DiDi asked a second question, "Why would you have seen Marguerite and why would you need to see her again?"

There was no time for a response. DiDi was already showing some impatience.

"Do you have something you want me to give to her if I see her again," she asked as if they were distant acquaintances.

"No," Garrison replied as he shook his head calmly, looking at the floor, and trying to depressurize the situation. He could tell that she was very suspicious. "There is nothing I have to give to her. I wanted to speak to her in person and ask her some questions regarding her son."

"You are Americans, yes?" DiDi replied.

"We are people," Garrison answered as he once again pulled the dog eared business card from his shirt pocket. "This is how we knew to come here. We saw Marguerite a couple days ago and she gave us this card. It is important that we see her again."

"Why should I believe you," DiDi asked. "You could be anyone. You could be from the government or the Brazilian Health Care System. You could be anyone."

"We could be, but we are not," Garrison said as he continued to do all the talking. "We want to see if we can get more details regarding Rigo's health and perhaps, just maybe, bring some solace to his life."

"Solace?" DiDi replied.

"Comfort," Randy replied.

DiDi fired back, "I know what it means."

Almost instantly, based on that comment, DiDi took an initial dislike to Randy. He was aggressive. He corrected people. He made direct and sustained eye contact. Unlike Garrison, Randy was not yet a master at gaining peoples confidence early in new relationships.

DiDi looked at the card and said, "I believe you, and I believe that you are not from the Brazilian Health Care System. This is good that you are not. They have not been helpful for Rigo. He is too young to die. He is such a good little boy."

After his prior conversation with Craig in the office weeks earlier, Garrison had taken the liberty of briefly looking into the health care system in Brazil. Craig was right, this was a burdensome system rooted more in process and paperwork than in care. There was reason to be skeptical. Perhaps not distrustful, but skeptical of what results this abhorrently over worked system could possibly provide a destitute young boy.

There are many countries around the world that have socialized health care systems. Great Britain and Canada are the ones that Americans hear about the most. In so many cases, people have a very hard time getting the needed services on the time table that will be the healthiest and the most advantageous to them.

Brazil is one of only a few countries on the planet which can stake claim to a totally free public health care system. With a system that big, especially in cities like Sao Paolo, one of the largest cities in the world, operational and logistical problems exist.

There are long waiting lists to see doctors for specialized appointments, long lines for emergency or general mezzanine maintenance care, cumbersome procedures to access patient historical information due to the sheer number of independent data bases that do not communicate with each other and a shortage of qualified health care practitioners. These are all common in social medicine and all play a part in delaying or furthering an *acceptable losses* mentality for the underprivileged.

To complicate the situation further, it had been a paper-based system for years. A tattered system that did not update captured data looking back. The government still does not have the ability to adequately forecast and train for births, deaths, surgeries and the like. Again, this lack of historical data added to the service gap in the present and for the immediate future. It will take a couple of generations of data to predict probable trends, and then there will be a demand to provide the training for the needed fields, which may take an additional generation.

The legislature in Brazil has enacted various privacy policies that were not in tandem with the need to integrate the point of care systems and; therefore, could not give the patient the most comprehensive care. In short, with every visit to the doctor's office, you started over again. This is a critical care nightmare, to say the very least, for people who are chronically ill.

The government is working on rebuilding their system, but it takes time, and time is one thing that Rigo just does not have.

As DiDi answered Garrison's questions about Marguerite, Randy was listening intently through her accent and hanging on every word of her almost perfect English. Randy found her apparent scholastics and annunciation to be very reassuring.

Both DiDi and Garrison had their best poker faces on. Garrison was getting a number of questions answered, but in conversation, he had already told DiDi too much. He had told her his name and Randy's name, why they were initially in Rio and how they came upon Marguerite and Rigo.

DiDi too, clearly an educated woman, did not want to answer too many questions. However, she has a healthy appetite for asking questions. With good merit, Garrison did not want to get her anymore involved than he needed to and DiDi could sense it.

"I do not know why you feel you can have an impact on Rigo's health, but I believe you are sincere. For this reason I will take you to them," DiDi offered. "It is early still and I do not have appointments until later. I will lock the shop and take you to her. Meet me outside the front door."

DiDi ushered them to the front door. As they exited, she locked the door behind them.

Once outside, Garrison remembered Randy's earlier question and thought that it was time he answer it.

"Randy," he began, "regarding your question on what the plan is, roughly it goes like this. First, find Rigo and his mother. Second, find whatever records exist. Third, understand exactly what his diagnosis is and find out how long he has been sick. Fourth, providing the records are accurate and reasonably current, understand what course of treatment may be beneficial, where it might be able to be provided and set course of treatment accordingly. Fifth, have him in treatment within a week."

Randy replied, "A week, that assumes you can help him here."

Garrison answered as they stood outside in the hot Ipanema sun, "Oh, I can help him, and it will most likely not be here in Brazil. We'll see."

Randy responded, "Good grief, are you sure we are not going to jail?"

51

DiDi pulled around the corner and stopped in front of the two men who were waiting at the curb. She was driving a newer model Nissan that almost perfectly matched her red glasses. The interior was a palomino colored leather. Like her shop, the car was clean, inside and out. Both Randy and Garrison got into the car.

"It is a short drive from here to Rocinha where Marguerite lives," DiDi said. "If you are really trying to help her, we should stop and get something for them from the grocery store before we go. They have very little to eat."

"We can do that," Garrison replied.

"Where did you learn to speak English so well," Randy asked, still fascinated by her command of the language and seduced by her accent.

"THEE Ohio State University," DiDi replied with a chuckle. "I was an exchange student. I missed my family so much, I did not finish and I came back home after three years. It was more important to be with my family."

"And now you are doing nails," Randy asked almost condescendingly as they pulled into the grocery store that was just up the street from the shop.

Garrison and Randy were both in the back seat. Garrison, irritated by the tone Randy was using with their number one contact person. Garrison, put his right hand on Randy's knee and pinched his thumb and middle finger together so hard at the knee that Randy thought the fingers would break through his femur and meet together in doing so. Randy winced, but was silent. He got the message.

DiDi was surprised by his comment, but responded in a rapid fire format as they all were getting out of the car.

"I am happy with what I do. I like my work. I do not spend every waking moment obsessed with my work like Americans do. In Brazil, work is not your life. Your family is your life. You work to provide for your family," she advised.

"Americans tend to love the time they spend at work, hate spending time with their family and are impressed only with war and material things."

"Ouch!" Randy exclaimed, as they walked towards the store. Randy felt like he was just schooled as a second class citizen on this planet because he was an American.

The grocery stores in Brazil are not like what they were accustomed to seeing in the United States. Aside from everything being written in Portuguese, there were many differences. The isles were very tight and the sanitation did not appear to be important. While it was not dirty, it did not appear as clean and well positioned for the consumer.

The entire store had the smell of freshly butchered meat. It was a bit overpowering. In the meat department, the freshness was evident, but so was the scent of a fresh kill. Partially plucked chickens with the heads still on them, fresh fish brought directly from the ocean that day, and meat being butchered right off of the hook.

The group shopped quickly, gathering up a few fresh fruits and vegetables and numerous shelf stable and canned goods. At DiDi's recommendation, they did not buy any meat. There was no refrigeration at Marguerite's flat, so there was no way to keep it from spoiling in the Brazilian heat. Anything perishable would need to be shelf stable and eaten within a couple days.

The bill was a little over fifty dollars US. This was a lot of groceries for a woman and a small boy who was to sick to eat. They bagged up their gifts of food and returned to the car. From there, they would make the fifteen minute ride back into the foothills to Rocinha, the shanty town above Rio within the South Zone.

DiDi revisited the earlier conversation they had before the stop at the store by asking Randy, "Do you know how to tell how 'American' someone is?"

Randy replied, "No. Is this a joke?"

DiDi continued, "It used to be a joke when America was a world leader in almost everything. Now it is a joke to everyone in the world, but the world is too afraid to laugh. It is not a joke any longer. You can tell how American someone is by how pretty their wife is, how fancy their house is and how nice their shoes are. All material things."

Randy responded, "Huh. His wife, his house and his shoes. I am single, I rent and I am wearing flip flops. How am I doing?"

Garrison was humored by the absurd comedy he was watching unfold before him. Randy was such a novice at the interpersonal relations and getting the most out of people. He was a great person and a formidable researcher, but not the best at winning people over.

DiDi responded, "You did not say you were an American. If you are, perhaps you are the one exception to the rule. At any rate, waving her hand as if dismissing his retort, my comment was directed at how Americanized you were regardless of where you were from."

Garrison wanted desperately to change the subject, but was not sure where to jump in. It was good trial and error for Randy. He needed to be challenged by a foreigner in his native tongue on just exactly how Americans are viewed. He needed to be better at influencing others. That is, as long as it did not go on too long or does too much damage.

Smoothly, to change the direction of the conversation and attempt to elevate the level of discussion, Garrison said, "Ohio State is a great University. I am sure they were lucky to have you, as well as other foreign exchange students there to help better understand each others cultures and the cultures around the world."

By this one sentence, Garrison was able to eliminate the banter. It was a compliment, an educated cultural statement and it was as if they had just met and were starting over again from the beginning with DiDi. Dale Carnegie's teachings on how to influence convince and sell others on your ideas or products were well applied here by Garrison, for Randy's benefit and Randy knew it.

The small talk about the scenery and education in the United States passed the brief time in transit quickly. Before they knew it, the car pulled off what appeared to be the main road and entered a narrow, debris laden dirt road.

"Are we getting close?" Randy asked impatiently.

"This winding road will take us up the canyon and to the village of Rocinha. You will not be impressed or feel comforted by the road, the garbage on the sides of the road, or the looks you may get from the people when we get to Marguerite's neighborhood." DiDi replied. "This is a very poor area with mostly pirated electricity, no trash services and very little law and order. Nobody seems to care much up here."

The bright red car was in stark contrast to the dull earth tones of the clay road, rusted out dwellings and weathered timbers. The colorless hues of poverty were undeniable here.

The car had to stop on a side street. DiDi informed them that there would be roughly a two block walk up a steep grade to get to Marguerite and Rigo's home.

As they walked up the narrow street, not even half as wide as a car, they received the looks that DiDi had spoken about. Well-dressed, well-groomed and cleanly clothed people were not usually seen walking around in this neighborhood. The smell of old and new trash filled the air. Garbage appeared to be stacked everywhere.

Most of the dwellings had no window glass, just openings. Most dwellings had doors. The people they saw appeared feeble and in poor condition overall. Residents were lingering, lumbering, coughing and generally milling about. No phone lines, no concrete sidewalks, no proper sanitation for human waste or otherwise. The living conditions were below third world.

"This is it," DiDi said as she extended her arm and opened her palm motioning them into the doorless opening. "We are here."

52

The three of them entered. It was quiet. It was like they were right back at the Redeemer. Marguerite was sitting with her back to the door holding Rigo. The room was dark and smelled musty. The floor of the single room shanty was dirt. There was nothing on the walls. There was a bed and a few small furnishings. There was a table that multi functioned as a kitchen counter, sink and as a dining room table.

"Marguerite?" DiDi inquired. "Marguerite?"

Jerking awake from her nap, Marguerite turned in her small wooden chair, a shrunken Rigo still in her arms. Marguerite, still not fully aware, looked at DiDi, then at Randy and to Garrison, then back to DiDi and back to Garrison. A smile came over her face. Her head tilted to the side, she stood as DiDi took Rigo from her arms.

Marguerite walked slowly to Garrison and gently lifted his arms and smiled angelically. She slipped her arms around his rib cage and gently hugged him, her head to his chest.

"Gracias," Marguerite softly said. "Gracias," she said again. Garrison did not need interpretation for that. He knew what she was saying.

Marguerite mumbled another sentence as she began to cry. DiDi also began to cry. Randy thought it all to be surreal.

"What did she say?" Garrison asked softly. "What did she say?" he asked again.

DiDi and Marguerite were sobbing openly Marguerite mumbled again the same sentence.

Garrison was standing in strange place, embraced by a stranger he had met only two days earlier, in what surely at this moment appeared to be one of the poorest places in the world, and looked back and forth between Randy and DiDi, waiting patiently for a response to his question?

Randy broke the otherwise awkward silent tears, "She said," choking up a bit on trying to get his words out, "from her mouth to God's ears. He has heard my call."

Garrison looked into her eyes and thought in that instance, people really believe in the statue? Is the statue a leap of faith…or is it a real manifestation of God's will.

DiDi turned and laid Rigo on the bed and nodded affirmatively with regard to the translation as she wiped the tears from her face. It appeared that Randy had understood the spirit of her words completely. DiDi stood looking at Rigo. He was so gaunt, so lifeless and so thin.

Garrison was showing little emotion. There was a task to be completed here and he wanted to get on with that task in an objective and judicious manner.

Some might see it as indifference, others as black and white, others, perhaps as sociopathic, but this was Garrison. This was his *let's get to the facts* way of doing things. As he saw it, there was little time to sit around crying. The sobbing would get little accomplished in the short run and every moment was precious at this point.

Garrison was focused and intense as he asked, "DiDi, I need you to be specific and translate a few questions for me. I need to know from Marguerite a few things."

"One, I need to know where I can get Rigo's medical records and what is his specific diagnosis and condition at present."

"Two, I need to know, right now, how long Rigo has been sick."

"Three, I need to know if he has a passport or any citizenship paperwork."

DiDi, slightly panicked and shaking, with eyes swollen from tears explained to Marguerite she would need to ask some questions and get some answers. Marguerite was focused on her words and tried to give good answers. Marguerite, tired and worn out, was not well spoken or well educated.

Trying to patiently ask the questions, while trembling, one question at a time, DiDi relayed the responses coming from Marguerite as Randy watched.

"He has some form of cancer she thinks," DiDi said. "She has some records under the mattress that the doctor had given her a while back when she told the doctor she did not think that he was doing a good job and she threatened to go elsewhere."

DiDi expressed outside of the translation while shaking her head, "Of course, we know she could not do that. The Health System would not allow it. She has no money for private care."

DiDi, still stressed, continued to ask the questions one by one, "Rigo has been sick for a year and a half, but she cannot say for sure, she does not track time very well."

DiDi was looking back and forth between Garrison and Marguerite.

Marguerite listened devotedly to DiDi's questions. They were hand-to-hand, eye-to-eye, and together as if in prayer, alertly paying attention to the questions.

DiDi hurriedly trying to translate as she worked through Garrison's request...stopped in mid-sentence as she relayed the next message. Her jaw dropped open in disbelief. She looked at Garrison. She looked at Randy and back at Marguerite. Shaking her head, she squeaked out the last response, "He has dual citizenship. He is an American." And after a slight pause she added, "and a Brazilian."

Randy, again the silence breaker, "How the hell can he be an American?"

Garrison turned to Randy and put up his hand as if to silently "shush" him as he calmly asked while nodding his head up and down, "He was born in the United States, yes?"

DiDi asked Marguerite if Rigo was born in the United States. The answer came in the form of an affirmative nod.

Randy was leaning forward, as if to be party to an interrogation, looked at Garrison, "How did you know that? How did you know he was born in the United States?" he asked of Garrison.

"You are smarter than this Randy. He is a young boy. There are very few ways to become an American citizen. Being born in a country covers about ninety-nine percent of them," Garrison responded.

Randy felt pretty silly and took a step back.

Marguerite was explaining simultaneously to DiDi that Rigo was born prematurely while on a trip to Texas with her late husband, as she made her way to the bed where the records and birth certificate were kept.

Under the torn and warn out mattress, as she had stated, was a packet of papers. Marguerite brought the papers to Randy who was still in a state of disbelief. He never took his eyes off her as he opened the large manila envelope. In the envelope was a binder clip filled with both typed and hand written medical record papers, the address of the doctor who had been treating Rigo and perhaps most importantly at this particular moment, in like new condition, a United States Passport.

"Un-be-lievable," Randy said in a soft tone.

It seemed that Marguerite, Randy and DiDi were all in amazement as to what the day's events were unfolding before their very eyes. Had you not been here to see it, you would not believe the contiguous chain of coincidences that had come to pass. Yet, here they were.

Conversely, Garrison did not seem to be amazed or surprised. You would have thought this was just another day at the office. He was confident, deliberate and definitely did not appear to be emotionally touched by the latest discovery.

"Let me see the documents," Garrison asked.

Many of the documents appeared to be in Portuguese, or perhaps Spanish. Some were barely legible cursive script. Fortunately, there was an extensive summary typed in English.

Garrison handed all but the typed English pages to Randy and read as he walked to the make shift table.

"I need a few minutes to read this," Garrison said as he gestured them aside as if asking them to excuse him for a moment while at the same time telling the others in the room what he intended to do. "I want to see what this says and know what we are up against here; besides time."

As Garrison began to read, the others except Rigo, stepped out of the shanty for a minute to get a deep breath of fresh air. Rigo laid silently on the bed.

53

After a few minutes, the others were back inside making use of time by preparing a light sandwich, cut fruit and storing away the balance of the groceries they had brought up the hill.

Garrison asked, "Ask her if the doctors knew Rigo was an American?"

Again, the response came in the form of a nod, yes.

"Dumb question," Garrison said under his breath while rubbing his forehead.

Garrison continued to read, thumbing through page after page of staging diagnostics and commentary. The diagnosis was pretty straight forward.

Rigo had initially presented in a chronically ill appearing state with a high fever and uncontrollable sweating. He has experienced a significant loss of weight from his already small frame almost two years earlier. A cervical node biopsy was performed and was found to positively identify nodular sclerosing lymphoma. In addition, a palpable mass was identified in the spleen and inguinal area concluding that a pathologic stage three B lymphoma was ravaging Rigo's body.

The report went on in more detail. Garrison was feverishly scanning for details.

His pulse was one hundred beats per minute and regular. There was shoddy cervical and bilateral auxiliary adenopathy which was not significant. There was mid systolic click with a late systolic murmur. The spleen was felt to be enlarged at roughly two cm below the costal margin. The balance of the physical examination was noncontributory.

Numerous blood tests were performed with varying results. A CT scan of the chest showed extensive anterior mediastinal and sub-carinal lymphadenopathy. A stereo chest x-ray was consistent with the CT findings. The CT scan of the abdomen revealed a spleen that was exceedingly generous in size and with substantial lymphadenopathy. A lymphangiogram was successful by injection on both the left and right side and confirmed enlarged iliac nodes. Bone marrow aspirate examination revealed significant hyperplasia with evidence of disease.

With these initial findings, a decision was made to complete an exploratory laparotomy. Garrison stopped for a moment and looked around the room. Sounds on track so far, he thought. He looked over at Rigo before he returned to his reading.

The diseased spleen was removed via a primary upper midline incision that extended slightly below the umbilicus. Disease was also found in the common duct and hepatic region as well as the splenic hilar region. There were some nodes removed that presented at four times the normal size.

The surgical record further anticipated that, while the patient was an unlikely candidate for radiation therapy only, vitallium clips were placed to mark the sites of the mediastinal and abdominal node removal, the wedge liver biopsies and the head of the bile duct. Hemostasis was satisfactory.

The mid-line fascia and peritoneum were approximated with interrupted vicryl sutures with one hemovac catheter being left in the subcutaneous space and brought through the lower pole of the incision. The skin was closed with a running subcuticular vicryl suture.

Garrison rose from the table and went to Rigo. He gently pulled up his shirt and validated the midline scar that was incredibly non-descript, yet clearly visible. Garrison retuned to the table as the others began to eat.

Garrison completed the brief reading and looked at the others. He had looked through all he was given that was in a familiar language. Garrison asked if there was more.

DiDi relayed that this was everything she had. Garrison shuffled the papers in his hands looking for more documents in English.

"There has to be more," he asked. "Ask Marguerite what came after the surgery," as he continued to shuffle.

"Nothing," DiDi answered without consultation. "There was nothing they could do for him. That is what they told us."

"You're kidding me," Garrison replied softly as he set the papers down, shaking his head and rubbing his eyes.

"He recovered from the surgery and seemed to be better for a few weeks after that, but it has been all down hill from there," DiDi answered.

Randy was looking at Garrison waiting for the next question. "What is the diagnosis Garrison?"

"He has lymphoma," Garrison said, speaking to both Randy and DiDi. "It is very treatable and has a very good success rate, even when caught late like Rigo's condition appeared to have been."

"He probably felt better after his spleen was removed," Garrison commented as he walked back over to Rigo and pulled up his shirt from the waist pointing out the midline incision that ran from the base of his rib cage to just below his belly button.

"His spleen was loaded with disease, but he was by no means going to get better on his own. Surely, he was sick when he was diagnosed at stage three with symptoms. Clearly, he is in stage four now. His bone marrow is likely compromised as is his soft tissue below the diaphragm. He shouldn't even still be alive at this point. Judging how much time he has left is impossible," Garrison cautioned.

Garrison sat on the edge of the bed next to Rigo for only a moment and pulled his shirt back down.

"Okay, we need to keep moving. So far we have found Rigo, found his records, identified how long he has been sick. Based on his diagnosis, I think it is worthwhile treating him with an experimental treatment that we have access to. Now all we have to do is get him home to be treated. We are off to a great start today."

Home, Randy thought. Now we are taking one of our own back home to receive a potentially life saving treatment. It felt cult like, clan like, club like. Like being part of an association that makes you feel a connection to people even if you have no connection to them at all; medical associations, car clubs, you name it.

You side with the people that have things in common with you. Most of the time, there is no real reason for it other than a particular product or a particular cause. This time, it was a young boy's hope. It was a young man, and the relationship, the association connection was his place of birth. He was an American boy.

A great start, Randy continued as he viewed things through his minds eye. Emotionally for him, from the moment he woke up, to their missing the ship, to getting grilled by DiDi, to this, he felt like the last few hours have been playing out over the course of a week. Nonetheless, there was more to be done today and into tomorrow.

With no other comments from others, Garrison continued as he looked at his watch, "It is almost noon. I have some calls to make to see what we can do to move Rigo to Minneapolis. Please ask Marguerite if we can take her son to the United States to try and make him better."

DiDi asked and Marguerite responded with a nod and comment, "You cannot 'try' to make him better. My child is a gift to all mankind from God himself. He must live and you have been chosen as the one who must find a way for him to survive. Look at this boy. He would not still be alive if not for the grace of God," DiDi relayed from Marguerite.

DiDi translated Garrison's reply to Marguerite, "Life itself is a risk. There are no guarantees Marguerite. Each day you live assuming you will be here to enjoy tomorrow, but none of us know that for sure. We hope and pray the decisions we make are good ones. Like the decisions I will make to try and save your son's life. Be assured, the lives of the citizens in all nations, regardless of where they may be or where they are from, everyone's son and daughter is precious to me. I will do my best."

Marguerite replied, "He must live!"

A bit taken aback by the deliberateness of her responses, Garrison asked, "Can we use the phone at your place DiDi?"

As if a stand-in for DiDi, Randy replied, "That will be good, what are you thinking? Who should we call? The airlines and try and get him a ticket?"

DiDi now replying for herself, "Randy, surely you had a professor at some point in your life that stopped you and told you to 'just answer the question' didn't you?"

DiDi was now looking at Garrison, "Yes, you can. I am already late for my appointments at the shop, but this is more important. I am alone today, but the shop is locked. People will have to understand. Family comes first. We can go to my house and you can use the telephone in private."

Randy was employing his selective hearing techniques, "Can we sleep there too? We have no place to sleep tonight."

"Ah, sure," DiDi responded with a look of consternation on her face, "That would be a good time for you to explain to me in more detail, how it is that you are here during Carnival', with no place to sleep, and trying to rescue Rigo."

DiDi was appreciative, but confused on how all of this could have transpired in the last forty-eight hours.

"Okay, let's go," Garrison said. As he walked towards the door, he continued to speak, "Tell Marguerite we will be leaving tomorrow, one way or another. It is my hope that we will have an update and some good news for you late today or tomorrow. He walked over to Rigo and gingerly ran his fingers through his fine hair.

"Hang in there young man," he whispered in the boys ear as he leaned over the bed. "I am afraid to let your mother down."

With that, the three of them were outside again, Marguerite in the doorway. As uneventfully as they had arrived, they were departing. In critically damaged English, Marguerite spoke, "Tomorrow me will see you all?"

"Yes," Garrison replied assuming she was asking a question and not making a statement. Garrison and Marguerite were making eye contact that was almost on a soul to soul level.

"Tomorrow I will see you!" he confirmed.

"Viva La Vida, Marguerite, Vive la Vida," Garrison said to Marguerite as he looked back at her.

They retraced their steps, documents in hand, to the car without making a sound. All three were reflective of what they had just witnessed. They were all prepared to be attentive to what their role in whatever the next step would be.

Their ship was sailing right about now. Garrison had already thought out how he would let the authorities know they missed the ship.

He had not thought out how he would get Rigo out of the country. However, this was seemingly easier now that he was a United States citizen.

Randy was thinking about how he and Garrison were going to get out of the country without going to jail.

DiDi, well, she was wondering who these two strangers were and why she said they could stay at her home tonight? How did they get to this point exactly and what had she gotten herself into.

54

Back in the car, Randy was the first to speak, albeit to himself out loud sensitively, "Celebration of Life. Good choice of words."

Garrison replied, "What?"

Randy responded, "Viva La Vida, celebration of life. A good choice of words."

Garrison continued, "Oh, I guess so," he said dismissively while continuing. "How far is your home from here DiDi?"

"Not far," she replied. "We should be there in less than an hour."

"We have to go by the pier in Rio," Garrison said.

DiDi looked at him in the rear view mirror and asked, "Why?"

"It appears that we have missed our ship," Randy explained.

DiDi smiled and shook her head side to side. "Let's go see if your ship has departed. It will be about forty-five minutes to the pier in traffic and another fifteen minutes or so to my home from there. Get comfortable back there."

The occupants of the car were quiet almost all the way to the pier. Garrison's eyes were closed and his head was back. Randy was looking out the window. Both were continuing their thoughts from the walk back to the car regarding how they would get back home and what would they do when they got there. DiDi concentrating on navigating the mid-day holiday traffic. Traffic moved continuously, but slowly and got progressively worse near the port.

Lifting his head to see why there was stop and go traffic, Garrison opened his eyes as they approached the pier. It was early afternoon, yet the streets were congested with people. Beer drinkers, sight-seers, vagrants and thrill seekers. A cross section from the entire South American society could be seen here in just a few blocks.

"The ship has sailed. Drop us off here," Garrison exclaimed, as DiDi pulled to the side of the road to let them out a block from the actual entrance to the pier. The pier was in sight and Garrison wanted to have a bit of drama in his entrance to add credibility to his ploy. A Rio police officer stood watching them from across the street.

"DiDi," Garrison said, "Wait about thirty minutes and pick us up exactly five blocks from where we are now on this same one way street. Got it?"

"Got it," she replied.

"And try not to answer any questions if you are approached."

"Why are you going all James Bond on us here?" Randy asked.

The two men got out of the car. The police officer was still watching them as DiDi pulled away. He appeared curious as the two men began to walk quickly towards the ship.

There were also two port agents standing at the pier entrance.

After they were sure they had been seen by the officer and the port agents, Garrison said "Run Randy. Run towards the pier." The two men started to run.

As they ran, Garrison quickly explained to Randy that they had to appear hurried to be credible that they had missed the ship. They could not just stroll up leisurely and inquire without raising suspicion. Garrison also informed Randy that he would do all of the talking to the authorities at the port. Randy and Garrison were both in pretty good shape so a run for a few hundred feet, back packs in tow, would not be too challenging.

There were two security agents at the pier. Slightly winded, Garrison put on quite an act as Randy kept looking towards where the ship was previously docked. Garrison acted panicked. How could the ship have departed without them? The hotels would be full and they had no place to stay! What were they going to do? How would they meet up with the ship? It was all part of the rouse. The agents listened, smiled and asked for their passports. Garrison explained how lucky they were to have taken the passports off the ship with them today.

The agent handed the passports back to them. With a smile on his face, the agent apologized for their having missed the ship. He explained that they were on their own to find lodging and meals until they met up with the ship or were able to make the flight home. After all, they were in the country legally and with the proper documentation. The agent further explained that there were rooms available in town, but they would be very expensive.

Garrison, acting disgusted, gave the passport back to Randy and packed his away. He turned to Randy and suggested that they get started on finding a place to stay. Randy thanked the agent as they walked to the curb.

"What next?" Randy asked as they walked.

Garrison replied, "We will stand here at the street for a few minutes looking up and down the street and making a few hand gestures. Then we will disappear into the crowd and go to meet DiDi."

Easy enough Randy thought.

As they stood there, the Police Officer they had seen when they exited the car was now walking towards the pier agents. He would look at the agents and then back at Garrison and Randy. Randy and Garrison both noticed that he appeared determined to speak to the agents.

"Give me a few more hand gestures like you are upset," Garrison said, "and do not panic and do not run."

The officer stopped to speak to the agents at the pier.

"What was the issue with those two?" the officer asked of the agents.

"Two Americans who missed their ship," the one agent responded.

"Hmm," the officer muttered as he looked towards Garrison and Randy standing on the curb engaged in what appeared to be some disagreement.

"Did you check their passports?" the officer asked.

"Yes," the pier agent said with a smile. "I also told them how expensive it would be to find a hotel room tonight in the city."

"Start walking," Garrison said, as he stepped off the curb, crossed the street and into the crowd. Randy was one step behind him.

The officer smiled back at the pier agent, "Very expensive. I hope we do not find those two gringos dead in the morning." As he watched them disappear from sight.

The agents were all laughing it off. The behavior was exactly as Garrison had predicted it would be.

Now out of sight, Garrison and Randy walked briskly to the meeting place they had set with DiDi.

Garrison was confident. Randy, feeling like he had just gotten away with his first criminal lie, had a knot in the pit of his stomach. He just knew the day would come when they would get caught.

Randy vocalized what was on his mind, "It was exactly how you said it would be."

"What do you mean?" Garrison asked.

"I mean they acted exactly as you said they would," Randy replied. "Exactly as you said."

"It was pretty predictable. There is nothing that happened here today that doesn't happen to travelers all the time. Cops just get indifferent to it," Garrison clarified.

"Well, I would say we have had a pretty eventful day so far," Randy replied.

"And we are only getting started," Garrison indifferently responded.

"There's DiDi," he added, as they made their way to her car and got in.

"Everything ok?" she asked.

"Oh, yes," Randy said, "Exactly as planned."

"To your house?" Garrison questioned. "We have some calls to make."

55

During the drive to DiDi's, Garrison explained to Randy that he was going to contact Pam Village at the Village Foundation, a non-profit network group that transports and makes accommodations for terminally ill children. Her foundation was similar to the Wish Foundation.

Garrison explained that he was going to personally sponsor a chartered aircraft from Rio to Minneapolis to transport Rigo. The aircraft will be medically equipped and Pam can cut through all but the heartiest red tape. With parental consent, Garrison paying the bill for the aircraft and Rigo's passport, she should be able to pull this off in a short period of time. Most importantly, Rigo would be in the U.S. legally.

A call to Pam, a few calls between Pam, the State Department and the air charter company with Rigo's passport information, and things were taking shape. Pam needed a confirmation from the Brazilian government allowing the plane to arrive and depart from Rio. She was confident she would have that secured in the next twenty-four hours.

She trusted Garrison and knew he was good for the donation check for forty-two thousand dollars. Pending the confirmation from the Brazilian government, the transport deal would be all set. It would not have been so swift if Rigo had not been born in the United States. Brazil usually stands in the way of these things, but Rigo was a U.S. citizen. As far as the child was concerned, all they needed was consent from the parent.

56

As night fell, the approval from the Government arrived. Pam and her global contacts were incredibly expeditious. It is interesting that governments rarely pay much attention to when people leave. The majority of all the attention is paid when people try to arrive. That premise was very helpful in this case. Rigo was departing. Anticipating a return, DiDi was also in possession of Rigo's Brazillian passport which would accompany him to the United States.

One could also argue that there is nothing that pulls heartstrings tighter than a terminally ill child. The aircraft would be inbound from the States within hours. The pilots would need rest, and they would be headed for Minneapolis by late tomorrow.

The story given to the foundation organizers was that before he took ill, Rigo was a huge *Nickelodeon* fan. They explained that Rigo only had weeks to live. His wish was to see the Nickelodeon Experience at the Mall of America, in Bloomington, Minnesota not far from the University. Sure, the plot was thin. It was all a fabrication for the paperwork, but it appeared to have worked.

It was late, "We are all set," Garrison said as he hung up from the last call of the night and turned to an impatiently waiting DiDi and Randy.

"DiDi, you need to have Marguerite and Rigo at this address at the airport tomorrow at 5:00 p.m.," as he gave her a handwritten paper with the private aircraft terminal listed on it.

"She will need to be prepared to sign a consent form to take Rigo to the United States. You should explain the consent to her on your way to the airport. You will need his U.S. and his Brazilian passports with you. Tell her that the plane will have medical care facilities on board also. I assume you think she will agree."

Garrison was trying to be sure DiDi was prepared.

"DiDi," Garrison continued, "Make sure she understands what is happening before you get to the airport. If they think anything odd is happening, they will not let him leave. She cannot say he is going to the States for treatment."

"Of course, she will agree," Randy interrupted. "She thinks you are one of the three Magi."

DiDi was tired, but did not seem as annoyed as earlier when Randy answered for her. It had been a long day. So much had happened. So much had happened on schedule. They were all tired. The apartment DiDi called home was small.

She agreed with Garrison's direction as she made a few notes.

It was time for everyone to go to bed. Garrison slept on the couch and Randy, he was the youngest, was content in the chair verses being sent out on the street.

57

The next day, they all were awake early. There was a lot of anxious anticipation in the air.

Garrison would need to confirm the inbound craft. He really wanted to be there when they saw Rigo off, but did not think it was wise. This was a tough decision. He wanted to be there when Rigo departed, but needed to be satisfied with just giving DiDi the basics.

Randy was in charge of letting American Airlines know that they missed their ship and that they wanted to go home tonight or tomorrow if at all possible. They wanted to be out of the country before anyone had a chance to put them together with the trip they had arranged for Rigo.

By noon, everything was falling into place. The Gulfstream IV aircraft had arrived from Atlanta and the pilots and medical staff members were resting as required by the F.A.A. The return flight for Rigo was scheduled to depart at 5:00 p.m.

Randy and Garrison were on standby for a 7:00 p.m. flight to Dallas.

DiDi had gone up to see Marguerite and called Garrison from her cell phone. Marguerite would provide consent.

Randy had arranged for two medical research interns to pick up Rigo from Signature Airport by ambulance in Minneapolis and take him to University Hospital's Medical Research Center.

As the afternoon passed, their plans played out in a scripted fashion. Garrison was a planner. Everything proceeded on schedule and as intended.

By 5:00 p.m., the Gulfstream was refueled in Rio. Rigo's flight taxied on the runway at 5:15 p.m. became airborne, with Rigo on it.

58

On the other side of the airfield, the commercial airport was not busy. There were plenty of seats available and the two colleagues cleared the international standby list quickly. Exhausted from their two-day marathon of events, Randy and Garrison walked to their plane having already passed through customs.

Randy asked, "Can you believe the luck we have had here?"

"Luck," Garrison replied, "I thought we worried about having to give me a manicure in jail?"

"I mean, we have such an opportunity to really help someone who appears to be in such a hopeless situation here. The fact that he is a fellow American is a bonus," Randy continued.

"Hope is a virtue most beneficially applied when things appear to be hopeless," Garrison replied and continued, "The fact that Rigo is an American is barely even consequential to what is taking place. We should always be mindful that we are making 'hope' based decisions and not 'fear' based decisions. It is far too easy to take the path of least resistance."

Randy and Garrison settled into their seats on the plane, on their way back to Minneapolis through Dallas.

Garrison looked out the window. Somewhat in disbelief, yet as empowered and liberated as he felt flagging down the cab yesterday, there was comfort in his actions. He had chosen wisely this week. His actions would have a consequence, that was for sure, but he had done the right thing.

He smiled and thought to himself. The custom's officer was right when they arrived in Brazil. He was returning from Brazil enriched. More importantly, he reflected on how proud Sally would be of him.

Randy turned to Garrison, eyes closed and head back in the headrest as the plane lifted off and said, "How do we get our stuff off the ship?"

Garrison replied looking out the oval window at Rio and *Christ the Redeemer* below, "They can keep it…or they can give it to the plumbers."

CHAPTER SEVEN
YOUR GOVERNMENT AT WORK

59

Cuda anxiously traveled directly by cab from the White House back to the United States Strategic Planning Commission offices. The Strategic Planning offices were only a few miles away. He had made arrangements to brief his boss, Alan Hoard, as to how receptive the new President was to his newest policy direction. Alan was equally anxious to hear how the new administration was going to behave. The Commission would need to immediately start making moves. They would also need to know if the President was on board with them or if they would be moving on with their agenda without him.

Alan Hoard is a complex and well-educated man. He is the Director of the United States Strategic Planning Commission. He too, like Cuda, had a role that was a bit self-perpetuating given the amount of pressure his tenure in position and experience on the job could bring to bear on virtually every aspect of American life and the United States Government.

In short, Hoard's role was to insure the long term financial viability of the United States Government. He had every possible resource available to him to help oversee the various pecuniary areas of the budget. Given the behavior of the Congress, this was a daunting task since September 11, 2001.

Hoard started as a young Special Agent and Liaison to the President when he was hand chosen to lead the creation and management of United States Strategic Planning Commission by President Dwight D. Eisenhower in 1958. He has been in the Commission's leadership role ever since. No one knows more about the Commission's role than Hoard.

He was in charge of numerous men, men just like Cuda, that worked for him on various strategic programs within the government. Cuda was the best and brightest that Hoard had to offer. From the best, the most was expected. Cuda was placed on domestic health care.

Like most men, power was a very seductive partner for Hoard. Hoard had the power and he knew it. His willingness to apply it was deliberate and measured. For most men, government control could suck the very life and integrity out of even the most educated, motivated and patriotic man, but not Hoard. He fed on it.

Cuda, on the other hand, had vast, but limited power and he clearly yearned for more. A lot more!

60

A Yale educated economist by training, Alan Hoard was getting on in years. He was very committed and consistent in his position, having spent just over fifty years in the same job. Some would argue that Hoard knew absolutely everyone within the beltway and everyone he knew owed him something.

Sure, there were also many who did not know him. The few that knew him personally and knew what his role was, a role largely hidden from the view of the public and press, thought he had as much power in Washington as the President himself.

Quid pro quo. Hoard was an expert at trading this for that. He was a master manipulator *magna cum laude*. He could influence all policies, assess cause and effect, and relate them back to the strategic long term financial plan of the nation. Power and influence were his greatest strengths.

Hoard, like Edward Cuda, had an interesting perspective on things. A perspective that shared many thoughts in common with Cuda on the pressing issues of the day. He was non-denominational and did not have a political party affiliation. He was very rigid in his thinking. Coming out of college in 1958 and moving directly into the Planning Commission role as a friend of the Eisenhower family, he has not spent any of his adult life working on any other issues other than Government and navigating the bureaucracy.

While he lived through the 1960's in his post college years, he was already a member of the *establishment* back then and; therefore, did not have the free-love spirit. He wanted control, as was the case of the government he represented.

His current thoughts, and the compelling thoughts of the Commission he directed, were that health care and legacy benefits were priority one, priority two and priority three for the nation today and for the foreseeable future. The full force and effect of his span of control would be focused on reforms that would put the system back in balance.

His primary objectives were very straight forward. The day of the country doctor and how they practiced medicine as a science and how that science was directed solely in the interest of the patient had long since passed.

Medicine today was a business, government business, and don't you forget it. He had taught Cuda to see life as a series of trade off's, a set of averages and a collection of decisions one based on another, non-chaotic, all having a calculatedly cumulative financial impact to the government. Financial impacts, with publically funded legacy benefit programs, could not be sustained.

His interpretation of the data was completely dispassionate. It was data. The patients in the system were only figures that were summed up into manageable statistics. He did not care if the people were eating their own dog food and taking right from the mouth of the family pet. He had a job to do.

Alan Hoard's legacy would be to train Ed Cuda on the in's and out's of the job. At some point, he would need a successor. Cuda was much younger, ambitious and indifferent. Cuda was a talented study and a formidable opponent who possessed negotiating and interpersonal skills of influence that were almost second to none Hoard had seen. He was a great candidate.

The over-riding strategy Hoard had employed over the years was to slow down the cures for degenerative and terminal diseases. By doing so, you could maintain a stable life expectancy, a predictable life expectancy that could be planned and accounted for. After all, medicine is almost one sixth of the G.D.P. in this country and growing.

Even moderate swings up or moderate swings down would cost or produce hundreds of millions, perhaps hundreds of billions of dollars of flex. We are at a time in our nation's history where the flex has to be favorable and it was his responsibility, in these challenging times, to help get the country there.

He attacked the strategy one disease at a time. Monitoring and adjusting, influencing the F.D.A. along the way. He would start, stop, approve, cancel and influence the progression of treatments that might cure cancer, end Alzheimer's, drastically reduce coronary artery disease, and other diseases.

Carefully anticipating what the public would accept and tolerate as progress along the way while adding information or disinformation as he went. To Hoard, these were all calculations of probability and outcome. *Quid pro quo*, from aging to obesity, he was in the loop in terms of the causes, as well as the cause and effect of any improvement or back sliding.

Hoard was often reminded of his cold war days when a Soviet leader had said to the world, that "capitalism would collapse of its own volition". Hoard was determined to see that this country did not collapse financially on his watch. He would not allow the country to fall into bankruptcy or worse; anarchy, rebellion or revolution.

Aging was of particular interest to Hoard, even now in his sunset years, he understood aging had to be controlled in all classes. Aging to Hoard was the sum of all diseases. Cure cancer, which accounts for twelve percent of all people that die in this country, you add three to five years to a human life span. Cure heart disease, which accounts for twenty-nine percent of all people who die in America and you add three to five more years.

Like scientists, these were high impact targets that Hoard watched faithfully, year in and year out, in terms of research and statistics. They varied slightly depending on who was doing the research, but they were very stable numbers.

The calculations regarding age and life expectancy are complicated. The outcomes, within reasonable margins for error, were predictable. The mighty weight of the Commission in play, over extended periods of time, he could slowly move the numbers as he felt appropriate.

As an example, was it a great mystery or a great mastery as to why the women, who live longer statistically, have had a progressively higher rate of cardiovascular disease since 1984.

Hoard could tell you he had to get the life cycle for women down. Women were living longer, independently and needing more assistance, due to the spouse passing earlier. They needed more specialized care as a result. It was very costly and he has been working on it for over twenty years.

In addition, thanks to the carefully engineered obesity revolution in America, obesity alone will net a negative three-to-five years in life expectancy. The result, if it actualizes over time, will be outstanding in Hoard's mind. To Hoard, the more people who choose not to take the time to manage their costly insulin treatments the better.

Hoard's feeling overall is that you cannot impact drowning, suicide, murders and accidental injuries, like fatally swallowing a chicken bone or falling off the roof, appreciably enough to have a statistically significant impact on the numbers.

Hoard often referred to a group of citizens that, through the latch-key generation of raising children, did not have a great ability to self-manage their own behavior. Hoard was of the mind that this generation would be very needy and their medical benefits would intensive in their later years. If we lost a number of them now, so be it. They would take more than they contributed over their lifetime. Hoard needed some *net gainers*.

Instead, manage the patients who are taking away from the system and who are adding costly treatment for long-term incurable disease. Manage out the ones that take more from the system than they give. That was the objective.

So, you can see, the objective was to manage and address the major cost impact issues on as broad a scale as you can. Manage epidemics like cancer, diabetes and obesity for example, and you can manage the life expectancy number up or down based on social acceptance and cost balance. That being said, any actions have to be socially acceptable and that is where the expertly maneuvered trade off skills of Alan Hoard came into play so perfectly.

The goal, happy, healthy and productive lives that terminate after a reasonable, but short stay on the countries legacy benefit program.

A great example of Hoard's work was the aggressive smoking cessation plans in the early 2000's. They were so well received. There was the elimination of smoking in bars and restaurants for example. It was what the people wanted.

Meanwhile, a half a world away, Hoard had arranged for our service men in Iraq to receive all the cigarettes and chewing tobacco they could handle. Every man and every woman could have all they could consume. Combine that with the stress of combat and we have an eighty-seven percent nicotine addition rate among returning service persons.

These are the trade-off's of social acceptance, cause and effect. The net end result was truly a passion for Alan Hoard and he had been honing his work for decades.

61

Coincidentally, Alan Hoard and Ed Cuda had arrived at the United States Strategic Planning Commission office at the same time. Both men were anxious to speak. There was much to be done.

"Alan, how are you today?" Cuda said as they merged together and walked up the large columned Romanesque stairs.

"I am fine," Hoard replied with a smile. "It is you who I was wondering about. I see you are not in jail as a result of your consultation with the President today. I suspect that is a good sign, yes?"

"All had gone pretty much as we had planned and predicted it would. There will be challenges for the President in the months ahead, but he now has a much better grasp on the implications of his actions and understands what needs to be done.

At the top of the stairs were the large bronze doors at the entry. They were very heavy and Cuda did the honors. He was compulsive about impressing the old man. In totality, he needed to be a relentless man of action. He needed to be a ruthlessly indifferent business partner and he had to be as silky smooth as James Bond when he was in the public eye.

The two passed through security quickly. Hoard was very well known and everyone was well aware that Cuda was the *heir apparent*. There was a pronounced opulence outside as it was around the various other feature attractions in the city. The inside of the office building was in stark contrast to the other government buildings in town. Hoard, ultra conservative, insisted that it was not a good use of the money to decorate lavishly with marble and stone when they were entrusted with the hard earned monies collected from the taxpayers.

There was little appropriation specifically for Hoard over and above a standard inflationary percentage buried in the general fund. His departments were very high return investments indeed.

Except for the most influential, many members of Congress had no idea who he was or what his department did. The influential members that did know him did not relish a visit from Hoard personally. When Hoard came to see you, he was expecting something big from you and all you usually got in return was some embarrassing moment removed from the public record or the promise of some future, yet to be determined compromise.

Hoard and Cuda walked into Hoard's office which was nicely adorned with pictures of the family he adored. The pictures spanned the decades. There was a neatly arranged line of pictures set out in chronological order for conspicuous viewing. A particularly impressive collection of photos taken over the years included Hoard with every President since Dwight D. Eisenhower through

George W. Bush. Each signed by the respective President with the same insightful phrase, "Thanks for all you have done." It was an odd sight.

"Tell me Cuda, what were the big take a ways from your meeting with the President today?" Hoard asked as he settled into his conservative Government issued office chair. Cuda too sat back and began to explain.

Trying to impress the boss and being very professional in his response Cuda said, "The President now has the understanding that this nation needs to manage life expectancy through a series of calculated and publically accepted trade offs. Trade offs which will prolong some productive lives and conversely eliminate numerous unproductive lives. He further understands that this course of management will take place within the framework of his health care initiatives."

"Does he now understand that all men are not created equal once they start being a burden on the system?" Hoard asked.

"I believe he does sir," Cuda answered.

"That's great news. That was a critical step. He has to understand that there are acceptable loses," Hoard continued smiling in approval.

Cuda continued to inform his boss of the day's events, "I explained to him that there are too many versions of the health care package he has floating out there now. Quite frankly, they do not all help resolve the issues we are facing. I have given him a number of objectives that I thought would be needed. Some beneficial and some, well, needed.

"I also explained the need to stay long winded in the bill so that we can have access to broad interpretation and too lose some skeptics in the sheer mass of it. I also said we needed to start working with party leadership to get on task and to be particular with exclusions. He understands that his initial objectives for legislation have definitely changed."

"This may not be a once and done pass at him Cuda," Hoard counseled.

"I know," Cuda replied, "but I needed to get things started before we are playing defense and a bill is up for vote. We have to ask for everything we can right now, given the dominant numbers they have in Congress."

"The legislation will not have to cover every complication Cuda, you know that right," Hoard said.

"I understand sir. I will stay focused on high value, high octane targets that will get the weak out of the system and get more of the younger and the stronger, paying in," Cuda clarified.

Cuda took several minutes to review with Alan the numerous legislative objectives that he covered with the President. In short and without all the details, Cuda reviewed the following as his takeaways.

* Demand a single payer system.

* The patient as a person needs to go away. Patients are numbers. They will need to be treated in accordance with their age and their sustainability of the treatment.

* Everyone must be on the government plan. No patient-centric plans.
* The costs will all be borne by the Government. We will take the patient out of the equation and therefore we will decide what care is best and most economical for the system.
* Government assisted euthanasia will need to be included.
* When we consider any treatments, people need to be allowed to expire from the disease, not the treatment at the single payer's discretion.
* The Government will need to set the pricing for all plans and it will be mandatory and compulsory to participate. You will be mandated by law to carry a health plan.
* There will need to be electronic recording of all medical records. E-record trends. We can then know what will be an issue in terms of life expectancy in the future.
* Terminate the stem cell research he recently approved.

"Those were the major issues I relayed to him," Cuda concluded.

"Can the one hundred and ten thousand pages of Medicare rules be dispensed within this Presidency as part of this legislation?" Hoard asked.

"Hard to say," Cuda replied, "We have to see the overall shape this takes. I will add it to the follow up notes for the President."

"That all does sound very good indeed. A good start," Alan suggested again nodding in approval and getting up to pat Cuda on the back before making a full trip around his desk and slipping back into his chair.

"Are you sure he understands that a single payer system will wield great buying leverage for the federal government and will create an environment that will allow us to accept and deny coverage or treatment better than we had ever imagined doing with Medicare which, as you know, cannot cherry pick patients like private plans can?" Hoard asked.

"I am sure he understands and I am sure he does not necessarily like it," Cuda replied.

"That's okay, he just needs to understand. You need to be sure he understands. This legislation and reform has to be favorable. We can no longer sustain the soaring medical costs in this country with little or no cost to the aging patient, huge cost to the government, and without patient responsibility or liability," Hoard reminded again.

"He understands," Cuda repeated.

Alan continued, "Government needs to be the one to decide if it is gainful for you to be kept alive when you are asking the government to pay for it. That's reasonable, right Mr. Cuda? It sounds reasonable to me. Since when is it a good idea to decide how you want to spend someone else's money?"

"I absolutely agree," Cuda responded in total agreement.

"Tell me about the euthanasia legislation discussion," Hoard asked.

"Like I said, I touched on it," Cuda replied.

"In this congress it should be a slam dunk. We have to get that passed. Add it to your list of needs to have. People need to be able to decide for themselves when they are a burden to others before we have to do it for them. That only makes sense Cuda, don't you think?"

"Absolutely sir!" Cuda replied again enthusiastically agreeing and wanting to be sure the boss knows he is a committed business partner.

"Okay," Alan concluded. "We need to move on to other matters. There are a few upcoming issues that I want to take a minute to update you on," Alan said as he handed a pen and paper to Cuda. "I know you thought you were coming here to brief me, but I have a small piece of other business to discuss."

"Of course," the upwardly mobile and outwardly ambitious Cuda replied now armed with pen and paper.

Alan started his list.

"There is a study taking place at the Sintar labs in Hanford that is rooted in the supercharging of mitochondrial D.N.A.. The science, as I understand it, is that they now understand what is making these cellular power houses fail over time. The failure advances the aging process. The lack of failure will increase life expectancy.

Needless to say, now that the research is showing a lot of promise we will need to be shutting it down. Overall, they do not feel they would be adding centuries to human life, but just one decade or even several years will be financially devastating to the cost matrix at this point. We need the funding eliminated. You decide why, but make it happen right away.

"I understand," Cuda replied as he wrote.

"That being said," Hoard continued, "I understand that damaged mitochondria can lead to a wide array of diseases and conditions. If that is the case, look into what they are talking about specifically and see if there may be options here to do something genetically to perhaps amp up the damages without long term care implications."

"Yes, Sir. I will look into potential cellular delivery of that option as well while I am at it," Cuda replied.

"Let's worry about delivery if you come up with something that is promising," Hoard reported.

"Yes, Sir," Cuda confirmed.

"Cuda, you understand that I do not mind extending life years if a person feels youthful, I mean, as long as they do not live any longer overall. You understand that is the objective, right? It is not our fault that we have been handed an unsustainable life-time benefit program for people who are on social security and medicare."

"I understand," Cuda nodded. "I understand we cannot afford to continue to support, by extraordinary means, aging related diseases and we cannot afford to socially pay the masses social security and medicare indefinitely when they are no longer healthy and productive citizens. If that is what you are asking, I understand 'it is a double whammy'."

"Good, it is important you understand," Hoard replied. "Seventy can be the new fifty as long as you do not go past seventy-seven point eight."

Both men smiled in agreement and moved on, picking up where they left off.

"I know a bit about D.N.A. damage and repair from a previous test we eliminated. I think it revolved around sirtuins and sirtuin enzymes, which are D.N.A. activators. I will look into it." Cuda replied.

"While you are there, check on what is happening with Reservatrol upgrade. It is said to be ten times more powerful and may be on the market in five years. Take a look and see. Let me know," Hoard added.

"Are you worried about the free radical experimentation?" Cuda asked.

"No. Not really. There are too many random factors for me here. Exercise, diet, calorie restriction, things we cannot control and things people and physicians do not take the time to care about. Remember, there is no profit in doing something *for* someone. Stick to the chemicals they are creating that override genetic mutation and cellular degeneration," Hoard answered.

Hoard continued, "On the life time-line assessment you have been working on, we need people to continue to think that we have all but reached a maximum human life span plus or minus a one-to-two percent margin for error. Your goal needs to be to continue to work towards that end. Continuing to make small incremental changes over time is best, but we have to hit hard at the legislative priority initiatives now while at the same time managing the research. We need to manage them together, at the same time. It is critical."

"Yes, Sir," Cuda replied.

"Next," Hoard continued, "The progress we have made in obesity is very encouraging for older adults. It appears that one in seven cancer deaths can now be related to obesity. Fat makes your cells insulin resistant, which results in more insulin being dumped into the blood stream, insulin motivates in a non-discriminatory fashion and promotes healthy and non-healthy cell division while at the same time inhibiting cancer fighting hormone production leading to uncontrolled cellular growth and tumors. This can be very promising if we can manage the long term aspect of the care and see that people in the later years die of the disease and not the extensive treatment."

Cuda added, "The childhood diabetes is starting to get some social push back."

"That's okay. It should be expected," Hoard noted. "As long as we can divide this along racial lines and continue to limit middle age life span among the middle to lower class Americans, we should still be ahead. We would have to put the numbers to it."

"Are you concerned about the kids, Alan? The reaction I mean, you know," Cuda asked.

Hoard, sat back defiantly and stood firm on his position, "I will be concerned about the kids when the parents care about the every day behavior of the children they are supposed to be raising."

"Got it," Cuda agreed without further questioning.

"Where are we at with the animal lovers funding these days?" Hoard asked.

"Animal lovers funding?" Cuda replied in a surprised tone.

"Yes, the animal lovers funding!" Hoard asked again.

"Not sure what you are asking about," Cuda shrugged. "If we are involved, it is not from my department."

"We are involved, I will take it up with Ethical Services," Hoard responded understanding that Cuda had plenty on his plate already.

"May I ask how it applies?" Cuda continued.

"Sure. When we need some added pressure on slowing down research, we put a little more gas in the animal lover's tank last year. The public seems to love to help slow down research that will save their lives to save little ole' Bowser's life instead," Hoard clarified.

"Hilarious! I understand," Cuda the student absorbed.

"Lastly, take a look at human vaccines in clinical trial. We really cannot afford to have any more than the twenty-five Class 1A major vaccines that are available world wide in production," Alan requested.

"Okay," Cuda affirmed. "No surprise that there have not been any significant human vaccine approvals in America for many, many years."

"No surprise. That should be all for today. I hope you are feeling challenged Cuda. These are times of great progress and even greater opportunity," Hoard concluded.

"I am definitely challenged and appreciative of all you have confided in me Alan. If I can be excused, I have to travel to Minneapolis. A contact I have there has provided some information for me. I understand that we have some people that may be using an experimental treatment that has been strictly prohibited."

Hoard replied, "I am aware of this. Do you know Dr. Garrison Keller?"

Cuda was surprised that Hoard was already aware of the Keller circumstance.

"I do not know him. How did you know that is who I was going to see?" Cuda replied.

"I am Alan Hoard," Hoard replied. "Remember who is working for whom here."

Hoard carried on intending to educate, "Listen carefully. Psychologists have been well versed for decades in the behavioral trend of people to substantially over estimate the odds of rare events, rare circumstances, and moreover, rare people. Dr. Garrison Keller is one of those rare people. You would be wise not to over estimate your hand or underestimate Dr. Keller. Be watchful of him. He is resourceful. He is ambitions and he is a formidable opponent. He is a crafty one."

"Yes, sir," Cuda responded as he got up from the chair and started towards the office door. "I will be careful."

CHAPTER EIGHT
THE TREATMENT OF
RIGOBERTO AYALA

62

Garrison and Randy traveled from Brazil safely and arrived in Minneapolis without delay. They intended to go directly from the airport to the University Hospital to see if Rigo had arrived before them and to assess his condition.

Rigo was to be admitted to the Medical Research Center according to Garrison's advance instructions. Garrison was anxious to see that Rigo had made the trip safely. If Rigo had arrived, Garrison and Randy were equally anxious to check on the lab work Garrison had ordered over the phone before leaving Brazil.

The two men were drained. It had been a couple of mentally taxing days. It had been emotional for them both in their own separate way. Rest continued to be a commodity that was in very short supply due to their one stop return flight home and a thankfully short layover.

There was not much conversation taking place, personal or professional, between the two men. Garrison and Randy were both contemplating their next steps even before the plane landed.

Throughout his life and career, Garrison had been looked up to as a confident and thoughtful man. He had always been equally respectful of the research and educational systems. The structured systems in America had consistently served him and the community at large in a fashion that he represented proudly.

Today, Garrison found himself lacking in the character traits that made him great over the years. He was apprehensive, nervous and worried. He was questioning the educational research practices and the American government's involvement in the system. He was questioning the systems mono and introspective focus. He was questioning the motivation of the system to serve itself in a strictly self-serving manner.

Was Garrison uneasy and hesitant because he knew that the course he was about to take was immoral or illegal? Could it be just the opposite? Was his uncharacteristically troubled and tense state of mind due to the fact that he knew what he was doing with Rigo was the right course regardless of how grave the consequences might be to his research, to all research, and possibly to him personally and professionally?

Could the death of Sally, the excesses of Brazil, the *enrichment* a young custom's agent referred to, the experience at the statue of *Christ the Redeemer*, dinner with Randy and the poverty in Rocinha all be converging into a single point of purpose and determination, potential defiance, for Garrison? Was there a calling, a collectively snowballing effect that was changing the configuration of Garrison's judgmental matrix?

Consequences be damned, he was committed. He was going to help Rigo.

63

Garrison and Randy efficiently traversed the familiar concourses and found their way from the terminal to the car they had parked in the airport's long term lot only days earlier when they were departing on the vacation of a lifetime. The subsequent ride from the Minneapolis/St. Paul airport to the Medical Research Center was only a few miles and would be brief.

Tired and edgy, they made their way expeditiously to the room to which Rigo was assigned. Rigo had arrived.

There was a nurse leaning over Rigo. She was taking his blood pressure. She looked up at Garrison and Randy as they entered the room. No eye contact was made by the nurse.

Garrison was familiar with this particular nurse. They had worked together passively for years. The nurse looked up at Garrison and she placed her stethoscope over her shoulder and around her neck. The two continued to look at each other as Garrison walked to Rigo's bedside. Garrison was seeking some comment, some motivation that was positive. Some sort of affirmation, anything. There was a faint left to right movement of the nurse's head.

As Garrison knows, good friends or professional acquaintances, the non-verbal expressions never lie. The critical care nurse assigned to Rigo had seen a lot of tough cases over the years. She was not very hopeful when it came to assessing Rigo's condition.

While Rigo had made the medical transport journey via Lear Jet without significant incident, little Rigo was clearly in a desperate condition. Rigo was weak. His pulse was faintly palpable, his breathing shallow and laborious. Intravenous and gastric tubes were attempting to get him rehydrated and stabilized as well as getting some limited, but needed, nourishment on board. He would need foundational metabolic strength to get him through the days ahead.

His general exam left only a few basic medical terms unmentioned, he was a very atypical young boy.

He had a fever of 102.2 degrees. He was sweating constantly and he was physically atrophic. Rigo's facial features were drawn and darkened. The dehydration and illness had forced his facial tissue features inward to appear bony and skeletal. His initial chemistry panel came back showing a patient that was drastically hemoglobin anemic.

His white blood count was so high that the lab staff retested the plasma specimen in an effort to confirm the accuracy of the initial test. Rigo's body was in a losing battle as it attempted to stave off his disease by flooding his system with white blood cells. It was a battle he just could not win on his own.

Rigo had never smiled, made a facial expression or even acknowledged Garrison's presence. He had dry, crusted lips, a careworn face with emotionless, hallow and sullen eyes. Rigo's eyes were as blank and glazed as a pair of ping pong balls. He looked deathly.

64

There is a term sparsely found in most medical books. A term usually reserved for specific types of strokes that occur low at the base of the brain near the spinal cord. The term for this condition is called "locked in". This individual presents in a condition whereby the patient is fully aware of their surroundings yet cannot speak or make expression. Sometimes they are unable to move a muscle. You are literally trapped in your own body.

Having this condition would be like standing in isolation on a flickering and dimly lit substation platform waiting for the non-stop train to hell, while knowing that you have to be on board the train. As you continue to wait, the train never comes. A never ending solitude while in the company of others with no apparent end in sight.

In this case, Rigo's nervous system was intact. His anemia, mal-nourishment, fever and general condition put him in a "locked in" state. Even as a young boy, you can only imagine the horror of his condition.

65

Randy had walked over to Garrison and was now at Garrison's side, next to the bed. They made a great team. Garrison was a man of action.

"I understand," Garrison affirmed as he looked at the nurse and now nodding his head slightly in an up and down manner.

"We will make him better," Garrison reassured the nurse in an understanding way.

"We need to get started Randy," Garrison counseled.

"Yes, Sir," as Randy took the chart from the end of the bed and prepared to dictate Garrison's medical orders.

"Randy," Garrison instructed, "We will be following an unconventional course of treatment that will need to be strictly followed."

'Yes, Sir," Randy replied. The atmosphere was professional and alert.

Garrison turned to the nurse and politely asked that she leave the room. Garrison followed her as she departed the small private room and closed the door behind her. Returning to the bed, Garrison unplugged and disabled the patient-to-nurse's station two-way intercoms.

"Listen carefully, Randy," Garrison said in a serious but calming tone. "I would like you to take two sets of notes here. Each set is critically important. One set of notes can go on the chart you have in your hand and be accessible to anyone who has responsibility for Rigo's care. This will be the medical chart of record that will contain only the legal and approved regimens. Do you understand Randy? You are to record only approved medical regimens in this chart."

"Yes, Garrison, I understand," he replied.

Garrison continued, "In tandem with this chart." Pointing to the chart in Randy's hand, "we will need a separate chart that will be the documentation and overlay for a second set of instructions that will be carried out by you and will clinically supersede the chart of record. The supplemental chart will contain a separate course of action that will consist of treatments that are not F.D.A. approved or are generally not accepted medical practices by way of the American Medical Association."

Randy asked, "Are you going to put to use any of the treatment protocols that have been canceled in the medical trials we have recently terminated?"

Garrison corrected Randy by stating, "Are *we* going to use any of the treatment protocols in the medical trials we have recently terminated? Is that what you meant to say? Are *we*?"

"Yes, Garrison. That is what I meant," Randy accepted the correction.

"In that case, the answer is both yes and no," Garrison replied.

Garrison continued with a reply that was as quick as it was educational,

"Actually, we are going to use treatments that have been canceled formerly and augment that treatment with some of the peripheral drug therapy that will enhance and boost the effectiveness of the experimental treatments previously documented."

"However, insofar as you asked the question directly, some of the supposition that will be incorporated into Rigo's advanced treatment will be applied as learned from the definitive outcome as a result of the Protein Suspension Radio Therapy and the Microwave Glucose Therapy Research," he continued.

Randy was focused and listening very carefully. It is complicated.

Garrison was getting off track and brought the heart of the conversation back to the present set of events and facts. There was no time to review the long chain of events that brought Garrison to the specific course of treatment that would be most useful, most beneficial, for Rigo.

Garrison continued uncompromisingly, "It is important that you manage these two sets of notes correctly for two reasons, Randy. One, is so that we will be able to explain what exactly we are doing if we are asked by the facility and the medical establishment here at the hospital. If what we log in the official chart works, it will be deemed a miracle. Two, to be able to keep track of what we actually have done that will really cure Rigo of disease. These two charts will be distinctively different."

"I understand," Randy confirmed. "I will take accurate notes and keep them separate as you have described to protect us as well as Rigo."

Randy would be careful to write diligently in the chart as Garrison played out the next six plus months of the treatment. Randy was always studious in his documentation.

Garrison continued to explain the treatment expectations to Randy, "We need to continue to aggressively bring on fluids and restricted nutrition. What I have ordered should be fine for today and tomorrow."

"Starting today, I would like to be aggressive with the Allopurinol, at least 400mg twice a day, so we will need to keep him hydrated, but I want to see big urine production as we start to treat him. His system needs to be constantly flushing the uric acid and other toxins. Keeping him flushed as we begin to dose him is critical. Doing so will assist in avoiding any organ failure from the initial stages of treatment."

Garrison continued, "Also, start today with a one and three quarter's full dose of the clinical trial daily recommendation dose based on weight of Bevacizumab. This will slow both the tumor growth and slow advancement to involved organs by limiting cell division."

Randy questioned, "This drug was approved years ago?"

Garrison replied, "I understand it was approved as an angiogenesis inhibitor intended to stop the creation of new blood supplies and capillary growth to developing tumors; therefore, cutting off their supply of nutrients."

Randy agreed, "Yes, and …"

Garrison concluded, "And it is much more effective in the higher dosages than was approved for the general population."

"One and three quarters recommendation?" Randy asked. "What about the side effects?"

Garrison responded as a matter of fact, "Some of the best results have come when this drug is used in excess of the documented dosages if tolerated. Rigo is in a great position to be a 'must tolerate' candidate."

"This sounds risky to me," Randy questioned as he looked at his notes and stopped writing.

Garrison again answered, "Randy, I understand there are side effects. The indication of strokes, heart attacks and blood clots are the least of his worries, believe me. He has a low platelet count now so his clotting will already be suppressed. If it makes you feel better add 325mg twice a day of acetylsalicylic acid to help keep any potential post secondary clotting down. Rigo will not have any noteworthy invasive procedures done anyway. He has already had a splenectomy. He should not have to worry about excessive bleeding as a result."

"Okay," Randy acknowledged.

"By the end of day tomorrow, I would like the following treatment to be documented in the chart. Dosage should be height and weight proportionate. Intravenously, over a forty-five minute drip in alternating femoral arteries, administer Mustaragen (nitrogen mustard), Vincristine, and Procarbazine.

Then add fourteen days of Predisone, say 200mg four times a day, orally. You should document the treatments to be given roughly four weeks apart as tolerated by the patient and as determined by the white blood cell deterioration, not to go below twenty-six hundred before the next treatment cycle is due. You will have been the person administering the treatment."

"The patient has a name," Randy replied trying to catch Garrison off guard.

"In the chart you are writing in, or should I say that you should be writing in instead of challenging me, Rigo is the patient. He is not your friend. This is a professional document," Garrison reminded Randy.

Without a care for being put in his rightful place, Randy replied, "That is a pretty old school treatment for lymphatic melanoma by today's standards and has a number of long term effects like secondary leukemia and others. I think they even gave it an acronym, *MOPP* combination therapy back then."

Garrison again had to refresh Randy on the plan, "Randy, I understand. That is why you are writing it in the official chart. You will not actually be giving him this relatively easy intravenous treatment. This will do two things. This will help us justify what Rigo is doing here. This would be a logical "knock down" treatment for an advanced disease like he has. It will also buy some time without attracting attention to get the treatment regimen logistics established."

Randy asked, "It will not help remedy the symptoms."

"Get with it Randy," Garrison reprimanded, "We are not treating the symptoms. Rigo is here for the cure. In the days, weeks and months ahead, we will deliver the treatment that will really resolve the disease."

Garrison continued with the plan. "Now, don't forget the anti-nausea documentation."

"Got it," Randy said.

"That is the official treatment plan in the chart. Are you with me Randy?" Garrison asked.

Randy was embarrassed. He had said he clearly understood Garrison's train of thought and planned pattern of official records documentation. He was not following along and replied, "I am now."

Garrison dictated firmly, "Play out the treatment of *MOPP* for six months, or six cycles, in the chart. We can monitor and adjust the official chart as we go."

"I understand," Randy replied.

Garrison carried on, "Let's now move to the second set of notes, these will be the ones that actually take us to the course of treatment for this and virtually all cancers."

"What do you mean?" Randy asked. "You have the cure for cancer?"

"I believe we do," Garrison replied.

66

Randy was star struck. Garrison would not have said he had a cure if there was not a relative certainty that he, in fact, had the cure at hand.

The mood in the room changed instantaneously. Randy was intent on understanding what Garrison had to share. Randy was now listening more carefully than ever. Randy was thinking, preparing for his inevitable line of questioning that would gain him the understanding of how a cure could truly be possible.

"Starting today administer the active cellular immunotherapy protocol that we had worked on last year. I would like to use the methodology outlined in test 163-2b as the standard for Rigo," Garrison instructed.

"You can find the complete details in my office within the text of the section labeled by the same name. Nan can get it for you. They are in my file cabinet. Take those documents with you when you leave my office and place them in a safe place that only you have access to," he continued.

"What about a copy for you?" Randy asked, "For your reference."

"I do not need a reference. I know what is documented there. I wrote them," Garrison replied and expanded, "Randy, understand; however, the treatment must consist of only the second set of notes and not the chart. Do you understand? Do not give him the *MOPP* treatment."

"I understand. I got it," Randy confirmed again.

"Through the chart we have to be able to explain what we are doing if we are asked. If we do what we are explaining in the official chart, Rigo will die," Garrison elaborated. "You must administer all treatment. No one else."

"I understand," Randy said. "I understand."

Being careful not to confuse the notes, Randy was recording only a few of his notes on the hospital chart. He simultaneously removed several pieces of paper from the back of the chart. It was there where he was writing his supplemental notes on the reverse side of the blank white standard issue hospital forms.

"Tell me more," Randy implored.

Garrison reported, "We are going to employ glucose and protein suspension microwave and radio therapy, but we are going to do so with a protein suspension agent that we had previously created, but that I have extensively modified."

"Generally, how will that work?" Randy asked.

"We are not at a point of generalities Randy," Garrison reprimanded and followed up. "I have developed a protein suspension serum that contains tiny units of D.N.A. that, along with an enzyme I have identified, will actively seal off healthy cells and make them immune to the radiology I am going to expose the unprotected cancer cells too. The cancer cells, which continue to reproduce in an unrestricted fashion and fail to die off normally, will not be sealed off and will be specifically targeted by the radio treatment. It is a sort of cellular reverse discrimination if you will."

Randy was fascinated.

Garrison continued, "Here is how you will follow through specifically. Today you will have already administered the active cellular immunotherapy protocol that we have just discussed. You will continue to do this for several weeks. We will watch his chemistry panel along with the effectiveness of the treatment and adjust until we discontinue this therapy based on how he tolerates the drug and how he makes improvements."

Randy was writing on the white paper backs. He marveled internally, the cure for cancer on the back of a piece of scratch paper.

"Okay," Randy said as he caught up with his dictation. He looked up at Garrison.

"This next step is important. You will need to simultaneously inject the glucose blocking agent I have developed into Rigo while at the same time expose him to exactly 434MHz of high frequency radio waves. This treatment will begin tomorrow in the Stereo Radiology Experimental Lab."

Randy gave pause. He sat and listened. His pen fell still. It was sinking in. He was consumed by the fact that he may very well be in the presence of the greatest social discovery since Columbus came to the new world.

"Are you going to write this down Randy?" Garrison questioned as he witnessed Randy's idle pen. "I said this was *important*!"

"Of course, of course," Randy said nervously while taking a moment to get caught up, "That was 434MHz. Correct?"

Garrison recounted and proceeded on, "Yes, that is correct. You will need to start daily at about 9:00 p.m.. The treatment will need to take place seven days a week given Rigo's condition and will take three to four hours a day. It is a slow, relatively painless process that will involve repeated exposure and an extended intravenous drip cycle."

Without looking up, Randy was writing as fast as Garrison spoke.

"I will understand if you come in late on some of those days," Garrison joked.

Randy never looked up or conceded the pun. He remained centered on his notes.

Garrison continued, thinking nothing of Randy's intensity, "In Rigo's condition, I would suspect that the leveling off would take upwards of fifteen weeks."

"I don't understand," Randy questioned.

"Which part, the four months of treatment?" Garrison attempted to clarify.

"No, the principles of why this treatment would be effective," Randy asked more directly.

Garrison took the time to explain, "Cancer cells, like all cells, need glucose. The fact is that cancer cells demand glucose at a much higher rate than normal cells and will readily mistake oxygen for glucose. A normal cell will not share the predisposition to mistaken identity. The blocking agent that I will be supplying to you contains an inordinate amount of passive oxygen. The passive oxygen will appear to be glucose."

"Due to the blocking agent, the oxygen will appear to be glucose to the glucose starved cancer cell. The cancer cell will rapidly, if not instantly, absorb the blocking agent the moment the cell is agitated by the microwaves. Already absorbed and then once affected by the microwaves, any remaining glucose is instantaneously burned off by the oxygen in the glucose blocking agent you have been administering and the cancer cells are terminated," he further explained.

Randy was again silent. This sounded like it would work. He was very curious about the chemical composition of the modified blocking agent that Garrison had developed. How would he ask Garrison where he could get this agent and what was in it?

67

Still at Rigo's bedside, there was not a movement, not a twitch, not a sound or motion made by Rigo. The machines continued to click away in the back ground as they carefully measured his vital signs and introduced the previously prescribed fluids.

Garrison closed out his explanation, "This non-invasive procedure will be continuously repeated until the normal cells have an opportunity to divide and repair any damage that was done and the diseased cells are incrementally and progressively eliminated."

"That is genius. Has this been tested for any long term success?" Randy asked.

Garrison glowered back at Randy. Had Randy not heard anything he had been telling him over the last few weeks? There was a self-conscious silence from Randy. Garrison was in soundless disbelief.

There was a break in the dictation; it was a moment of reconciliation.

Randy looked back at Garrison inquisitively, "I get it, there are not any long term results because there was never any long term trials allowed. No one in control will ever let it get that far!"

"Now you are starting to understand it Randy. I am glad you came up with that on your own this time." Garrison replied. "I continued to research the glucose blocking agent and protein suspension modification research on my own. I will clarify, while the microwave treatment was not my idea in concept or in research, I believe that I have perfected the corresponding critical interface characteristics of the protein suspension and glucose blocking agent."

"Will this be effective on all cancers?" Randy asked.

"Insofar as cancer and cellular division are dependent on glucose, lactic acid and the conversion of one to the other for effective healthy and unhealthy cell division alike, and insofar as healthy cells do not mistake oxygen for glucose, I believe so. All malignancies have this characteristic in common," Garrison educated.

Randy could not help himself. He could not wait any longer. He needed to know the names of the people who knew about this discovery, what was in the blocking agent and how he could get his hands on it.

"Who have you told of this discovery?" Randy asked.

Garrison was taken aback by the question. He had told no one. In the heat of the description of the process, it was a question that was very out of context for this discussion. Why would Randy be interested in knowing who else was aware of the discovery? Why would that matter? Why would he care? What motivates a question like that to be asked? It was a concerning question.

Randy sensed Garrison's discomfort with the inquiry and moved directly to another question to help relieve the mild uneasiness Garrison was representing. Garrison filed the comment in his mind for the moment.

"What side effects might I observe if I am going to be in the lab alone with the patient?" Randy asked.

Garrison shot back. Still slightly troubled by Randy's comment, "Very good. He is the patient."

Garrison continued without vacillation with an answer to his question, "The very resonance action, created by the microwave, which will make the cells hungry for the blocking agent also creates heat from the reverberation which will, in turn, creates warmth in a normal cell.

"Cancer cells do not radiate normally and; therefore, as treatment continues, the more healthy cells you have, the warmer the patient will be post treatment. That is why the treatment takes several hours each day. Rigo will be hyperthermic, but symptomatically this will dissipate within a couple hours post treatment as treatment goes into the later weeks."

"I see," Randy said as he reached for another sheet of paper to continue his note taking.

"Like I said, you will be working nights for a while," Garrison said with a smile, "but you will be very proud of your work."

"Other effects?" Randy asked.

Once more, Garrison was troubled by the follow up question from Randy. No acknowledgement of the treatment, the good that could be done, he just wanted to absorb the next step and the treatment course. There seemed to be a primary interest shift in Randy. It was a shift towards commandeering the total treatment regimen and details. Garrison wasn't quite sure what to think of it.

Garrison was starting to feel like he needed to be more guarded in his conversation. Randy was eager to ask questions that were not relevant to the immediacy of the initial treatment. The questioning almost seemed self serving. He trusted Randy though. He needed Randy now.

Garrison replied calmly and in a controlled and skilled voice, "Yes. Yes, I suspect there will be other minor effects. The mild warming brought on from the treatment will kill red blood cells naturally. We will need to watch his anemia."

Garrison contemplated the question as Randy sat impatiently waiting for a response.

"I think that," Garrison replied and paused in thought.

"I think that given the severe state of the anemia with which Rigo has presented, we should plan to transfuse him early in the treatment and then again in a few weeks. His marrow is compromised, but it should recover. We will be able to play it by ear based on his chemistry. Get his blood type and set it up," Garrison stated confidently after some deliberation and specificity in semantics.

"Okay," Randy acknowledged eagerly.

Garrison added another component to the treatment as Randy reached for another piece of paper, "Strange as it sounds, to avoid any glucose starvation to the brain, Rigo must get to a point soon where he can eat by mouth, more importantly, and he will need to eat red meat daily. This will help bind healthy cell glucose in his system. As long as we have ongoing treatment, the sooner the better and as soon as he can tolerate it, he needs to eat cooked red meat daily."

"Okay," Randy scribed.

"Lastly," Garrison continued. "No selenium or vitamins A, E or C. See that his drips contain a minimum IU of these vitamins. Antioxidants will have a negative effect on the glucose blocking agents that I will provide you with."

"Where can I obtain the information on the glucose blocking agents and what their chemical composition is specifically? I want to be able to understand how they work."

Damn it Randy, Garrison thought to himself. Why does it matter?

Garrison snapped, "Why are you so curious all the sudden as to where I am keeping information and what my glucose blocking agent is made of? I have a protein suspension agent too. Do you want that also? How about my old Mustang? Want that?"

"Whoa! Easy Garrison! Why are you so upset? I am your business partner here," Randy defended.

"You are asking too many questions about the 'what' and not enough questions about the 'how'."

Garrison continued. "Is there something you are not telling me Randy? Is there something I need to know?"

Randy was surprised by the sudden onset of paranoia. Garrison's brow was tense. There was a mistrustful feeling in the air. Garrison had never treated Randy this way before. Randy had never given Garrison a reason to question his integrity. Randy was always careful not to give Garrison a reason to mistrust him. Randy was always careful to be respectful and cautious in his conversations with Garrison.

For a second time in this conversation, Randy would find himself changing the subject to help eliminate any questioning of his motives.

"Okay, how about diet" Randy asked.

There was a long pause as Garrison stood at the bed looking at Rigo. His concentration had been broken. Garrison turned to look at Randy. In a somber and educational tone, Garrison took a deep breath and articulated, "Diet will be critical."

Garrison handled stress by educating. Garrison overcompensated for his frustration with Randy by starting to preach as he stared blankly. He was careful not to look Randy in the eye as he spoke.

"Calorie restriction was first started in the 1930's. It was really thought to slow metabolism. What it really did, we now know, is to activate the SIR2 gene, a yeast cell that can extend a normal cells life by fifty percent or more."

Randy sat in the chair next to the bed. He was afraid to probe Garrison again right now. He would come back to getting the answers he needed, just not right now.

Garrison continued to pontificate, "Randy, I am sure you will recall that a calorically restricted monkey can have half the incidence of cancer and heart disease as a normal monkey, much less an over weight or obese monkey. We have proven this over and over again and yet society makes it very convenient to over look this basic fact about diet."

People do not understand or appreciate the basic principles of the Krebs cycle. They do not give credit to their own ability to manage their metabolism. When the ratio of carbohydrates, fats, proteins and glucose is out of balance, so is the path to creating energy and burning calories.

It is a vicious circle creating fatter and fatter people with more and more health problems and no one seems to want to help them change. We just want to take the money for treating the symptoms and complain about the cost of treating those same symptoms. We are right back to doing something to someone verses doing something *for* someone.

Randy was poised to write, but while this was interesting, it was not note worthy.

"Rigo will need a low calorie diet. A low calorie, but nutritious, diet will switch on the SIRTI gene which controls many other gene networks. It is Rigo's very malnutrition that has probably turned on the army of proteins that have prevented other damage from occurring even faster and have kept him alive to date."

"Like Reservatrol?" Randy asked.

"Exactly like Reservatrol. Garrison came alive as if awakened from a stupor, but he continued to preach. "Reservatrol is a capsulated molecule that switches on the SERTI gene. However, in test cases, the hypothesis it was created for was intended to slow aging."

"However, it had another pleasant side effect," Randy said as he attempted to lighten the mood.

"Sure," Garrison agreed, but failing to see the humor. "Dozens of companies have been pursuing molecular based anti-aging pharmaceutical applications, but they have not really gotten any clinical footing with the F.D.A. and we know why."

Garrison added, "I would like to enhance the diet and Bevacizumab regimen we already discussed by adding 10,000 mg per day of the Reservatrol A-52 the natural form."

Randy insisted, "I have access to the natural form that was tested and not the synthesized version. You are right. You need over 5g per day for effectiveness."

Garrison repeated, "Ten grams, he needs at least ten grams of the natural form. Without a very high dose, which was not published in the trial, it will not reach the blood concentrations needed to be effective."

Garrison thought to himself. He was quickly assessing the comment made by Randy so that he would not draw attention to the hiatus. Garrison too had access to the original test forms of the drug. He had access to a highly potent A-52 form of the drug as a matter of fact.

Continuing to think to himself, where would Randy gain access to natural A-52 Reservatrol? As this clinical conversation drew on, the entire exchange had become more and more suspicious as it got more and more detailed in the application of medication, the documentation, the treatment and now the access.

Garrison debated for a few seconds if he wanted to question Randy's ability to gain access to the tightly restricted and subsequently discontinued anti aging pharmaceutical. If Randy's credibility, loyalty or confidentiality was a concern to Garrison, Garrison did not want Randy to know it. This had the potential to be the "end game" issue and Garrison did not want to miscalculate any play calling.

Randy was a trusted friend and colleague, but this was a cure for the ages. This was big business, big money and big consequences, positive and negative, depending on your point of view. The inner circle of information, just exactly how much he was willing to share, and with whom, would need to be carefully calculated.

"You have access to some?" Garrison casually asked an anxious Randy who sat, looking up at Garrison, one leg crossed femininely over the other.

"You said you have access? I did not hear you tell me where you have access to it from exactly," Garrison asked again.

Randy responded in an attempt not to escalate the situation, "What I meant was that we may have access through the research lab or through a couple adjunct labs on the east coast. I think we could get some."

"Hmm," Garrison muttered.

Randy was changing the subject again. "Have you thought about stem cell treatment? As you know, stem cell research is tricky in the United States but we could test that. Stem cells have tremendous potential," Randy said.

Randy was now going to educate the boss, "Nano-particular stem cells migrate through your body, repairing anything that may be cellular defective. It is marvelous."

"Randy, I have a treatment that will cure him. We are not testing anything else at this time. What I have will work."

Garrison dismissed the mis-start that Randy had in changing the tone and directional reception of information. "We will be using Sipulev-T1A, This is the active cellular immunotherapy treatment I referred to in my notes. You can find the notes in my office under the same name in the same file cabinet. Take the clinical documentation with you."

Garrison suspended the conversation for a moment. He knew that none of this information would be helpful if the protein and glucose suspension serum he alone had so industriously developed was not available to Randy.

The recipe for which resided in Garrison's mind and in Garrison's mind alone. There was no reason to hesitate further with Randy. Much of the product was synthesized and could not be replicated through chemical analysis. Garrison and Garrison alone had the key to the cure.

"You don't have any of this on disk so that I can see the path of the discovery," Randy asked.

Again, Randy was unable to resist trying to gain access to the trail of the discovery.

Garrison smiled. Confident in the understanding he had the knowledge needed to facilitate the treatment and that he may be grossly over estimating any unfavorable intentions that Randy may harbor. He was a good friend. Either way, Randy did not and would not have the missing link.

Garrison replied, "I have only paper and you and I will have the only copies of it. With regard to the Glucose blocking agent, I will keep the chemical composition to that confidential for the time being."

Randy smiled back at Garrison in a cat and mouse *tit-for-tat* exchange.

"Okay," Randy replied. He was unsatisfied, but he needed to be content for now.

Bringing closure, Garrison elaborated on the last component of the treatment, "T1A is a super T-cell killer that seeks out tumors. It is fairly toxicity neutral in the application I am proposing."

Randy looked through the pages of notes that he had taken, thumbing through the handwritten pages front to back.

"Do you have it all documented," Garrison asked.

"I think so," followed by a quick reply. "Nutritious, but calorie and antioxidant restricted diet, Bevacizumab and Reservatrol combined with Sipulev-T1A."

"These will be indicated as you have described. Most importantly will be the glucose and protein suspension serum that will be accompanied by the daily microwave treatment," Randy concluded.

"That is correct. The beauty of this entire treatment is that it can be applied and re-applied as often or as infrequently as needed depending on the needs of the patient due to a very low toxicity and very low incidence of residual effect."

"Is there a point of diminishing return?" Randy asked.

"The diminishing return is when there is no more cancer in the patient to treat. If you continue to treat or if there is a recurrence, there are few if any side effects in the long or short term, perhaps only the need for transfusions of plasma. If there is a reoccurrence, you simply begin treatment again. "

"I will need the serum," Randy blurted out.

"I know Randy. You have made that clear. I am well aware of that. I will supply you with an exact amount of the blocking agent that you will need each day," Garrison repeated. "That will be for yours, mine and Rigo's protection,"

Garrison said as he looked down and into the open but vacant eyes of Rigo.

"I will not have access to the drug?" Randy asked.

"You will not have access to the drug other than to administer what I give you daily in its entirety."

Garrison again clarified as he continued to look into Rigo's eyes.

"I see," Randy replied in disappointment and gazing aimlessly out the window. "You do not trust me on this one, Garrison. We have been friends and professionals together for years!"

Garrison put his hand on Randy's shoulder and was quietly sympathetic for a moment. What Garrison knew is that what he had was a powerful tool. A tool that could change the world, create great wealth and topple governments.

Randy was only human after all. Trusted or not, he did not want to put him in a position of making a decision that may alter the course that was being taken. He knew Randy well, but given the situation, how well really. How would any one man act when actually given the ultimate bargaining chip? The trump chip! A chip that would contain the hope a hopeless man would die for or may die without.

"Randy, I love you like a son, but I have told you what you need to know," Garrison said as he tried to comfort Randy.

Randy stood from the chair where he was seated. In an admonishing voice he reprimanded Garrison, "That is pretty disappointing Garrison, but you are who you are."

Garrison did not respond.

Randy collected the papers that he had been writing on. He haplessly placed them at Rigo's feet at the end of the bed.

"I will get these notes cleaned up and organized. I will be sure they are placed in a safe spot," he added.

Garrison was unsure of what to think of the comment and what was running through Randy's mind. It gave Garrison comfort to know Randy did not have all of the pieces to the puzzle and that the treatment for Rigo had been put into motion. In the next few days, the clock would most surely be ticking in Rigo's favor.

CHAPTER NINE
THE SCHOLAR VS. THE SYSTEM

68

Twelve weeks had passed since Rigo had made the journey from Brazil to the University Medical Research Center in February. Garrison and Randy had been getting along well. As expected, Randy had been meticulously attentive to Rigo's care and treatment. Besides Randy, no one at the hospital was asking too many questions.

The hospital room was being funded by Garrison's department and his care was *pro bono* thanks to Randy and Garrison's University employment and expertise. The medicine was, of course, courtesy of the clinical trial community.

This was a teaching and research facility after all. There was non-conventional case management that took place here all the time. All in all, they didn't expect many questions, but the official chart of record was up-to-date nonetheless.

Garrison had been working in his office all morning. Craig had become annoying. He was asking an inordinate amount of questions regarding research documentation, funding and reporting responsibilities. In fact, Craig even seemed like he had an even greater proclivity for the details than usual. He had been wearing Garrison out for a week with his non-stop "what if" and "where it came from" line of questioning.

Randy and Garrison were speaking daily about Rigo's care. Garrison went to the hospital yesterday for the first time in a week and was amazed at the progress. Rigo was unrecognizable when compared to the emaciated and non responsive boy who was admitted. He was alert and talkative, if not a bit restless. He spoke relatively good English and Garrison was able to converse with him.

Garrison was as proud as a father with a new born. He could not take his mind off of the boy and the physical momentum that he was gaining in his recovery. Be assured, Rigo was far from cured, but it was a compelling story to date. If you were close enough to the treatment, like Randy and Garrison were, and knew the true improvements of his condition, it was exciting.

Garrison decided to take a break from the probing he was taking from Craig again today. It was an easy ten minute walk through the tunnel system that connected his office, the administrative office building to the hospital itself.

Garrison went up the elevator and to Rigo's room.

Randy and Rigo were past the halfway point of what they had anticipated a full regimen of treatment to be. Randy was at the nurse's station making his daily contribution of fictitious notes in the chart. He had spent all night with Rigo in the Radio Lab and was ready to go home for the day. Garrison said hello as he passed Randy and walked into the room.

The room was silent and Rigo was sleeping peacefully. Garrison had walked to the same bedside where he had stood only twelve weeks earlier. Randy followed him from the corridor and stood just inside the doorway.

They booth stood quietly so they did not interrupt Rigo's sleep. Rigo too had been up most of the night. Garrison began to run his hands through Rigo's dark black hair.

"Have you spoken to his mother," Garrison asked quietly, not taking his eyes off the boy.

"I have spoken to her each week," Randy replied from the doorway. "I have arranged for DiDi to place a call each week to me directly and DiDi is relaying the information to Marguerite."

"Very good," Garrison said calmly.

"Are you keeping up the chart?" Garrison asked.

"I am keeping the chart at the hospital current as we discussed," Randy reassured.

"Okay," Garrison said softly still gently adjusting Rigo's hair. "and the actual documentation of the microwave therapy and glucose blocking serum injections?" Garrison asked.

"I had Craig type up my notes from the initial meeting. I have been dictating his progress and Craig has been inputting my comments into the data base each day. Craig has found it very interesting."

Garrison pulled his hands back from Rigo. He momentarily stared out the window and an air of frustration came over him. He broke his stare and turned to Randy, "What have you done?" Garrison asked. "You have jeopardized all we have worked for."

Garrison was furious. This was not a high school experiment that he wanted to have everyone involved in.

"You were not listening Randy! Why did you involve someone else?" How is Craig's computer a safe and secure place?"

"You should have done this yourself, Randy, by hand as I asked. You should not have involved anyone else. You should have asked me first?"

"Damn it Randy!" Garrison was visibly shaken, "I trusted you with this information," he said softly as he thrust an open hand at Randy.

"You do not understand the range and scope of the people who follow these trials Randy. They have access to the data bases. These are very aggressive people when it comes to getting things started and stopped. Do you understand me? Why do you think I have been so careful? Why do you think I have shared only parts of the information? Is this a game to you Randy?"

Randy stood in the door and remained calm. Was Randy tired or was he indifferent because Garrison was not sharing all of the treatment details with him.

"What is your point, Garrison?" Randy said in a condescending tone.

The room fell still. There were no longer any machines in the room. Rigo was eating by mouth and had no intravenous attachment. All you could hear was his heart monitor thumping consistently in sinus rhythm. Garrison stood fast looking out the window in disbelief. He turned to Randy. They looked at each other.

"Maybe you did this on purpose Randy. Maybe you did this because you are part of the system? Is that it Randy 'ole friend. Are you just here to keep an eye on me?"

Randy was puzzled by the suggestion that he was somehow not the friend and man of character he had convinced Garrison he was. As Randy stood in the doorway, he showed no emotion. He was listening to Garrison. This lack of reaction was tantamount to an admission in Garrison's mind.

69

The weighty silence in the room was interrupted by a short young man edging Randy from the doorway. The man spoke rudely once in the room, "I am looking for Dr. Garrison Keller?"

"Are you Dr. Keller?" the man asked aggressively of Randy before anyone had a chance to reply.

Absent of comment, Randy looked at Garrison.

The young man, unlike Randy, was an expert at interpreting facial expression and non verbal communication. Instantly, by seeing the vacant look on Randy's face, not knowing if Randy should identify Garrison for the young man or if Garrison should be allowed to indentify himself, the young man knew.

There is no substitute for *in person* non-verbal communication and this young man knew it too. That is why he was here. That is why he made the trip to Minnesota. Just seeing the way Randy looked at Garrison, the man turned and concluded definitively, "So you are Dr. Keller!"

Garrison replied, "I am Garrison Keller. How can I help you?"

"Please explain to me the scope of this young immigrant's care," the young man questioned.

"Please keep your voice down, the boy is trying to sleep," Garrison said in response.

"What is your relationship to this boy and what creates your level of interest in his care?" Garrison asked, knowing that the only people who had a legal right to know were either in this room or not available.

The young man continued as he closed the door, "I have reason to believe that this boy may not be getting the appropriate level of care!"

Appropriate level of care, Randy contemplated to himself calmly as he watched this conversation take its course from just inside the closed door. Who could say if the care was appropriate or not, this boy was deathly ill and his care is documented! Better yet, who would be asking in this manner? Randy had been part of many medical inquiries in the past and they never began or took shape as this one did.

Garrison replied administratively, "Insofar as I know that you are neither the father nor mother of this young boy, I do not need to disclose anything of this boy's care to you unless you have their consent, which I would find unlikely."

"Is that so Doc. Quoting Health Insurance Portability and Protection Act (H.I.P.P.A.) regulations to me now are you?" the young man smiled and raised his voice in an obvious effort to inflame the discussion.

"Perhaps you can take me to this boy's parents then? I can speak to them directly and not go through the middle man."

"Oh, c'mon," Randy slipped in a faintly audible tone causing the young man to turn and give him a cursory gaze, clearly acknowledging the comment, followed by a turn to stare back at Garrison.

Not exactly a question that Garrison wanted to answer at this time.

Garrison had to have some understanding of why this man had come into Rigo's room. Why this room, this boy and this boy's care specifically? There was a lot at stake here in terms of completely facilitating the timely care for Rigo. He did not need interruptions. Was this man from the State Child Welfare Board or Health and Human Services? How did he even know Rigo was even here?

Garrison did not recognize him as part of the Medical Center's administration staff. Who was the man anyway? Garrison needed a try to get back in control of the situation.

"I did not catch your name or why you have interest in this patient?" Garrison asked.

"My name is Ed Cuda."

There was a pause.

"Okay, Ed Cuda. I will ask you again, what is your relationship to this patient and this patient's care specifically?"

"I really have no interest in this patient at all," Cuda replied in a normal tone with his usual apathy and indifference.

Saying again in a low tone while looking down at the sleeping Rigo, Cuda repeated, "That is accurate. I really have no interest in the boys care whatsoever," as if to reassure himself that he was speaking truthfully.

"My concern is that the care he may be getting here may be in violation of the covenants of your medical facilities charter and outside the bounds of what has been approved by the F.D.A. as acceptable medical practices by a physician or a research facility in the United States."

Randy was wide awake now and he was listening to every word. This sounded serious. Randy was nervous. What had he started in motion? Ed Cuda was obviously a person that knows the system, medical facility levels of certification and the requirements of proper notifications to government agencies. Could it be that Cuda was just a great confidence man, Randy thought?

"I see," Garrison said.

"I also understand that you have been to Brazil recently?" Cuda added.

Garrison and Randy were both silent. There was a good answer for that question right now.

Garrison commented, "I went to Brazil. Is that a crime? I went there legally."

Cuda expanded, "So you are the great teacher Dr. Garrison Keller," Cuda said as he arrogantly picked up the chart from the end of the bed.

"Well, teacher, give me a lesson today. I will need to see…"

Garrison interrupted as he ripped the chart from Ed Cuda's hands, "Mr. Cuda, you have yet to show me what medical jurisdiction, or justification period, you have to even be in this room. You have yet to show me any reason I should be speaking to you at all. I will not be showing you any medical records without first knowing what agency you represent and, within the H.I.P.P.A. protections afforded this patient that you already seem to be aware of, a parental release of information."

Cuda was not easily frustrated. Even though electronic medical records were not yet mandatory and were therefore not yet readily accessible for any government official to peruse at their leisure, Cuda knew what Garrison was up to. Documented or not, he knew this boy was treated with experimental procedures that were not approved for use.

Cuda had access to all the medical records he needed. There was a boy in front of him that was making great strides in recovery with an antiquated treatment regimen and the antiquated regimen in the chart did not follow the same course as the treatment being recorded in the research data base.

Even though this was a teaching hospital, legitimate e-medical records retention was not accessible for the general public. The lack of easy access to electronic records was another restriction that Cuda did not like and he would see that this would change in future legislation.

Randy was still in the doorway. He was tense for all the right reasons. Rigo, still sleeping soundly, Cuda asked, "Perhaps we can continue to have this discussion in your office Dr. Keller."

Garrison replied, "Randy, please see that Rigo's chart is current. I will be returning to my office with Mr. Cuda."

"You do that Randy old pal. I appreciate your help," Cuda said with a Grinch like grin.

Garrison stared angrily at Randy. In return, Randy stared back defiantly at Garrison. They were both at a loss for words. Garrison did not know what to think of Cuda's comment and simultaneously, Randy did not know what to say to Garrison as he exited the hospital room, Cuda in tow.

Speaking as he walked out the door, Garrison informed Cuda, "You can follow me Mr. Cuda. My office is only a couple blocks from here."

Cuda obediently followed Garrison past Randy, giving Randy a perfunctory wink on his way out the door. Randy smirked in disapproval.

Cuda followed a couple steps behind as Garrison lead the way through the tunnel system and back to the office. Garrison became more incensed with every step he took.

Garrison maintained a swift pace as he transcended the stairs and entered the office lobby. Craig was sitting at his desk pounding away fastidiously on his key board. Craig looked up as Garrison passed. Garrison gave Craig barely a hurried look. Cuda was tracking right behind Garrison.

Craig's concentration had already been broken by his boss's rapid entrance and quick passing. As Cuda walked by, Craig and Cuda made eye contact. Craig nodded at Cuda as he passed. Ed Cuda gave a suspiciously confirmatory nod back.

"Hold any calls that may come in," Garrison said as he whisked past Nan who was also sitting at her desk working industriously as the two men passed.

"Yes, Sir," Nan replied as Garrison entered his office.

Due to his hearty pace, Garrison did not see the nod from Craig as he breezed by. Having given a suspicious smile and a nod to both Nan and Craig as part of his silent high school style of greeting, Cuda was still smiling as he followed Garrison's into his office. Cuda had an infuriating nature about him.

Cuda crossed the threshold and took the liberty of slamming Garrison's office door behind him. The loud crack echoed in the small office as the door came to an abrupt stop latching in the closed position. The crashing interruption to the quiet office caught Garrison, Craig and Nan, one and all, off guard.

Garrison spun around, surprised by the irritation that Cuda had just willfully created. Ten feet from each other, Garrison and Cuda were fixated on each other. The room was once again quiet. Cuda was still smiling faintly as he walked past Garrison stopping behind Garrison's desk.

"I decided to set the stage for our conversation," Cuda said as he wiggled his back side comfortably into Garrison personal chair that sat behind his desk.

"Comfy place you got here chief," Cuda added while casually taking a visual survey of the room.

"Have we met?" Garrison said insolently, still troubled by the line of questioning over the last half hour.

"Oh, we have met alright," Cuda replied fumbling through his shirt pocket to retrieve a wrapped tooth pick, peal back the plastic and start to clean his teeth.

Garrison stood quietly observing Cuda sitting comfortably at his desk. Cuda tossed the tooth pick wrapper on the floor. Garrison was puzzled. He was being sarcastic. He was certain they had never met before. He was sure of it.

Garrison remained silent. He thought it best for the time being that Cuda start any meaningful conversation.

Yes, in dee dee, we have met," Cuda responded again to the same question staring straight into Garrison's eyes as he pompously picked his teeth.

Garrison was contemplative. "Yes, in dee dee"? Was this a coincidental comment or did he mean DiDi? Was he making a charitable attempt at being funny? Surely this was not a laughing matter. Garrison was unsure of a method within which he would be able to calculate just exactly how challenging an opponent Cuda would be.

"Dr. Keller," Ed Cuda began as he leaned forward in Garrison's chair, "I know what you are up to here."

Garrison listened.

"And you know," examining the point of his weathering toothpick, "I understand what you are doing. I do! I really do! I understand that people like you and people like me are different and that is ok by me."

Garrison continued to listen.

Cuda continued in an animated manner, waving his hands about, "Yup. Different is okay by me. People like you are out to make this big difference in the quality of people's lives. You want everyone to live happy and healthy lives. You want to change the world in varied and long lasting ways. Everyone lives happily ever after in your world, right?"

Cuda collected his thoughts for a moment. Garrison continued to save his words.

"Mr. Cuda, have we met before?" Garrison asked again.

"Please, call me Cuda. My friends call me Cuda," Cuda counseled.

This man was hardly my friend Garrison thought. But why was he here? Who had sent him here and how could he get him out of the way without sharing too much information. For that matter, how much information did Ed Cuda already know? Was he already in possession of enough information to be in a position to just play games with Garrison? Was he just toying with him for pleasure?

"What is it exactly that you think I am doing?" Garrison asked.

Cuda studied Garrison's face. Now we are getting somewhere, Cuda thought to himself, failing to take his eyes off Garrison.

After a moment of pensive deliberation, out came an abrupt reply blurted out by Cuda as he became restless in his seat, "I think that you are trying to test and perfect a cure for something. Cancer maybe? That's what I think."

Cuda sat up erect and attentive in the chair.

Cuda repeated himself without waiting for or giving a chance for Garrison to reply, "Yes sir! That is what I think. A cure? You seek the cure. That is the type of man you are."

"That is absurd," Garrison stated, being careful not to break eye contact or to look away at this critical moment.

"You're a rebel Garrison Keller. That's what I have heard. A rebel! A play by the rules closet rebel," Cuda replied. "A closet rebel!" Cuda repeated out loud.

"That's funny don't you think?" as Cuda amused himself. "Closet rebel."

"There is nothing funny about you making accusations about the integrity of this facility or me personally. Let's get that straight first. Second, I have devoted my entire life to making practical application and useful discovery," Garrison defended. "I am not fearful or ashamed of that."

"Is that so?" Cuda questioned, becoming more relaxed with every question. "Don't you understand that these discoveries have limitations?"

Cuda has the moral character of Rasputin. He could make your blood boil with his provoking comments. That was his game. He was cool under fire and would not let his emotions show. The more he could get his opponent to become angered or frustrated, the better his game worked and the more information he was likely to get.

"Why are you here?" Garrison asked of Cuda with a raised voice. "You still have not told me why you are here, what you are looking for, and who do you work for or on what foundation you have built these lofty assertions about the nature of my work?"

"I work for the United Sates government. The Secret Service to be exact," Cuda replied confidently. "Would you like to see my badge?"

Cuda picked a small leather billfold from his pants pocket and began to make a superficial attempt to show Garrison his badge and identification. Garrison was standing close enough that he moved forward slightly and ripped the badge from Cuda's hand.

Garrison examined the badge and identification. They appeared to be legitimate. Garrison had dealt with governmental departments before and was familiar with the watermarks and holograms that are generally in place for authentication. Cuda was for real.

Garrison tossed the wallet back on the desk in front of Cuda. "What could the United States Secret Service possibly be interested in here at this hospital or with me for that matter?" Garrison asked as he turned and took a few steps, stopping at the front of his desk.

"Great question," Cuda said with a slightly larger dose of smugness added in for effect.

"I am here by order of the President of the United States, as his Special Liaison, seeking verification of information that may have, and I say may have, significant national security implications. Does that tell you who I work for and why I am here?" Cuda concluded.

Cuda did not work directly for the President even though that was the title of his position and that was the sub title on his identification card. Cuda took full advantage of the title. It was a convincing piece of the confidence game that he played and it certainly added to his self-assurance and coolness in conversations like these.

While Cuda was truthful, he was not willing to divulge too much to Garrison, not yet.

Both men were careful not to disclose too much information about what motivated them to continue to be in each others' company. Garrison wanted to know just what Cuda already understood about Rigo's treatment so far. More importantly, if he knows about the treatment regimen, how did he find out? Cuda on the other hand, was seeking as much information as he could get. Cuda and Garrison were both playing a pretty close hand.

"I am a teacher. I want to educate and make useful contributions to the daily quality of American lives. I came to this profession to heal," Garrison continued. "These are challenging times for people."

"Sure you have," the perpetually indignant Cuda replied. "You're an educated man Dr. Keller. You are a man of means that seeks the common good. A very smart man in complicated times. A philanthropist, is that what you are telling me?"

"I try to put my professional training, education and resources to good use," Garrison added.

"Your training," Cuda riled as he pointed to the various commendations and documents on the shelves in the office, "Let me tell you something. There was a time when high school was job training, so all of your diplomas in today's self-serving world do not mean a whole lot to me. Street smarts will prevail today Keller. Street smarts! We both have a job to do here. You know it and I know it. I would guess you even know what my job here is?"

"And as I have been asking, what is your job here exactly?" Garrison asked.

"Given all of the parchment in the office that bears your name, your ignorance is disappointing. Let me explain it again. I will use small words this time," a spiteful Cuda replied smugly.

Garrison was feeling the pressure inside his chest start to accumulate. He had never been spoken to this way before. Cuda continued the humiliating and disrespectful means of making his point.

"I am here," Cuda said oscillating his finger back and forth, pointing at himself. "To see that you," pointing at Garrison. "You are not getting too far ahead of the system."

"Are you with me so far?" as Cuda stopped and asked for an attention check with Garrison.

Garrison did not respond to the insolent treatment he was getting.

Cuda continued in sound bites now pointing at Garrison, "Of the approved treatments."

"Established by …"

Cuda was intentionally speaking clearly and in small words that he thought would be best for Garrison to understand.

"The United States g-o-v-e-r-n-m-e-n-t."

"As it pertains to disease management," Cuda said with fervor.

"Was that clear enough?"

Cuda continued his comments with passion, "I am here to see that you do not over step your small and narrow research perspective. I am here to prevent the unforeseen consequences that your, shall we say, irresponsible actions may have on this country and the citizens that your country is here to serve."

"That sounds serious," Garrison antagonized, trying not to show that he was angry right down to the marrow.

"You are treating this boy illegally," Cuda puked out in a belligerent manner. "You know it and I know it, so let's stop playing cat and mouse here."

"I am treating a boy with approved methods. He is an American citizen. He is ill. I wanted to make his last days here better and I had the means to do so. Why is that a concern of the United States government?" Garrison replied.

"It is a concern because I think you are lying," Cuda smiled. "You are a liar, pure and simple. You are treating this boy by illegal means. I know it," Cuda added as he continued to interrogate using one of the oldest techniques known to man, which is not allowing the person you are questioning to know what you already understand to be fact or what you are still seeking to discover.

"If this is what you think, then prove it to me. What am I doing illegally?" Garrison asked with measured confidence.

Cuda paused. Garrison was uncertain as to the intent of the pause. Was this a stare down and did Cuda just blink? Cuda was either unwilling or unable to commit to his next step. Cuda is a tactician and he was assuming a mental fall back position. He took a blind eye to Garrison's apparent generosity.

Garrison speculated that Cuda was unsure, unwilling or unable to reply based on the facts he had. Perhaps Cuda was less informed than he initially thought and did not have as much information as Garrison was presuming.

Cuda spun the chair around, manipulated the subject and lectured, "You bring a young boy here, all the way from Brazil, to see that his final days are comfortable. I am supposed to believe that?"

Garrison responded in kind by changing the subject again, "Brazil is one of the richest developing nations in the world. The people should demand better care for their fellow countrymen, don't you think?"

"They are a rich nation indeed," Cuda agreed. "Think about what you have just said. The nation is rich. The people are not rich.

The air in the room was still.

"How do you think the nation got that way?" Cuda asked making quotation marks via hand gestures using his index and middle finger on each hand bringing emphasis in *air quotes* to the word nation.

Garrison did not reply.

Cuda continued, "Did they get there by giving free health care to illegal immigrants? Maybe they got there by keeping terminally ill patients on the dole for more and more tests in the hope the cure is right around the corner."

Cuda waited for a reply. He waved his hands in front of his own face, making motion to the effect that Garrison was not listening.

"Hey," Cuda snapped his fingers. "Helen Keller, you in there?"

Garrison did not reply.

"No, my dear friend Garrison, the cure is not coming and it certainly is not coming from you.

Still no reply from Garrison.

Cuda continued, "Now, listen up. Brazil became a rich nation by applying the twenty-first century version of natural selection. They provide for the healthiest and the best able to serve and contribute to society. Period! There are acceptable losses Garrison. This is a sacrifice and service that we are obligated to perform as countrymen. We should feel good about it!"

"Why are you here speaking to me in this tone of voice?" Garrison asked.

Cuda thought through his response, "Let me start by giving you a little lesson here today, Dr. Teacher. You may have gotten into this profession to heal, but the health care and research vocation is business. It is big business indeed. Face it Keller, whether you like it or not, and it's a business that is as corrupt as our own members of congress. Ouch!"

"It is not all about the money and the business side of it," Garrison said.

"Is that so," Cuda reminded. "Are you not aware that the U.S. spends a greater percentage of G.D.P. on health care than any other industrialized nation? That is business my man. Government is business. Government is control!"

"We have a system that makes health care available to citizens who need it regardless of whether or not you can pay for that care or not. You are not denied treatment," Garrison replied.

"That is the 'happily every after' part I was talking about. You people want the nation to pay for the care, the treatment, the testing, even if the odds of survival or success are slim," Cuda stated.

"I do. People deserve a chance!" Garrison responded.

Cuda glared back at Garrison and evaluated his response for a moment. "Let me make my perspective clear Keller. I think that a premature baby born at twenty weeks should be allowed to die in their mothers' arms rather than forcing an unwilling nation to pay two million dollars on critical care. Have another baby for God's sake, and take better care of yourself to insure full term next time. The kid will have nothing but costly problems later in life anyway."

"That is barbaric," Garrison barked.

"Then try this one on for size. The older you are and the younger you are, the less likely extraordinary means will be employed to save you. Too young, the nation has not invested in you yet. Too old, you have reached your shelf life expiration and you will begin to take more from the system than you put in. Simple Simon it seems to me," Cuda finished.

Garrison was speechless for the moment.

"Don't look so surprised there Helen Keller. You probably figured this out a long time ago. You just could not accept that is was true," Cuda blabbered.

"I am aware that health care and long-term benefit costs are very high in this country, but I didn't think that the government would go to such drastic steps to change the course of mortality," Garrison responded.

"I was aware it was very high," Cuda mimicked Garrison's response. "Nice response from an educated man like you. I thought your role was to know these things and to be aware," Cuda said.

No response from Garrison.

"Now then, Helen, let me ask you this again, now that you are more *aware*. Do you think health care is big business?" Cuda added.

Garrison needed to defend his profession. Not to Cuda per se, but he needed to defend his own belief and self respect to himself.

"There are no guarantees as to how any one individual man will apply the Hippocratic Oath Mr. Cuda. There are good men, there are great men and there are bad men. We try to do well by the patients."

"I am sure you try. When you speak of good men and bad men that surely are noble, what you are missing is the role of government," Cuda stated.

"How do you mean?" Garrison was asking for clarification.

"I am sure you think that you have affected so many people so favorably over the years. Don't you?" Cuda questioned.

"I do. I think we have conducted ourselves over time with great vision and with great result," Garrison replied.

"Indulge me, Garrison. Name one of these great visions for me?" Cuda requested.

"Taking statins," Garrison replied while waving his hand dismissively.

"Ah, yes. Taking statins! I see," Cuda replied. "Taking statins is a great example. I am glad you have chosen this one. I know this example well. Let me tell you Dr. Keller, statins are no magic bullet. You may have lowered your cholesterol and you may have even cleared some arteries, but the medicine never addressed the underlying issues that were in place that would have negated the need for statins to enter into the main stream of medicine to begin with."

Garrison listened.

Cuda grinned confidently and nodded his head up and down, "You never addressed the underlying issues of poor diet, fast food on every corner, inactivity, diabetes, you name it. All the bad habits stayed on the bus. You failed Garrison. Yes, you failed."

Garrison was listening in disbelief.

"You see Garrison, the government's plan was to give you the easy way out, a pill, to make you think you were healthier. You would not do anything that would actually change your mortality. More people would get fatter still and only some would take statins. Net gain to the government."

Garrison was still listening as Cuda was planning an essay on medical theory. Medical theory that Garrison himself was worried was true.

"The introduction of statins was a zero sum game. Statins were the confidence man selling you wart elixir or one size fits all shoes from the back of a covered wagon. By the time you realize you have been had, he is gone. The wagon was on to the next small town," Cuda continued.

Garrison realized he was now being given a lot of the same lines of thought, albeit different examples, from a government official none the less, that he had given to Randy at the Barra Grill over dinner. It served as disappointing confirmation of the suspicions he had been harboring for years.

"Garrison, for such a smart man, like I said, I am surprised that you did not suspect a sham all along. The statins were never intended to step in when you blew your diet. No, no, no!" Cuda said as he waved is finger back and forth in his customary prevocational manner.

"They were intended for you to think that you would be in the same place as if you had succeeded with your daily work out and less self indulgent diet. It was really a *false sense of security* pill," he continued.

"That is a wretched way to strategize," Garrison retorted

"No, this is just big business Dr. Garrison and the big pharmaceutical companies are happy as clams. You have given, and we have approved, a real winner with this one. Great example. Do you have another example for me?"

Garrison responded, "There are benefits to these drugs. I have seen the results. You are just attempting to morally bankrupt a culture."

"Whatever," Cuda replied, "I think you will find that if you check your data, patients in studies abroad taking this medication suffered fewer heart attacks and fewer strokes, so you were successful. You sure were," Cuda added.

"I have seen the data. It is a good drug," Garrison once again clarified.

"It is interesting though that the averages say they seemed to have died at roughly the same age from a number of other causes," Cuda concluded with this surprise tidbit.

Garrison countered, "People have a right to live a natural life with the excellent care that research has developed over the years."

"No," Cuda corrected. "You are wrong. People have a right to live in peace without being a burden to family or society. I told you, this is not personal in any way. People live and people die. Some die sooner than others, and so goes the way of the world."

"But enough of this, I have my facts straight now. I think you do too," Cuda said still comfortably seated in Garrison's chair.

"Garrison, this has been very inspiring for me, but I have to get going. So let me leave you with this," Cuda sounded off.

"And what would that be?" Garrison replied.

Cuda swiveling back and forth in Garrison's chair and elaborated, "Death will always be there for all of us. It is like those eyes on the girl from the portrait in the hallway in the house you grew up in. Those damn crazy eyes, always following you around. It used to drive me wild thinking about her following me around, back and forth, every time I passed her picture."

Cuda paused for a second and regained his pinpoint attention and focus on Garrison, "but as time passed, you learned not to dwell on her constant staring. Death is like that old picture; it just keeps staring at you. She is always there, staring. She is always there. She is there staring at the young and she is there staring at the old. Those crazy eyes!"

"Your point is Cuda?" Garrison blurted out.

"You can't save everyone and you just cannot let yourself dwell on it," Cuda coolly replied.

"I know of what you are speaking Mr. Cuda. I have seen the look on many patients' faces the moment they are told it is an unavoidable fact that they are going to die soon. I know what they feel in their hearts when you tell them. I also know that I have the ability to help many of them," Garrison responded.

Untouched by the dialogue, Cuda sat back in the chair. However, Cuda was very concerned by this comment. He was sure that Garrison was holding out on some material information. Cuda never took his eyes off of Garrison. Neither one of them so much as blinked.

"Well," Cuda added as he fidgeted, still looking at Garrison.

Garrison had called his bluff. After all this, what was Cuda going to do about it anyway? Cuda stood up and spoke, "You may have your way this time Garrison. You may save this one pathetic little boy."

Cuda took a couple steps towards the door, "Yep, you just might save this one little bastard, and I do mean bastard. Who could say for sure at this point, right?"

Garrison was still.

Cuda nervously looked at the back of his hands. He made a fist and then relaxed his hands as he stared at them. He made the same motion again. And looked at Garrison, "The question is, how can you save yourself?" Cuda asked.

Garrison looked impassively at Cuda. He was not precisely sure how he should take that last comment. Was Cuda threatening him? Had Garrison pushed someone, somewhere, too far by treating Rigo?

"What is that supposed to mean?" Garrison questioned.

"Oh, your profession I mean? Of course, your profession! We are all professionals here," Cuda said with contempt for everything that Garrison stood for.

Cuda sensed the awkwardness of the interaction and attempted to clarify if only to comfort to the discussion at present, "Of course, Garrison, your profession. Relax. You know what you have done here. You know the difference between legal medicine and illegal medical practice as defined by the United States government and the American Medical Association. You know the difference between right and wrong. Don't you?"

"I do know the difference between right and wrong," Garrison responded.

Cuda lashed out by chastising Garrison and with another abrupt change of emotion as he raced through the following comment, "Good. From where I sit, I can see that you have clearly violated numerous charters, codes of ethics and Federal laws here. The F.D.A. is rigorous when it comes to their clinical trials for cancer and immunotherapy. Treatments that are tested on young boys, even if they are tested on experimental immigrant boys that you are using as human guinea pigs, must have been proven 'unequivocally' to be beneficial. You know where you stand and what the consequences will be. Correct?"

"I have acted in good faith. The F.D.A. requires long term data to substantiate the trend lines and they are not willing to extend tests long enough to get the data, so I am precluded from using the treatment," Garrison responded.

"Good faith," Cuda laughed. "You are not even in the same church with me on this one Dr. Keller. Faith! Funny!"

Cuda was ready to up the ante, "We need to look at one world at a time here Garrison. Like Thoreau said, 'One world at a time'." Cuda reiterated.

"Mr. Cuda, it is as you say. You and I are different. I see a human race that has a vaccine for Alzheimer's. I see a world where drugs are created that will improve memory. I see a world where gene and stem cell therapy will make paralyzed people walk and put an end to clinical diseases of almost every sort."

"That is not the world Thoreau spoke of and by that definition Keller, it is a world you will never see," Cuda replied.

Cuda continued after a brief respite, "You may never have the capacity to understand what the big picture is all about Keller. I just don't think you have the capability to understand it. But I can tell you, it all leads back to one place."

Garrison requested, "Where is that Mr. Cuda?"

Cuda replied, "It all leads back to money. The big money is in disease management and aging and we simply cannot afford it. We can no more afford the millions invested in a premature life, than we can afford the billions in infirmary care for people on legacy benefits."

Garrison was silent.

Cuda continued, "Aging, more particularly, is the one inescapable human solution that will end American civilized life as we know it if it is not managed. Paradoxical don't you think? The very thought of the long life we seek will be the end of the prosperity that we have come to expect from it. It is a contemptuous situation."

Silence.

"How do you see yourself Garrison?" Cuda asked.

Garrison replied, "I see myself as a patriot and a scholar. To be a patriot you have to brave. I am not speaking of the stuff Purple Heart recipients are made of. I am speaking about leading courageously and advancing the cause of great health. Being a good compatriot to your neighbor's quality of life should be a commitment we are all willing to make severally and interdependently."

Cuda was giving the appearance that Garrison was making a personal connection with him.

"You have to ask yourself, Cuda, was your overall objective when you got into this job, and came to this discussion, to add to, or take away from, the greater service you are providing to society?"

Cuda looked at Garrison with distrust, smirking in a sort of one sided smile, and replied, "Dr. Garrison, you are a fool. Unless you have discovered a way to turn terminally ill citizens of all ages into battalions of *mission, men and me marching soldiers*, the fruits of your aging and cancer cure research will likely fall on deaf ears. The government just has no use for sick old people."

"You are insane," Garrison implied.

"Am I?" Cuda interjected. "Life is a terminal solution that can be managed in terms of who and how. Soon, through the efforts of the Congress, it will also include *when* and *at what cost*. You should have completed your minor studies in history. Governments and dictators, hell, even nomadic tribes, have been applying this concept in both civilized and uncivilized ways throughout all of recorded history."

Garrison had heard this before and from his own lips none the less.

Garrison asked, "Are you worried about the cure you say that I am seeking for the people or are you worried about a cure for the ailing economy which our government created for and by itself? Is this the cure for the people, the economy or for governmental control over the very lives the government has sworn to protect?"

Cuda listened.

"And I too know what you are doing, Cuda. You seek the cure for the sake of the power. The power over the people! Absolute power corrupts absolutely," Garrison reprimanded.

Remembering the words Alan Hoard said to him, and recalling that Hoard suggested psychologists have been well versed for decades in the behavioral trend of people to grossly over estimate the odds of rare events and rare people, Cuda contemplated his next comment.

"When we were twenty years old Keller, things always seem to be so clear. We were all so smart at that age back then. We knew so much. Now that we are older, things are not so clear. Why is that do you suppose?"

"It is because self-serving greediness and power take-over as we grow older. Deception takes careful thought. A youthful truth comes out freely," Garrison replied.

Cuda concluded as he stood on the doorway transom, "You would be wise not to over estimate your role Doc. The deaf ears that hear your story for the last time, in the end, may be your own."

Cuda walked out the door and wished Nan a good day. As he walked by Craig's work station, with an exiting wink and nod for Craig, he heard Garrison call out from Nan's desk, "My quest for a cure cannot be stopped!"

CHAPTER TEN
INSIDE THE INVESTIGATION

70

Chris and Jude were at the Sheriff's department annex in Plymouth. Chris was having trouble merging the facts of the case. There were far too many dead ends. The merits of virtually every material fact, circumstantial or otherwise, were a total disconnect with what had been his perceived end result to the case. Dr. Garrison Keller's death, improbable as it seemed, was apparently a suicide.

The two sat together, calmly ruminating fixedly at the battered white board they used to accumulate and examine the facts of the case. The white board was a tradition with the Sheriff's department. Mastering an analytical perspective was an art. The large white dry erase board with the hand written summary, gave detectives a great overview to any case. The white board had been used in the department for years.

The board was larger than life and served as an objective operations status report and a great thinking tool. Over the years, to the crime solving appreciation of the community as a whole, this method had helped visualize and solve many mysteries.

Both Jude and Chris stared at the board. Chris was vigorously running his hands through his hair.

"Jude!" Chris said breaking the concentration.

There was no response from Jude who continued to scan the facts in front of her. Facts that had been compiled on this case going back to the night they were interrupted from dinner to investigate Dr. Keller's untimely death.

"Jude," Chris said again a little louder with his fingers interlaced and his hands on his head, "yeah, I heard you. What?"

"Let me get this straight. What I see in front of me is a grossly lop-sided collection of murder suicide data. Maybe the most lop-sided evidence I have ever seen," Chris stated with a perplexed look.

"It is," Jude, with her inordinate attention to detail, agreed.

Chris began to read down the list of leads and events.

"The house was locked and the alarm was set. How do you explain that? There was no forced entry and there was no apparent theft at the home. He shot himself on a Friday night, a time when it was not likely that anyone would find him, or miss him, for a couple days," Chris explained.

"He shot himself right before a weekend after telling numerous people he would be sailing. He had hoped for good weather to get one more good sail in because he needed to get the boat out of the water. His colleagues at the office were very tight lipped. Nan had nothing to share of value at all. Craig and Randy seemed like they were holding back. I will say that did bother me!" Chris said becoming animated.

"Randy and Craig both had good alibis and were not suspects. They just seemed to be holding something back!" Chris continued. "Either way, the people that worked with Garrison adored him. That was obvious."

"According to those who share his calendar, he was free and clear of any commitments for the weekend."

"He had cancelled two trips that were coming up. No, we don't know who cancelled them. They were cancelled on time and it was not traceable due to an old doss based reservation system."

Chris continued as Jude followed along and listened to him read down the laundry list.

"He goes to Maynard's for coffee. We stop in and talk to the server who waited on him the day he died. He was upbeat and commented on how much he loved the fall colors. How much he loved this time of the year."

"Yup," Jude replied.

"He had everything to live for. A nice home, plenty of money, a life full of accomplishments, work he loved. What am I missing Jude? He was in good health and spirits. He was not distressed and yet there was not any compelling evidence that there was foul play," Chris asked.

Jude was the one driven to examine all of the details and the motive. Chris on the other hand jumped right into what he thought happened and then looked for the facts to substantiate his gut feeling.

It was unusual for Chris to be taking this much interest this far into the investigation. He was usually checked out by now. Chris liked the simple cases. For some reason Chris was taking this case more personally than usual.

"Chris," Jude commented, "He presumably used a gun that no one knew he had."

Jude continued the analysis of the objective and material matters on the board, "The bullet used came from an inexpensive aluminum cased shell that was made twenty years ago. That could be when Dr. Keller bought the gun."

"The bullet we recovered from the wall was fired from the gun that was in his hand on the desk. The gunshot wound was a through and through. There was gunshot residue on his hand. The laser study concluded that the trajectory angle of the bullet is consistent with a self inflicted wound that was generated from his sitting position," Jude explained.

Chris listened reticently, his head gently moving back and forth in apparent disbelief or disagreement.

"Sure," Chris interrupted. "He could have bought this gun and shells twenty years ago, and he could have become manic overnight, but I think it would be very unlikely."

Chris continued while Jude remained focused on the white board, "Immigration stated he went to Brazil twice in the last year. Did we ever figure out what that was for?"

"He went to Carnival'," Jude replied.

"Wow! That is one hell of a party for an old man," Chris cautioned.

"Who knows why a man his age goes to Brazil for Carnival'? I will say that I don't think it is wise that you assume it to be the same reason that old Englishmen go to Thailand with their buddies," Jude admonished with a smile.

Chris understood the satirical comment and the assumption of deviance that Jude was accusing him of. The point, while difficult, was well taken. Chris moved on.

"If he never leaves the lake in the summer, why did he go back to Brazil for two days in August?"

"Good question. He went alone," Jude replied.

The white board once again became the center of attention for Chris, "He mails his house payment that is due the first of the month five days early. Does that sound like a man that is going to whack himself?"

Jude replied, "It sounds like a responsible man."

"Okay, then, if Mr. Responsible did kill himself, why did he still have the boat in the water and why did he speak of having to take one more sail this weekend? Why would he tell anyone that?"

No response from Jude.

"And then, if he was going to kill himself, and he truly loved to sail, why not take that one last sail first? He never took his final voyage from what we can tell."

Without comment, Jude walked over to stand next to the board as if to get a closer look at the already oversized handwriting.

"Makes no sense to me," Chris continued.

"Jude, can't you see it? Garrison Keller was a man who had something to do, he had work that he loved, people he adored and he had plenty to look forward to. Something to do, something to love and something to look forward to. These are the key elements to any productive and happy life. Why would he commit suicide?"

"Maybe he had *something to love* and not *someone* to love," Jude cautioned.

Chris was impassioned. He was speaking from the heart. He could not believe that someone with so much to do and so much to give would take his own life in such a tragic and demeaning way.

"You just don't decide to kill yourself overnight," Chris continued.

Chris was getting more and more excited. He was now standing next to Jude at the white board waving his hand demonstratively as he continued, "And then …," Chris stuttered nervously, "and then, he goes home and kills himself five days after he was taking steps to keep his life on track while at the same time telling his friends, colleagues and strangers all the things he was looking forward to."

"I suppose you don't think he killed himself," Jude replied jokingly making fun of his passion in a professional manner.

"You damn right I don't. The good Dr. Keller was murdered and I have no idea how to prove that I am right," Chris replied adamantly.

Jude smiled.

71

Chris was searching the board for what he had missed. It had to be here. The only lose end that may have some value appeared to be that second trip to Brazil and anything that Randy or Craig may be holding back.

"What do you think of this Cuda character?" Chris asked of Jude.

"How do you mean?" Jude returned.

"I mean, why was he there? How did he get there so fast?" Chris responded.

"He said that he was already in town and that he was with the Secret Service. Dr. Keller was an important man involved with influential research," Jude replied.

"I get that part. How did he get here so fast? How did the men get here so fast to start emptying out the house before we got here? How did he get the access?" Chris asked.

"I don't know the answer to that Chris," Jude said.

"I don't like him Jude and I don't trust him. He is at the center of my investigation, I can tell you that. Him, Randy and Craig, they are all on my list," Chris continued.

"Are you suggesting we put the United States Secret Service on the white board or should I just put the President of the United States on the board? What do you think?" Jude said in jest, yet understanding that he was serious.

Chris looked at Jude and mulled over a reply. He knew that Jude was joking, at least in part, but Chris was serious. He needed to be careful though. There was not any real evidence here that would be particularly damning to any one. His reputation and the reputation of the department, not to mention the credible legacy of the white board, might be at stake with a flippant entry.

"I don't think that we need to add the entire Secret Service," Chris replied looking over at Jude. "Do you?"

"Are you suggesting that we..."

Chris interrupted, "I am suggesting that Ed Cuda should be considered for the board insofar as he works for the President. He may be considered as a key player or suspect at a later date."

Jude remained calm. In her mind, based on the evidence, there certainly wasn't anything that would even remotely implicate either of these two men. After all, there have been dresses with Presidential D.N.A. on them that have not risen to the level of definitive evidence. What they had in hand was certainly far less compelling.

Jude wanted to be thorough, leave no stone unturned, but she needed to be rationale. She needed to keep Chris and his passion in check.

Jude replied, "I understand that Agent Cuda was in town to review with Dr. Garrison Keller the high profile nature of the research that he was involved in and the high value of the grant money he had oversight for."

"Are you kidding me, Jude?" Chris asked. "Are you out of your blonde skull? Since when is the United States Secret Service involved in grant money research? The Secret Service largely serves to protect the President of the United States and those agents serve at the pleasure of the President."

"I understand," Jude confirmed.

"I don't think you do. Do you know what serving at the pleasure of the President means?"

"That statement is not exactly true," Jude replied, still responding to the first comment that Chris had made. "The Secret Service also investigates counterfeiting and a few other policy issues."

"Serving at the pleasure of the President means that when he says jump, you say how high. It means that the minute that the President has lost respect or confidence in you, for any reason, that you are gone. You are out, man. That's it!"

Jude listened.

"It is just like serving at the pleasure of the Queen. You must do exactly as you are told and you do not ask questions," Chris explained.

"We do not have Kings and Queens here," Jude explained. "It is not like that."

"Whatever, Jude. It's exactly like that. It is policy, protocol and ego." Chris said with a tone that Jude was not familiar with. Chris had overcommitted himself personally to his investigative quest.

Chris was convinced a murder had taken place and he was further convinced that Ed Cuda and maybe the United States government were in on it as well. Unfortunately, for Chris, there were no real, tangible facts to support his theory.

"You are naïve, Jude. Travel the world a bit, you'll see. It's like this in every government. Call it what you like, but every country has power hungry people. In some governments it is just harder to find who is really in charge, that's all."

Jude was an idealist. She disagreed with Chris on almost every account and assumption in this case. There were few facts to support his theory. For starters, you are innocent until proven guilty in America. She did not appreciate the zeal Chris had for convicting Cuda in the court of his personal opinion while at the same time ignoring the evidence before them.

"Don't you think it was odd that Cuda did not offer to help get to the truth Jude?" Chris asked and continued. "He felt he knew what he wanted the truth to be. He was not offering to examine what happened objectively. He knew what he wanted the facts to be. He offered to help bring timely closure to the case and was scooping up the evidence for God knows what reason. Who knows if we even have everything?"

"Given all of the hands that were on the files in his office and the objects removed from the home, we might only be in possession of the things that people want us to have. We may only have ten percent of what was removed. Who knows? The most helpful, most compelling or most damaging information might be in third party hands as we speak," Chris surmised.

"I think your imagination has run wild," Jude responded.

"And like I said Jude, you are naive. You think that your government is above reproach. You think they have *your* best interest in mind. They don't. The government, all governments, serves their own best interests," Chris reminded.

"Explain to me Jude why the maid was sent home?"

"I cannot explain that," Jude replied.

"Explain to me why we were not told that *sent home* meant deported to Mexico. We cannot even speak to her. For all we know, she did it. For all we know, she is also dead."

Jude replied again, "She was illegal!"

"So what? There are illegals all over this city that no one is in any rush to deport. Why deport the one you need to talk to most?"

"I can't explain that either," Jude replied.

"Exactly," Chris concluded.

They were once again at an impasse. They had not written the President or Cuda's name on the white board. Their opinions were not going to come together. The evidence all pointed towards a confirmation of suicide, although there were numerous suspicions that had yet to be resolved. Both knew that it was unlikely that these suspicions would be satisfactorily resolved. The only loose end they had was the purpose of the second trip to Brazil and anything that may be gained from another conversation with Randy and Craig.

Perhaps Chris was right in his approach to cases. He was feeling he had over committed to this particular case. It was not going to get any easier from here. Chris began to be a let down in his level of commitment.

72

The Sheriff came into the room and asked how they were doing, "Good morning," he stated. "Are we making any progress?"

"Not really," Chris said as he backed away from the white board, removed the magic marker from behind his ear and tossed it on the desk.

"It appears to be a suicide," Jude added.

It appears to be a murder, but I do not have clear motive, any evidence or any suspects at this time," Chris commented in defiance of Jude.

Jude smiled.

The Sheriff stood looking at the white board. He scanned it back and forth and spoke concisely. "I have received a lot of calls on this case."

"Is that so?" Chris said, paying half attention.

"Yep. I sure have," The Sheriff continued. "I have gotten calls from people that have no business asking questions and no apparent interest in the outcome other than curiosity."

Chris turned, now with increased interest, "Interesting! Like who?" assuming that someone was perhaps trying to return to the crime scene.

"Well, I have had calls from damn near everyone who is anyone in the federal government. I have had calls from the Speaker of the House of Representatives, the F.B.I., some *smart ass* named Ed Cuda from the Secret Service, and the F.D.A., you name it."

Looking at Jude, "I told you Cuda was still slinking around. What have they asked about?" Chris asked.

"They all seem to want to know the same thing. They all want to know how the investigation is going. They all want to know if it was really a suicide and they all want to know if I have any information on what Dr. Keller was working on."

"Very interesting," Chris said in a drawn out tone.

"What do you conclude from these calls?" Jude asked.

"I conclude that there are a lot of people that have a lot of interest in how this man died and what he was working on and, for whatever reasons, they want to know what I know. They want some sort of validation of cause of death evidence and they want to know if I have any data in discovery in terms of what he is working on."

The Sheriff continued, "I have come in and looked at the board during the last few days and I don't see any clear picture of what happened here either. Well, other than a man who took his own life."

The Sheriff paused.

"Do we have any information in discovery that shows us what he was working on that does not fall into the well-documented programs that the government already has access to?"

"We do not," Chris replied.

"Do we have any evidence that says he didn't kill himself?" the Sheriff asked?

"We do not," Chris replied again. "Well, just this Cuda fella. It sounds like you have spoken to him also. I have a bad feeling about him. The removal of evidence bothers me. The maid that went missing bothers me and Cuda having just been in all the right places bothers me," explained Chris.

"Me too," the Sheriff agreed.

That was exactly what Chris wanted to hear. The Sheriff was seeing things exactly as he was thanks to the white board and the suspicious calls the Sheriff had been receiving. Maybe Chris would put in just a little more effort just to be sure.

"I had to put Cuda and his boss in their place this week," the Sheriff added.

Jude and Chris looked at the Sheriff and waited for additional comment. The Sheriff looked at the white board with greater intent. His back was turned towards Chris and Jude.

Chris and Jude shrugged their shoulders at each other not knowing what the Sheriff had just said. Jude would be the one to clarify the context of the comment.

"Put him and his boss in their place. How do you mean?" asked Chris.

"After denying Agent Cuda information about the case, I can tell you he was very upset to say the least. He wanted to know all of the details of the investigation. After I vetted his credentials, I reached out to him and told him that while I had the updates from the two of you, he would not be getting those updates until we concluded our investigation," the Sheriff clarified.

"Who was his boss that called you?" Chris asked.

'The President of the United States," the Sheriff replied in a matter of fact manner.

"Whoa! Are you sure it was him?" Chris asked.

"Oh, I am sure it was him alright. He asked a lot of the same questions and I gave him the same answers. He was slightly less pleased than Mr. Cuda was," the Sheriff replied.

"You told the President of the United States to go fish?" Chris asked.

"No, I told him that we were conducting an investigation. The information was confidential at this time. I explained that we had a cause of death, but there were unresolved issues related to motive and suspicions about whether it was a suicide or not. It was at that point that he demanded answers and started telling me who he was, who elected him, who paid my salary."

"I cannot believe the President called you!" Jude exclaimed.

"I know. It was the damndest thing," the Sheriff replied laughing.

"I couldn't tell him the facts of the investigation. It just would not be right at this point. Quite frankly, based on what I have seen on the white board and read in your notes, I am surprised that you don't have Cuda on the board by now. Seems like it is at least possible that he may be involved here in some way and if, and I mean if, there is foul play."

Chris looked at Jude with a grin that stretched from New York to Los Angeles. Jude shook her head in disbelief, but shared a smile in return.

Chris was so thrilled with the Sheriff's response he could hardly stand it. He was obviously eager to hear how the Sheriff had handled the President on the phone.

"So what did you tell the President?" Chris asked as he sat down to get comfortable and enjoy the storyline.

The Sheriff turned and faced the two detectives.

"After the badgering I took, I told him nothing about the case. What I did tell him was I had taken an oath of office. An oath I took to uphold and defend, preserve and protect the Constitution of the United States of America."

"No kidding!" Chris exclaimed giddy with equal parts of respect and anticipation.

"I reminded the President that this was the same oath he took and the same oath he expects our soldiers to take at home and abroad.

"I further explained that the Sheriff has the ultimate authority in his jurisdiction and not even he, as President, could tell me what to do within the confines of statute application in this county," the Sheriff stated with pride.

Jude commented, "This is what I started to tell you about earlier Chris."

"Tell me more," Chris requested, eager to hear more.

"It is pretty simple really. The Tenth Amendment fundamentally says, in Article One, Section Eight, what the powers of government are reserved for. This section tells the bureaucracy what they can and cannot do. Basically the Tenth Amendment says, that if we forgot anything, you probably should not do that either. The power needs to be left to the States. It is our *police power* of the States."

"Of course, as a lawyer himself, the President did not want to hear my thoughts on constitutional law. After some more name dropping and threats, I explained that as far as I was concerned the Sheriff is the most powerful person in the United States and the Sheriff has the ultimate power and authority in his county. No one can displace the Sheriff's power, not even the President," the sheriff instructed.

"Is that true?" Chris asked while Jude stood nodding her head affirmatively.

"It is true for the most part. The Sheriff's discretion is very broad. There is legal precedence, especially when there is national security involved. There is case history on the matter, not that he knew that," Jude replied.

"The civics lesson here is that state legislators have to enact hurdles against the Federal Government. The Tenth Amendment is a constructive protection against any violation or corruption against personal freedom," the Sheriff concluded.

"I suggest you and Jude continue to work this case for a few more weeks. See what you can dig up on Cuda and take another swing at Randy and Craig."

"Excellent!" Chris responded. "We don't have a lot to go on, I know. We need to tie up a few loose ends. I do not know where it will lead us, maybe nowhere, but we appreciate the latitude you are giving us to get the job done."

"The truth is never wrong, right Jude?" the Sheriff asked.

"Yes, sir."

Time will tell if this added time and interest will prove beneficial.

CHAPTER ELEVEN
THE GOVERNMENT'S RESOLVE

73

There was a lot of tension at the Strategic Planning Commission Offices in Washington. Summer was coming to a close, mid-term elections were right around the corner and the economy was not improving. The ambitious new President was not bringing closure to his health care reform. His ambitious political agenda was stagnating and lacking movement. The country was becoming increasingly frustrated.

There was not any real expectation of the economy catapulting into a full blown recovery in the short term and there were many culturally divided issues that had to be resolved legislatively. Not the least of which was the broad-based heath care reform Hoard and Cuda needed to have this term to support their plans.

Compounding the complications brought on by the up-coming elections was some field intelligence information that was coming directly to Alan Hoard. Hoard, at his own request, was getting a direct feed from some of his agents in the field on an issue that was becoming increasingly more disconcerting.

At issue was a researcher that had potentially become a rogue disciple searching for the cure of soft tissue cancers. It was Dr. Garrison Keller. Hoard knew he could not be underestimated. He was a veteran researcher.

Dr. Keller was already being followed closely due to the unfavorable visit from Cuda weeks earlier. Now, separate and unrelated, he is getting independent feedback indicating undesired and unaffordable behavior from Dr. Keller. He was attempting to advance a cure for cancer. Worse yet, his actions would put his discovery at risk of becoming public.

Dr. Keller appeared to be on a mission of mercy. A mission he had undertaken personally to advance some of his own research in an unapproved environment and by using his own personal means to do so.

The information that was coming in locally regarding Dr. Keller's work appeared to be in order. At least what information Hoard could get his hands on, appeared in order.

There were numerous inconsistencies when it came to the recorded treatment of a few patients. In the case of one young boy in particular, the treatment, the predictable outcome, and the results achieved, did not correlate.

There were several cases where the application of the treatment in a patient's chart that did not match the patient needs and certainly had a very favorable outcome.

On a separate, but related note, the President was not ramming the health care legislation through Congress as he had agreed to do. It was making Cuda look bad and gave the impression the President was stalling.

This was a huge financial crisis in the making for the fiscal outlook of the United States in the intermediate and long-term. The stars may not align in a congressional fashion like this again for decades. There was an urgent need, even if it meant cramming legislation down the opposition's throat, to get this universal one payer system of health care passed. There had to be caps placed on how much care would be given to whom, and for how long.

The issue of managed *mortality based on cost effective returns* had now become a two front war for Alan and The Strategic Planning Commission. On the eastern legislative front, there was the legislation that needed to get passed. On the western front, he now had to deal with a scientist that may have developed a treatment that could add decades to human life.

On the legislative front, what Hoard had assumed would be a slam dunk was now taking longer to execute and there were too many compromises being made. The President was not getting the job done.

On the research front, Hoard needed all age advancing research stopped, regardless of how much it cost in public opinion equity. This was a true crossroads.

Hoard was concerned to the point that he summoned Cuda back to his office to discuss both Dr. Keller and the President specifically. Looking toward his future role in the organization, Cuda wasted no time getting to Hoard's office.

74

"Good morning, Alan," Cuda recited as he entered Hoard's office, walking right past Hoard's assistant and into the open office. Alan's assistant was expecting Cuda's arrival and gave a cordial and accepting wave as he entered.

Hoard was all business.

"What have you done to follow up with your initial visit with the President on this damn health care initiative?" Hoard asked.

"Nothing," Cuda replied.

"And just why the hell not?" Hoard demanded.

"I have been following the bill as it takes its course and it appears to be on the road to Committee. The President understands what needs to be done," Cuda replied.

"The President doesn't understand spit. He has people in his own party putting up road blocks. He will want to go ahead with what *he* committed to when he was on the campaign trail. He doesn't care about what you told him unless you reinforce it."

Hoard continued, "Presidents get elected by giving people the run around. This President is that way, the last President was that way and the next President will be that way. Every President since Kennedy has had to be made to understand the *why* in our plans."

"What are you saying?" Cuda asked.

'Read into it what you wish," Hoard replied.

"What do you mean reinforce it?" Cuda again questioned.

"What the hell is your problem? Why are you being so ignorant? Perhaps I have overestimated your ability to make things happen around here Cuda. I thought you are a man of action. Do I have to spell things out for you?"

"No, Sir," Cuda barked back.

"Then get your ass over to see the President and tell him he needs to bring some closure to this health care legislation or else," Hoard ordered.

Hoard was obviously upset. He prided himself on managing a controlled and well thought out master plan. Things had a way of falling into place for Hoard. This situation had the appearance of getting out of control.

Cuda expressed some concern, "The only obstacle I see is the ability to get this forced through a strict party line vote and the issues revolving around the constitutionality and the costs of forcing a single payer plan on people. This may be a stumbling block we need to find our way around."

"We will manage the constitutionality after the fact. Don't come in here and talk to me about stumbling blocks," Hoard returned. "The *we* we are referring to is the President. He is the President of the United States for Christ's sake. He has to find a way through that. This is junior league stuff."

"Do you feel like the situation is out of control?" Cuda asked.

"The only time I feel like things are out of control is when they *are*. That being said, you tell me."

Cuda stared down at the floor. Hoard was right. He had missed a great opportunity to follow up.

Hoard continued, "What I am telling you is that there are ways to get things done in this town and there are ways to just spin your wheels. For those who think that it will be unconstitutional to require them to carry the single payer plan, we will simply price and regulate the private sector out of business.

"Regarding the costs, the cost benefit will only show up if you look at the long term Congressional Budget Office (C.B.O.) analysis. No one is looking that far out. When we eliminate the low return testing and maintenance for those with a low likelihood of survival, only then will you see the big savings. It will cost more in the short term, but in the long term the C.B.O. numbers I have seen are staggeringly favorable," Hoard instructed.

"Besides, this government will tax the hell out of everything anyway. They will make up for excess costs there too."

Hoard took a moment and reflected, "What did I read? They want to add a value added federal tax in addition to the sales tax, income tax, property tax and whatever other buckets are already out there. Plus, through their new "Czar" regulatory body, they are even proposing a tax on soda pop."

"Seems ridiculous," Cuda indifferently added to the conversation. "Not my idea. I am trying to address the spending side."

"The net of this is that the health care reform legislation needs to get passed and we need the single payer system. There are too many company plans popping up addressing health care gaps in the proposed legislation and we need to get our arms around it starting right now. If that means by way of an unfair competitive advantage in the governments favor, then so be it. No privatization," Hoard reprimanded.

Hoard looked at the papers on his desk. There was quiet in the room for the moment as both men knew what their respective roles would demand of them.

"There is no other way Cuda," Hoard said, putting down his paperwork. "This plan will be funded by slashing Medicare and slashing research for new drugs. No doubt about it."

"We will start letting people die of the disease rather than the treatment," Cuda responded.

"Exactly! Can you handle this assignment Cuda?" asked Hoard.

"Yes, sir," Cuda confirmed as he got up from his chair.

"Sit down!" Hoard exclaimed adamantly. "I will tell you when you are excused. There are other items on your list. Other issues, that I might add, you have not managed very well either."

Cuda was getting a full force reprimand. Hoard was not happy to have to intercede into these matters at an operations level. Hoard was the equivalent of the CEO of this organization. He was not expecting to dole out specific responsibilities. It was his role to lay out the objectives. It was his role to see that things got accomplished and hold people accountable. It was not his role to execute the tactics which would lead to getting the strategy accomplished.

Cuda dropped back into his chair as if his legs had been cut out from under him.

"I will finish with my comments on the President first," Hoard called out.

"You have to understand the President owes the unions and the associations a lot. He has been, and will be, under a great deal of pressure. He will want to be serving many masters. He may not understand the financial objectives of this government are the sole and most important ones that matter right now."

Cuda listened studiously.

"You can help the President through this with careful coaching," Hoard contemplated.

"What do you recommend?" Cuda asked.

"We can help him with both the unions and one association in particular," Hoard began.

"Go on," Cuda took note.

"Through his influence, the President will be able to see that the screen door is left open to unionize the health care program to almost one hundred percent in a single payer system," Hoard concluded.

Cuda removed a small note book from his shirt pocket and began to write.

"What the hell are you writing?" Hoard asked.

"I am taking notes on what you are asking me to do," Cuda responded.

"I am going to tell you three things. You cannot remember three things?" Hoard snapped.

"I can," Cuda replied.

"The last thing we need to have happen is to have some "Heidi Fleiss" set of notes show up for someone to read. Keep it in your head Cuda for Christ's sake. You're no rookie at this," Hoard explained.

"Yes, Sir," Cuda spouted.

"That should take care of the unions for now. Greedy bastards! They'll be back," Hoard continued on with his strategic thinking. "Secondly, the associations are formidable opponents."

"They are indeed," Cuda agreed.

"I have given this some serious thought. We will have to start a bit of a scandal. I love good scandal, Don't you?" Hoard asked of Cuda.

"I do," Cuda responded with a tense smile.

"This will be a scandal the President will actually appreciate and get some relief from," Hoard advised.

"Okay," Cuda replied anticipating the plan.

"I have come up with a scandalous plot that just may virtually eliminate the need for an association post election pay back," Hoard explained.

"How do you plan to do that?" Cuda asked continuing to show a grin of premature appreciation and anticipation.

"Why is it that I am doing all of the thinking Cuda? I thought you would have gotten some of this strategizing done for me," Hoard said sternly as he continued to admonish Cuda.

"It was not my intent to disappoint," Cuda responded.

"Don't come in here expecting relief by offering some sappy sympathetic whimpering about intent and disappointment. You need to be the one who gets things done."

"I understand," Cuda replied.

"I thought you *understood* last time you were in here. I don't want to have to go through the need for urgency and action with you again. You have to make things happen. I cannot and will not spend my time holding your hand," Hoard instructed.

"I understand," Cuda forcefully replied.

Hoard took pause for a moment and concentrated his attention on Cuda. He was not sure, not to an absolute certainty, if Cuda was going to be able to get the job done on his own. Surely, there was no doubt that Cuda had been a competent asset and a loyal servant to the organization for many years. But could he make the leap from being a good field agent who was able to execute the strategy to the person who was making the strategy and holding others accountable for the end result. It was a time of growing pains for Cuda.

On the other side of the desk, Cuda was determined, at all cost, not to disappoint Hoard again. He would take matters into his own hands and make sure that Hoard knew he was effective. He would now take the approach that he would make decisions as he saw fit and ask for forgiveness rather than come to Hoard and ask for permission. Worse yet, he would not be accused of not taking action.

Hoard shared the strategy regarding the association, "I have arranged for a couple of junior journalists to take a run at creating a documentary, an expose', of some shady transactions by the association. The two of them will take a hidden camera into a couple of their offices and provoke some controversy."

"Do you think we will get some damning information?" Cuda asked.

"Of course, I think we will get some damaging information. I would not be doing it if I did not think there was opportunity. It should not be hard to find shady dealings in this or any of the other nationalized pro-pet project activist groups. Their loyalty is to the cause, not to what is right or wrong. We will expose and broadcast whatever negativity we find and the need for any payback will evaporate. You can tell the President our plan."

Cuda questioned, "If I tell him, he may attempt to stop it."

"He will appreciate the relief, believe me. Anyway, with the news media, particularly *FOX News* station, he will not be able to stop it once we leak the videos," Hoard said.

"Do you have the people in mind?" asked Cuda.

"Like I said, it is already arranged. It may be taking place as we speak, so the clock is ticking."

Cuda was absorbing the information. He wanted desperately to write things down so that he would not forget anything.

"That was subject one. Are you ready for subject two?" Hoard asked.

"I am," Cuda replied.

"You have to get over to the F.D.A.," Hoard began. "I need you to follow up on the Oncology Drug Advisory Committee (O.D.A.C.) meeting that happened this week. I have set you up to meet with the committee director today at 3:00 p.m.. They are getting together again tomorrow. There are several new chemotherapy agents that are coming up for approval and I want all three of them shut down."

"On what grounds?" Cuda asked.

"On what grounds?" Hoard asked defiantly. "because you said so! What do you think the grounds would be?"

Cuda reflected on Hoard's words.

"On the usual grounds!" he continued."Too toxic! Not effective enough! I don't give a damn what grounds you choose to use to justify the action; just make it happen."

"Is there an even trade we can offer?" Cuda asked passively.

Hoard continued to be annoyed by the context of the questions. Cuda was supposed to be the one to think through the actions needed to fulfill the objectives set by him.

Hoard thought through his response for a moment. Would this be a pivotal learning moment in Cuda's professional growth or would this be that watershed moment where Hoard decided that Cuda, while good at what he did, was not capable of taking his career to the next step.

"There are no even trades in life that are truly even Cuda. These are the worst of times. The financial issues before us need to be leveraged in our favor with the perceptive slant favoring an even trade. We need to make these drugs appear to be unfavorable and the director needs to write it up that way. You need to make certain of it. Is that clear?" directed Hoard.

"Clear," Cuda replied.

"Good," Alan continued. "Drug companies will not spend research monies on products that will not be brought to market, condoned by the medical profession and supported by health care providers. Wall Street will not allow it. From our perspective on this issue, control the research and you control the patient."

"Got it," said Cuda.

"Control the patient treatment, particularly among the young, old, especially those on legacy programs, and you control the budget."

"Got it," Cuda replied in agreement a second time.

"Perfect. Are we ready for subject three?" Hoard asked.

"I am," Cuda repeated.

"Are you sure you can keep all this in your head?" Hoard asked sensing that Cuda would be much more comfortable if he were allowed to write things down.

"I have to be," Cuda replied.

"Exactly right!" Hoard replied. "The third issue ties into the last subject regarding the O.D.A.C."

"Okay," Cuda responded.

"More specifically, it deals with Dr. Garrison Keller."

"Dr. Garrison Keller? I have spoken to Dr. Keller," Cuda advised.

"I know you have. I had read your brief. After reading that brief I took the liberty of putting a couple of my other agents on Dr. Keller and tasked them with seeing what exactly he was up to these days," Hoard informed.

"Agents other than me?" asked Cuda.

Now was a good time for Hoard to leverage his agency and the people in it. He was unsure as to what the true capabilities and career boundaries were for Cuda. Hoard was about to make the stakes a lot higher and at the same time create an additional degree of separation between him and the master plan.

"You have been disappointing me lately, Cuda. I needed to take some of your responsibilities and give them to others," Hoard instructed.

"I can handle Dr. Keller," Cuda reassured.

"Can you? Do you really think that?" asked Hoard.

"I can. I don't trust him, but I can handle him. You have to believe me Hoard. Tell me the assignment and I will get the job done," Cuda assured him.

Hoard replied with careful thought as he worked a self-serving and objectively targeted strategy, "I will tell you the end result; the overall objective. You will need to determine the tactics on how to get there.

"Okay, fine, either way. I can handle it," Cuda assured his boss once again.

"You will have to," Hoard advised. "There is a lot depending on your actions."

Hoard gave pause for a moment and continued, "There is a mountain of circumstantial evidence that implies that Dr. Keller is operating outside of the bounds of what has been approved for cancer treatment in this country. In addition, some feel he may even have developed a cure for soft tissue disease."

"That would really complicate matters," said Cuda.

Hoard continued, "Yes, it would. If a case for a cure is being made, we cannot allow him to further develop it or allow him to get to a point where he shares his findings and results with his colleagues here or his colleagues abroad."

"I have not come across any colleagues abroad," Cuda replied.

"Well, he has gone to Brazil at least once this year that we know of. What was that for?" asked Hoard.

"I don't know why yet, but I have been asking," Cuda replied.

"It is your job to know why," Hoard bellowed. "You will need to meet with Dr. Keller again and step up the pressure. I have very good reason to believe the accounting of his activity is true. He cannot be allowed to continue."

"I know he was treating a Brazilian boy. Are there others?" Hoard asked.

"We are not sure exactly," Cuda answered.

"Again, it is your job to know the answer to these questions. I just know that we cannot afford a ten-year favorable impact on mortality," Hoard replied.

"I understand," Cuda again stated.

"Do you? Do you understand this time?" Hoard asked.

"I think I do this time," Cuda returned.

Hoard continued on with a brief history lesson as support for his critical position, "When social security was created by Roosevelt there were twenty people paying in for every one receiving benefits. At that time, the average life expectancy was sixty-four years of age."

"I know. Times have changed dramatically," Cuda responded.

"Now, there are four people paying in for every person getting benefits and the average life span is well into the eighties," Hoard instructed.

"I understand we cannot afford the legacy benefits any longer and I understand why," Cuda reassured him.

Hoard added, "And in the midst of all of this financial turmoil, economic unpredictability, health care debate and not to mention an international instability crisis in the Middle East, the Chinese are suggesting that they may want loan guarantees for the three-trillion dollars in federal securities we currently owe them."

"Wanting is one thing, that doesn't mean they will get them," Cuda added.

Hoard nodded affirmatively with a grin, "True."

Cuda smiled and continued by trying to make a joke of it, "I would recommend we give them Michigan if they want loan guarantees. Perhaps they will do a better job there with the auto industry and the economy than our people have over the last twenty years."

Hoard did find a moment of humor in what had been a very serious conversation, "That's funny! Good one Cuda. Good one! The world has come a long way *Mr. Cuda* since the Chinese invented gun powder. They have loaned a lot of money to us. It was risk capital that they sent over here. The United States has been a low risk venture over the last one hundred years. It will be an even lower risk once this health care initiative is passed. We owe them nothing."

Cuda gave summary, "I will get over to O.D.A.C. for the 3:00 p.m. meeting today. The President is in town and I will get in to see him tomorrow morning early. I can make that happen."

"Good, and Dr. Keller?" Hoard asked. "My source says he is in Minneapolis all week."

"I should be able to see the President in the morning tomorrow so I will book a flight out tomorrow afternoon and see Dr. Keller this week. I will find him and we will talk. I will get to the bottom of what he is doing."

"I know he was treating the boy. Do you have a disposition on the boy?" Cuda asked.

Hoard replied with indifference, "From what I understand, the boy is being treated for some disease that was not thought to be curable at his late stage, but he is making a miraculous recovery. The damage done by treating this boy for his ills, however critical, is inconsequential to the damage that may be done if the treatment theory expands. Let the care play out...he may not survive anyway."

"That was my thinking and what I relayed the last time I spoke to Dr. Keller. The boy is an American citizen," Cuda added.

"He sure is, but the boy has already been undergoing treatment. The issue now is with Dr. Keller. The boy himself cannot do us any harm now. He does not know how or with what he was treated?"

"Sure," Cuda replied.

"Now you may be excused," said Hoard in a dismissing manner.

Cuda got up slowly.

"Be assured, I will not disappoint you again Hoard," Cuda advised.

"I know you will not disappoint on purpose, but I will tell you Cuda, I have double covered myself here," Hoard replied.

Cuda looked confused. "How so?"

"Like I said, you are not the only agent I have on this case. I am getting information from several sources and have a back up plan in place just in case you cannot complete the task."

"You won't need a back up plan for me Alan. I can get the job done," Cuda assured him.

"I always need a back up plan. You would be well served to always have one also," Hoard grinned.

75

Alan Hoard was not a man without a plan. He was notorious for covering and double covering himself. He had to deal from a position of strength in the complex and ever evolving role he had. This was a winner take all game and he was out to win on behalf of the country as a whole, albeit from strictly an actuarial standpoint. Money was not everything to Alan, but on the job, as the saying goes, it was the only thing.

Hoard's mind could not compare things sympathetically. A mother suffering during the loss of a son with a terminal disease had a value. The hip replacement in an elderly woman had a value. A prematurely born infant had a value. Each situation could be compared in and of themselves to the value associated with the contribution in the coming years divided by the sum of the cost of their survival and their current age.

There had to be a benefit to investing in their continued existence and that benefit had to be in the governments favor. Period! No personal exceptions would be heard based on emotion.

Through Hoard's eyes, you had to see things as part of a comparative advantage. Hoard was; therefore, perfect for his role. There is no such thing as an even trade. Not anywhere in the world. For any transaction to take place, even the transgressions of government, both parties need to feel like they are getting some gain for themselves. This was a perception in the public eye that Hoard had orchestrated and mastered over the years.

However, given the number of issues at play in this very complex set of circumstances, this particular subset was more worrisome. If a cure was found, if single payer control was not achieved, the results would be catastrophic.

"Who are the other agents assigned to the job," Cuda wondered.

"I don't think that is in my best interest to tell you," Hoard snarled.

"Okay," Cuda countered."I will see Dr. Keller no later than the day after tomorrow."

"Excellent," Hoard replied pleased with his direction. "I will expect to hear from you after you have met with the President and spoken to Dr. Keller. If you are traveling tomorrow and seeing Dr. Keller the day after, I expect to see you back here in this office with an up-date within the week. Set up an appointment with my assistant. I am looking forward to hearing back from you."

"Yes, Sir," Cuda repeated.

Cuda made his way to the door and opened it.

"Cuda," Hoard called out.

Cuda turned, door handle in hand and looked back at Hoard.

"I am watching you closely. I am expecting great things from you. Do not disappoint me on this one. Time is of the essence," Hoard instructed.

Cuda continued to look back at Hoard.

"The President needs to take action and Dr. Keller needs to be stopped from developing a cure for anything, any illness, which we have not calculated into the plan," Hoard concluded.

"Yes, Sir. I do understand. You can count on me," Cuda replied.

"My thanks in advance," Hoard replied.

Cuda faced the door as if he was exiting and stopped short of actually leaving the room, turning back to Hoard with another question, "Alan," Cuda queried.

"Yes," said Hoard.

"What do I tell Dr. Keller when he asks how we can consider this course of action an act of protecting the people when we are holding back the course of the research?" Cuda asked.

"You tell him that we are improving the quality of the lives while they are here and not prolonging the lives of those who have a substandard quality of life to live," Hoard responded.

"I see," Cuda acknowledged.

"Listen to me Cuda. In our current state of affairs we have a nation that is divided by healthcare. In due time, we will create a healthcare system that is divided out to a nation," Hoard advised.

"I see," Cuda again acknowledged.

"I do not expect Dr. Garrison Keller to understand the objectives we have and the end results we expect. I just expect him to abide by the rules or face the consequences," Hoard added.

"Yes, Sir," Cuda repeated.

If nothing else, Cuda is an uncharacteristically respectful man when he was in Alan Hoard's office. One would suspect that this is probably two parts respect for the power Hoard wielded and one part ass kissing because he wanted Alan's job so bad he could taste it.

One thing was clear to Cuda, he had to get the job done or Hoard would have someone in place to do it for him. The question in Cuda's mind was the timetable. When would he have to prove definitively that he had handled Hoard's request. Vague and noncommittal, in a manner that did not implicate Hoard in any wrong doing, Cuda had to get the job done.

Looking back, he had already threatened the President of the United States in his own oval office. How hard would it be to manage the outcome of Dr. Garrison Keller's research?

Hoard sat solemnly at his desk quite literally twiddling his thumbs as Cuda walked out of his office and closed the door behind him. He painstakingly considered the future that Cuda might have in the organization and if he was up for the task at hand.

In the end, concerning Dr. Keller and the President of the United States, Hoard had set himself up quite nicely. Time was marching on and the end result was all but pre-determined at this point. All Hoard had to do was fill in the names of who executed what directive.

CHAPTER TWELVE
INVESTIGATION WITHOUT PROGRESS

76

Weeks had passed since the Sheriff encouraged Chris and Jude to continue the investigation. Chris was once again searching the white board for what he had missed. The answer had to be here somewhere. There wasn't one lead that had panned out since the Sheriff's interjection. The only thing he knew for sure was the fact that Dr. Keller was dead and there was no doubt about that. The question was why did he die and by whose hand? If he could determine why he died, he could then start piecing together who had killed him.

He had gone back and spoken to Randy and Craig. There were no new developments there. The two office colleagues were very tight lipped. His attempts at speaking to Ed Cuda were equally unsuccessful. Cuda simply said he began an investigation and subsequently turned over all of his information to the Sheriff's department.

The only lose end that may have some real value appeared to be that trip Garrison took to Brazil only days earlier. Why did he return to Brazil?

There was a boy from Brazil he had been treating named Rigo. Rigo had already been returned to his mother in Brazil after completing his regimen of treatment. He was disease free and had gained enough weight to be height and weight proportionate for a child his age. Could seeing Rigo have been worthy of another short notice and brief trip to Brazil?

Chris and Jude had both agreed earlier in the day on one point. Randy and Craig were likely holding back pertinent information. What they could not agree on was whether the two of them were holding back to cover for their boss or were they holding back because they were somehow associated, one or both, with Dr. Keller's death.

Chris could just not seem to let go of his obsession with Cuda. No matter how unlikely a suspect, Chris was compelled to following his instinct.

The fact remained, Cuda was an agent of the United States government after all and his credentials checked out. He was indeed a Special Liaison to the President himself, but how did he fit into the big picture of all of this? That question was still a mystery.

Exactly how did he arrive at the crime scene so fast on the day that Garrison was discovered dead in his home? Why did the Sheriff have to pull rank to take over the investigation when it should have been a county crime scene to start with?

Clearly, it was the Sheriff's jurisdiction. Was evidence removed intentionally, that has now gone missing, from Dr. Keller's home by Cuda or by Cuda's agents before Chris and Jude arrived at the crime scene? If so, what evidence was removed?

The review of the numerous boxes of evidence logged into the county that night eventually resulted in no useful information whatsoever.

Chris scanned the white board in solitude. He recalled Dr. Keller's office at the University being intact other than a damaged laptop that he understood was dropped in the lake. Testing of the laptop; however, did not show any biological marine material on it? Maybe it did not fall in the lake at all, he thought. Maybe he said it fell in the lake because it sounded less careless than spilling a glass of water on it.

Nan and Craig had written statements suggesting there was some unauthorized intrusion into their office computers, but they could not say what, if anything at all, was missing.

It would be nearly impossible to merge and reconcile the variance between their remaining saved work products with the body of work on the University main frame to look for missing data. That would be like reconciling the internet looking for missing information.

Even if there was missing information on the office computers and assuming the laptop was damaged intentionally, he still was missing a motive that could potentially lead him to a prospective suspect. What was he looking for exactly?

He threw his marker at the white board in frustration. The marker crashed and fractured before it fell harmlessly to the floor in front of the white board that had served him so well in the past. The case had gone cold and there were increasing demands, even from the Sheriff, to either produce some new evidence, or close out the case on the intrinsic worth of what it appeared to be, a *suicide*.

Looking intently at the white board, he thought to himself. Well, of course, there was the possibility that Dr. Keller's death was in fact a suicide after all. It was unlikely in his professional opinion that Dr. Keller would have pulled the trigger himself, but he certainly could have. It would not be the first time that someone who had everything to live for decided to put an end to their life by their own hand.

Jude entered the room carrying a fresh cup of coffee, "Here, I brought this for you."

"Thanks," Chris said.

"I know you are frustrated Chris, but there is just no place else to look. We have spent months on this case and have not turned up anything new in weeks," Jude said.

"That exact point is what is so aggravating," Chris replied. "There is always some place else to look. Everybody loved this guy. He had money and fame. He had everything to live for and he just gets up one day and shoots himself in the head?"

"Everybody we have spoken to loved him," Chris advised.

"Everyone, but Cuda," Jude replied.

"He loved him too if you take his words at face value. He just did not happen to know him from what I can figure out. It sounds like he might have been at the hospital from what I can tell. But from the statements I have from Craig and Randy, other than a visit or two, he was not acquainted with Dr. Keller."

Jude was indulging Chris. She was a good friend and a good listener. She didn't think there was much more to be gained from continuing to pursue the increasingly smaller list of dead ends. She knew he was exasperated with the stagnation of the case, but wanted to hear him out. By doing so, closure would be sooner than later.

Chris continued, "Still, if Cuda didn't like him, why didn't he like him? It's not like the President is going to send an agent to Minnesota to kill some researcher."

Jude thought for a moment, "Yea, I suppose not. The President seems to have plenty on his plate right now. A University researcher would seem an unlikely target."

Jude smiled.

"You're toying with me again," Chris confided.

"No, I am listening and hoping that we make some new progress Chris. I just don't see it. I think it is time to hang it up. The guy took his own life. We can work this case well into retirement and still not get one single new lead."

Chris was getting ready to give it up. He had insisted on being unusually spirited and unusually energetic with this case. He did not like Cuda and there was surely more information to be gotten somewhere. He knew it. He had been determined to keep looking, but it appears, not being good at or interested in cold cases to begin with. Enough is enough.

"Jude," Chris said seriously, "I am not ready to close this case yet, but I will. There is more here but I am not the one to keep looking for it. Someone will find it, it just won't be me."

"I know. That's fine Chris. I understand. You tell me when you are satisfied. Tell me when you are ready. I will support you until then," Jude encouraged Chris.

"Thank you, Jude. You are a good partner," responded Chris.

"No, I am a great partner and don't you forget it!" corrected Jude.

CHAPTER THIRTEEN
THE CONSEQUENCE PHASE

77

The meeting at the Director of the Oncology Drug Advisory Committee

Cuda made good time traveling by cab across town to the F.D.A. offices from Hoard's office. It was at the F.D.A. headquarters where he was to meet with the Director of the Oncology Drug Advisory Committee (O.D.A.C.). The Director and his assistant were expecting Cuda as Hoard had already arranged for the conference. It was 3:00 p.m.

Cuda entered the O.D.A.C. facility and went straight to the Director's office.

"Good afternoon," welcomed the pretty young woman cordially as he entered the Director's reception area.

Cuda walked up to the reception desk and locked into an intimidating eyeball-to-eyeball stare down with the young woman behind the counter.

"My name is Ed Cuda. I have a 3:00 p.m. appointment with the Director," Cuda replied abruptly, assuming he would save time as he bypassed the pleasantries.

Cuda had little time to spare in the next couple days. He had a meeting planned with the President in the morning, an afternoon flight to catch tomorrow, a surprise meeting with Dr. Keller the next day and then a flight back to Washington to debrief his boss. It would be an intense couple of days and there would not be time for any unproductive distractions.

"He will be with you in just a few minutes," the young woman said nicely, calmly.

"He will be with me now!" Cuda shouted.

"I have an appointment at 3:00 sharp and he will see me at 3:00! If he is busy with someone else, tell him he has a bigger name on another line," Cuda said abruptly in a resonating and impatient, controlling, yet matter of fact, voice.

Cuda was obviously succumbing to the pressure and was expressing it by the means he knew best. Belittling and breaking down the people who were in his line of fire.

The young woman was speechless. She looked at Cuda and did not say a word.

"Hey, lady! Are you deaf?" he said as he snapped his fingers in front of her face. "Do I need to go and buy you a watch or what? It is 3:00. Don't just sit there and look at me. Take me to him or go get him and bring him to me, but by all means, get up and do something."

Never taking her eyes off of Cuda, still focused on each other eye-to-eye, the woman rose from her seat slowly.

The Director assumed that he, Cuda, and his assistant would all be present at the meeting today. He and his assistant were running a little late as they took extra time to see that the meeting room was properly set. They felt they really needed to give a great impression today. Hoard told the Director the nature of the meeting and the Director had prepared a case for the research they had been doing. Hoard failed to tell him the outcome was pre-determined. In addition, little did they know, Cuda could care less about what they had to say or how perfectly they had intended to prepare!

"Follow me," the young woman said as she started down the short hallway to the meeting room where the Director and his assistant were putting the finishing touches on the appearance of the room.

Entering the meeting room, the young woman said, "The gentleman said that he has a 3:00 p.m. appointment and was adamant that I bring him back to you immediately," the young woman advised.

"Thank you," the Director said kindly to the young woman, feebly trying to disguise his surprise. The young woman quickly departed the room to return to the reception area.

The accommodations were arranged neatly and meticulously set for three. There was water, coffee, scones, pen and paper at each seat as well as a tasteful arrangement of fresh flowers all smartly placed on the oversized round table. It seemed that every attempt at salesmanship and hospitality was being played out by the Director.

"Good afternoon," the Director greeted. "My name is…"

Cuda interrupted, "I know who you are. Sit down. We do not need to waste time with introductions. I won't be here very long," Cuda ordered.

"Excuse me," the Director said.

"Let's get down to business," Cuda replied as he sat down in the chair and pushed the note pad aside.

The Director and his assistant were still standing. Both looked at each other in disbelief as they watched Cuda pour himself a glass of water and reach for a scone.

"Please, sit," Cuda ordered again.

"Can I introduce you to my assistant?" the Director asked.

Cuda looked up at the Director and then at his assistant. She appeared over dressed for the occasion. The assistant had mistakenly assumed that *dressing for success* in anticipation of the meeting would be beneficial.

The miscalculation was two fold. First, her semi-formal attire was too dramatic for the setting. Secondly, she was dressed as if she was going out clubbing. For a middle-aged woman, she had misjudged how well she looked in suggestive clothing and she definitely underestimated the indifference of her audience.

Cuda reflected for a moment. He wanted to be sure that what he was about to say was appropriate for the setting and the tone he intended to set. He needed to have the right people in the room for the short meeting that was about to take place.

"An introduction is not necessary," Cuda said as he took a bite from his scone. With his mouth still full and looking directly at the assistant, in his usual arrogant fashion, he continued, "You can tell your *fly girl* she is excused."

"That's enough. You will not come in here and speak to my employees in this manner," the Director blurted out, astonished by the ill-mannered behavior Cuda displayed.

Cuda set down his scone and took another drink or water to clear his pallet. He knew he had deliberately decided to be disrespectful. He waited patiently for a moment to see if there was anything else that the Director had to add.

"You're right," Cuda replied. "My apologies, Ma'am. Please close the door behind you on your way out."

The assistant was all too eager to leave the meeting room which seemed to grow smaller with every word that was spoken. The Director and Cuda were alone as the door closed behind the Director's assistant.

Cuda again began to pick confidently at his scone, never taking his eyes off the light snack as he nibbled. The discomfort the Director was feeling was obvious. The room was silent, if only for a moment.

"I came here to review the numerous chemotherapy agents that you and your committee team are considering for approval," Cuda stated.

"That is correct. They offer great promise and we should be able to fast track them to market given the favorable results they have shown to date," the Director instructed with pride of accomplishment.

"Is that so? The information that the balance of the F.D.A. team has provided to me suggests that these drugs are too toxic and do not show the effectiveness needed to continue to offer the governments support in completing further clinical trials and documentation of results." Cuda said as if to knock the wind out of the Director's sails.

"I do not understand how that can be?" the Director replied. "I will have to check with those departments you are speaking about. Tell me who you have spoken with."

Cuda continued to be confident. "There is no need to check my homework.

I am right and you are wrong. I am convinced that what I understand to be the case is in fact true. You will need to stop all of the trials related to these agents immediately."

"On whose authority?" the Director replied defiantly.

"Did I mention I will need a full accounting of product inventories, compositions and test names and that you will cease all use of them effective immediately?" Cuda continued.

"You cannot come in here, treat my subordinates like dirt and dictate research protocol to me and my agency," the Director warned.

"Well," Cuda replied. "As a matter of fact I can."

"On whose authority?" the Director repeated.

"And as a matter of fact I just did," replied Cuda.

"On whose authority?" the Director repeated again.

"By order of the President of the United States of America," Cuda instructed.

The Director laughed lightly and with a chuckle in his voice, "You do not represent the President of the United States. He would be proud of these discoveries. I have spoken to him before on the promise of our research here," the Director replied.

"Yeah, I am sure he would be. This would be a great ego stroke for him. Major strides in research on his watch would be great. However, he feels that it will do more harm than good based on what he has seen to date," returned Cuda.

"More harm than good. Are you kidding me?" the Director responded. "Canceling these programs will have real consequences for real people. People will die as a result of not continuing the existing treatment testing and not continuing the research. Does the President understand that?"

"I believe he does," Cuda said.

"You do not represent the President of the United States," the Director repeated again in disbelief.

In an almost joyful manner, Cuda pushed his scone aside, pulled his badge and ID from the breast pocket of his sport coat and presented them to the Director for his review. Indeed, Ed Cuda was a Liaison to the President of the United States. The question was, would a Liaison to the President misrepresent the President? It was a risky question the Director was willing to ask. He had to ask.

"I do not believe you," the Director questioned.

"Really," Cuda replied. "Director, do you realize that you serve, in this office, at the pleasure of the President? I am not sure that he will appreciate you questioning his authority."

"I am not questioning his authority. I just want validation of his intention," the Director snapped back.

"Did you hear what I just said?" Cuda reminded.

The Director was silent.

"That is surely a funny way of putting it. We are actually saying the same thing. It is a matter of semantics. You are telling me, to tell the President, he needs to put it in writing to you, because having me relay his words is not good enough for you. Is that correct?"Cuda clarified condescendingly.

"That is correct!" the Director instructed.

"I will get it in writing for you, no problem," said Cuda.

"Thank you, Mr. Cuda," the Director said awkwardly.

"No problem. No problem at all," Cuda said as he rose from his chair and took another drink of water.

"I am curious to see how that works out for you though," Cuda stated in closing as he gave the Director his characteristic smirk, turned and left the room.

Cuda was done for the day. He winked as he walked past the Director's overdressed assistant who was standing by the receptionist at her post. He exited the office and left the building. From there, a cab was hailed and he was headed home for the night. He would be prepared to meet with the President early in the morning prior to catching his flight out to Minneapolis.

The Presidential Consequence

78

Cuda arrived early at the south entrance to the White house. It was 7:30 a.m. and his appointment was for 8:00 a.m..

The President had informed Hoard's assistant there would only be a half an hour available for Cuda this morning. Cuda was sure he could cover his subject matter in a half hour, but the timeline was likely a typical politician's diversion. A diversion intended to restrict your time so that you would not be able to share your issues. Without regard to the President's schedule, Cuda was prepared to get the job done in the time he had.

The security at the south gate was particularly slow today. There seemed to be a lot of commotion. Cuda could not be late. He did not want to give up any of his time with the President, so he made his way to the front of the security line.

There was a new agent at the South Gate. A new agent he was not familiar with. The new agent appeared to be fumbling as he manned the screening booth. Cuda looked for the second agent. There were always at least two. It was a rare event indeed that Cuda did not know a Secret Service Agent at the White House. He had trained with and been close to so many over the years.

He made that comment to the agent. He explained he was meeting with the President at 8:00 a.m. and would like to get in front of the line. The new agent did not recognize him and said he would need to get in line with everyone else. Cuda was adamant. He was not going to wait in line.

Unfortunately, the new agent was equally inflexible. A minor disagreement ensued.

It was just then the second agent showed up at the gate. Cuda was familiar with the second agent and they exchanged a brief greeting.

Needless to say, Cuda and his almost infinite influence, was moved to the front of the line. He showed his badge and moved efficiently through the turnstile. That was the good news.

Cuda asked the new agent, "How long have you been here son?"

The agent replied, "This is my first day at the gate, Sir."

"I suppose it is stressful, securing the White House and all," Cuda chided.

"Not really, Sir," he replied. "I am sorry. I did not realize you are a Secret Service Agent also. My mistake, Sir. I was called up from Quantico yesterday and given this assignment today."

"Well, congratulations. I am sure we will show you the ropes. Who was the

Commander that called you up son?" Cuda asked. "Maybe I can put a good word in for you."

"It was the funniest thing. The President himself called me. I was at the top of my class and he needed some great talent," boasted the new agent.

'Really," Cuda replied. "That must have been inspiring."

The green new agent was being played. Cuda was trolling in deep water and by chance, totally unexpectedly, he snagged a whopper.

"I couldn't believe it myself," stated the new agent "The President called and said he was going to work me through the positions at the White House."

"Great," Cuda replied.

The rookie agent came close to Cuda as he whispered, "And I was supposed to make the south gate a real cluster this morning. He had someone coming to see him that he wanted to delay them until after he departed," the naïve agent informed.

Cuda looked around as if he were trying to identify this mystery person.

"Really," Cuda replied. "Who do you think that person is?"

"He wouldn't say," stated the new agent. "He said he would give me the all clear signal by 9:00 a.m."

Cuda continued to scan the growing line giving the appearance he was being helpful.

"Well, you keep up the good work," Cuda advised. "I will let the President know you are taking care of things as he asked."

Now here's the bad news! Cuda knew the person the President was referring to was none other than Cuda himself. That was bad news indeed for the President this morning.

The bad news for this new agent was that this was the new agent's last day on the White House security detail. From this day forward, all this particular agent would be doing was following counterfeiting leads from an office desk. Cuda would personally see to it.

From the south gate to the Oval Office was only a short walk. Cuda stopped to exchange personal comments and well wishes with several White House security detail agents on his way through the grounds and into the Oval Office.

He had met an old friend in the hallway outside the President's office. He was new to the White House. Cuda was glad to see him, ask about his children and joked about the time when they took a vacation together back in the days when he was *just one of the guys*.

Cuda was on time, well rested and in position to meet with the President.

The President too was punctual. He had a busy day ahead of him. Unfortunately, his plans for the day did not include meeting with the unpredictable and personally volatile Cuda. He was very surprised to see Cuda in his office.

"Good morning, Mr. President," Cuda stated as the President entered the Oval office.

The Secret Service Agent that was keeping Cuda occupied until the President arrived was excused.

"I am fine this morning Mr. Cuda. Thank you for asking," the President relayed in a calm, but surprised manner.

"To what do I owe this pleasure? Are you here to tell me what to do again?" the President said sarcastically.

"No, Sir. I did not tell you what to do last time I was here. I recall you making a decision," Cuda said respectfully.

"Well, I am sure I can guess why you are here, Mr. Cuda. You are here regarding the health care reform legislation. So, let me take some time now and tell you what we have been doing to promote the new bills that are in committee. It is a bit of a long story," the President stated confidently.

The President was attempting to control the thirty minutes by getting started with a rambling dialogue about how he has been navigating the shark infested waters of the Congress. This is a very common practice among politicians. They want to tie up your time with dribble so that they do not have to take time to actually hear your issues.

"No, thank you, Sir," Cuda replied with a big smile. "I am well aware of the politician's handbook chapter that describes exactly how to talk about all the things you are working on rather than what you have accomplished. I am well versed in the knack politicians have for making small talk, asking about family and God knows whatever else, so that it comes time to talk about the constituent's issues, there isn't any time left on the clock. At that point you are promptly dismissed."

"So now you are a constituent?" asked the President.

"Sure," Cuda replied smugly. "I am a constituent. I am a voter and a party to the good will and the long term security, prosperity and peaceful existence of this country."

The President was indifferent. "I am confident that you are," he replied.

The President was feeling a bit more comfortable than was perhaps appropriate given the circumstances. While there have been many things that the President was not aware of, Cuda had not done anything that he knew of to follow up on their previous meeting.

"This time, the constituent is here to do something for you," Cuda offered.

"Is that so?" inquired the President.

"You bet. It is time for me to give back a little," Cuda stated.

The President's confidence grew just a little bit more. Why was Cuda here on short notice to do me a favor, he thought? Perhaps Mr. Cuda feels he had over leveraged his hand? Perhaps the President had assumed Cuda had greater power than he did?

"I would love to hear what you can do for me," the President said, now semi convinced he was dealing with a person who was back peddling. After all, the President had taken the liberty of having his entire security detail, within the White House proper, changed out.

"Here is what I can offer to you, Mr. President. I am offering you a chance at political survival. Let's call it a sort of, well, survival buffet!" Cuda instructed.

"Oh, my," the President exclaimed. "I love a good buffet. I am sure I am going to love to hear this. You best get started, you only have twenty two minutes left," he said attempting to catch Cuda off guard and create a sense of urgency that would in turn cause him to misspeak.

Cuda started off egotistically as the President listened, "As an appetizer, I have created a situation that will all but completely discredit your largest financially contributing association and virtually negate any post election responsibility you may feel to them."

"That does not sound very likely to me," the President replied as he snickered.

"It is more than likely. It is a virtual certainty," Cuda replied.

"And just how are you going to serve this appetizer to me exactly?" the President asked.

"Not so fast Mr. President. Eating this buffet too fast will give you some serious indigestion," Cuda toyed. "Let's just say I have it tactically in place. It is better you don't know how the logistics will play out."

Cuda was depending heavily on the direction that he was given by Hoard. He was over stepping his intelligence just a little, but gambling on Hoard was always a pretty sure bet.

The President sneered with skepticism and distrust. He again thought that perhaps Cuda was joking with him. Perhaps playing a high stakes game of chicken.

"Okay," the President replied. "I suppose I will hear about it when everyone else does, on the morning news?"

"You are correct, Sir," Cuda replied.

"I can't wait. I owe them a lot these days," the President laughed. "It would be a relief."

"What else. You still have twenty minutes left," the President's confidence grew.

"On to the soup and salad," Cuda continued to toy. "I will help you make this next step possible. Well, actually, you will make this policy. The new health care provisions will make the supplemented single payer government plan completely unionized at a lower cost base rate than any proposed peripheral privatized plans."

"Interesting," the President replied.

"I thought you might like that part," Cuda added. "Both plans will be driven by unionized jobs. Driving the unionization will make it almost impossible for every day citizens to afford their own privatized plans at out-of-network union rates."

"That is a great suggestion," the President stated. "To my knowledge, the obligatory unionization has not been addressed in the current version of the plan."

"I am here to help. We will avoid the lock out issues that happened to Reagan during the air traffic controllers strike; largely because you are not Ronald Reagan," Cuda added.

"That is for sure!" the President replied not knowing Cuda had just insulted him.

"What is my main course?" the President asked growing impatient.

"Sure, Mr. President. I was just getting to that."

Cuda continued, "I am sure you were expecting me to come see you eventually. I am sure you were expecting to give me the standard run around the block."

Cuda paused.

"Mr. President, respectfully," Cuda began. "I don't need the exercise of any more trips around the block Sir. We had an agreement that you would get your party rallied around you and you would get your party aligned."

The President was tolerant of Cuda's matter of fact dialogue.

"You further agreed that you would get the health care legislation passed on a party line vote if needed. Yet, here I am, months later, and you have not gotten the job done. I am questioning your competency and commitment as Commander in Chief, Sir," Cuda advised.

"Are you?" the President said, resentful of the implication.

"Yes, I am," Cuda stated.

"Have you considered the consequences to the country if I, as President, follow through on the numerous requests you defined so clearly for me when you were here last?" the President said as he pulled out the notepad from his desk. The same notepad where he had listed Cuda's demands previously.

"Mr. President, we have gone over this already. You had made a commitment," reminded Cuda.

Confidently, the President corrected Cuda by resetting the stage, "I have gone over this list and I find it to be unreasonable."

"I don't give a damn what you think is reasonable, Mr. President. You have committed. I have committed, We are committed," Cuda emphasized.

"So what! Is this the first time in your life someone has disappointed you and broken a commitment? Get used to it," the President replied.

"You seem to be having an information retention problem right now, Mr. President," stated Cuda. "Let me refresh your memory on the hardship you are trying to avoid. I have explained that your own Congressional Budget Office (C.B.O.) has agreed that the intermediate and long-term viability of my plan will save billions of dollars at or around year ten. You are looking at the short term view. You are only thinking about your short term poll results."

"As President, I have to be aware of what is happening during my term as well as after my term. In this case, at this time, I am more concerned with what is happening during my term," the President advised.

Cuda responded quickly, "Imagine that, a self-serving politician. You are prepared to create a long term problem so you can look good in the short term? You're an idiot."

"Watch your language in this office," the President demanded.

Cuda was not even going to acknowledge the reprimand from the President. He had wasted enough time. It was time to drive his point home. This conversation was going nowhere fast. Like Hoard said, the President needs to have his commitment *reinforced* and Cuda, again, was the man who would be the enforcer.

"Mr. President, I am glad to see you in action first hand. I, like most of the country, am surprised at how exactly we put you in this office. Now hear me when I tell you this, it took millions of this country's citizens to vote for you and elect you to the Presidency. Isn't that correct?" Cuda asked.

"And I plan to serve them well," the President answered.

"How many citizens will it take to remove you from office, Mr. President?" asked Cuda. "Perhaps it would take several million to overthrow you in an internal government rebellion? Maybe it would take a few thousand men in another country when you are traveling abroad and your security detail is over run? Perhaps it would take only a few hundred Al Qaeda who storm the White House and bomb it into a huge hole in the ground with you in it at the bottom."

"Are you threatening me again?" the President stated alarmingly. "It seems you were intending to come here and do things for me and to be helpful."

Cuda continued without hesitation, "Perhaps it would take only ten men, the wrong ten men, on your personal security detail."

The President was silenced and once again fearful as he felt the faint notion of a lump in his throat. He shot back, "Good try, Mr. Cuda. I have changed my entire personal detail after your last visit. It makes me more comfortable in my own house."

"I know you have, Mr. President," Cuda advised.

The President interrupted Cuda, "Then suppose you take your boney ass out of my office and go find someone else to try and bully, because you are not going to do it here anymore."

"I still have twelve minutes remaining," Cuda said. "You did not let me finish."

The President did not want to tangle with Alan Hoard, so he was willing to be tolerant with Cuda for another twelve minutes.

"What I was saying is, I know you changed your detail. What you did not let me finish saying is that I could not have picked a better bunch of men had I done so myself," Cuda grinned.

The President was confused by that statement from Cuda.

"Then again, maybe I did pick most of them myself. I practically know each and every one of them personally," Cuda stated.

The President was once again on the short end of the stick. He called out to the hallway for his door agent to come in. Failing to use the intercom and just shouting out.

"Maybe there was one at the south gate that was not a good fit. He surely was not able to slow me down as he had been told to do by the Commander in Chief," Cuda added.

The President looked towards the door in anticipation of his agent entering the room.

The Secret Service agent quickly opened the door and stood in the doorway, "Yes, Mr. President," he said.

"How long have you been on the White House security detail?" the President asked.

"Only a month, Mr. President, Sir," he responded.

"Do you know this man?" the President asked as he pointed at Ed Cuda.

The agent smiled and looked at Cuda with a *Gomer Pile* sort of appreciation, "Yes, Sir. That is Agent Cuda. I know him very well, Sir."

The President rubbed his forehead with both hands, "You are excused," the President said to the agent.

"Why don't you stop wasting our time," Cuda continued. "The fact remains that it will not take thousands or tens of thousands of rebels to remove you from office. It will take one talented man. It may even take just one well-trained woman. It will take one person with the right access, at a time when there is a momentary lack of concentration, for someone to have the opportunity to deal with your insubordination and arrogance. At that point, we can deal with your incompetent patsy of a Vice President full-time. Quite frankly, it is pretty appealing to me right now after the stunt you pulled at the south gate."

The President was gutless. He had lost his courage and resolve once again. He was truly a coward at heart. He was more concerned with his own personal safety than he was the personal conviction to serve a nation on the platform that got him elected.

"What do you need from me?" the President asked.

"Let's see, what do I need from you? I need you to take the notebook you have in front of you and I need for you to get this God damned legislation passed as we discussed last time I was here. I am not going to come here and hold hands with you on this issue again. If I do not see a full court press to get this passed, I will assume you are not on the team and you will suffer the consequences. Is that clear?" Cuda asked.

The President could not speak. He was not well versed at handling a threatening and adverse environment at this level.

"I oversee your personal safety. I will not guarantee your personal safety if you do not follow through. Do you understand me?" Cuda repeated.

Cuda picked up the notepad from the President's desk that contained the items they discussed on their last visit together when Cuda dictated the events and the parameters of what he expected in the legislation, among other things. He was looking it over and considering if he needed to review it again, point-by-point.

"I understand, but there are constitutional issues," the President responded, breaking the silence.

Cuda tossed the notebook disrespectfully at the President, hitting him squarely in the chest.

"Look, I don't care if it takes an amendment to the Constitution to get this Legislation passed. Make it a budget reconciliation action if you have to. That only takes fifty votes and not sixty. You need to take care of it or I am sure we can convince that spineless Vice President of yours to get the job done for us. You're the President, start acting like it!" Cuda shouted.

The President picked up his phone and began to dial. It was clear he was waiting for someone to pick up on the other end. Cuda was unsure of who he was calling and for what purpose. In an instant, there was an uneasy fretfulness that had come over Cuda. Had he gone too far?

The President spoke to the person on the other end of the phone, "This is the President of the United States."

There was a pause while the President listened for a few seconds.

"Why, thank you," the President responded to the voice on the other end of the phone. "I am calling for the Speaker of the House. Please give her a message and tell her that she needs to be in my office at her earliest convenience."

Internally, Cuda let out a sigh of relief, careful not to let the President know he was relieved of his momentary angst.

The President continued, "I appreciate that she may not be in Washington, but tell her to travel here immediately. That is why she has her own plane."

There was another brief pause as the President listened, "Thank you. Please have her office let me know when I can expect her here."

"Another good call, Mr. President. I wish you would have followed through the last time we spoke."

There was no retort from the President.

Cuda looked at his watch and now turned the tables on the President, "Oh," he said sarcastically pretending to be concerned about the Presidents schedule, "I am almost out of time. There is one more thing I need from you."

Cuda pulled a paper from his jacket pocket. It was a one page document written from the President and directed to the Director of the Oncology Drug Advisory Committee. At the top of the page it stated *Top Secret* in bold red print.

"And what might that be?" the President asked.

"I have arranged, at your direction, for the termination of several chemotherapy and cancer treatments medical trials. I have listed them here specifically on your personal White House letterhead. I just need your signature," instructed Cuda.

The President looked over the document.

"I have not asked for these tests to be terminated," the President said, surprised by the request.

"Huh," Cuda replied looking at the paper. "Says here, and I quote, 'By order of the President of the United States of America, you will cease use of the following agents and forever abandon their use until otherwise directed by this office'."

The President continued to hold the document in his hands. "The F.D.A. just presented these to me a week ago and they were very promising."

"Then you should have listened to our first conversation months ago and you would not be in a position of appearing to be in conflict with your own approval," advised Cuda.

"On what grounds are we terminating these tests?" the President asked.

"Mr. President, I am having enough trouble with some hot shot researcher in Minnesota who thinks he can circumvent the rules and provide the world a cure for cancer. I don't need to hear it from you too, do I?" Cuda asked.

"Someone has found a cure for cancer?" the President asked.

"They may believe they have. That is why you are sending me to Minnesota today to see this man," Cuda instructed.

"What is this man's name?" the President asked.

"Dr. Garrison Keller. Hopefully, he will conduct himself the way you have assured me that you will be conducting yourself or we will lay out similar consequences for him," Cuda snarled.

"Who are *we*?" the President asked.

"Well, insofar as I work for you and you are sending me to see him, I guess *we* translates to *us*. I hope nothing happens to him while I am there. It will look bad for both of us," advised Cuda.

"I see," the President replied in disbelief.

"Do you want to know more or do you want plausible deniability," Cuda asked.

The President needed no more information on Dr. Keller at this time and repeated his earlier question, "On what grounds are we terminating these tests?"

"On the grounds that you have ordered it to be terminated, Sir" Cuda explained.

"How will I explain this to the citizens when it becomes public?" asked the President.

"Have you ever attended any civics classes, Mr. President?" Cuda pointed out.

"Question withdrawn," Cuda replied to his own query. "Let me tell you a little tidbit here for future reference about how things work around here from a confidentiality stand point."

Cuda continued mockingly as the President looked over the paper. "When it says *Top Secret* on the top of the page, all parties are bound, under penalty of treason, not to disclose the details of the document for fifty years unless your office releases the documents."

"When will the people see this document and who else will sign it?" the President asked as he attempted to be sure his personal political safety net was in place.

"You will sign it, Sir," Cuda instructed. "The Director of O.D.A.C. over at the F.D.A. will sign it and then it will not be disclosed to the public for fifty years. You really do need to learn to listen."

Without further delay, the President, relieved of personal consequence for the foreseeable future, signed the document.

"Thank you, Sir," Cuda added.

Cuda picked up the document and turned towards the doorway. It was just like before, only a few months later. He was leaving the President's office and he felt just as victorious.

He turned and looked at the President before he opened the door, "I am counting on you, Mr. President."

"I will get it done," he replied looking at Cuda. "I will get it done."

"You will have to this time," Cuda assured.

Cuda opened the door and found the Oval Office Secret Service agent and two of the hallway agents standing in front of him. To the President's consternation, the agents all merrily greeted Cuda as he left the office. Two of the men did not know their good friend Cuda was in the building.

Looking back over his shoulder at the President, Cuda smiled at the President. Cuda confidently pointed at the President with his index finger. With his thumb acting as the hammer to a pistol, he winked and dropped his thumb. The President got the message.

Cuda was on a tight schedule to get a couple of minor matters resolved before he would depart for Minneapolis later in the day.

The Return Trip To See Garrison

79

Garrison was exhausted, yet unable to get a good night sleep. He had tossed and turned most of the night. Tired, fitful and restless, it was time to get up. The very least he could expect from himself would be to get up, take a hot shower and go into the office. There was plenty of work to be done given everything that was going on. Perhaps he could get some uninterrupted work done before the phone started ringing and the other staff arrived.

As he traveled to the office, he thought about how proud Sally would be of him. He had taken actions that would save a few lives in the short term, but given the circumstances, the best he could do for the many lives that potentially hang in the balance, was to insure his legacy was passed on somehow.

This was not the time or the place to make a stand. It surely was not the political environment. He was sure that Sally would understand.

While he was not fearful overall, he was concerned. His visit from Cuda was intimidating. It was unclear to him just how far the government would go to prevent him from applying his life's work if they were to know exactly the scope and breadth of his cure. That being said, given the uncertainty, he was glad he had taken steps to secure the cure that he had developed, yet he was becoming more certain every second that the steps he had taken to date would not be enough.

It was not the time to go public with his discovery, he thought. It certainly was not the time for him to be the one to bring it to the forefront.

The time passed quickly and before he knew it, he had arrived at the University. His thoughts had been racing and the adrenaline had overcome the sluggish start to his day. He had been so focused on Sally, Rigo, Cuda and the government, that he had arrived at the office without recalling much of the ride into the city from the lake. As each mile passed, he felt a greater level of anxiety coming over him. It was only 6:00 a.m..

By the time he arrived at the office, the thoughts of Rigo and the government were consuming him. He knew that Rigo was doing very well, remarkably well. He was very pleased.

On the other hand, the government would not be so pleased. Garrison knew that somehow the government was following his treatments. Cuda simply knew too much. There must be someone in Garrison's inner circle that has been spoon feeding him information. What other explanation could there be.

How could Cuda be so well informed? The government would rightfully assume that Garrison had perfected a cure and that was a real problem. Clearly, the government would be very interested to know how the boy responded so quickly. Garrison was consumed by paranoia.

His obsessively mistrustful thoughts this morning bordered on frenzied and neurotic by the time he entered his office. Was it a matter of coincidence, compulsive thought, or just good planning given his experience and methodically driven nature, we may never know for sure.

This morning, in an obsessive compulsive systematic race towards removing exculpatory information, he would take the next step. Today's actions, combined with what he had done to disguise Rigo's treatment, would all but insure that there was no absolute trail to the specifics of his serum. He alone would be the keeper. He alone was the only one he trusted.

Over the next several hours, he logged on to each of the office computers and deleted all relevant information regarding the treatment of Rigo as well as the precursors to the serum development. He cleared every file in his office that could be related to the path that got him the serum development and shredded the pertinent documents that were on site.

He removed his laptop from its docking station and walked it over to the sink in the small kitchen area. He plugged the sink and filled it with water and proceeded to place the laptop in the water to soak.

He thought for a moment about any documents he may have at home. His laptop was his only connection between his work life and his home life. There were not any documents on his home computer systems that would compromise his work. For that matter, there were not paper files in his home that would be of benefit either.

He walked from the small kitchen back to his office. Once again, he systematically rifled through each file in his office looking for any information others might find useful or might connect to his serum, then promptly shredded any potentially useful information.

He had sent Randy some of the information earlier in Rigo's treatment, but none of them included the all important staging serum.

He smiled as he shred the last of the documents he was concerned about. Sally would be proud of him now as well. He marveled as the cross shredder ate the documents. He was at first in awe of his work, his accomplishment and the great discovery he had made.

Secondly, he was in wonder about why he was taking such drastic steps to destroy the evidentiary trail of such a great find.

Lastly, as he ran the final set of documents through the shredder, he was filled with trepidation, apprehensive, and the anxiousness of what might happen next.

It was almost 9:00 a.m. He sat in his high back office chair and relaxed. His adrenaline was tapering down now as he felt more comfortable with his actions. He had been running around like a mad man for the last few hours. He was satisfied, secure in knowing that he had saved himself from possible prosecution and possible persecution based on his actions.

Yet still, he knew there was one person who had the recipe, had the cure, and he knew where that person was. That person was himself.

Just then he heard the office door open. It was Nan. Garrison sprang from his chair and bolted to the kitchen. His laptop was still steeping in the sink. He pulled the laptop from the water, unplugged the sink and quickly wrapped it in a towel from the counter.

Nan called out, "Garrison? Are you here?"

Garrison was fumbling to drain and dry the computer. Luckily, Craig walked into the office, distracting Nan.

"I am here," Garrison replied, as he carried the laptop under his arm and returned to his office, carefully placing the wet laptop on the towel at the corner of his desk.

Nan and Craig were exchanging some small talk as Garrison emerged from his office.

"Good morning," Garrison said, as he wiped his still slightly damp hands on his pants.

"Good morning," they both replied.

"You're here early," Nan commented as Craig made his way to the kitchen to start a pot of coffee.

"Yeah, I couldn't sleep," explained Garrison.

The door to the office abruptly opened and in walked Ed Cuda. Cuda's arrival surprised both Nan and Garrison. His visit, as Cuda wanted it, was unexpected.

"Well, well," Cuda said. "Glad to see we are here on the job early today," unaware that Garrison had been here for hours.

"How can we help you?" Garrison asked.

"We need to talk Keller," Cuda barked.

"And why is that?" asked Garrison.

Nan was uncomfortable and returned to her desk. Craig returned from the kitchen.

"Hello, Ed," Craig said as he passed.

Garrison was instantly suspicious of Craig's comment. Since when were these two on a first name basis? Garrison's eyes followed Craig as he took his seat.

"Good morning, Craig," Cuda replied.

"You have got to be kidding me," Garrison exclaimed. "Are you two best friends or something?"

"Dr. Keller. Dr. Keller, easy now. Jealousy will get you no where. He just knows me from when I was here last time. Right Craig?" explained Cuda.

"Yes, Sir," Craig confirmed innocently as he made himself comfortable in his chair.

Garrison continued to be uneasy, but thankful for how he had spent the last few hours.

"What do you need to talk to me about?" Garrison asked.

"Step into my office," Cuda arrogantly replied as he started to walk towards Garrison's office.

Garrison's tolerance for Cuda was at an all time low, but he had covered himself to the best of his knowledge. There was little that Cuda could do to Garrison professionally.

As Garrison followed Cuda to his office, Craig barked, "Hey, someone has been on my machine?"

Cuda stopped and turned back to Craig, "What do you mean?"

"I mean that someone has been on my machine. It appears that they have erased some files and they have also deleted my trash and scraped by hard drive erasing some of my files permanently. I will have to check the mainframe to see what I am missing."

Cuda returned to Craig's desk leaving Garrison in the hall. "Show me."

"I cannot show you anything," Craig replied.

Cuda fired back, "Show me what was erased."

Nan called out, "Mine too."

Cuda turned to look at Nan. He then looked at Garrison. Garrison shrugged and raised an emotionless eyebrow.

"It appears as though someone had copied my material, deleted the documents, and replaced the material on my machine with empty folders."

"Is that so?" Cuda responded as he continued to stare at Garrison and then turning his attention back to Craig.

"Whoever did this knew what they were doing," Craig added.

"Do we know when it was done?" asked Cuda.

"No," Craig answered. "Based on how they did it, I cannot tell. They were good. The machines parameters have all been reset."

"Looks the same here," Nan replied. "I seem to be missing data also and some of my icons have been moved, but I cannot tell you exactly what I am missing."

"Do either of you have hard disk data back up?" Cuda asked.

"Only for e-trails on the server. Not for research documentation. It is not allowed," explained Craig.

"Do we know if you are missing e-mail trails or research data?" Cuda continued to question.

"Like I said, I don't know what I am missing. I just know that my machine is different today than it was yesterday and it appears that data has been moved or removed," Craig replied.

"Same here," Nan added.

Cuda turned to Garrison again, "Interesting. This should make for an interesting talk Keller," Cuda stated as Cuda once again lead the way to Garrison's office.

Cuda slammed the door behind him for effect. Garrison was unimpressed and un-startled this time by the childhood antic.

"Feel better," Garrison commented as Cuda attempted his usual intimidation routine.

"I sort of like you, Keller," Cuda began. "You're a real man. You have money, accomplishments, and a nice home on the lake, a great job. You have it all."

"I am not sure how you know that I live on the lake?" Garrison pointed out. "However, this I am sure of, you haven't come here to compliment me on all of the things I have done right in my life!"

"You're right. I didn't," Cuda answered as he picked up the wet laptop from the desk.

"What happened here?" Cuda asked.

"I dropped my laptop in the lake," Garrison advised.

"You dropped your laptop in the lake? That's funny. How convenient," Cuda stated.

"It certainly is not convenient for me," Garrison replied. "There was a lot of information on that laptop."

"I am sure there was. Probably a lot of information that a lot of people would want to see, don't you suppose?" Cuda questioned.

"How do you mean?" Garrison replied unassumingly.

"I mean that your story here seems to get less and less believable with every added piece of information I gather. Mysterious cure from treatments that should not have been effective, late night trips to the radiology lab, trips to Brazil and now, missing computer information and a laptop that fell into the lake. Seems to me a lot of quirky things have been happening around here lately. Maybe you are just unlucky. Who knows?" Cuda cross-examined.

Garrison responded to his subtle accusation, "Perhaps I am having a run of bad luck."

"Everyone who describes you does so by referring to you as the luckiest man they know, and also the most prepared. Things just seem to come to you at the right time."

"I have been lucky in my life."

Cuda made himself at home in the chair opposing Garrison's desk and pondered his approach. Did he want to advance this meeting by taking a standard line of questioning approach or did he want to just come out and say it like it is. Cuda's impatience would win out.

"I think that you have something to hide. You may have a lot of things that you are hiding. I can't say for sure just yet, but I think your luck is about to run out though."

"What would I be hiding?" Garrison asked.

"Let's see, Cuda said. "For starters, how about the fact I think you have developed a cure for cancer and soft tissue malignancies."

"That is absurd," Garrison responded. "There is no such protocol. There isn't even any advanced testing for a macro-application, cellular-based, malignant resolution."

"Like I don't know that already," Cuda replied. "Let's not play games here, Dr. Keller. I do not have the patience to argue with you. I am here to make sure that you are not advancing any treatments or testing or experimentation, or whatever you want to call it that will support a cure for cancer, soft tissue disease or anything else for that matter."

"Okay," Garrison replied.

"Am I clear?" ordered Cuda. "Everything you are working on goes through the F.D.A.?

"Clear," Garrison replied again.

"I don't like your smug attitude," snarled Cuda.

"Okay!" Garrison replied.

"Are you going to stand there and give me one syllable, one word answers?" asked Cuda.

"I have agreed with everything you have asked me so far. I thought that is what you wanted. No?" Garrison replied.

"You should speak freely Keller. It will help you learn," said Cuda.

"Is that so. What will I learn today Cuda?" Garrison inquired.

"Do you have any understanding of the size of the problems that face this great nation today? Do you have any clue as to what I am trying to accomplish here?" Cuda asked.

"I think I have a grasp on both. I just don't agree with how you plan to get there. I don't think that holding people back will help them move forward," Garrison replied.

"There you go again. It's all about the *people*. You talk about the people, but you are focused on one person at a time," Cuda cited.

"Isn't a group of people just the sum of the individuals?" Garrison questioned.

"This country is too big for that. People need to be handled in aggregate. Everyone herded through an equality funnel. This country was built on equality," Cuda reminded Garrison.

"What you are saying sounds like socialism to me," Garrison responded.

"No. No! It is equal application of resources. It is good investment in healthy people. It is survival of the fittest. It is not putting a bet on a dead or dying horse. There is only so much money to go around," Cuda defended.

Garrison thought for a moment. "I am mistaken. I am not sure if socialism is a strong enough word. This sounds more like *Mein Kampf*. Do you have a master plan Cuda? Is that it, a master plan?" asked Garrison.

"I am saying that people in this country are just big numbers in little boxes to a government this size. People need to be treated equally and with the financial resources that we have. We can no longer invest in those that are not going to produce goods and services and who will only siphon off precious capital from the system," Cuda spoke from his soap box.

It was as Garrison had expected at dinner. His fear was founded prior and definitively confirmed now. Just as he had discussed with Sally from time-to-time and as he had confided with Randy at the Barra Grill earlier in the year, the government was in charge and they could not be entrusted with making decisions regarding the public's well being. It was a game of financial gain for them. From health care decisions to legacy benefits, this was a problem of *Herculean* proportions and they would stop at nothing to gain control.

If there is one thing that government has always excelled at in this country, it was the ability to find self-preservation. Whether by war, riots, legislation or election control, this country was built on a foundation of governmental survivors. The integrity of the people as individuals far exceeded the collective integrity of the people and motivations of those in elected office.

"Let me get this straight," Garrison queried of Cuda. "Somehow you are seeking the involuntary redistribution of health, wealth and resources as a gift. Call it charity, from those who are unhealthy or less fortunate to those who you feel may make a greater contribution. Is that right?"

"Not exactly," Cuda responded. "You will not be giving anything back to the people. You are giving the wasted money back to the government for their redistribution; as they see fit."

Garrison could not believe what he was hearing from a representative from the government, much less one that represented the White House. Speechless was an understatement.

"I don't know what to say," Garrison confided.

Cuda was becoming indifferent to Garrison's unwillingness, or incapability to understand what he was being presented with.

"Look. You must understand the *why* in what we are doing Garrison," Cuda explained.

"And why is that?" Garrison asked spitefully.

"You are the teacher here. Of all people, you should know that students learn their roles better when they understand the *why* of their actions," Cuda continued.

Garrison listened and Cuda applied a basic learning principle to the babble he was trying to sell.

"You have to evaluate the *why* verses the *how*. *How* only gets you in the door. The *why* is the hardest part for people to understand, especially when things are complicated."

Cuda continued, "With all of your education and protocols that have been set, why do you think that the rules don't apply to you?"

Garrison was getting agitated. "Who said I don't think the rules apply to me and just *whose* rules are you referring to? The rules of the States, the Federal Government's rules, the rule of morality, the Hippocratic Oath or the rule of a patient's privacy, the rule of law?"

"You know the rules, Dr. Keller," Cuda replied.

"Seriously, what rules are you referring to? The rules that will dictate and insure that this government will be around another two hundred and fifty years. *Those* rules?" Garrison defined.

"Yes. *Those* rules," Cuda clarified.

"What about the next two hundred and fifty years? What about being progressive world leaders in technology and human policy? Who will manage *those* rules, *you*?" Garrison asked.

Cuda refrained from comment. Garrison's frustration just might lead to a comment that may be useful.

"What about the progress you can make with the people and for the people? What about doing what is right?" Garrison continued.

"We have allowed over twenty years to be added to the American survival rate. We think that is progress. Not fast enough for you, Dr. Keller?" Cuda replied to the rapid fire questioning.

Garrison collected his thoughts for a moment.

Cuda continued, "In some cases, the people may feel they are making progress on specific life enhancing issues. Simultaneously, the Government may feel that they are at least standing still in terms of life expectancy. It's a trade off you see."

Garrison understood what he was saying. In fact, Garrison had said the same words himself, but this time he was not buying it, but continued to listen.

"Mull it over, Keller. It's true, you see. Right down to the most disadvantaged people. Right down to the most disadvantaged people," Cuda repeated as he fiddled mindlessly with the paperweight on the desk.

Looking up, staring Garrison right in the eye, "You call it. It's your time to shine. Make a decision here," staring him down and hesitating, "The cost of new opportunity is, at a minimum, the status quo. It's the only way!"

"No. It's not good enough. If you are telling me this mortality rate is a totally regulated number, and the government is the regulator, then no. No it is not good enough. If that is the case, you know it and I know it, it is just not good enough," Garrison replied

"Not good enough? What do you mean not good enough," Cuda answered. "Adding to the aging population in the increments greater than this will break this country"

" We have probably gone too far already," Garrison countered.

Garrison was exasperated by the lack of interest and indifference that Cuda expressed towards the individual.

"People should be allowed to live as long as their physical self can support life and by whatever means is available to assist them. If that cost falls back on the government, then so be it. It is the government's role to protect the people, not destroy them," Garrison pointed out.

"Of course, it is! In your perfect little *Polly Anna* world. You are right," Cuda responded. "We can inch up the average age and wouldn't that be great. And wouldn't it be great if all we were worried about is the incremental growth of the average American's lifespan. However, the picture is bigger than that. What about immigration? What about all of the benefits we pay to the people who contribute next to nothing? What about the roads and infrastructure?"

"Are you trading roads for lives?' Garrison replied horrified. "It is about the cost of the programs? It is all about the money?"

Cuda responded sharply, "It is always about the money."

"What about the cost of human lives?" Garrison pleaded.

"I am saying that there is only so much money to go around. Take your human life and a dollar to the grocery store with you. You cannot even buy a loaf of bread with the combination," Cuda advised.

"That is because government wastes so much money," Garrison responded dismissing Cuda's lack of respect for human life.

"Look Keller, money is not the root of all evil. The love of money and the power it brings is the root of all evil. The lack of having enough money is the root of all evil. There are plenty of politicians that love their money and their power. I will get things done my way and within the confines of the law," Cuda spouted out.

"It is always about the money, not the benefit," Garrison said audibly, but under his breath.

"Money is a funny thing," Cuda added to Garrison's confusion. "Money is material to people in many ways. Money is what you make of it at the time you have it. Money takes on many forms to many people and is more or less valuable depending on your own personal sustainability and circumstance at the time.

"Hell, cigarettes in prison can serve as money. A primitive concept, but money is what ever you have to trade for whatever you need at the time. The sustainability of money is to transitory to measure depending on your personal situation."

"It's still about the money. It is about the wasted opportunity that self-serving people squander in the spirit of a personal cause," Garrison replied in a depressed tone.

"That is an argument for another day," Cuda advised.

Garrison reflected for a moment on the dinner he and Randy had in Brazil, the look on Marguerite's face when he told her he was an American doctor and the feeling he gets when he can give good news to a patient. Garrison was solemn for the moment.

"Immigration can be legislated," Garrison added, referring to the previous comment from Cuda.

"It can be, but it's not legislated. That's why you have checks and balances in a Democratic government. That is why you have me," Cuda added confidently as if he was the nation's savior.

Garrison, continuing to be somber, replied, "I have seen the excess in government both here and abroad."

"On your trips to Brazil," Cuda asked, pitching for more information about his time spent there this year.

Garrison did not answer.

"You can pick a lot of countries. There are a lot of them that have this new age perspectives regarding how they treat their elderly and their infirmed; Brazil, Canada, and England," Cuda added.

"Sure," Garrison replied, "and what do their governments think of this program?"

"I am sure the governments think things are great," Cuda responded.

"And the people?" Garrison questioned.

"We don't ask the people. I suspect the people will not be asked about the discoveries you have made, mainly because they will never know about them. All too often the people don't know what is best for them. So you don't ask them. It just clouds the objective view. Too many cooks spoil the soup as they say."

"Is that so," Garrison replied.

Garrison was now more committed than ever to find a way to pass what he knew to the next generation. There had to be a way to pass the cure on to someone who would know what to do with it.

"I think we are doing the citizens of this country a favor actually. That's what I think. We are allowing them to expire when the quality of their life makes life not worth living without the legal hassle of euthanasia laws," Cuda coached.

"And that timeline is for the government to decide?" Garrison asked.

"It is," Cuda responded. "In my opinion, it is."

"That is not an acceptable answer. The government is not entitled to sentence people to death like this."

"No!" Cuda exclaimed and continued in an angered tone. "This is not a cruel and unusual punishment issue Keller. This is an issue of government assistance beyond the means of the government."

"Why do you think that major private endowments for research are at an all time high? Why do you think that the F.D.A. takes so long to approve new treatment applications?"

"Why are some great drugs never getting to market? Huh, why Dr. Keller? Why? Is it because researchers are not doing their jobs?"

"That's not *why* and you know it," Garrison responded to the run on questioning from Cuda.

"I am not saying what is right here. I am just saying what has to be," Cuda explained.

Garrison had heard those words come from his lips before and he did not like being on the receiving end them. When he said these words he hoped they were wrong. It was an over reaction on his part. When Cuda said these words, he knew they were wrong. It flew in the face of everything he stood for.

"I understand that a lot of these new treatments don't make it to market because you have shut them down, just like you are shutting this one down," Garrison said under his breath continuing to be subdued.

"What did you just say?" Cuda asked.

It was a slip of the tongue for Garrison. Garrison referred to a treatment shut down and Cuda heard him.

"Nothing," Garrison replied.

"What program are you shutting down?" Cuda asked. "I am not shutting down anything here. Are you working on something I should be concerned about? I think you are hiding something from me Keller and one way or another I am going to find out what it is. You can be sure of that!"

"Good luck," Garrison replied as he picked up the towel and began to gently wipe the moisture from his computer.

Garrison wanted to keep listening to make some sense of this conversation with Cuda. It was getting increasingly challenging for him to continue to sit through the badgering. He could no longer hear any reasonable argument coming from Cuda.

"How do you see yourself?" Cuda asked Garrison.

"You have asked me that question the last time you were here. I see myself as a scholar," Garrison replied without hesitation. "I also see myself as a *patriot.*"

"A patriot. Really? Were you in the military?" Cuda laughed.

"To be a patriot, you have to serve GOD and country, Cuda. I can say I see you as serving neither. It is also advancing the cause of your nation. As I said before, it includes being a good compatriot to your neighbor's quality of life," Garrison spoke with pride.

"You have an interesting perspective on things, Keller. I respect that about you. You are consistent. I will say that about you when you are gone. But you have it all wrong," cautioned Cuda.

"I ask you, was your overall objective when you got into this profession to add to, or take away from, the greater service your government is providing to society?" Garrison requested.

"You asked me that last time. Now we have both repeated ourselves. We're even. Look Doc, you are in no position to quantify my intentions or my contribution to the government or the people the government serves. You are playing to the wrong audience here and you need to get with the program," Cuda snapped.

Finally, tiring of the controversy, Garrison had had enough of Ed Cuda for today.

"You're too late Cuda. My work here is complete. Now get out of my office, Garrison ordered. "If I never see you again … it will be too soon."

"You still don't understand do you," Cuda responded to the mandate. "You really think that the rising tide of genuine health care improvement will lift all boats. I am here to tell you that the tide you seek is a financial tsunami heading for the people of this country and it just may bring down an entire government."

"Is that why they call it health care reform and not health care improvement?" Garrison clarified.

"Could be! You know what wordsmiths those congressman on the hill are. They take pride in the deception, but you have to know that they are always looking out for you," Cuda added with his signature grin.

"And we will all live to tell about this great historical circumvention?" Garrison asked.

"Will we?" Cuda questioned.

"Now you have turned toward intimidating me again?" Garrison asked.

No reply from Cuda.

"Get out!" Garrison blurted out for the second time.

"I am not threatening you, Keller. I am not saying how long you will live either. I am just saying that you will surely be there when you die," Cuda advised.

"Will *you* also be there when I die," Garrison asked.

"That is only for you to know. I cannot see the future or speak for other parties involved. Most of all, I do not know exactly how much damage you have done," Cuda concluded.

"Like I said, my work here is complete. Get out!" Garrison again ordered.

"I cannot be responsible for your safety from here on out, Dr. Keller," Cuda stated.

"My safety, when were you ever responsible for my safety," Garrison asked.

Cuda was silent.

"Well, it is too bad that you cannot assure my safety. In return for your lack of commitment to my safety, I want you to know that I cannot assure you that I have not created and distributed the cure," the overly fatigued Garrison said intending to deliberately annoy.

Cuda was furious. What would Hoard think? What would Hoard do if he knew that Cuda had let the cure slip through his hands and create a virtual melt down of the U.S. economy over the next decade? Once a cure was in the hands of the public, you could not un-ring the bell.

The men had truly reached an impasse. The conversation was finished. Garrison knew that he had sealed his fate in some fashion, but he was not sure if his fate would be in the hands of Cuda.

Cuda knew that Garrison too was serious. He knew in his mind that Garrison was capable of creating the cure, but he was not totally confident as to whether he had actually done so or not. Was Garrison bluffing just to antagonize or was his work already complete. If it was complete, where could it be found? Surely the information would be worth a fortune and, like legislators, not even Cuda was above reproach if it came to seeking compensation for the cure. It could be a a huge financial windfall for who ever possessed the cure and a real geo-political game changer.

CHAPTER FOURTEEN
PAYING IT FORWARD

80

Garrison was relieved to have gotten Cuda out of his office. Cuda was a frighteningly fearsome opponent with alarmingly covert capabilities. Garrison was confident he had not fully come to appreciate all that Cuda was actually capable of undertaking to insure things were done his way and his way only. Cuda may have given the intermittent and fleeting impression of being collaborative, but Garrison was sure it was the twenty-first century version of a confidence man's ploy.

Further, looking up the chain of command, Garrison certainly did not understand how far the *people* Ed Cuda reported to would go to insure their objectives were also met, whatever those objectives would ultimately be in the end game.

Garrison was exhausted, but exhilarated. He took pleasure in his forethought which had put him well ahead of Cuda in terms of managing the data that Cuda was so concerned about getting his hands on. He had run around like a wild man this morning removing and collecting data from various storage mechanisms. It was a virtual certainty he had removed any evidence of any perceived wrong doing on his part. He was equally certain he had removed any evidence of the serum replication protocols from the records, paper or electronic.

As he sat and wondered what steps Cuda would take next, he realized that by removing all of this information as thoroughly as he did, he had created two new issues for himself.

First, and most importantly, if something were to happen to him personally, how would the serum someday be brought to the public? It would have to be rediscovered, from scratch more or less, if not somehow left for someone to replicate.

There were very few people, no one he could think of at first blush, he would trust with such a powerful social and economic tool. Surely anyone who came forward with the cure would instantly have the world media establishment beating down their doors, not to mention the opportunity to gain a gazillion dollars overnight.

Secondly, he was so thorough in his sweeping attempt at removing information from the records, if something happened to him personally, there would likely be no one to point fingers at. He had left nothing, not a single report or electronic trail, which would point to the government, to Cuda, to the serum or to a cure. If he were to pass suddenly, there would, in effect, be no motive, no smoking gun so to speak. As far as he knew, he was well liked by his friends and colleagues.

It was through his careful thought along the way, as he developed the serum, that there was such ease in erasing the pathway to the cure. From the beginning, Garrison knew how powerful this treatment would be. He was premeditated and intentional in how he collected, stored, documented and selectively routed the compartmentalized documentation of his finding. If not for this planning, he would not have been able to erase the information in a matter of a few hours.

Likewise, he was able to summarize the information just as efficiently and place it on one chip for future retrieval. That chip was in his possession.

Garrison was comfortable with the decisions he had made, but was there an immediate need for him to be concerned about his personal safety. He would just need to be more careful and he would need to be more aware of his surroundings going forward.

As he reflected, thinking of what would happen next, he continued to wonder about his personal safety. He remembered there was an old handgun that had been given to him by a friend when he was in college. The gun was at his home. There were even some old shells in the closet. A novice with a handgun, he was pretty sure that bullets didn't go bad with the passing of time. Perhaps he should dig it out, just in case.

Sally was not a gun advocate and did not allow guns in the house. Garrison, while not a gun supporter either, was unsure what to do with the firearm after it was given to him. After considerable debate, in the end, he decided it would do less harm in his closet than it would do anywhere else. Out of sight was out of mind for Sally and Garrison both.

As uncomfortable and unfamiliar as a loaded firearm in the home was to Garrison, in this case, it might provide some measure of consolation in the weeks and months ahead as he became more familiar with how serious the situation with the government might be or how greedy some of his coworkers might become. Generally speaking he favored being in public places, by and large he surmised, did he need to be particularly worried?

81

Why am I so worried about my safety and why is my safety consuming my thoughts right now, Garrison thought to himself, still sitting alone in his office with the door closed. He was again bordering on delusional paranoia to be sure. Yet still, Garrison knew, he had foresight. Looking back, he had only been paranoid in the past when he had good reason to be so. His swift thinking and careful planning had always kept him out of harms way. This time would likely be no different, he resolved.

It was time to make a conscious decision to be more productive with his thought, but at the same time, keep his own personal safety in the front of his mind.

He could not see what tomorrow would bring or what role his emotions and psyche may play. He needed to stay focused.

He continued to think through the proactive and preventative actions he had taken today and where he could have made any mistakes. If there was ever a time for error free work, this was it.

The documentation of Rigo's treatments at the radio therapy lab, while falsified, was only known to be inaccurate to Randy. Randy had witnessed a real miracle and would undoubtedly be sure the cure was effective. Over the last few days, it was questionable as to whether Randy was still a trusted friend or if he was somehow connected to the crazed trail of information the government was getting.

Garrison was fairly sure Randy would keep the information regarding Rigo's treatment to himself. If he didn't, Randy would surely run the risk of losing his medical license. With regard to the issue of wanting to actually get his hands on the serum, the cure, Garrison was not so sure. Randy may prove to be as ambitious as the rest of the American public when it comes to fame and fortune. Their friendship would only take them so far together.

Craig was a different story. Garrison thought he knew him pretty well, but that greeting in the office with Cuda was troubling indeed. Garrison was confident they have spoken outside of the office. Craig had been exposed to some daily summaries of Rigo's treatments early on, but Garrison eventually put an end to that distribution. He was not sure how much attention Craig would have paid to the information that was coming through anyways, unless, of course, he was involved at a higher level than Garrison was employing him.

Regardless, they have been removed from Craig's computer now. No harm done there. This thought had created a more compelling reason for Garrison to be suspicious of Craig. Think back, upon starting up his computer, Craig knew instantly he was missing data, but was unable or unwilling to say what he was missing specifically. Garrison knew what information was missing. After all, he was the one that had removed it. The question was, if Craig was not tracking the information or working on it daily, how would he be able to know it was missing first thing in the morning. Then again, maybe some icons were rearranged, or something less damning that Craig noticed. Maybe Craig's comment was more generic, as he had indicated.

Either way, the paper and electronic trails that might lead back to the treatment and documentation of Rigo, as well as a few other precursory patients to the same treatment, had been removed, replaced or destroyed. Now, he contemplated, was that a good or bad position to be in.

Garrison was not only comfortable with the decisions he had made, he was proud of the decisions he had made. Very proud!

Only weeks earlier, He had successfully sent Rigo home to his mother, cancer free and in full remission. He was not able to make the trip. He thought it would attract too much attention. The combination of his protein suspension serum and the radio therapy had incrementally knocked down and eradicated the disease from Rigo's body as he had suspected it would.

As he sat at his desk, he thought of a saying his mother had imparted on him years ago, "what does not break you, son, will only make you stronger. You have every reason to be confident". It was a far cry from encouragement back then, but it had stuck with him and served him well over the years.

He had often thought, while positivity is a good perspective to have, to many very smart people will see a positive approach as actual fact, naively taking the "glass half full" side of things too literally. Often times the "break you" potential was over looked.

It was Garrison who thought that sometimes we needed to be "broken" in spirit and principle to grow as human beings. It was only then, at the breaking point, at the rock bottom of your moral and ethical unease, that you would be able to clearly identify who you were at the core and therefore define your own interpretation of right verses wrong. At that point, it would be up to you to lead courageously.

This path would inevitably separate you from the rest of the herd. Often times this road would lead you in the opposite direction of conventional wisdom. This path was seldom smooth, but it had the potential, if you were able to avoid the pitfalls, to lead you to your sense of self. The end of the path, the destination you would seek internally, would be to consistently make decisions based on your own set of principles and therefore not be the second best someone else.

It was at that instant a new moment of clarity came over Garrison. His sense of self, sense of purpose, and his principle driven decision making had revealed another opportunity that was before him. He could not let the cure waste away into obscurity for someone else to discover some day, perhaps in the very distant future.

Invariably, if someone was to stumble onto the same cure that he had discovered, there would be obstacles. He supposed that would be true regardless of who had come across the information, but he needed to be willing to take a calculated risk. Someone who would have a greater than even chance of having the right moral fabric, understanding of the good that can be done, and the desire to seek liberation with the cure versus money, power or fame. He needed someone that would be personally vested in the discovery.

Instantaneously, these thoughts all converged on a single point. He had decided. It could be a blessing or a curse, he may or may not have the moral fiber needed in the years ahead to handle such an ethical burden, but Garrison would leave the cure with Rigo. The imposing question was, just exactly how could Garrison possibly leave the cure with Rigo without someone taking the cure from him. How could he safely leave his legacy with Rigo, he was just a boy.

He sprang from his chair and walked to the door. He was belting out his command to Nan, who was quietly working at her desk, before the door had even fully opened.

"Nan!" Garrison ordered. "Get my travel agent on the phone."

Nan, startled at the abruptness of the request, replied that she would do so right away and send the call to his desk. As quickly as Garrison's office door had opened, it had now closed. Garrison once again had a long way to go and a short time to get there.

There was not a moment to waste. Within a few minutes, he would have a trip planned to Brazil. The issue with the Visa was quickly resolved. He had paid for a twelve month visa when his initial Visa for his trip to Carnival' was planned. He had lawfully entered the country within the sixty days required and; therefore, his Visa was still valid and would be for a couple more months.

While on the phone with his agent, she had asked about a couple of other trips Garrison had planned. There was one coming up in the next few weeks. Garrison was unsure of what the next few months would be like at work. He thought for a moment.

"Give me the tracking numbers for these trips," he asked.

The travel agent complied, giving the information. Garrison wrote them down on a pad and placed them on his desk. Doodling, he wrote down his Delta password, "2169".

"Can you fax the e-tickets to my office?"

"One more thing," Garrison asked in closing his conversation with the agent. "If any of my staff calls to ask about where I am spending my time off this week, I would like you to tell them that you were not able to book the trip I wanted. I had just called and requested information."

The travel agent agreed.

82

The very next day, Garrison would be on his way to Rio to see Rigo. There would be a lot of things that needed to come together in less than twenty four hours for his trip to be a success. He would be able to sleep on the plane tomorrow, but for now, he needed to get the information, tools and personal items gathered for the trip.

Garrison hastily called and spoke to DiDi to inform her he was coming to town. This was a critical step. He would need DiDi to do some translation and relied on her for transportation. Garrison had arranged to take a cab to her salon to meet her. As long as he was confident he was not being followed, he would land at the airport and travel directly to see DiDi.

The plan was for DiDi to arrange for a meeting with Garrison and Marguerite at their tiny lean-to in Rocinha. Garrison explained to DiDi he would need to spend some time with Rigo and his mother at their home. DiDi was welcome to be there if she wished, but he needed a ride either way. DiDi, appreciative of all Garrison had done for her friends, quickly agreed.

He also gave DiDi a list of a few minor medical provisions that he would need when he arrived. The main thing he needed from DiDi when he arrived was iodine. She was curious, but did not ask what he would need it for. She was anxious to see him.

Garrison collected the fax from his travel agent and placed it next to the confirmations and his password. He stared at the paperwork, finally paper clipping them together and placing them on the corner of his desk. What was he thinking? These were the most uncertain of times. He had no business planning a trip anywhere for pleasure. Nonetheless, he would wait until later to decide if he should cancel them.

Finishing a couple of other calls from his office, including one to the hospital lab, Garrison departed the building. He told Craig and Nan that he would not be in for a couple days. He needed to take some time for himself and do some sailing. It was getting to be his favorite time of year. He needed to recharge his batteries. This was odd for Garrison to make such a request and they both knew it. His time was often committed to others, leaving little time to account for his own piece of mind.

Racing out of the office, he carried with him a small microchip that he removed from his office desk. It was on this small chip that he had recorded the path through which he had come to his conclusions about the cure. The cure, the serum, the process and all of the supporting documentation, almost six gigabytes of data, had been reduced to a chip smaller than the size of a dime.

From his office, he had called a colleague at the laboratory over in the hospital building. He would need to stop at the lab to pick up a couple of other items he would need before making his way home to finish collecting his personal belongings for the trip.

83

Garrison's stop at the hospital lab was lengthy and time consuming. His adrenaline was pumping as he drove home. It seemed like a lifetime would pass between now and tomorrow when he would see Rigo. He drove home and rushed through gathering the right clothes for his two-day trip. It was well after midnight. He had a plane to catch at 7:00 a.m.. Time was wasting.

As he packed his bag for the all day and subsequently all night flight, he once again thought about his safety. He scrambled down stairs, locked the doors and set the alarm on his way past the kitchen. Feeling somewhat more comfortable, he ran back upstairs to locate the handgun he had stashed out of Sally's sight.

Right where he had left it, his gun was in the closet on the top shelf, stored in a tattered handgun bag and packed in an old shoe box. In the bag was the nickel-plated .357 Magnum his friend had given to him before he joined the U.S.O. over thirty years ago. Also in the small bag was a handful of cheap aluminum jacketed bullets.

With his hands shaking, in the privacy of his own home, Garrison loaded six thirty-eight caliber shells into the large revolver. The handgun was bigger and heavier than he had remembered it to be. He could not recall the last time he had held a loaded firearm.

He became even more panicky as he handled such a lethal weapon. So much damage could be done with a handgun like this one. This firearm, in the right hands, had the ability to quickly save a life. Perhaps even faster, this weapon had the ability to terminate a life. Hell, he thought, more neutrally and autocratically, this weapon would be able to end a troubled life.

The power of life and death that this weapon wielded for so many was not of any interest to Garrison. He was unsure if possessing this gun gave him strength or made him weak. It would depend on how you applied the use he supposed. To be sure, it made him feel differently when it was in his hands. Garrison was somnolent and reflective.

The time on the clock continued to slip away. He packed up his toiletries, clothes and the items he had collected from the hospital. He had a couple hundred dollars worth of *Riise* left from his earlier trip. He salted those away in his billfold. He was sure they would come in handy. The chip too was safely tucked away in the zipper pocket of his wallet. He double checked his passport and Brazilian Visa stamp and walked his suitcase down the stairs, placing it by the front door.

Garrison was getting tired. It had been a very long day. Racing around the office, up and down stairs, totally focused on what would happen next throughout the entire day. He wasn't seventeen anymore. He was physically and mentally spent for today. His tank was running on empty.

84

He deliberately walked back up the stairs, slowly placing one foot in front of the other, walking back into his office as he sat at his desk. His back was to the door, the recently loaded firearm lay in front of him. He looked out the window of his office into the pitch dark night before him. He looked at the gun and looked at Sally's picture on his desk.

"I am sorry Sally," he said out loud in a depressed tone of voice. "I miss you so much. The time we had together was so fulfilling for me. I miss the times we had together. I never wanted to let you down. In all of the years that we had been together, I can honestly say that with all we had and all we had done, there was nothing that had any value until I shared it with you."

Garrison continued to stare at Sally's picture. He missed her so much. He wanted to be with her as much as he wanted to relive the good times. What he would give to be with her again.

"I hope you know, Sally. Everything I do, I ask myself first what you would think of my actions. You have been a great filter for me over the years. Everything I am, I owe to you. I hope you know that. I look forward to us being together again someday."

There was an eerie silence. Garrison could hear the house creak in the cool crisp night. It had sounded as if someone were walking on the second floor of the house. He felt the light touch of a hand on his shoulder. Startled, he spun his chair around and flailed his arm up as if to push the strange hand he felt away from his shoulder.

No one was there. He walked to the threshold and looked into the hallway. Again, there was no one. The house was empty. He had set the alarm. The house was quiet. Garrison listened. The creaking had stopped. Perhaps it was Sally's spirit touching his shoulder in approval and consolation for the agonizing decisions he had made or the agonizing decisions that were yet to come. Who was to know for sure?

Garrison turned and gazed into the darkness that lay outside the window. There was a glimmer of light reflecting off of the water as he peered over the lake.

"I know you don't like guns in the house," Garrison remarked, "but perhaps it will make a difference for me."

"Know that I love you," Garrison again spoke out loud, hoping Sally could hear him. He could only hope that she would somehow respect the decision he had made at that moment and forgive him. It was never his intent to let her down.

With that final thought, Garrison looked at the clock. It was 3:30 a.m. He placed the loaded handgun meticulously at the head of the desk, rose from his chair, walked out of his office and down the stairs.

He wrote a brief note for the maid and left it on the counter. She would be in to clean the house. She knew the alarm code, everything would be fine. Collecting his bag at the door, he reset the alarm and departed the house.

He wouldn't have a lot of time to spare. He should leave now to catch his plane. There was international security, even though he was connecting through Miami, who would be asking questions given the short notice of his ticket.

On the way to the airport, thinking of every possible complication, Garrison conjured up some self-deprecating story about a sentimental piece of jewelry, a Rolex watch, Sally had engraved and given to him prior to her death. He had reported it lost in Brazil when he was there earlier in the year. He fabricated it was lost and he had been contacted about picking it up now that it had been found. They demanded he be there in person with his certificate of authenticity. Luckily, it was a story he would never need to use.

85

The routing through security was swift this morning in Minneapolis. The flight was on time from Minneapolis, but the layover in Miami would be long. Very long! Too many hours too long. It was the best they could do on short notice for a flight that he wanted to be direct from Miami to Rio.

Garrison was able to nap on the first leg of his flight to Miami, but the hours he had to kill once he had arrived in Miami were wearing.

The Miami airport, while comfortable, was not a place for an aging man to catch up on sleep. Eventually, the security check and personal inspection was similarly swift in Miami. His bag was checked in, the chip was in his wallet and he departed on time for Brazil.

Garrison was able to book a seat on the one flight traveling from Miami directly into Rio de Janiero. This saved him the trip from Sao Paolo to Rio. Unfortunately, it did come at the expense of a long wait in Miami and it would still take an all night flight to get to Rio.

Upon arriving in Rio, and unlike Sao Paolo, the walk through the Customs inspection area was quick and efficient. The luggage appeared to have passed through inspection quickly and was waiting for him at the carrousel. As planned, he hailed a cab for Ipanema. Another Portuguese speaking driver was at the wheel, ready to take him to DiDi's shop. Garrison was careful to insure that he was not followed.

As he repeatedly looked back over his shoulder, remembering the cars that were behind him with each look, he snickered at himself out loud. He was becoming a paranoid schizophrenic. No one but his travel agent even knew he was going to Brazil. It was such short notice. Who would follow him anyway? To Garrison, his paranoia was laughable.

The surroundings and the variations in the culture were recognizable to Garrison now. The narrow streets, the inattentive driver, the drive to Ipanema, all were recognizable on this, his second trip to Brazil.

The cab arrived in Ipanema at the salon. Garrison retrieved his bag from the trunk of the car and paid the driver his fare. He had now spent all, but the last of his local currency.

Garrison looked up and down the street suspiciously before he entered the salon. The bells chimed as he entered. DiDi was attending to a customer, but stopped to come over and greet Garrison with a hug.

"You have made it," she exclaimed, in perfect English.

"I have indeed," explained Garrison.

There were two other people working in the salon. It was early morning and business looked a lot better today than it did the last time Garrison was in the shop.

"You are a little early," DiDi called out. "Let me finish with this woman. It will be only a few minutes. She is my only appointment I have for the day."

"Business looks good," Garrison commented, waving his hand in a passive gesture affirming that a wait for a few minutes was not an inconvenience to him in the least.

The two other employees looked back at Garrison and smiled.

"Things are good here in Brazil," one of them commented responding to his rhetorical comment.

"I am sure they are," Garrison replied as he took a seat by the door, again looking up and down the street curiously.

Within a few minutes DiDi had completed the work she was doing for the woman and promptly cashed her out at the front register.

"I am ready," DiDi stated. "I will meet you at the front."

"Do you have the iodine?" Garrison asked, taking another gaze outside and then looking at the two women in the salon chairs through the mirror.

"Oh, yeah. I almost forgot. Yes, I do," said DiDi.

"Bring it along," Garrison replied.

DiDi pulled her car up to the front door just as she had done before. Garrison collected his bag and placed it in the car.

"Do we need to stop and get groceries again?" Garrison asked seriously.

"No. I was up to see Marguerite yesterday and brought her groceries, but thank you for asking."

Garrison removed a crisp one hundred dollar bill from his wallet and placed it on the center console as a token of his appreciation, and in some way to help cover the cost of what he assumed DiDi spent the day before.
He then removed the rest of his *Reais* from his wallet and placed them in the center console.

"I won't be *needing* this money anymore," Garrison commented as he placed his wallet into his back pocket.

"U.S. dollars?" DiDi exclaimed with a laugh. "You don't need U.S. dollars anymore. If you cannot use them, what am I supposed to do with them? No one wants them here either."

"You'll figure it out, you are a smart lady," he replied.

They continued their short trip up the mountainside to Rocinha where Marguerite and Rigo were sure to be waiting.

They talked about the progress Rigo had made and the difference in Marguerites spirit. The boy had made an astonishing recovery and a lot of people had taken notice. Marguerite was like a new woman. She was eating better and trying to take better care of herself. Unlike before, now she really felt she had something for which to live.

86

Arriving at the side street where they would park, they pulled over and got out of the car. Garrison asked for DiDi to open the trunk. There were a few items he needed to get out of his luggage before they walked up to Marguerite's.

Once he opened his suitcase, he was able to collect his things. He placed numerous items into a smaller bag which he had also packed, He seemed to be meticulously retrieving specific items from his checked bag and placing them in the smaller bag; items that appeared to have been strategically placed in his luggage.

Once he was packed up and zipped up, they started to walk to Marguerite and Rigo's home, what there was of it.

As DiDi had described to Garrison, Rigo and Marguerite were anxiously awaiting his arrival at their home. As they walked up the dirt street, Rigo came charging towards them and embraced Garrison in a hug.

"Oh, man. Let me look at you," Garrison commented. "You look great."

DiDi translated as Marguerite watched from a distance. Rigo turned to DiDi to listen to what Garrison had said. Rigo then gave her a big hug too. The three of them held hands as they walked the few hundred feet back to the front of the shanty where Marguerite was standing.

"Thank you for giving me my son," Marguerite said in broken English.

"He was always your son," Garrison said modestly as DiDi translated. Marguerite smiled shyly and nodded as she began to cry.

"These are tears of joy, yes," Garrison asked.

After a quick translation, Marguerite nodded, yes. They were indeed tears of joy.

Everyone converged on the front entry simultaneously and, one–by–one, entered. Marguerite had gone above and beyond her means. She was really trying to show her appreciation and squeeze out every drop of hospitality that was available to her. Her surroundings fell far short of modest, but between her and DiDi yesterday, they had put on quite a show for this neighborhood.

There were fresh flowers on the table. There was an air pot of coffee. There was some cooked chicken and some pie from the grocery store.

They all sat, ate, gave thanks to "Christ the Redeemer" and shared conversation.

Garrison was very appreciative, especially given the limited means that Marguerite had to work with, but he needed to get down to business. There was limited time. He needed to transfer the information he carried with him to Rigo and he had a plane to catch later that afternoon.

"I have come here to try and give Rigo an even better chance at survival," Garrison commented.

"How is that?" DiDi asked after sharing his abrupt comment with Marguerite.

"I have one more minor operation to perform on him. I will need your permission to perform this operation."

The two women looked blankly at Garrison. Operation? Here? How could he do an operation here they thought.

Garrison continued, "This operation will help with his long term treatment. I would like to insert a small device in his lower ankle area. The device must stay in place. When he is older, maybe around twenty-four years of age, he can have this taken out. It is critical that it stays in place until then if he is going to survive."

Marguerite and DiDi listened. DiDi was an educated woman and was not sure what to think of the proposition that Garrison was conveying. How could a small implant help his survival? Then again, who was she to judge? She would have never thought Rigo would still be alive today had it not been for Garrison.

"How will it be done?" DiDi asked.

"First you have to understand that it cannot be taken out. You have to understand that you cannot tell anyone the device is there. Rigo's survival will depend on it."

"We understand," she replied continuing to confer with Marguerite.

"I will have to make a small cut into Rigo's lower right leg, just above and behind the ankle bone. I will insert a small piece of material that I have brought with me. Once inserted, I will stitch the tiny incision in such a way that you will not need to have the stitches removed. Within a few weeks, he will not even know that I have implanted anything in there. It will heal completely without even so much as a scar. The implant will not bother him as he grows older."

Without hesitation, Garrison continued, "Can I have your approval?"

Marguerite nodded happily in approval. She had all the confidence in the world in Garrison. She was totally resolved to the fact that Garrison was here only to help. He would not do anything that would bring any harm to Rigo.

Garrison promptly laid open his bag and removed a sealed and sanitized scalpel in vacuum packaging, a pair of latex gloves, a needle and some sutures. From another small wrapper, he removed a pre-packaged syringe.

Removing the safety cap and turning to Rigo while speaking to DiDi, he asked if Rigo would jump up on the table. Rigo responded to DiDi's command. Garrison then positioned himself to be steady. He swabbed the skin with an alcohol swab and carefully injected a topical anesthetic to numb the skin just behind Rigo's ankle. He made the injection in several places.

As he waited for the numbing agent to take effect, he removed the hermetically sealed chip from his wallet. Garrison then unsealed a small bowl from its wrapper. He poured the iodine in the bowl. Garrison then placed the sealed chip in the iodine to steep.

Before leaving the hospital a couple days earlier, Garrison had arranged the tools he needed to perform this minor out patient surgery on Rigo. It may not have been in time of war, although the room resembled M.A.S.H. field unit conditions, he was prepared enough to have it done safely.

After gathering the tools for the operation, Garrison went to the hospital's lab and created a silicone sealed case for the chip he would implant in Rigo. It was touchy because it was so small. By using the implant lab technology, he was able to completely seal the chip in a manner that only increases the volume of the chip by twenty percent. It was still a very small implant.

Marguerite and DiDi watched as Garrison worked methodically. He was preparing his work, step-by-step, insuring that he was efficient at managing time and procedure.

Garrison unpacked a set of long handled tweezers and whisked the chip briefly in the fluid. It appeared to be ready. There was no evidence of any leakage in the lab and there did not appear to be any leakage now.

Garrison turned his attention back towards Rigo. He asked that DiDi tell Rigo that he might feel some gentle tugging, but this would only take a few minutes and would not hurt.

Everything was set. The sutures were ready, the chip was ready and the scalpel was ready. Carefully and methodically, Garrison lathered his hands with an antibacterial solution from his bag. Garrison had applied the fluid liberally and shook his hands to remove some of the excess liquid. The product he used was self drying and quickly dissipated.

He turned to DiDi as he put on his latex gloves, "Bring the iodine," he asked.

Coaching DiDi, she poured iodine on his hands and he gently rubbed his hands together. There was no running water at Marguerites home. This was the best sanitization he would be capable of here. He then asked her to pour some on a specific spot in the ankle area of Rigo. The same area he had injected minutes earlier.

Garrison was careful not to touch anything.

Looking Rigo in the eye, Garrison asked, "Ready?"

DiDi translated and Rigo nodded as Marguerite looked on.

Garrison confidently and expeditiously cut a three quarter inch incision into the skin just behind Rigo's right ankle. He then removed the sealed chip with the tweezers from the iodine solution where it had been soaking. The chip slid smoothly into the spongy tissue.

Rigo sat angelically as he watched in amazement. Given all he had been through, this event was not particularly taxing.

Garrison gave the implant a couple pinches with his thumb and forefinger, insuring it was positioned in such a way that the muscle and bone would keep gravity from forcing the implant lower.

Garrison promptly executed six sutures to close the incision. He opened a small sterile bandage from the package and set it to the side as he poured a little more iodine over his handiwork. Allowing excess to run off to the side and dry, he then placed the bandage over the stitches.

"Done," Garrison called out. "He will need to keep this dry for a week. No baths, no swimming and no getting it dirty for a week."

DiDi relayed the information to Marguerite. She agreed to watch Rigo closely.

Garrison began to pack his tools in the bag. He had intended this bag to be disposable and would leave it in the nearest trash can once they left Rocinha.

"Are you leaving so soon?" Marguerite asked.

"I have a plane to catch to go back home. There are people who will be expecting me back at work in a couple days. I don't want to let them down."

Garrison continued, "Now, remember, no one can know of this implant for years to come. This will need to be Rigo's secret. Keep it clean and keep it dry."

"I understand," Marguerite replied.

"DiDi, I need you to translate this secret I have for Rigo."

"Sure," she replied.

"Tell him this. You have every reason to be confident. Never forget that. In good times and in bad, the decisions you make that affect other people are the most important decisions you will ever make in your life. I have given you a great gift today. Choose your life's path wisely as you grow old."

Word for word, DiDi relayed the message. Rigo was alert and attentive to every word she spoke. For a boy of his youth and upbringing, he was an astute young man. Someday, he would have choices to make in his life. Would he be able to escape the meager environment he grew up in and contribute to a life spent making the world a better place? This was now a solution that only time would determine.

There were heartfelt tears and apprehensive goodbyes in *Rocinha*. More of the same took place at the airport. For the three of them, there were no words that could be said and no actions that could be taken that could appreciably put into perspective the thanks they all felt for Garrison.

A chance meeting at the statue of *Christ the Redeemer* had set this collection of people on a course to be forever grateful to each other. Rigo has again been granted the gift of life. This time, the gift was not just for him.

Marguerite, while there are no guarantees, had her son for years to come and DiDi was able to see the suffering of a true friend come to an end, while at the same time come to appreciate the fragile nature of life.

As for Garrison, he was able to face the implied fear that the system puts in all of us. He was able to face the power the system threatens to apply and stare it down. His cure may not come to market today, but he believed he had taken the steps available to him to insure that his work would be passed from one generation to another.

There would be plenty to think about on the trip back home. It was another long flight, but it was unusually peaceful. Garrison was not sure if the peacefulness was a result of him having successfully completed the transfer of information from his mind, to the hermetically sealed chip, to Rigo's lower ankle, or was he just too weary to be motivated.

87

The aircraft's wheels touched down onto the Lindbergh Airport runway in Minneapolis where this incredible series of events had started months ago. It had been quite a journey. Finally, Garrison thought, back safely in Minnesota. In an hour, he would be back in his own home. He would be in his own bed. His affairs were now in order. They were comprehensive, well thought out, and were capable of being executed given the challenging circumstances.

After the short drive home, Garrison was exhausted. He looked forward to some much needed and well deserved rest. Tonight, barring any unforeseen consequence, would be the best night's sleep he had gotten in the last few months. A little channel surfing on the television, a glass of red wine, and he was sure to fall asleep.

Relaxed at home, sitting on the couch, there was a knock at the door. Garrison was anxious. He was exhausted and home alone. Who would come to see him at home at this late hour? He got up from his comfortable position on the couch to see who it was. He peered through the two-inch blinds and could not see the face at first.

In his paranoia over recent events, he stood for a moment at the base of the steps near the front door and debated running up the stairs to get the handgun he had recently removed from the closet and loaded. He knew he had left it on his desk. Garrison glanced at the alarm panel. The alarm was disarmed. He looked up the stairs and then looked at the front door.

As he approached the door, the figure standing outside came into better view. He was relieved to see a familiar face. Garrison whisked the door open and greeting his unlikely guest.

"Come in Craig. Man, am I glad to see that it is you. You scared me half to death."

CHAPTER 15
IN CONCLUSION

88

The pictures of Garrison and his wife still hang on the walls in his unoccupied office. So too did the numerous *Certificates of Accomplishment* he had achieved and collected in his storied and productive life.

Chris and Jude walked with the dolly full of boxed documents to the evidence storage locker. Each box carried the date that Garrison had died and the words, **Case Closed**. Chris had succumbed to the fact there was nothing else to prove. After all, it was just another case. This was not personal for Chris, he just had a slightly greater interest in this case than in others. To be sure, there was plenty of other work to do.

Hoard, Cuda and whomever the other agents were that Alan had assigned to follow up on Garrison, were all happy with the end result. They never spoke about what exactly happened to Garrison. It was better that way. Hoard and Cuda were both determined to objectively carry out their respective roles and go about their work as they each saw fit to do so.

As ambitious as Edward Cuda was in this project, only time would tell if there was really any upwardly mobile opportunity for Agent Cuda. The Health Care Reform Act was all but implemented in its entirety just as Cuda had outlined. The nation would soon be on course to be more fiscally sound, albeit at the expense of many of the less than fortunate citizens who were too sick to be supported at the government's expense.

An ungrateful nation would soon come to see the ramrod legislation for what it truly was; an ugly step sister borne of the basterdized and criminally negligent father that our government had become. It was the poster child for what a Congress with a thirteen percent approval rating stood for.

Rigo had been safely returned to Brazil, a healthy boy, unwittingly possessing what was tantamount to the cure for all soft tissue diseases. He was getting ready to celebrate a birthday no one thought he would live to see. His mother was eternally grateful. She was more committed to her religion than ever before. After all, *Christ the Redeemer* had delivered her only son from the grip of a certain death.

The circumstances surrounding the President and the Presidency were definitively less fortunate. In the early days, this new President was clearly the *chosen one*. A nation anxious for change had bought into this administration the notion of a more promising future on his watch. The citizens were depending on his connectedness, commitment and exuberance to deliver them from the global issues of the day. Yet somehow, the high energy campaign and mission to unite platform on which he had been delivered to the office had quickly turned into a single minded, mono focused and ultimately secular Presidency. One must certainly ask why such a charismatic and youthful young candidate had developed into such a fearful and intimidated leader of the free world.

Looking back, what had happened was all too clear. The President had changed his course. We all know that it is not unusual for a *candidate* to act differently than the elected *official* they would become. But this change was different. This change was due in part to his true beliefs coming to the forefront and in part due to his lack of courage to stand up for what was right in the face of adversity. He was a conceited and self-serving leader. He cherished his own personal safety and that is how he would be viewed in history's eyes more than anything else.

The re-positioning that overtook his administration was nothing more than political spin created in the wake of personal and political survival. If nothing else, this clearly demonstrated what a clear communicator fear can be. Perhaps also a lesson, one more time, that history confirms the notion that in any system, 'absolute power will corrupt absolutely'.

This President failed to realize that the beating heart that lives in every presidential legacy depends on its ability to act with integrity and pump jobs into the nation's economy. You could call it the President's pulmonary ejection fraction. The weaker the pump, the less healthy the patient becomes as a result of that weakness. The integrity of the pump was failing. The ability to deliver on his commitment to unite a country was failing. This President failed to faithfully execute the office of President of the United States and did not, to the best of his ability, preserve, protect and defend the Constitution of the United States or the people whom he was elected to serve. He failed to eliminate racial and class divides and…he had now become complicit in a *Failure to Cure*.

Before Garrison had passed on, he had reflected to himself during his last days. He was proud of his life and he was proud of his work. He was equally proud of his contribution to mankind.

In the final analysis, Garrison theorized, we are all judged by the body of work we have created throughout our lives. Whether we are judged by family and friends, by colleagues and supervisors or by God himself, we are all judged by what we have done with our time and how we have impacted others. Somehow, somewhere, Garrison believed there existed a scale.

A scale of the most basic weights of subjective human values by which all contributions were measured. The measurement was our contribution to mankind. He knew it was up to each of us to manage our way through life's gauntlet of varied temptations in an effort to have a heavy purse filled with achievement when approaching the pearled gates.

It matters not if you are a poor man or a rich man, a government official or simply a token example of one of the local town minions with little influence on the future of our culture. It matters not if you grew up in a stable or unstable family environment.

What matters most is how you managed yourself. Did you have a compulsion to do well by yourself and by others? Were you admired by loved ones and emulated by colleagues? Did you lead a loyal and patient life that was sensitive to the needs of good friends and strangers alike? Did you seek education and use that knowledge to impart wisdom on the behaviors and achievements of others? Did you seek a legacy that benefited the common good or were you concerned only with the privileged few?

Once again, we all hit the crossroads where we must collectively and severally understand, people have choices in life. Garrison too had choices. He had consciously chosen to do well by others regardless of the pressures of every day life and the politics that inescapably accompanies it. His choice was to deliver people from illness and to provide some salvation and solace for those less fortunate. His choice was to create an environment of being more compassionate and caring in an unsympathetic and increasingly apathetic and financially driven world. Garrison was successful, at least for Rigo, in breaking the cycle of past indifferences.

While Garrison had no children of his own, he would leave one child behind that would carry with him, quite literally, the cure. It would be up to Rigo now, some day, to manage the legacy that Garrison had willingly, covertly, left for him to deliver.

One boy's secret would be carried forward to a new generation. Rigo was now armed with a recipe for a secret genetic serum that only Garrison knew how to perfect. Could Rigo make the ultimate contribution to humanity that Garrison was not able to see to completion? Perhaps Rigo too would be a doctor some day.

Could Rigo someday be transforming a system that will forever alter the future of how medicine is seen by the people in power? Will governments around the world be forced to stand up and take notice? If he could not change the perception of universal care, could he change the reality of the care that was restricted by the financial constraints of a cash strapped. misappropriated and greedy government? Could Rigo provide the cure or would Ed Cuda get to the cure first and once again make it about money and the obsession for power and control?

Perhaps of paramount thought for all of us is this. Can the government, any government, even ones that are governed *by the people and for the people* like the one in America, be trusted to be your life's timekeeper? Is your government beyond reproach? Do they have your best interest in mind at all times, in good times and in bad? Only you, the constituent, can be the judge of that.

Think now, would your choices have been different? Would your choices have been any more considerate, any more responsible, any more impactful or any more memorable? Will you have left a legacy to be proud of and admired.

Action takes interest. Action will also often take courage. Courage takes hope; hope that there is a better way and a solution to your plight.

Hope and courage are best applied when things appear to be hopeless. Things are often what they appear to be. Be equally cautious when choosing when to act and when not to act. The failure to act can also have consequences. The final judgment awaits you. A space where time *is time without end* awaits all of us.

Most importantly, as we close this story, will you be able to recognize that possibly the most enduring disappointments we have in our short time here in this life may very well be a result of decisions, inaction, and choices we have made for, and imposed upon, ourselves. It is up to you to make a difference.